1-2022

Tacos for Two

TACOS FOR TWO

BETSY ST. AMANT

THORNDIKE PRESS
A part of Gale, a Cengage Company

LIBRARY OF CONGRESS CIP DATA ON FILE.
CATALOGUING IN PUBLICATION FOR THIS BOOK
IS AVAILABLE FROM THE LIBRARY OF CONGRESS.

ISBN-13: 978-1-4328-9332-3 (hardcover alk. paper)

Published in 2021 by arrangement with Revell Books, a division of Baker Publishing Group

Printed in Mexico
Print Number: 01   Print Year: 2022

To my husband,
who is always willing to watch
You've Got Mail
just one more time.

PROLOGUE

LOVE AT FIRST CHAT DIRECT MESSENGER

Stongerman99:
We have to stop meeting like this.

> **ColorMeTurquoise:**
> You mean, anonymously
> through a computer?

Exactly. I actually spent a long time trying
to think of something better to say than hi,
but now I think that would have been better.

> LOL. I applaud your effort. Am I the
> first one they've matched you with?

Second. 😩 That sounds worse than it is.

Not when I tell you that you're my fourth.

Yikes.

Does that make me look bad?

Actually, it makes the app look bad. They've failed you three times. You should demand a refund.

I like the way you think.

So what was wrong with bachelors #1, #2, and #3?

A lady never tells.

Smart. Because then I could go out of my way not to repeat the same mistakes and you'd never know if I was genuine.

Ooh, I'm already worth a potential masquerade? That's what I call a good first impression. It's only been three minutes.

Are you going to ask me what was wrong with bachelorette #1?

I'm assuming you're too much of a gentleman to tell me.

You stole my line.

I'm sure you've got more.

Care to stick around and find out?

I think I will.

StrongerMan99:
Do you like cats?

ColorMeTurquoise:
I feel like this question is loaded.

It is. No pressure.

I don't have a cat, if that's what
you're asking.

It's not.

Drat.

You're getting closer. That rhymes with
cat, but it's still not an answer.

I guess I'm really more of a dog person
if anything. 🐶 Pass or fail?

Pass. Flying colors.

What if you hate the color turquoise?

I could never.

ColorMeTurquoise:
Favorite ice cream flavor? Mine's
mint chocolate chip.

StrongerMan99:
Cookies 'n cream.

I suppose I can overlook that.

That just means more for you, right? We
would never have to share a pint.

The fact that you thought sharing a
pint was an option in the first place
makes me think perhaps Love at
First Chat made another mistake.

I'm enjoying this mistake far more than the
last one.

ColorMeTurquoise:
Did you ever have any doubts
about this app?

StrongerMan99:
You mean, did I ever doubt that an online

10

matchmaking program could quiz me, run a background check, slap up a profile, and immediately match me up successfully with a complete stranger who lives within a sixty-mile radius of me but who I've never met before on my own and cause me to fall in love and live happily ever after? Of course not.

Me neither.

StrongerMan99:
Romantic comedies are underrated.

ColorMeTurquoise:
Now you're just trying to impress me.

I mean it. Fantastic story lines. Happily ever after. Solid actors. It's gold. Besides, who wants to watch heavy stuff? Isn't real life hard enough?

You had me sold at happily ever after.

It doesn't always work out that way, though, does it?

Not in my experience.

Mine either.

Favorite novel?

Sophie's Choice.

You joke.

Are you laughing?

Yes.

Mission accomplished.

ONE

If Rory Perez could find a way to wad all the cilantro in the entire world into a ball and hurl it into outer space, it still wouldn't be far enough removed for her preference.

"That's enough, right?" She pulled her turquoise sweatshirt up over her nose and turned pleading eyes to Grady, who stood by the food truck's efficiency stove and sprinkled the vile weed into a bubbling quesadilla mixture.

Grady shook his head, humor dancing around the laugh lines by his eyes — wrinkles Rory was pretty sure she was responsible for. Probably responsible for the gray hair streaking his dark temple too, even though he was only in his early forties. "Calm down, hermana. He asked for extra. Besides, who's the chef here?"

"You are." Rory reluctantly dropped her sweatshirt from her face and reached to hand him the spatula she knew he'd need

13

next. Grady was more than her late aunt's longtime food truck assistant. This past year, he and his wife, Nicole, had been Rory's sanity as she struggled to keep the inherited business booming — and other things from exploding.

She cut her eyes at him. "By the way, I'm not your sister."

"Close enough — and good thing, or I'd have kicked you out of this food truck a long time ago. You know I wouldn't keep up this charade for just anyone." He wrinkled his nose at her as he adjusted the heat on the stovetop burner.

She crossed her arms. "I don't think *charade* is the right word."

"Fine. You like farce better?"

"More like assumption."

"Right." He clicked his tongue in mock disapproval. "Customers assume you cook like your aunt and assume I bus the dishes."

Rory's neck flushed as the truth of the statement lingered. "They do not."

"Sure they do. Fortunately, Nicole keeps me man enough to take it." He winked. "And I'm not complaining. Most of our male customer base would vanish if they realized you weren't the chef around here, and hey, men eat a lot. Now, can you hand me the —" He stopped as Rory waved the

14

black utensil in his face. *"Gracias."*

"See? Maybe I'm not good at cooking, but I'm good for something." If she were typing that in a DM to StrongerMan99, she'd have added *#kidding #notkidding*. Maybe. She hadn't dared to be quite that vulnerable in their online chats. But they were getting to that point. There was something so appealing — so *safe* — about anonymity. Grady might be as close as family, but it was hard to go there with him. One, because he turned everything into a big brother compliment-fest, but also because, technically, he was her employee.

Technically, she owned the Salsa Street food truck.

And technically, she couldn't cook to save her life.

He pressed the tortilla flat against the skillet. "You're good at a lot of stuff, Ror. Probably more than you know, if you'd ever get out from behind your computer. What are those boards you stab?"

"It's *pin.* You know — Pinterest?" She bristled. "At least I'm organizing and planning. It's not like I'm some obsessed gamer or something."

"Hey, now — what's wrong with gaming? Everyone needs a break from reality now and then. Me and Nicole play online pool

15

together. She's getting pretty good." Grady flipped the quesadilla.

The too-familiar aroma of spicy chicken and peppers filled the cramped space. Rory's dark hair had smelled like smoke for almost a year now. Just one of many things that had changed in the past twelve months.

"Exactly — a *break*. That's what my Pinterest boards are for me." Everything made much more sense on her computer screen than it did in the kitchen. There were colors on her party-planning boards. Angles. Patterns. And they all fit together like a puzzle, a dazzling palette of turquoise — always turquoise — and gold and silver and peach. She liked when things lined up and looked neat.

Too bad there weren't any parties to plan. Not since her cousin's event last year. Before everything changed. Pinterest was an escape. The food truck, however, served as a frequent reminder of the pressures riding Rory's shoulders like a pageant queen on a hometown parade float. She couldn't get lost in that. It smothered. Like the smoke from the stove.

"I'll admit, the updated truck skin you designed for Salsa Street is legit." Grady reached over and clicked on the vent, raising his voice over the sudden whirring. "I

16

knew you had more in you design-wise than those online boards."

"Whatever." She straightened the crooked oven mitt hanging on its peg by the stove. She'd learned to hate compliments. She'd gotten good at batting away the "you're so pretty" ones. Now, the ones she truly needed — the compliments that referenced her strength or character or other beyond-skin-deep attributes — seemed to ricochet right off while she flailed around to catch them. Her ex-boyfriend, Thomas, had done a great job helping her flick them away.

Rory paused to align the salt and pepper shakers against the straight edge of the counter. "Besides, until we have the money to actually put the skin on the truck, it doesn't really matter what I design."

Grady shot her a knowing look. "Don't stress out."

"I'm not." She guiltily stepped away from the seasoning shakers.

He pointed with a carving knife. "You're organizing things. Which means tomorrow I won't be able to find them. Relax — we've got the food festival coming up. That always brings in extra dough."

According to Grady — and Aunt Sophia's sales records — that was the case every year. But could they depend on that alone?

Columns of red numbers danced in Rory's mind. It seemed foolish to put all their eggs — make that tacos — in one basket. But wasn't that what she'd done when she quit her pay-the-bills job in insurance and took over the food truck last year when her aunt's health declined?

It had started in increments. Rory had filled in while Aunt Sophia was too weak from chemo to work the truck. Grady kept things running, but one man couldn't take all the orders, fill them, and keep up with the business side of things. Rory had filled the gaps, thinking it would only be temporarily, until one day they all realized it wouldn't be. The decision was made, the will was signed, and a few months later, Aunt Sophia was gone.

"Like I said, hermana, you're good at a lot. But for now, why don't you be good at scooting over. You know he'll be here any minute." Grady nudged her out of the way of the stove with a bowl of freshly grated shredded cheese.

Rory glanced at her watch. Wednesday, June 2. "It's the lawyers' order again, isn't it?" The last few Wednesdays, without fail, the Worthington Family Law Firm ordered enough food for an army and insisted on a rush job. Heaven forbid they order ten

18

minutes sooner instead to make up the difference. The runner they sent each week — a pale, lanky college kid — always looked as harried as a third monkey trying to board the ark.

And yet every Wednesday she and Grady hurried around during the lunch rush, all at the whim of some rich society family thinking they were too good to wait in line like everyone else. What was that saying about insanity? Something about doing the same thing over and over but expecting different results?

The walls of the food truck crushed in a few inches, and Rory inhaled deeply. Speaking of insanity — a food truck owner who couldn't cook. But she was there to carry on Aunt Sophia's legacy. There for her cousin Hannah. For all the people depending on her. Salsa Street wasn't only a popular restaurant on wheels. It was an heirship.

Even if it did constantly reek of cilantro.

Grady glanced up from the stove, calm and steady as always, despite their fast-paced morning. "Ready for the box."

She was already holding it open.

His warm, big-brother smile of gratitude reminded her to take another deep breath. "She'd be proud, you know. Aunt Sophia."

Rory cocked an eyebrow at Grady.

"Don't do that. You look even more like Fiona when you do."

She twisted her lips to the side. "That's so annoying."

"Oh, yes, poor thing. It must be tragically difficult to be constantly mistaken for a beautiful Hollywood star." Grady rolled his eyes as he expertly transferred the quesadilla to the waiting black Styrofoam box.

"It is, actually." That's why Rory had signed up for Love at First Chat in the first place. Total anonymity. No pictures allowed. At least not until the app's self-designated progression of communication declared it time.

Step One: Connect via matchmaking pairing through the app's trusted formula.

Step Two: DMs.

Step Three: Personal texting.

Step Four: Photos shared.

Step Five: Meeting in person.

She'd memorized the steps, yet at the moment, she had no intention of sliding past number two anytime soon. It was too risky.

Rory artfully arranged slices of yellow and red peppers atop a pile of rice, then secured the lid on the box, added it to the to-go bag of other orders, and turned to the pick-up window just as the lanky law firm runner rushed up, shirt half untucked and shoelace untied.

"Laces." She jerked the bag out of his reach.

"Not again." He sighed as he bent to quickly whip them into knots. Then he straightened and held out his hands.

She shook her head. "Shirt."

He rolled his eyes and shoved it haphazardly into the loose waist of his slacks.

"You know your boss would lecture you. I'm doing you a favor." She surrendered the heavy bag to his waiting grip.

Grady joined her at the window, straight-faced. "Fly."

The kid's eyes widened, and he quickly lowered the bag a few inches south. Grady snorted. "I'm kidding, man. It's a joke. They don't do that where you work?"

He sighed. "If you count laughing *at* people as joking, then yes. The partners are regular comedians."

Grady tilted his head back and roared, the contagious sound radiating from deep within. Tension melted off Rory's shoulders. It always did when he laughed. It reminded her of Aunt Sophia. Joy, personified. She could hear her now. "*Cooking brings me joy, hija.*"

Rory wished it did the same for her.

21

Maybe it would if she could do more than burn grilled cheese.

Grady leaned farther out the window. "You're funny. What's your name?"

The guy hefted the bag to hang on his elbow. "Alton."

"You going to be a lawyer one day, Alton?" Grady shoved a handful of napkins at him. "Don't forget those sample cups of jalapeños."

Alton dumped a few lidded cups into the bag. "No way. It's just a job. Beats minimum wage somewhere."

"You should always do what you love," Grady said. "Then it's never truly work."

She kept her eyes on Alton, bumping Grady intentionally with her shoulder. "But also remember that commitment is important."

"So is finding joy in the everyday." Grady pressed closer to the window, raising his voice over hers.

She ignored Grady's elbow in her ribs. "Yes, but so is financial security and supporting the people you love."

Alton backed away slowly, wary eyes darting between them like ping-pong balls. "So, is the life advice free, or will you add that to the company's tab?"

"Oh, we're adding it." Grady straightened

22

with a grin. "They can afford it."

"They can also afford manners, and yet . . ." Alton's voice trailed off as he lifted one hand in a wave and walked away.

Grady chuckled in his wake. He cupped his hands and shouted after him. "You're gonna be fine, Alton!" He shook his head, still laughing as he began cleaning up spilled cheese. "And you too, by the way." He raised his brows pointedly at Rory. "Even if you keep working jobs you hate."

"You trying to get rid of me?"

"Of course not. I need you."

The sentiment was meant to be kind, but it felt more like a noose. Salsa Street did need her — and so did her cousin, Hannah.

Rory helped him clean, swiping the mess into her hand with a napkin, her mind drifting to a happier place. StrongerMan99 would get a kick out of the exchange they'd had with Alton when they talked tonight. She couldn't share any names, though. No hints of anyone or any places that would lead to recog—

"You're doing it again." Grady snapped open a new trash bag.

Rory cinched the full bag and lifted it from the can. "No, I'm not." She hated when Grady read her mind.

He ignored her. "Are you ever going to

23

meet this guy? Or should I tell your computer congratulations and get Nicole to buy you guys a toaster?"

"Look, we can't all marry our high school sweetheart and live happily ever after the traditional way like you and Nicole, okay?" Rory hefted the bag and opened the truck door. "Some of us have to get creative."

"*Have to?* Hardly. You could walk down that street right there and have any date you wanted." Grady gestured to the alley behind them. Then his eyes darkened. "But don't do that. That's dumb. You know not to do that, right? Bad example."

"Relax. I'm not desperate. I'm not even looking." Rory hesitated at the top of the truck ramp as she shifted the bag from one hand to the other. "I just like chatting. Keeping it casual."

"Casual, as in perfect strangers."

"It's not like that." In fact, she felt like she knew StrongerMan99 a lot better than most of her in-person friends — and they'd only been talking for a few weeks.

She knew StrongerMan99 ran 5Ks and enjoyed classic literature like she did. She knew he had one brother, his favorite NFL team was the Saints, he was addicted to the Food Network, and he reluctantly knew all the words to "Ice Ice Baby," which had won him a karaoke contest back in college.

She just didn't know his name. Or phone number. Or where he lived, except for somewhere within sixty miles of Tyler, Texas. The odds of him living in her own small town of Modest, Texas, were slim. After all, she knew just about everyone here. Which meant he could even be as far away as Tyler.

"You ever going to meet?" Grady repeated his question, the one Rory thought she had so carefully dodged.

She shrugged. "We have a good thing going now." She didn't want to jeopardize that. There was something safe about having a friend — a flirty friend — who knew so much about her yet didn't know the less attractive, in-person parts. The rejectable parts.

She'd had enough rejection.

"But what if you could have a better thing going?" Grady gestured with the damp rag he held. "You know. Marriage and kids."

She wanted those things. One day. But . . . "I don't like change."

His expression softened. "I know. There's been a lot of it lately."

She nodded, blinking back the memories. Sophia had served more as a mother figure to Rory over the years than an aunt. She didn't deserve to die in her fifties. Didn't deserve the cancer that stole her hair and her health but never her smile. If Rory turned into even half the vibrant, vivacious, caring woman Sophia was, she'd be doing well.

Rory might be one-fourth Mexican, but as it were, she wasn't remotely one-fourth of the way to being as good of a woman as her aunt.

Grady's voice cracked. "I miss her too."

Rory lifted the bag, her throat tight. "I've got to —"

"I know, I know." Grady held up both hands in surrender. "Too mushy." He called over his shoulder. "I'll just go light this cilantro-scented candle I bought for you."

The knot in her throat slid back down a few inches, and she cast Grady a grateful smile before heading for the dumpster. She knew her blessings. He was one of them. Sophia had been another, and Rory would do all she could to keep her aunt's legacy — the best part of Rory's heritage — alive.

Even if that meant spending her days with endless cilantro.

They never put enough cilantro on his quesadilla.

Jude Strong Worthington swiped his

mouth with a napkin, the cheap paper catching on the five-o'clock shadow that always sprung up around noon and was the bane of his father's clean-shaven existence.

Which meant if his beard was a puppy, Jude would have given it a treat as a reward.

Hollis Strong — never "Dad" during business hours — raised dark brows at Jude across the gleaming boardroom table. "Did they get your order wrong again?"

"Nah. I asked for extra cilantro, but it's no big deal." Jude shrugged before diving back into the deliciously cheesy concoction. Nothing was ever right — or good enough — for Hollis. Jude had learned long ago to let the little things slide. When you grow up without a mom and have the world's most domineering father and a pretty-boy society brother, you figure that out quick. Unfortunately, Hollis had yet to catch on. Besides, Salsa Street's food was delicious, even without the extra cilantro. He'd taken to eating there once a week months ago, but once his family jumped on board, they'd insisted on creating obnoxious rush orders.

Apparently, it wasn't enough to be one of the top law firms in North Texas. The infamous Worthington family had to leave their mark everywhere they went.

"Figures they screwed it up. I don't know

why we keep going back to this Salsa Street place." Hollis sprinkled a few jalapeños onto his salad.

Jude gestured toward his meal. "Because it's fresh food, and if the doctor finds out you keep eating burgers and fries three times a week, he's going to lay into you again."

Hollis scoffed. "What he doesn't know won't hurt him."

"It'll hurt *you*, I believe is the point."

"Salsa Street isn't that great," his brother, Warner, chimed in. "The chips are always stale."

"They're not stale, they're organic. Besides, you think you can do better?"

"No, but you probably do — Mr. Taco Boy, always watching Food Network and helping our housekeeper when we were growing up." Warner snapped his fingers. "What was her name?"

Maria. Her name was Maria, and she'd been the only mother figure in their household for most of their childhood until she retired and moved back to Mexico when Jude turned eighteen. Warner knew her name — he was just being rude.

Jude fisted his napkin. Lately he'd been picking his battles with Warner, and while Maria was worth it, getting Warner to

28

change his spots was impossible. "She made good tacos." The best he'd ever had. Salsa Street, while consistently pleasant, couldn't come close to Maria's authentic, four-generational family recipe. His mouth watered thinking about them.

"Well, I'd much rather have the burger and fries. I'm sick of this Salsa Street place — they never know what they're doing." His father muttered a racist expletive. Warner snickered his amusement.

Jude dropped his napkin. "For the hundredth time, don't *say* stuff like that."

"Why not? The walls have ears?" Hollis crunched his taco salad with a fork.

"Yeah. Yours." Warner flashed a polished smile that earned a chuckle from their dad. "What with that new security system you put in last week."

Jude ignored his brother. "Because it's racist. Or, at the least, bigoted." Knowing his dad, it was both.

"What, am I on trial now?" Hollis laughed. "Save it for the courtroom, son. You need the practice."

Jude shoved another bite in his mouth to keep from saying something disrespectful. Some days he couldn't believe this was his family. Other days the framed Ivy League degrees on the walls proved it was in his blood, and escape felt the opposite of imminent.

In fact, when he half closed his eyes, the walls felt like they might be slowly moving together, like that carnival fun house he went to when he was ten. The one that Warner abandoned him in, thinking it'd be hilarious. That night was the first and only time he heard Maria cuss at his brother. Good thing Warner hadn't known Spanish back then.

He opened his eyes. The walls, with their custom crown molding and mahogany chair rails, remained in place. But the weight of his load felt a dozen times heavier. He had to get out of there. Not for the afternoon but permanently. Yet as usual, any plans he conjured with that goal in mind always dissipated like a mirage on the horizon. How did a man fight his destiny?

Hollis tossed his napkin onto the table. For someone who allegedly didn't like Salsa Street, he sure had devoured that salad. "How's the Blackwood case coming?"

Speaking of heavy loads. Jude couldn't muster the energy to mask his sigh. "It's coming." His dad had given him a complicated scandal for training, and it was taking most of Jude's evening hours to investigate it as thoroughly as he needed to. And he wouldn't even get credit for it since he wasn't licensed to practice yet.

"How enlightening of an update." Hollis's tone dripped with sarcasm. His attention shifted to Warner. "What about the Steiner case?"

Warner straightened in his seat. "It'll be wrapped and ready for trial in three days."

Jude fought the temptation to roll his eyes and settled for finishing his quesadilla in two forceful bites. The way they seasoned their chicken was exactly on point. Cumin, cayenne pepper. He chewed slower. What else was he tasting? Maybe —

"You still with us, baby brother?" Warner tilted his head toward Jude. "Who is she?"

"Who is who?" Jude shoveled in a forkful of rice and beans. *He* knew who she was. Well, her username anyway — ColorMe Turquoise. But Warner had no idea he'd been chatting online with a woman, and he'd like to keep it that way.

"The girl on Love at First Chat."

Jude's eyes narrowed, and he set down his plastic fork. "You've been monitoring my internet usage?"

"I just said the walls have Dad's ears." Warner spread his hands wide. "Regardless, personal time should be spent during personal time, am I wrong?"

31

"You're not the boss." He immediately hated how petty that sounded. But Warner had crossed a line with the privacy invasion, and now his heart pounded faster than at the final lap of his 5Ks. His conversations with ColorMeTurquoise were one of the highlights of his evenings. The last thing he wanted was for Warner, of all people, to poke his haughty nose where it had no business being.

Warner bristled. "Maybe I'm not the boss *yet*."

Hollis snorted. "Hey, I'm still very much alive and well over here."

Warner ignored him and pointed at Jude. "You know, maybe you need to study more instead of drifting off into la-la land over some chick."

"You're one to talk. *You* have a girlfriend."

"I didn't when I was taking the bar years ago. Yours is in less than a month."

"I'm aware." Jude boxed his trash and tried to keep the grit from his voice. Warner knew how to push his buttons. It was a matter of staying calm. Staying in control. Not giving in.

Warner ignored the hint, per usual. "You know me and Dad both scored a —"

"I *said* I was aware."

"Don't get testy. Sometimes I go weeks

32

without seeing Maddison." Warner slammed his bottle of sparkling water on the table.

It had always aggravated his brother that things came a little easier for Jude in school — he had earned his master's six months faster than Warner had. It wouldn't be a competition, except Warner insisted on making it that way. He was probably ready for Jude to get the bar over with simply so he could relax in knowing he'd made the better score.

Warner's scowl deepened at Jude's silence. "We all have to pay our dues to get where we're meant to be."

Jude swiped a stray piece of cheese from the table. "And I'll pay mine."

At the moment, his entire life felt like paying a debt — or maybe more like prison labor. Cutthroat lawyer blood didn't run in his veins. But carrying the last name Worthington didn't give him a choice. The embossed name on the firm's intimidating doors ran up the ancestral ladder all the way to the legacy his grandmother had left behind — and it carried expectations.

If there was a way out, Jude would have taken it by now. He didn't fit in here. But leaving meant abandoning his place in the family will. Hollis didn't play. And Jude had nothing else to fall back on.

"I haven't seen you crack a book in two weeks." Warner refused to drop it. "I *breathed* law for literally nine months in preparation for my bar."

"I don't see how you could breathe at all, with your head so far up Dad's —"

"Boys." Hollis's voice boomed. "Enough."

Boys. Exactly how they were acting. His brother always brought out the worst in him, and Jude hated that he let him. If he tried hard enough and passed the bar with flying colors, then maybe — *maybe* — he could earn their respect. Even earn Dad's favor over Warner, for once.

He just wasn't sure he wanted to anymore.

What *did* he want? Not the bar. Not another plaque on the wall. Not another rat race paired against his brother, striving to earn their father's empty praise.

And somehow, under all that, he couldn't stop wondering about that dang quesadilla. What *was* that other ingredient?

He offered a halfhearted apology to Warner, more for the sake of his own conscience than for any true attempt at achieving peace. Warner brushed it off as expected. And naturally, his brother didn't return the gesture but rather set his jaw and averted his gaze.

Jude shoved away from the table. He'd had enough, all right. Enough of all of it.

TWO

Rory sat in bed, her laptop perched on the pillow in her lap as she typed in Love at First Chat's messenger app.

> Do you ever feel like the walls are closing in?

She should have been sleepier than she was, given the fact that it was almost midnight. She'd left her girls' night out with Nicole early to come home and crash with sweatpants and her favorite romantic comedy but found herself unable to stay away from StrongerMan99's DMs.

He was quickly becoming the best part of her day — even more so than Tom Hanks and Meg Ryan. She paused the movie, then took a sip of green tea as she waited for him to respond to her question.

Wall, huh? You mean literally or figuratively?

She hesitated, then resumed typing.

Both.

I experienced that today, oddly enough.

Literally or figuratively?

Both.

She leaned back against the padded headboard, comfort seeping through the quiet space. Being understood was priceless. Suggested progression timelines or not, if her friendship with StrongerMan99 never went anywhere else, that alone would be enough.

He got her.

Sometimes I feel so trapped in what I do.

What do you do?

She hesitated.

I thought we couldn't share specifics?

That was part of the rules of the site. Of

course, they could break them anytime they wanted to — that was up to them. But the blind concept of the site and its suggested progression course were there for a purpose. She and StrongerMan99 had both signed up for a reason.

And a few weeks of connection probably wasn't long enough to override reason, even if it was starting to feel like she'd known him forever.

Dots formed, then vanished, then started over as he responded. She held her breath as her thoughts battled each other over his question. What did she do — or what did she *want* to do?

She was fairly certain those were two different answers. She beat him to the response.

> Well, my coworker tells me all the time I should do what I love.

> So that means you don't currently do what you love?

> No. But it's not that simple.
> I have responsibilities.

Like protecting her aunt's legacy and

38

decades of recipes passed down through the family.

Dots formed. Then he wrote,

> I understand that. Ditching the specifics, what do you do? In general?

> In general, I own a business.
> Did I ever tell you that?

Would he pick up on the *You've Got Mail* reference? She smiled at the movie paused on her TV.

> Is this my cue to tell you to go to the mattresses?

She laughed.

> I knew you were a keeper.

Her fingers flexed over the keyboard. Too far? They'd never pushed the limits from appropriately flirtatious into future references. But tonight, she craved connection. She pressed on, heart pounding.

> I like daisies too, for the record.

> Duly noted. I've heard they're the friendliest of flowers. 😉

39

She couldn't stop the matching smile tugging relentlessly across her own cheeks. She typed again.

> So what do you do? Generally.

Family business.

> Discount bookstore featuring overpriced coffee? F-O-X?

Funny.

The dots formed again after a brief pause. Was he, too, trying to filter how vulnerable to be?

No books, unfortunately. Let's just say it's not a business I want to stay in.

> Is that why the walls moved on you today?

They do that a lot around my dad. He's not the easiest person to get along with.

Dots formed again, then stopped and didn't return. He couldn't — wouldn't? — say more. It was her turn. She thought a moment.

My mom died when I was little, and ever since then, my dad has traveled a lot for his work in the oil and gas industry. We're not very close either.

She knew deep down if she needed her dad for something major, he'd be there — probably. But she had the feeling that her father preferred the distance, so she rarely burdened him. He'd left so much of her parenting up to Aunt Sophia, especially during her tween and teen years. And with each failed relationship she'd endured, the absence of his attention always felt a little rawer.

Families can be tough, huh? I never knew my mother at all.

She inhaled slowly. Things were getting heavy. This was a next step for them — but a step to exactly where, Rory wasn't sure. She started to respond, but he beat her to it.

Didn't mean to go all Eeyore on you. 😳

No problem.

She wanted to offer so much more, but her fingers wouldn't move. She wasn't sure

41

where to go from here. Even thanking him for being there felt too mushy. But wasn't she always afraid of that — of being vulnerable? Grady would say so.

She ran her fingers over the keys.

> After all, if you can't talk to a total stranger, who can you talk to?

> LOL.

She pressed on before she lost her nerve.

> I'm here anytime you want to vent.
> Vague vent, of course.

As much as she enjoyed talking to StrongerMan99, she also really enjoyed the rules. They were safe — and they kept their developing friendship safe. In a way, it'd be nice to be able to see the person on the other side of the screen. Did he have dark hair? Blond? Was he telling the truth about his age?

She knew the risks. Knew he could be anyone, anywhere in the world, masking as a single guy in her radius. But that was unlikely since the site's staff background-checked each applicant and canceled accounts without refund if caught lying.

But at least he didn't gawk at her. "Has

anyone ever told you that you look like Fiona Stone?" She'd heard it on every date she'd ever gone on — and after each one, she never knew if the guy was interested in her or in her best physical features. This site was perfect. No photos, no identity except the true one of the heart. Or however their cheesy motto went.

He typed again.

I appreciate it.

And she appreciated him — more than he'd ever know, and probably more than she'd ever be willing to say.

Favorite *popsicle* flavor? Mine's grape.

And just like that, the heaviness of their conversation faded. She loved this part of their signing-off routine — taking one last step to get to know each other before saying good night. It was lighthearted, fun — and best of all, it conveyed the message that he wanted to keep learning about her.

She responded.

Orange. Grape turns your mouth purple. Favorite gum flavor? Hint — it's either mint or you're wrong.

43

Cinnamon. 😬

She snorted.

    Well, it's been nice chatting with you.

    Hey, now. Don't forget, opposites attract.

    You have a chance to redeem this.

She looked up at the movie.

    Do you prefer Meg Ryan's hair
    short or long?

    Short, obviously.

    Redemption secured.

They said good night, then signed off.
Rory slowly closed her laptop. The warmth
of their interactions always lingered deep
inside, easing the ache like a hot shower
after a cold jog. Grady had a point. Eventually, they'd have to meet for their relationship to go any further. But for now, she
craved stability, and StrongerMan99 was
always a DM away. So far, he wasn't treating her like she was too much and somehow
not enough all at the same time — like
Thomas had.

Maybe that meant he wouldn't run away after realizing she was just a small-town woman who hated change . . . a food truck owner who struggled not to burn toast . . .

And a girl who couldn't ever get a man to stay.

"Mayonnaise!"

That was it. The ingredient in Salsa Street's quesadillas he hadn't been able to figure out. Jude shoved away from the stove and yanked open the refrigerator as the front door chimed. Quesadillas would be his next experiment. For now, he had to finish these tacos.

"What in the world are you doing?"

Jude turned, meat-laden spatula at the ready, and shoved it toward his best friend as he entered the kitchen. "Try this."

His longtime friend and college roommate, Cody Austin, held up both hands in defense as he rested his hip against Jude's stainless steel kitchen counter. "I think I just turned vegan."

Jude extended the sampling of seasoned ground beef farther. He could only imagine what his friend thought, coming over to help quiz him for the bar and finding Jude in an apron, the kitchen a total disaster. "If you hate it, I'll eat a bite of raw onion."

"Like an apple?" Cody raised his eye-brows.

"Like an apple."

"Deal." He opened his mouth.

Jude handed him the spatula, and Cody shoveled in the bite. He chewed, hesitated, swallowed, then hesitated again. "Totally awful." He pointed to the peeled onion sitting on the cutting board. "Your turn."

"You're lying." Jude snatched the spatula back.

"I'm lying." Cody nodded. "I tried to hate it, but man, that was good. Excellent, really."

"I knew it." Jude resisted the urge to fist pump, then went ahead and did it anyway. This was cause for celebration. He hadn't cooked Maria's beloved taco recipe in about six years, and he'd been afraid he'd lost his touch.

"The cilantro might be a bit heavy."

Jude scowled. "Impossible."

"Not everyone loves it like you do."

"Well, they should."

"So, are we studying or playing Martha Stewart?"

Jude untied his apron strings. "I got hung up on this one section in the book and wanted a snack, and the snack turned into . . . well." He gestured to the cilantro covering the island like confetti, the dishes

46

stacked in the sink, and the hamburger meat wrappers piled by the overflowing trash can.

"You know, there are people out there who do this cooking thing for you. And even bring it to your door, for an extra fee. It's an amazing time to be alive." Cody swept a handful of cilantro into his palm and dusted it over the sink.

"That's the idea." Jude stirred the skillet of meat with a clean spatula. He cast Cody a glance over his shoulder. "What if I was that people?"

Cody squinted, as if trying to follow. "That people?"

"Well, *those* people."

"Those people?" Cody echoed.

"Dude. You're not a parrot."

"And you're not a chef. Or a deliveryman. What are you saying?"

"I'm saying, I could be." He nodded toward the flyer lying on the kitchen counter. "Look."

Cody picked up the blue flyer and read the big block letters in a monotone voice. "Announcing Modest's Food Truck Cook-Off, sponsored by Coined Bank & Trust."

"Not the contest part. Keep reading."

"The annual food festival?" He blinked at Jude. "But isn't the festival for food trucks?"

"Yes."

"You don't have a food truck." Cody glanced over his shoulder, as if checking to see if one had pulled up and parked in the living room.

"Not yet." Jude rubbed his hands together. It was crazy. But he felt a little crazy. Because working for his dad had made him crazy. "But I could."

Cody tapped the flyer against the counter. "Is this like a midlife crisis a decade early? Wouldn't it be easier to, like, rent a convertible and drive up the California coast or something? I'll chip in for gas money if that's the deal."

Midlife, no.

Crisis? Nearly.

"No gas money necessary. Unless I need gas for the food truck." Jude frowned. "I guess I need to figure out how that works."

Cody face-palmed.

When the flyer had come in the mail that afternoon, Jude had almost thrown it away. But the exchange with his family at lunch yesterday and his conversation with ColorMeTurquoise last night had gotten his bar-weary brain churning with what-ifs.

What if he didn't take the bar?

What if he didn't stay in the family business?

What if he opened his own food truck —

48

or one day, a restaurant — and actually enjoyed his career?

If he wanted out of the family legacy, it was now or never. He'd never had a shot at it before, but this seemed to be a true opportunity. Or maybe, for the first time, he'd finally mustered enough courage to go for it. Regardless, the festival would be the perfect time to launch into the industry and make a name for himself.

Jude shrugged. "Look, there's a lot to figure out, but I can do it. I've always loved cooking." There was a special joy in creating something and having someone else find pleasure in it. Something comforting and warm. He couldn't tell that to Cody, or his brawny, former-football-playing best friend would go into testosterone overload and march right out the door.

But he could be real with ColorMeTurquoise. She'd get it. In fact, he'd tell her tonight. As much as he could, anyway — no specifics. But he could tell her he was finally chasing a dream and that she was partly responsible for giving him the courage to do so. Their conversation yesterday had sparked new initiative in him. Asking her what she did made him reevaluate what *he* did, and he didn't like what he saw.

And he wanted her to see the best in him.

Cody handed back the flyer, doubt glazing his expression. "Your dad's cool with this? Quitting the family firm to drive around tacos?"

"I'm not driving around tacos." His smile faded. Cody had a point. Hollis wouldn't just let him leave without consequences. There'd be vague — but intentional — threats using words like *trust funds* and *rewritten wills* tossed around if he even tried.

Which meant he somehow had to make his dad think this was *his* idea. That it was somehow better for the firm if Jude went this route instead of taking the bar — at least for now.

The meat sizzled. Jude reached over to click off the burner and removed the pan from the heat. "Does it ever bother you that you went to an Ivy League university, yet you're back here in Modest?"

Cody tilted his head. "The same can be said for you."

"I didn't mean it like that." Jude shook his head. "We're only here because Grandmother grew up in Modest before moving to Dallas later in her life with all their oil money. Her family helped found this town, so she carried out all the Worthington traditions. As the only son, Dad feels an obligation to keep that torch burning."

50

"Grandmother?" Cody shook his head. "You never called her something more familiar growing up? Like Nana or Mammaw?"

Jude squinted. "You never met Emma Worthington, did you?"

"I can only imagine."

"Let's just say she was more pearls and pedigree than cookies and throw pillows." More firm pats on the back than warm hugs. Maybe it was no wonder his dad was so stiff and unaffectionate. Still, Grandmother had been generous to the town of Modest with both her time and her money and left behind a legacy that demanded respect for reasons far beyond wealth.

Unfortunately, Hollis wasn't living out the same. He might have donated annually out of obligation, but doing so was more a power play than true generosity. Grandmother had loved the landscaping around downtown Modest and had spent countless hours beautifying the town with her own hands, gloved though they were. She hosted garden parties and book clubs — which was the reason he'd been introduced to Austen, Hemingway, and Dickens at a young age — and created a nonprofit that supplied art supplies and instruments to the elementary school. She donated funds and first-edition literature tomes to the museum, started a monthly women's Bible study at the country club, and made frequent efforts to create awareness about and protect local honeybee colonies.

The only thing Hollis ever wanted to protect was his own backside.

Cody shrugged. "I'm pretty happy with the construction business I started."

Jude pointed. "Exactly. *You* made your own decision, *you* started a business, and *you're* happy."

Cody handed Jude the colander sitting on the counter and stepped back as he drained the meat. "What's your point?"

"The point is — you chose, and you're reaping those benefits."

"So you're saying being a millionaire in *Grandmother's* hometown isn't doing it for you? Why not stay in Dallas then, in your other family mansion, and do law there?"

Jude turned on the water to rinse the grease from the sink. "Because I love Modest."

"Dude, you're losing me." Cody ran his hand over his jaw. "What are you getting at?"

Jude set the colander on the counter and turned to face him. "I never got to choose."

"And you're not happy."

"Right."

"You know, a girlfriend could help with that."

Jude shot his friend a look.

"Okay, so to sum up — you're not happy, and now you're choosing tacos over the family business."

"I don't know. Maybe."

"What's it gonna be? Should I quiz you on the bar? Or is my new duty official taste tester?"

What *was* it going to be?

Jude hesitated. He was most likely diving in over his head. He knew nothing about any of this. He'd never even cooked for more than a few people at a time. It was going to take more than simply figuring out a few secret ingredients and stuffing his own fridge with tacos. He needed a cooking class — probably several. Maybe he could sign up for one of those YouTube courses, take a master class online.

An idea suddenly flared in his subconscious, morphing slowly into possibility. He didn't know a lot about starting a business, but he knew a great business that already existed. And he didn't know much about cooking anything other than Maria's recipe, but he knew an existing food truck that did a stellar job. And right now, he had the funds to invest in learning.

Hope rose against the odds — stubborn like a Worthington. Jude shoved his textbook out of the way, then pointed to one of the barstools on the other side of the counter with a confidence he didn't quite believe but desperately needed. Decision made. "Have a seat and grab a fork."

StrongerMan99:
Favorite TV show?

ColorMeTurquoise:
I love *King of Queens* and *Friends* reruns.

Would it be weird if I said the same?

No. You still like sports, though, and I'd rather watch grass grow. Actually, watching golf is sort of the same thing.

Fair enough.

First memory?

Hmmm. My dad took me and my brother to this restaurant when I was little. They threw rolls at you from across the room if you asked for one. It was a kid's dream and a parent's nightmare.

LOL. I've been to one of those before.
I got smashed in the face with a roll.

What's your earliest memory?

I don't know if it's my first memory, but
it's an old one. My dad and my aunt
took me to Disney World with my cousin.
I just remember the parades and the
spinning teacups.

Is barfing allowed in the happiest place on
earth?

Allowed or inevitable?

It'd have to be both if I rode one of those.
😆 Okay, new game. Would you rather . . .
be able to tell the future or read minds?

Hmmm. Read minds.

Even right now? With us?

Especially right now . . . with us.

You don't strike me as a risk-taker, and
that seems risky.

You make me feel safe.

I'm honored. Also, I have to point out, I'd choose tell the future. We should combine our powers for good and rule the world.

Deal. Now, would you rather let a tarantula crawl down your arm or eat a ghost pepper?

I hate spiders.

That's cliché.

No, really. I HATE spiders.

I hate spicy food.

More than spiders?

More than anything.

Can I tell you that you're an absolute weirdo and you not be offended?

I already knew you were going to say that.

THREE

"I've never understood the appeal of mole sauce."

"And I've never understood your aversion to authentic Mexican food." Grady shot Rory a look as he measured chicken broth over a mixing bowl. "Also, if you pronounced it correctly — meaning *not* like the animal that tunnels underground — it might have more appeal."

She tilted her head, considering. "Doubt it."

"Can you at least stop eating that Hershey's bar now?"

Chocolate was her favorite stress snack. She pinched off one more bite, then handed over the remainder of the dark chocolate bar. Grady shook his head as he appeared to fight the grin stretching across his face. "You're impossible, hermana."

"I prefer incorrigible." She wiped the

corners of her mouth to remove the evidence.

Hannah stifled a laugh from the bottom of the open truck ramp, where she was set up with a card table and folding chair, carefully creating origami in the late-morning sun. "I think she's both."

"Thank you, Hannah." Grady bowed toward her, and she wrinkled her freckled nose in response.

"Don't start ganging up on me now." Rory pointed teasingly to her cousin. She loved when Hannah got to come hang out at the truck — her mom's old business. Hannah had been at Unity Angels, a home for people with Down syndrome, for almost seven years and loved it. They treated her like family — made sure she knew she was valued and important. A little over a year ago, Rory had volunteered to plan the party the care center hosted to celebrate each resident's annual achievements. It was the last event Aunt Sophia had been well enough to attend. Rory still remembered her aunt's proud smile as Hannah walked the stage and accepted her certificate.

When Hannah was around, it was as if Sophia still was too.

Rory smiled at her. "You're supposed to be on my side, remember?"

"I'm on the side of the swan." She held up her latest creation as a proud grin split her rounded cheeks.

"That's amazing." It really was. Hannah had a natural gift for origami, sort of like Grady had a natural gift in the kitchen. Rory, well — she was naturally gifted at dialing for takeout.

"You know, Rory, you could actually learn to cook rather than stand by bemoaning that you can't." Grady turned to the next counter to continue slicing strips of chicken on a cutting board.

"Hear, hear!" Hannah piped up.

Rory hiked her eyebrows as she leaned one hip against the oven door. "Remember the last time you gave me a lesson?"

Grady winced. "Ah, right. The dish towel."

She demonstrated the fireball with her hands. "Whoosh."

"Went right up in smoke." Grady handed her a package of bread crumbs. "You're right. Never mind. Just measure me out a fourth of a cup of these."

"I can manage that." Bread crumbs made her think of Hansel and Gretel. And Hansel and Gretel made her think of fairy tales, which made her think about her conversation last night with StrongerMan99.

The banter had been fun as always. But

the best part was the end of their conversation, when he shared that he'd decided to go after a new career goal — and she'd been responsible for giving him the boost to do so. He said the magic words she'd been craving . . .

"You seem to really get me. And that's not typical of most people in my life right now. So, thank you."

She didn't know where this thing between them was going, but he already had her looking forward to the journey. Trying to hide her lingering smile, Rory finished pouring the bread crumbs and handed back the mixing cup.

Grady started to dump it into the boiling pot on the stove, then stopped. "Rory. I said a fourth of a cup."

"Right." Rory pointed. "One-fourth . . . oh." She'd measured one *and* one-fourth of a cup. She grimaced. "Sorry?"

"Like I said. Impossible." He shook most of the bread crumbs back into their package and dumped the rest into the pot.

This time she didn't argue.

A knock sounded on the window. Rory jumped, eyes darting to the closed partition. "We're not open yet."

Grady checked his watch. "Five 'til. Someone's hungry."

60

"I know I am." Hannah held up one hand and waved it. Grady slipped her a piece of the uneaten chocolate bar with a grin.

"I saw that." Rory slid open the window, then inhaled sharply. It was the lawyer from their infamous Wednesday order — the younger one. Jude. The one she'd always begrudgingly admitted was the most handsome of the crew, although she still insisted the entire family was one to generally avoid. Alton's insider-scoop testimony the other day had only sealed her opinion. "Good morning."

Further words fled her vocabulary. What was he doing here? Was Alton sick? She checked her watch. Wait. It wasn't even Wednesday.

He smiled, his teeth as white and straight as a toothpaste commercial. For some reason, the sight made her immediately wary of his genuineness. No one was that perfect. "Good morning. I know I'm a few minutes early, but I was hoping to get a little help."

He didn't seem overly entitled, but she kept her guard up. After all, he had knocked before they'd officially opened. She kept her tone friendly and even. "Sure. Quesadillas, right? Extra cilantro. And a taco salad."

"No, I'm not here to order. But good

memory." The wind sent a gust of warm air into the truck, and a shock of dark hair slipped from its gelled position to drape down his forehead. He brushed it back, the tousled look even more appealing.

Rory stiffened a little, annoyed she'd noticed. Despite their unconfirmed status, she felt loyal to StrongerMan99. Besides, Jude wasn't simply part of the Worthington Family Law Firm — he was part of an entire family society. The community magazine featured the beautiful brothers in almost every issue as they split their time between Modest and Dallas. Their father, Hollis, was a shark in local waters when it came to legal matters. He never lost. But what he lacked in congenial personality, his sons more than made up for in good looks and public charm. They were the whole package.

If someone were to notice that kind of thing.

She cleared her throat. "So you don't want food? I'm confused."

"That's my fault." He smiled again. "Let me start over. I'm here because I'm a big fan."

A fan? Her crossed arms dropped to her sides. "Of Salsa Street?" Her voice pitched.

"Of course."

Of course. A blush crept up her neck. She craned her head to see if Grady could intervene and save her from further humiliation, but he was busy making the mole sauce and didn't even seem to notice Jude standing in front of their truck. This was why she needed to date online — she was a hot mess in person.

"Thank you." Not that she could take direct credit for the food. She self-consciously reached up to adjust her ball cap.

"You guys have the best quesadillas. And I've been thinking about taking some cooking classes." Jude hesitated, shoving his hands into the pockets of his navy slacks. "I was wondering . . ." His voice trailed off in another gust of wind.

Rory leaned slightly out the window to hear, but she'd already missed it. She racked her brain for an appropriate answer based on what little context she had. "There are usually a few summer cooking courses at the community college in Tyler."

"Well, I was hoping for something more one-on-one. From someone who I know knows what they're doing." He laughed, the sound more awkward than she'd have expected from someone of his wealth and status.

Wait. Was he *nervous*?

The thought brought a rush of validation, and she straightened. She'd have to let him down, but she'd put this compliment in her pocket for many weeks to come. One of the famous Worthington lawyers wanted cooking classes from Salsa Street. She had to tell him the truth, though. "I'm flattered, but I actually don't do the cook—"

"I'm willing to pay private course fees." His smile dimmed in wattage at her hesitation. Probably because he wasn't used to being told no. "I understand it's asking a lot at the last minute, and I'm happy to compensate accordingly."

The rebuttal died in her throat. Salsa Street needed all the financial help it could get right now. Business hadn't been the same since losing Sophia's magic touch. This could pull them through until the festival, when hopefully their numbers would shimmy back into the black. Depending on what he wanted to pay, anyway. She had no idea what to charge for something like this.

Jude must have taken her silence as further rejection because he pressed on. "A couple of classes should be plenty. I'm a fast learner, and I'm mostly interested in various kinds of tacos. Nothing fancy."

That was the problem. It was all fancy to Rory. She could teach him how to burn towels and mismeasure, sure . . .

Then Jude voiced the amount he was willing to pay, and her stomach clenched.

She tightened her grip on the counter as she stared at Jude and Jude stared back, eyebrows raised, waiting on her response. She should tell him — right now — that she didn't cook. That it was all a farce, or an uncorrected assumption, really, on behalf of the community since Sophia had passed away. But her throat closed, refusing to release the confession. Once word got around, could it affect business even more? Sophia had been so proud of their heritage, of their family line and the passed-down recipes from her grandmother and her grandmother's mother before her. Everything was authentic and unique to the Perez family. Wasn't that why Sophia had left the truck to Rory in the first place, and not Grady — because of heritage? Family didn't leave family.

A memo her father had never received.

Rory owed it to Sophia to figure this out. After all, she was supposed to know how to do this by now — it was in her blood, whether she liked it or not. Perez blood. Bloodlines that stopped after Hannah and

Rory were gone, if they never married or had children.

No pressure.

She gulped a breath of fresh air, her thoughts spiraling out of control as she fumbled for an explanation. Grady, oblivious to the conversation happening at the window, hummed under his breath as he stirred the mole sauce.

Grady. Rory sucked in her breath. That was it. He could help her. Wasn't he just saying she should learn to cook for real? Well, they could kill two birds with one stone, all while saving face. He could be the voice in her ear — however they had to rig it to coach her along for these classes with Jude. Didn't they do that kind of thing in the movies all the time? She just needed a pair of quality earbuds.

"In that case, I'm Rory — your new teacher." She stuck her hand out the window to shake on the deal before she could talk herself out of this craziness. "There's a community kitchen at the rec center, and local licensed businesses have access to it if you'd rather do lessons there and have more space. I can reserve it for us."

She'd been there a few times over the past year with Grady when he would try out new recipes and needed "elbow room," as he put it. Truthfully, though, it was more of an excuse for him to cook messier and sing louder.

Jude's easy smile remained in place as he shook her hand. His palm felt warm against hers, shooting a quick tingle up her arm. She dropped his grip as he responded. "Here is fine. I'm sure that'd be easier for you, right? You'd have all your familiar utensils and ingredients and everything. I don't want to be any trouble."

He didn't realize that her attempting to cook wouldn't be easy, regardless of where she was. She nodded, rubbing her affected palm as subtly as possible. "When do you want to start?"

Relief flooded his expression. "As soon as possible."

"Tomorrow after the lunch rush?"

He nodded. "Great. I'll be here by two thirty."

"Perfect." As perfect as this foolish escapade could possibly be, anyway. Rory slid the window closed.

Grady turned then, spoon dripping over the large pot of sauce. "Who was that?"

She opened her mouth, then shut it. Then she smiled her best little hermana smile. "Do you happen to own a good pair of wireless earbuds?"

■ ■ ■ ■

He'd done it. Taken the first step toward his zany adventure into the world of food service. His dad, at best, was going to think he'd lost his mind — if Jude ever figured out a way to tell him. But ColorMeTurquoise would be proud. He wished he could tell her the specifics.

One day.

Jude tapped his fingers on the mouse, watching the blinking cursor on his computer monitor. Ever since leaving Salsa Street and making arrangements for cooking lessons with Rory, he hadn't been able to concentrate. He was really doing this.

He opened the browser on his phone and went back to skimming the business plan he'd googled earlier that day. He'd decided to purchase a used truck so that it would be ready to go and had already inquired about several online. The festival started in two weeks, and there was a ton to do. So much, in fact, that he couldn't think about it too long or he got overwhelmed.

And speaking of work — there was still plenty to do in the office today. He reluctantly went back to his desktop computer and finished his reply email to his father's paralegal. He hit Send as his intercom buzzed on the landline. "Mr. Worthington?"

His secretary. He'd told her a dozen times to call him Jude — with three Mr. Worthingtons in the building, it would be easier. Besides, he was starting to hate the name association.

He pushed the button to respond. "Yes, Rachel?"

"Mayor Whitlow is here to see you."

Jude frowned as he quickly scrolled through his online calendar. "The mayor? We don't have an appointment . . ."

"How's the local gentry?" Mayor "Whit" Whitlow barged through the door and landed in one of the chairs in front of Jude's walnut desk. His red bow tie, perfectly centered as always, stood out today against a crisp white button-down. He crossed one slacks-clad leg over the other, loafer bouncing.

"Mayor." Jude reached across the desk to shake his hand, nodding subtly behind him to Rachel, who shrugged helplessly and mouthed an apology from the doorway. "Doing well. To what do I owe the pleasure?"

He settled back in his chair as Whit did the same. A broad grin creased the mayor's face. He was forty-two, single, and didn't look a day past twenty-eight. "You know I don't like appointments. Is that okay?"

It didn't matter, regardless. Whit marched to his own tune, which, thankfully, had led the town of Modest well so far — three years into his first term. Although a handful of townsfolk still wondered if it was more akin to the tune of a pied piper. Regardless, the Worthingtons had supported the mayor every year. Jude appreciated Whit's knowledge of historic renovations and the way he kept the nostalgic parts of the town preserved in as many ways as possible. "It's never a problem, sir."

"Stop with all that *sir* nonsense." Whit lifted his chin a little. "If you want."

Which was code to not stop. Got it.

Whit continued, reaching under his sleeve cuff to fiddle with his Swatch. "This is sort of awkward." Whit rubbed his hands down his pant legs. "You know we value the Worthington family here in Modest."

Jude nodded. "Never doubted it . . . sir."

"And we realize you could spend all your time — and funds — in Dallas, but you choose to keep a residence here that benefits our community. For that we are grateful."

"Of course." Had he memorized this little speech before he came in?

Whit rubbed his palms a little faster. "It

seems that this year we've yet to receive the Worthington family's annual donation to the Town Beautification Fund."

Ah. So that's what this was about — his dad hadn't cut a check yet to Modest. The one that earned them a certificate or a plaque on a stepping-stone in the town square every year. "Sorry about that. It was probably an oversight. I'll see to it." Jude began making a note on his orange sticky pad.

"I'm afraid it might be intentional." Whit tapped at his dark brows in time with his bouncing loafer. "That's the awkward part."

"Intentional?" Jude's pen hesitated over the notepad. "I can't imagine —" But then, he could. Hollis was never beyond surprise. In his mind, any slight offense could justify holding a grudge — or holding back a donation. But that money went a long way each year to beautifying the town square, paving streets, or supporting other efforts that benefited Hollis as a citizen and kept up Grandmother's legacy. Last year the donation single-handedly rebuilt the collapsing gazebo in the center of town where Jude's grandparents had once renewed their vows. Surely Hollis wouldn't stoop so low as to penalize his own city?

"I'm not convinced your father is" —

Whit's voice dropped to a whisper so low Jude had to lean across the desk to hear him — "behind my upcoming . . . you know."

"Reelection?"

"Shh, shh," Whit hissed. He waved his hands, as if the erratic movement could alter the volume of Jude's words.

"He's not here." Jude gestured to the empty office. Then he remembered the whole "walls have ears" security system Warner had mentioned the other day. Still, he had to know what the mayor meant. "Why do you assume so?"

"Because he said so." Whit's voice pitched, and he cleared his throat.

"He said so?" Jude repeated the absurd declaration, trying to grasp it. His dad's MO was more mind games and manipulation than blatant disrespect. He'd talk about someone behind their back for months before being rude to their face. He valued his own image, if not his own character.

Besides, who would run against Whit?

"If you could ask him about that donation, the council and I would really appreciate it. If he isn't contributing this year, well, it changes our budget projection, to say the least."

"I don't understand. Did he tell you himself he wasn't supporting your campaign this election?"

Whit hesitated. "Not directly."

"So . . . indirectly."

Whit looked off to the left, toward the wide bank of windows overlooking Spruce Street. Several shops with colorfully striped old-fashioned awnings lined the road. The drugstore still boasted an antique soda fountain, complete with spinning stools and black-and-white-checkered floors. The corner grocery. And the more modern makeup store attached to the local salon — where Warner's girlfriend cut everyone's hair.

"Maddison Bussey?" Jude blurted out before he could censor.

Whit's gaze darted back to him, and his eyes confirmed what his voice wouldn't.

Jude nodded slowly, still bewildered as to what could have possibly upset his dad enough for him to withdraw his financial donation — and why Maddison of all people would have told the mayor. Wouldn't Jude have heard about it himself? If his family liked anything, it was griping about people. Plus, the tax write-off alone was motivation for someone like his father to keep donating. He wouldn't give that up for nothing.

"I'll look into it, but I really don't think —"

"I've always liked you, Jude." Whit leaned

forward in his chair, his brows furrowed. "You're approachable, you don't beat around the bush, and you seem like you couldn't be less interested in politics."

"Guilty." Jude chuckled. "But is that really a good thing to a mayor?"

"It is when you have the resources your family does. You don't seem bent on using those resources to get your way."

Everything started to click into place. "Mayor Whitlow . . . did you owe my dad a favor?"

Whit tapped his finger against his lip. "I believe I do now."

StrongerMan99:
I'm trying something new tomorrow.

ColorMeTurquoise:
New like tucking in your shirt
or new like skydiving?

😆 Somewhere in-between.

That doesn't rule out very much.

Okay, hint. I'm taking a lesson.

Musical?

Nope.

Sports?

Nope.

Singing?

Isn't that musical?

I meant instrument when
I said that earlier.

Voices are instruments.

Is yours?

Heck, no.

So, no.

No.

Is this actually a game of twenty
questions? Because I'm not sure
I can think of seventeen more.

Hint. My father will think it's ridiculous.

That hint would be more effective
if I knew your father.

You're better off this way.

Gotcha. Enjoy your housecleaning lesson tomorrow, then.

Nope.

Have fun at scuba diving lessons tomorrow.

Still no.

Drat. I'm apparently not good at games.

Sure you are.

One more.

Hint: it involves food.

Enjoy your doughnut-eating competition tomorrow.

That's sort of close!

Sweet. I like where this is going.

Me too.

FOUR

The air smelled like a mix of lemon Pledge and an apple spice candle.

"Always nice to see you, Rory." One of the nurse's aides waved from her station as Rory strolled the halls of Unity Angels. The floors gleamed and the blinds were pulled wide, letting in ample morning sunlight. "I believe Hannah's on the back porch this morning. We had a lovely sunrise."

Rory tucked the box of doughnuts against her hip and smiled. "Thanks, Angela." She couldn't ask for a better setup for her cousin. The staff genuinely cared about their residents, and more than one had gone out of their way in the months after Sophia's death to check on their entire family.

"You tell Miss Hannah she knows what to do with any leftovers." Angela winked as she pointed to the box of treats with her clipboard.

The porch was unoccupied, save for Hannah and a young man who looked to be in his thirties, running a pencil lightly over a sketchpad. Hanging pots of flowers framed a beautiful view of the lake in back of the property. Outside, on the manicured lawn, two residents played Frisbee. Peacefulness flooded the facility. Rory paused and took a deep breath, letting it soak in.

Across the screened-in porch, Hannah looked up from her perch on a wicker rocking chair and beamed. "Rory! Are those for me?"

"Of course. Though I hope you'll share." Rory sat in the rocking chair next to her cousin and set the box between them on a table. Hannah scooted a small potted fern out of the way, then opened the lid and carefully secured a glazed doughnut from the row of still-warm pastries.

Hannah took a bite, then swallowed. "Why did you come?" she asked as she wiped glaze from the corners of her mouth.

Rory loved Hannah's bluntness. If only everyone else would say exactly what they thought and meant. Then the irony of that struck, and Rory reached for a doughnut. If that were the case, wouldn't she have admitted to Jude that she couldn't cook? Then she wouldn't be gearing up for this afternoon's faux lesson.

She shook off the thought and focused on her cousin. "Because I wanted to see you."

"Ta-da!" Hannah gestured with her arms out to the side, as if pointing out Rory could now, indeed, see her.

Rory tapped Hannah's knee and laughed. "When are you going to start a comedy hour here?"

"I'm much too busy with my origami to pursue comedy." Hannah's face turned serious again. "I'm better at that."

"I think you're good at both." Rory nibbled on the side of her doughnut as Hannah went for a second one. She cast her cousin a glance from the corner of her eye. "How'd you get so confident, anyway?"

"I know who I am." Hannah tilted her head, studying Rory as she chewed. "Who are you?"

"I'm your cousin."

Hannah waved her doughnut. "Yes, but not just that. Who else are you?"

"I'm . . ." The only thing she could think of was that she was currently a big fat pretender. A wave of uncertainty washed over her. Maybe she should cancel the cooking lessons with Jude. Was it worth the charade to earn a little money? It would help Salsa Street, sure, but if Grady's projections about the festival were accurate, they should be able to keep going with the boost in sales.

Until . . . well. Until they couldn't.

"Oh, good, you're still here." Angela bustled out onto the porch, saving Rory from answering further. She held up an envelope. "I'll just give this to you now instead of mailing it." Then she hesitated, her brow furrowing. "It's somewhat time-sensitive."

"No problem." Rory took the letter, officially addressed from Unity Angels, and began to tear open the flap. Hannah offered Angela a doughnut, which she politely declined — then eagerly accepted at Hannah's insistence.

The dark-haired nurse tore off a bite and grinned. "You should run for office, Hannah. You're very influential."

Hannah returned the same honest answer she'd given Rory. "I'm much too busy with my origami to pursue politics."

Angela threw her head back and laughed. "You have my vote anyway, sister." Then she turned what seemed to be sympathetic eyes to Rory. "Let me know if you have any questions." She pointed to the letter before slipping back inside.

Hannah gestured with her doughnut before Rory could even fully remove the letter from the envelope. "My tuition is going up."

"It's *what*?" Rory glanced down at the letter, then back at her cousin. Insurance had always paid the bulk of Hannah's cost of living at Unity Angels, and Sophia had made up the mild difference. When they settled Sophia's estate, the bank account designated for Hannah's caretaking was revealed — with somewhat dwindling funds. Because of how meager Sophia's life insurance policy was, Rory and Grady had agreed to keep funneling a percentage of Salsa Street's earnings into Hannah's account just as Sophia always had. That way, the account balance shouldn't ever be a problem — unless the fees went up.

Rory turned her attention to the letter, skimming it before absorbing the full impact of the announcement. She let out a slow breath. It could have been worse — Hannah's insurance was still covering the bulk of the tuition, thankfully. But it wouldn't pay more than it had been. At the new rate, Rory and Grady would need to up the percentage of funds from Salsa Street that they moved into Hannah's account every month. Funds that, based on the past few months of sales, they weren't guaranteed to continually have.

Perfect calm coated Hannah's voice as she cheerfully brushed doughnut glaze from her hands. "It'll work out."

"Of course it will." Rory tried to make her tone as assured as Hannah's while she traced the logo on the doughnut box with one finger. Her mind raced. So much for canceling Jude's lesson. They really needed the extra funds now. But Hannah didn't have to know that or stress over it. In fact, Rory would do anything it took to keep her from finding —

"I know you stress over money, Rory." Hannah met her gaze straight-on. "That's pretty pointless."

Rory flinched. "I'm not stressing —"

Hannah pointed to the way Rory had just absently rearranged the contents of the end table, so that the straight edges of the square pot and the doughnut box lined up perfectly.

"Oh." Rory held up both hands in surrender. "Don't worry. I have a plan."

"I'm not worried." Hannah shrugged. "Maybe you should tell yourself?"

Rory inhaled deeply, shoving her shoulders up and back to release the tension. Then she shook out both arms until Hannah giggled. She shook out her legs next, until Hannah was doubled over, laughing.

"Please don't quit your job to be a dancer, Rory."

Rory kept her smile in place, grateful that Hannah's was fully intact, and tried to ignore the realization crashing over her.

That was just it. She couldn't quit her job at all.

Ever.

"Do I need an apron?" Jude self-consciously patted the front of his polo shirt. He'd worn his favorite casual one — gray with the wicking fabric so he didn't sweat to death in the tight confines of the food truck. On second thought, he probably should have taken Rory up on her offer to cook at the local community kitchen. He hadn't realized how crowded the truck would be.

Or how cute Rory would be in her ball cap, ripped-knee jeans, and oversized T-shirt knotted at her hip.

His chat with ColorMeTurquoise last night ricocheted through his mind, pulling him away from the dimple in Rory's cheek. Not that he and ColorMeTurquoise had a real relationship — yet — but he felt loyal to her while they investigated this tenuous thing they had going on through a screen. Every time they chatted, he felt more connected to her — to the point where he caught himself frequently opening the dating app on his phone throughout the day, checking for DMs.

As Warner used to say back in junior high about the head cheerleader — he had it bad.

"Do you need an apron?" Rory raised her dark eyebrows at him until they disappeared beneath the brim of her green hat and grinned. "That depends on if you plan to be messy."

"I don't really have a plan." He winced as the truth nudged him. "Except, you know, this one semiambitious plan." In honor of full disclosure . . .

"What's that?" Rory set a mixing bowl on the counter and then reached for a spatula hanging on a peg over the stove.

"The plan where I'm hosting a dinner party for my family to show them what I've learned."

She pursed her lips as doubt flickered through her eyes. "So, like, next month?"

"How about next week?" It was a bit crazy to expect so much in so little time, but he was a quick learner. He'd been cooking for himself for years, so he already had the basics down and could even experiment with recipes and taste testing. Really, he just needed to know the ins and out of public food service and how to cook in bulk. Right?

Plus, whatever other tricks Rory might have up her sleeve that had put Salsa Street in his speed dial. The woman knew what she was doing in the kitchen.

At the moment, though, she looked a little bewildered as her arched eyebrows lowered into a dark furrow over her hazel eyes. "That's semi, huh? I'd be interested to see what a *fully* ambitious plan looks like to you."

He shrugged. "It's sort of a time-sensitive issue." With his family, it always was. Except this time, it wasn't his dad's impatience demanding precedence — it was his own ticking clock. If he didn't have a solid business plan in place to escape taking the bar exam ASAP, he'd be skipping Taco Tuesday to sit in a classroom for hours. He had to get going. Now.

"That's a new one. Learning to cook Mexican food being an urgent matter." Rory checked a piece of paper lying on the counter — a recipe for taco meat seasoning, it looked like — and then shot him a curious smile.

He stepped out of the way as she opened a drawer and removed a whisk. He couldn't tell if she was inviting further conversation, demanding an explanation, or simply being polite. After all, she was getting paid, regardless.

He cleared his throat. "What can I say? We're a quirky family."

He almost missed hearing her mutter "I'll say" under her breath, but she definitely did.

"I'm sorry?"

A red flush tinted her neck. "No, I'm sorry. I didn't mean to say that."

"Out loud . . ."

She rolled in her bottom lip.

"But you meant to think it."

She opened her mouth, then closed it. "Busted."

He smiled first, giving her permission to do the same, and they chuckled together, hers containing more than a measure of relief.

"The rush orders are annoying, aren't they?" He looked around the small truck, stooping to peer out the service window. "I never even thought about it from this perspective." More like the perspective that Dad was hangry, so order quick to hush him up.

"Most people don't. It's okay." She shrugged it off.

He hated when people did that. He saw it all the time in law — clients pretending something was fine because they didn't want to deal with the consequences of the truth. "But it's not okay. We shouldn't do that to you guys, especially during a lunch rush."

She opened the refrigerator and removed a package of hamburger meat. "It does make things stressful some Wednesdays. But I'd say the bigger burden falls on poor Alton."

"Alton?"

There went her eyebrows again. "Your firm's runner?"

"Oh, right. Alton." He just then, in that moment, realized he'd never known the kid's name. A knot tightened in his stomach. Was he already turning into his father and brother, toting around a better-than-you attitude simply because they were born with money and reputation?

He saw the same question in Rory's eyes and suddenly wanted to clarify. But it wasn't her business. He wasn't there for counseling — he was there for tacos.

He briskly rubbed his hands together, fighting the urge to defend himself when he wasn't on trial. "So what's first, boss?" He grinned, hoping the switch to humor would kill the judgment clouding her hazel gaze.

It did, somewhat. She hesitantly handed him the package of meat, reaching up to fiddle with an earring. "Start cooking this." She coughed, adjusting her earring again. "I mean, browning."

"You do realize you owe me for life, right?" Grady hissed in Rory's ear via her earbud. "And for heaven's sake, tell him to stop stirring so hard. I can hear him. He's not sautéing the onions, he's taking out a personal vendetta on them. He's going full Count of Monte Cristo."

Rory bit back a snicker, turning it into a cough. Even to her untrained eye, Jude was rather enthusiastic with the spatula. "Maybe ease up a little."

She unwittingly placed her hand on his forearm, and the feel of his muscles cording beneath her fingers jolted her palm. She quickly withdrew it. "You don't want to smush them."

She could practically hear Grady, stationed outside in the parking lot in his car, rolling his eyes. "Smush?" She'd glimpsed him earlier when she'd taken out the trash — reclined all the way back in the driver's seat, sunglasses in place despite the summer cloud cover, hat brim pulled low. He somehow managed to make subtle look incredibly conspicuous.

Thankfully, Jude seemed oblivious. He

laughed. "I do that at home too."

"You've been cooking at home a lot?" She still couldn't wrap her mind around why he wanted lessons in the first place — he already seemed to know what he was doing far better than she did. She could, however, wrap her mind around the check she'd be able to deposit into Salsa Street's account when the lessons were over.

"Yes, I have been. Mostly for my friend, who serves as a guinea pig. I swear he's gained ten pounds." Jude grinned, glancing up from the sizzling onions. "But I really need to learn to cook for a crowd."

He must have a big family — more than just the brother and father she knew about from the media. She opened her mouth to ask, but Grady interrupted.

Frustration tinged his voice. "If you haven't chopped the bell pepper yet, now is the time."

Right. The peppers. She gestured to the cutting board and knife on the counter. "Next step, pepper chopping." She infused more confidence into her voice than she felt. Hopefully he'd buy it.

"I can guarantee you he isn't holding the knife right. Make him do it like I do it," Grady barked.

Rory reached toward Jude's arm one more

time, then hesitated. She couldn't demonstrate without looking like a fraud — she knew what Grady did but didn't dare position her own hands in a like manner for fear of chopping more than pepper.

She also didn't dare touch Jude again. She told herself it was for fear of interrupting the knife's blade, but deep down, it was more to avoid the shock of chemistry.

He finished cutting the pepper — growing in confidence with each knife stroke — and proudly scraped the bits of green into the waiting bowl. *"Voilà."* He presented the bowl to Rory.

"Well done," she guessed. Not that she'd really know. She did know that his beaming smile was like a proud little kid showing off his first-grade art project, and she couldn't help but smile back. There was certainly more to this stuffy lawyer than she'd ever have guessed. Maybe he was a normal guy — okay, a ridiculously wealthy guy — who wanted to learn to cook for himself and his large family. She could respect that.

Apparently, the rest of said family was able to stay out of the spotlight and not be involved in the law firm that gave Jude, his brother, and their father a lot of local status that she was beginning to think Jude didn't necessarily like. Little comments he'd made throughout their lesson gave her the impression that he didn't quite fit on the same page as them. The sudden consideration of the rush orders, the way he'd mentioned Alton in a positive manner two more times as if trying to make up for not knowing his name, the way he actually blushed when a female teenager ordering a quesadilla gawked at him through the service window . . .

"I can't help but notice that you guys seem to offer a little bit of everything on your menu — authentic Mexican and Tex-Mex." Jude stirred the bell pepper and onions into the sizzling meat, jolting Rory from her thoughts. "That's kind of unusual, huh? I thought food trucks typically downsized and stuck to one thing for lower costs."

"That's typical, but Aunt Sophia was not." Rory smiled at a memory from her late teen years. "She started out solely authentic — tostadas, pozole, the works. But the community gradually started requesting more and more Tex-Mex, and so she eventually said, 'Let them eat cake.' " She shook her head. "Ever since then, we've had a rotating menu that covers a little bit of it all."

"I see. She sounds like a special lady. I hate that I didn't discover Salsa Street sooner." Jude's eyes softened. "I'd have

91

loved to have met her."

"She was." Rory swallowed back the emotion crowding her throat. No mush allowed. "So, pop quiz. How many tacos should this batch make?"

"Coward," Grady whispered in her ear. "You know feelings won't kill you, right?"

"Shut up," she hissed, then widened her eyes at Jude, who thankfully hadn't heard her as he tilted his head and studied the skillet.

"Fifteen? Eighteen?"

Thankfully, she knew the technical details of Sophia's beloved recipes, even if she couldn't execute them well. She exhaled. "Twenty-five."

He squinted with doubt at the meat. "Really?"

Grady sighed again, this time longer and louder. "Tell him you don't ever want to overfill a taco. It'll get soggy and crack." *Duh* tinged his voice. He crunched something in her ear — a stakeout snack, apparently — and Rory adjusted the earbud volume as he continued. "And he can turn off the burners now. Unless you guys want to start another fire."

Jude turned off the burner without being told, and Rory raised an eyebrow at his instincts. In fact, he'd done that two other times with different tasks since they'd started the lesson. He didn't seem to need nearly as much help as she'd anticipated.

Or, more likely the case, she wouldn't recognize it if he did. If only Grady had a way to be the eyes inside the truck during the lessons too, instead of just the ears. She could screw this whole arrangement up — quickly.

But the grin on Jude's face didn't lend to the idea that he might view their lessons as pointless. In fact, he looked downright jubilant as he sprinkled the beef mixture over a soft corn tortilla, rolled it up, and took a giant bite.

"You've got to taste this." Joy lit his eyes as he turned the taco around to the unbitten end and held it up to her mouth, palm cupped underneath to catch any drips.

Rory hesitated, then leaned in and took a bite. Exactly like Grady's. Exactly like Aunt Sophia's.

He'd done it.

She chewed slowly and their eyes locked, the scent of onions and cumin mixing with a spicy hint of expensive cologne. For a minute, he didn't look like Jude of the Worthington Family Law Firm. He didn't look like the haughty man she'd seen in tailored suits featured in the local newspaper and on social media pages, or even like the entitled jerk who treated staff like paupers and demanded others' time for his own gain.

He simply looked like the guy next door who had accomplished a goal and was hoping for a gold star.

From her.

Grady's warning about starting a fire echoed in her ears, and she quickly took a step back. "Good — good job." She averted her gaze, clearing her throat in an attempt to hide the stutter.

"Oh, man." Grady's high-pitched, surprised tone grated in her ear. "Are you —"

She clicked off the earbud volume with a stealthy swipe of her finger and turned what she hoped was a neutral smile to Jude, keeping her gaze on his chin and away from his chocolate-brown eyes. "I think it's safe to call it a day."

FIVE

She'd been wrong. There was nothing safe about Jude. Certainly not the way his proximity in the food truck for lesson number two tugged at her stomach. Or the way his laugh echoed in her ears and made her want to earn it again. Or the way her skin sizzled like fajita meat every time he reached around her for an item on the counter.

This wasn't going to work. She felt like a traitor. And a liar.

Rory rubbed her hands, tainted with grease, down the front of her apron, then smoothed back loose strands of hair that had escaped her ponytail. She'd worn a different hat today than the last time they'd worked together, a burgundy one that read "Kiss the Cook" in white stitching, which Grady and Nicole had gotten her as a gag gift last Christmas. It'd come in handy for her rotation of required hats during her shifts in the truck and usually made her laugh at the irony.

Now, however, standing this close to Jude in front of the refrigerator, it felt like her head was on fire. Why in the world had she grabbed this cap? She stepped back, away from Jude and his cologne, and hoped he didn't notice the heat in her cheeks.

He slapped a green oven mitt on the counter and grinned. "Now we wait."

"Now we wait." She repeated the confirmation, subtly adjusting the volume in her earbuds. Grady had coached her through the lesson earlier, as he had the other day, but had recently excused himself. Bathroom break? Ice cream truck? With Grady, there was no telling. But she had never been this alone with Jude before and desperately wished she'd invited Hannah back over for another origami session.

Rory scooted as far away as possible, ticking off their accomplishments on her fingers to give her something to focus on. "We've gone over cooking in bulk, how to use the deep fryer, and now we're warming the taco shells."

Checklist: Avoid close contact. Business only. Prevent emotional connection. StrongerMan99 would be waiting in her DMs that evening, and she had no intention of betraying him because of some rogue chemical reaction she kept experiencing.

"It's been a productive lesson. Oh, and don't forget the cheese trick." Jude casually crossed his arms over his chest, and she couldn't help but wonder if he worked out or was naturally in shape.

That wasn't following the checklist.

She nodded briskly. "Right. Layer the cheese in first so it melts on the shell and holds it together." That was one tip she remembered hearing Aunt Sophia talk about frequently while cooking. She'd teasingly referred to the cheese as "shredded glue" sometimes, which had always made Grady gag and Rory laugh.

A knot of memories tightened in Rory's throat and she coughed, willing Grady to hurry back so she could wrap up the lesson. She felt vulnerable, exposed, standing there in the kitchen in front of one of the state's most eligible bachelors, waiting on tacos to cook and hiding from a tidal wave of emotion — and guilt. Hiding the truth about her cooking ability felt a lot less justifiable today during lesson number two, and a lot shadier. At this point, she just wanted to get it all over with — for multiple reasons.

"I really appreciate you doing these lessons for me." Jude stepped closer to her, his eyes catching hers. She fought to free herself from his open gaze, but her eyes refused to obey her brain. "I know it's been inconvenient, at best."

"Not at all." She inched backward, raising her chin slightly as if projecting confidence could make her feel it. "Service provided for money rendered, and all that."

She mentally face-palmed herself as Jude's expression faltered. What was wrong with her? There was a fine line between maintaining a professional demeanor and being a distant jerk. She was dangerously close to the latter. She tried to smile. "I meant, it's helping me out of a jam too. You know. Financially."

Now she literally covered her face with her hand. Revealing their financial situation was as unprofessional as she could get — and embarrassing. Jude was the definition of wealthy. What if he thought she was hinting for more money?

He nodded tightly. "Right. I'm glad to help." He shuffled one foot against the cheese-sprinkled floor.

There. The floor. That was her out. "I better clean up." She quickly opened the supply closet and grabbed the broom. But before she could start sweeping, Jude reached to take it from her. "Let me."

His hand reaching for the handle brushed against hers, and she dropped the broom like it was on fire. It clattered to the floor, narrowly missing his shoulder, and knocked an open spice container off the counter. Now a dusting of garlic powder coated the floor along with the cheese. They were one lettuce incident away from having an entire salad.

Rory squeezed her eyes closed, waiting one heartbeat, then three, then nine. She opened them. Jude was sweeping, casting a slightly concerned, slightly amused glance her way. "You okay?"

She stepped backward, away from the mess. Away from him. She didn't want to guess what he was thinking. Her own thoughts seemed to link elbows and spin in a confusing dance of attraction, embarrassment, and guilt. She'd led him on. She'd lied. She'd made a fool of herself.

All those unfortunate facts jumbled together and spun on top of each other until she couldn't find a safe place for her gaze to land or a rhythm for her heart to beat to.

"Rory." The broom stilled. Jude's steady gaze held hers, his gentle tone more unnerving than if he had yelled or teased. He seemed . . . concerned. Genuinely concerned. About her.

With every ounce of dignity she could muster, she politely thanked him. Pointed out where he'd missed a spot. And then hightailed it down the ramp outside.

No mush allowed.

Jude was accustomed to the best of the best when it came to first-class traveling, tailored clothes, and five-star restaurants. He'd eaten fresh lobster straight from a boat in Maine, homemade lasagna on a flagstone patio in Italy, and hot baguettes on the balcony of a Parisian bakery.

But right now, he'd trade it all for a single box of Oreos.

"Dude. Why are you so stressed?" Cody crunched another tortilla chip as he dodged Jude's frantic transition of the tortillas from the stove top to the granite island. "They're just tacos, right?"

"Of course not." Jude donned a striped mitt and pulled out the taco shells he'd been keeping warm in the oven. "Right now, they're tickets." Golden, crispy tickets to freedom. He set the cookie sheet on the stove with a clatter. His mind raced. He still needed to grate the cheese. And slice up a few jalapeños. What else had Rory taught him that he'd forgotten?

Ah, Rory. Their second lesson the other

day had been interesting, to say the least. He'd learned a lot, but something had been off. It was almost as if Rory had been a totally different person. Their formerly easygoing kitchen camaraderie from the first lesson had been replaced by stoic professionalism and a withdrawn, overly polite demeanor on her part. Had he somehow offended her?

He truly didn't have time to figure it out and honestly — with that crazy spark that repeatedly flickered between them — it was for the better. He had a natural chemistry with Rory that he couldn't afford. Not while he was in the middle of changing careers and getting to know ColorMeTurquoise. He refused to be the guy who entertained two women at once. Those tricks were more Warner's style.

Cody took another chip from the open bag on the counter. "So how's this going to work again? You're going to feed your family tonight and be like, by the way, I'm abandoning the law firm to go into the food industry, so please don't cut me out of the will?"

More or less. "I should have made flash cards."

"Honesty is the best policy."

Jude shot him a look. "You must not

101

remember my dad."

"Oh, I remember. I still get hives from the look he gave me that night after high school graduation when we ordered too many tequila —" Cody sobered at Jude's raised eyebrows. "We were kids. I'm fine, really. Totally over it."

"We've all grown up since then." Thank goodness. Now, he had a proper head on his shoulders, one born of lessons learned and mistakes hard-earned. If anything, his relationship with his brother had taught him a lot of "what not to-dos," and so had a good bit of postcollege time spent in church.

He finally knew what he wanted in life — and that didn't include taking the bar.

He snagged a chip from the bag beside Cody. "Unfortunately, Dad is going to see this new business plan as a major step backward for me professionally."

"Is he right, though?"

Jude narrowed his eyes. *Et tu, Brute?*

"First of all, I haven't read Shakespeare since college, so whatever." Cody shrugged. "And secondly, I mean, are you sure you don't want to think this over one more time? You're taking a major risk in the long term. You've got a good recipe and a lot of energy, and you took a few cooking classes from that Salsa Street girl. But what else?"

"Her name is Rory." The retort automatically flowed from his lips, and he pointedly kept his gaze away from Cody's, willing him not to jump on the accident. But his friend's eyes lasered into his profile with precision.

"My bad, bro." Cody held up both hands in defense, a knowing grin spreading across his face. "I didn't realize you two were on a first-name basis already."

Jude shrugged. "She helped me out. That deserves some respect, is all I'm saying." His heart pounded, and he took a deep breath to slow the erratic pace. "Rory's nice, that's all." Was he trying to convince Cody or himself? He grabbed another chip.

"She's so nice you're going to steal her business away?" Cody crunched loudly.

"Of course not."

"But you're planning to open a competition food truck." He waved his chip back and forth, as if trying to connect dots Jude couldn't see.

"I'm just making tacos. Salsa Street offers a variety of Mexican cuisine *and* Tex-Mex. It's totally different." Jude dismissed the concern. Salsa Street served tacos, sure, but also tostadas, quesadillas, Mexican pizzas, taco salads, chimichangas, burritos . . . He wouldn't be a threat to them at all.

If anything, it'd be the other way around.

"So back to my question, before you got all riled up." Cody dug into the chip bag. "What else are you bringing to the food truck table of success here?"

Jude had asked himself the same question that morning while shaving, so he was ready. He ticked off the points on his fingers. "I have my start-up money. A hungry community. And a big festival to get me immediate customers and publicity."

"You have to get customers to try your food for that to matter." Cody pointed with his chip. "And it has to be good."

"It will be." Jude pulled a few tomatoes from the fridge drawer. It would be. Right? He also grabbed the block of cheese he'd picked up that morning from the corner grocery store. "Don't forget, I've been watching Food Network for years. I'm looking into taking some YouTube classes too."

"Learning how to cook online. What a time to be alive." Cody rolled his eyes. "What about tonight? How are you going to share these fun facts with Pops?"

"Don't worry. I have a decoy topic ready." He thought about the conversation with Rory in the food truck during their first lesson — how his family was quirky. Hollis wouldn't take that as a compliment. He wanted prestige. Power. Quirky, to him, would be considered weak and vulnerable. And now there was the matter of the missing donation check, which wasn't exactly giving their family a good reputation in political circles. For whatever reason, Hollis might not be a big fan of Whit — but he'd never approve of the mayor and the entire town council thinking poorly of the family name.

Grandmother would not only roll over in her grave, she'd come right up out of it.

Jude began grating the cheese over a plate. "It seems the firm has been getting some negative chatter lately, so I'm going to sell this to Dad tonight as a PR opportunity."

Cody raised his eyebrows. "How so?"

Jude framed his hands to signify reading a newspaper. "Local lawyer competes in community food festival; feeds tacos *and* goodwill."

"I'm glad you're not pursuing a career in media with that train wreck of a headline." Cody didn't look impressed as he brushed crumbs off his shirt. "And you're out of salsa."

"Which is precisely why I hid a jar from you in the back of the fridge." Jude slapped his hand with an oven mitt as Cody reached for the refrigerator handle. "But you have to go. My dad and brother will be here any minute."

"Yikes. Cue foreboding music." Cody held up both hands in defense. "And hey — for the record, it smells good in here."

"Thanks." He ushered his friend toward the front door.

"For what? Eating all your chips and lending moral support?" Cody grinned as he stepped over the threshold onto the woven welcome mat.

"Something like that." Jude started to shut the door.

Cody leaned in, talking fast. "I'll take any leftovers you don't —"

He shut the door. The meal had to be perfect. If that didn't help break his father in gently, nothing would. It was a lot of pressure to put on a taco, but he trusted Maria's recipe.

He wiped his hands on his apron and started back to the kitchen. Hopefully the PR plan worked — or he'd be stuck with a ton of tacos and a major loan as constant reminders of his failure.

Not to mention that Warner would ensure he'd never live that down.

"Tastes like chicken," Warner joked around a second bite of a taco. A bit of juice dribbled onto his chin, and he dabbed at it.

"What's the big deal?"

"Well, for starters, if this cow tastes like chicken, I've stumbled on something revolutionary." Jude refrained from rolling his eyes as he took a sip of water. "That's a beef soft taco."

"Now what do they call these? *Street* tacos?" Hollis stared at his food with as much intimidation — and disdain — as he did when peering at a witness on the stand.

" 'Street' is in reference to the size, not where I picked it up from." Jude sighed. "Focus on the taste. How are they?" Dealing with these two was like herding cats. He drummed his fingers on the table. He hadn't shared his plan yet. He'd been waiting to let the tacos speak for themselves first.

Unfortunately, they only seemed to be whispering.

Warner wiped his hands on one of the cloth napkins Jude had scrounged up from deep in a kitchen drawer. "Like I said. Chicken."

His family was the worst.

Hollis plucked a chip from the towering stack on his plate. "I don't know why you bothered to cook instead of ordering out. Do you not have a maid anymore?"

"Housekeeper, Dad. And yes, she comes once a week, but that doesn't mean she

107

cooks too."

"Mine always does both." Hollis shrugged.

Yes, Maria always did everything — cooking, cleaning, and oh yeah, helping raise Jude and influencing him to have an actual beating heart rather than the pulsing bank vault that thumped inside his dad's and brother's chests.

He started to push away from the table, then took a deep breath. He'd already told ColorMeTurquoise tonight was the first step in accomplishing his goal. He couldn't log on later that evening and admit failure. He cleared his throat in a feeble attempt to dissolve the tension. "I was thinking that —"

"That you were going to take the bar early?"

Jude ignored Warner's verbal jab and kept his gaze on his father. "I've been hearing some negative chatter about the firm lately, and I had an idea."

"What kind of chatter?" Hollis wiped his face with his napkin and glanced around. For more tacos? That could be a good sign.

Jude stood up and grabbed the baking sheet from the counter, where the remaining hard-shell tacos rested. "We're apparently not giving the community a good impression lately. Our reputation is being hit." He scooped a taco onto Hollis's plate.

"Reputation as what?" Hollis snorted. "Winners?"

"Reputation in general. People around town see us coming and run, so to speak."

"That's good." Hollis provided a brisk nod before taking a big bite. "I've always told you boys that intimidation is a plus," he mumbled. "We need that in court."

Jude's plan was unraveling in his lap. "But they're calling us quirky."

"Hardly. We're way more distinguished than most of this Podunk town," Warner huffed. "Sometimes I wonder why we don't live in Dallas full-time."

Hollis gestured with his taco. "It's cheaper to live here and split our time. And there's the tax write-offs to consider. Plus, we have a solid reputation in two counties now."

Jude set the baking sheet back on the counter. "Modest isn't a Podunk town, whatever that means. It's community centered and family friendly. Travel magazines call it charming."

"It's nothing like Dallas."

"Your own girlfriend is from here!"

Warner lifted his chin. "She's destined for bigger and better things."

As a trophy wife, no doubt. Jude fought the urge to roll his eyes. Maddison wasn't necessarily beautiful in the traditional sense, but she was striking and had a commanding presence. Perfect for Warner's career aspirations. Plus, she inaccurately believed Warner hung the moon.

"Besides, why are you defending locals? I thought you started this conversation to defend *us* from them." Warner raised an eyebrow. "I'm confused."

Jude was too. Conversing with his family started so many conflicts, he forgot which battle he was currently fighting. "I brought that up to let you two know I have a plan to fix it."

Hollis spoke up. "Hopefully you mean a plan to pass the bar and officially join the team."

Jude's last bite of taco lodged in his throat. "Actually . . . the opposite."

A storm cloud of imminent danger darkened Hollis's face. "I know you didn't cook up some random Mexican fare and invite us over here only to tell me you're delaying the bar."

Yes, that was exactly what he was doing. And his window of opportunity was about an inch from slamming completely shut. But the most important part was not letting his dad smell fear.

Jude settled back into his chair, casually

wiping at a spot of grease on the table with his napkin. "I came across a good public relations opportunity. We could use it."

"What we could use is another lawyer on board." Hollis's tone rose in volume with each word.

Fear was blood in the water. Jude inhaled slightly and tilted his head, pressing forward as if Hollis hadn't spoken. He kept his voice even. Factual. Emotionless. "The annual food festival is coming up, so I bought a truck. I'm going to sell tacos at the festival — and some positive press for us. It'll be a win-win."

They both stared at him like his head had turned into a giant taco shell. He swallowed hard, waiting. Counted to three. Waited again.

They kept staring.

He kept waiting.

"A win-win for who?" Hollis finally asked.

"The community. The firm." *Me.*

They resumed the staring standoff.

Jude coughed. "I'll get the firm's name printed on napkins, generate some good publicity, do a few YouTube videos to promote us. You know — make us more approachable."

Crickets might as well have invaded the kitchen for all the response he got.

He tried again. "There's a contest this year sponsored by the bank, with a cash prize big enough for storefront money, so all the local food trucks are really bringing it. It's a community hit. We could capitalize off that and finally show our clients a softer side of the firm."

Silence reigned.

Finally, Hollis spoke. "Why?"

"Why?" Jude repeated. "Why would we *not* try to cushion some of these family porcupine quills?"

Hollis exhaled, long and slow. "You're not thinking in the right direction, son."

Most fathers didn't say "son" as a dig, but his did. Jude frowned, unable — or maybe unwilling — to hold back his frustration any longer. "You mean, like the direction of backing out on annual donations the town depends on?"

Hollis's gaze darted to Warner. Something flickered in his usually pristine poker face.

Jude's frown deepened. "Don't play dumb. I know you decided not to support Whit in this next election."

"I wouldn't say that, exactly." Warner chuckled.

Great. Whatever it was, Warner was in on it.

"Nothing has been decided — yet." Hollis

grinned. "Only threatened."

"Why?"

"Leverage, my boy. Leverage." Hollis brushed crumbs off his lap. "Mayor Whitlow didn't agree with me last year on how the donation should be channeled, and because of that, I had to break a promise to a big client."

The pieces began to click into place, and the picture the puzzle created wasn't pretty. "So unless the mayor agrees to use this year's funds for what *you* want, you won't support his upcoming election?" Jude frowned, still missing one piece. "But why? If someone beats him, you can't guarantee being able to control their decisions either."

Hollis raised his eyebrows. "Can't I?" He looked at Warner, who grinned.

Oh no.

"Don't be so dramatic. The mayor will get his money. I'm waiting until the last minute to remind him who's in control. If he doesn't go with my suggestion, then he'll get some competition this year." Hollis pointed a triumphant finger. "Now *that's* what you call a win-win."

Jude pinched the bridge of his nose, that last taco churning in his stomach. "Warner, you don't even like this town. You just said so. Why in the world would you even want to be mayor?"

"Power." His brother casually bit into a chip. "You don't have to like something to want to be in charge of it." He said it so matter-of-factly, so coldly, Jude had half a mind to check for a pulse. "Besides, it won't come to that. Whit will shape up."

Jude buried his face in his hands and refused to look up. "Dad, I'm not taking the bar."

Warner stopped crunching. Quiet reigned. Jude risked a glance. A muscle jumped in his father's clenched jaw.

Warner collapsed back in his chair. "Listen, baby brother. I get it. You're scared. The bar is tough, but don't do something crazy out of a fear of failing."

It was perhaps the closest thing to empathy Warner had ever shown. Unfortunately, it was totally inaccurate. Jude met his gaze. "I'm not afraid of the bar."

The slight softening in Warner's eyes hardened back into a defensive shield. "Then what's with all these dumb tacos?"

Clearly, the public relations angle wasn't going to work. He'd forgotten his family didn't care what people thought of them because they thought themselves better than everyone else. Time for Cody's suggestion of honesty.

114

Now he really wished he had some flash cards.

Jude scooted his plate away and braced his forearms on the edge of the table. The thought of ColorMeTurquoise cheering him on gave him a boost of courage. He wanted to give her a good report tonight, no matter how difficult it might be to get there. "I don't want to take the bar."

Hollis lifted his chin, peering down at Jude. "This month?"

"At all."

Color drained from Warner's face, and even he had the decency to avert his eyes. Jude waited for the crackling of lightning, the boom of thunder as Hollis traced the beige striped pattern on his napkin with a burly finger.

He was thinking — which might be scarier than an impulsive outburst of rage. Calculated bursts of rage were far worse.

Finally, Hollis lifted his head, tapping his finger twice on the napkin. "If Warner ends up in politics, I'll need you on the team more than ever."

That wasn't Jude's problem — and all the more reason for them to stop this ridiculous ploy before it fully began. He opened his mouth to point that out, but Hollis didn't let him.

115

"I think you're right."

Jude blinked. Those words had never come from his dad before.

"But I won't *actually* end up in politics. Right?" Warner asked, frowning.

Hollis ignored him. "For Warner to win — if Mayor Whit chooses poorly and it comes to that — we'll need positive publicity for his campaign. If there really are these alleged disgruntled community members, we'll have to fix that. There's only one solution — you will enter the contest."

No. He didn't want to enter the contest, only start the food truck and get his feet wet in the industry — prove he could do this on his own, without the help of a trust fund. He needed that personal accomplishment for himself — something his dad and brother would never fully understand. "Dad, I don't —"

"If you win, you're done in the firm. Free and clear, no hard feelings."

Jude released his breath.

"Winning will revive our name in the community and show me you have the ability to pull this off and make it another Worthington family success. But if you lose . . ." His dad's voice trailed off, half-threatening, half-terrifyingly factual. "You'll take the bar immediately and join the firm for the dura-

116

tion of your career. No further questions. Do we have a deal?"

The words his father wasn't using rang all too loudly in his head. Not agreeing to this stiff deal would mean no more inheritance. No place in his father's will. All the vague threats from the past that held Jude loosely in his leather office chair would become all too real. This was it. If he didn't agree, he'd be stuck. If he lost, he'd be stuck.

He had to win.

Hollis held out his hand to shake, dark and challenging eyes boring into Jude's.

Warner's mouth gaped in Jude's peripheral vision.

He took a breath. Then clamped Hollis's hand in his before he could change his mind and shook it firmly. "Deal."

SIX

Rory scooted a turquoise vase of daisies a little closer to her laptop and buried her face in the cheerful white blooms. She had set her computer on the patio table on her back porch for the night's messaging session with StrongerMan99. It felt like a date. She had even strung several strands of twinkle lights strategically across the ceiling and poured herself a half glass of sparkling cider.

And she had the flowers.

She couldn't keep the grin off her face as she typed.

> You'll never guess what I got via an Amazon Locker today.

Black roses?

She winced.

That would have certainly elicited
a different reaction.

A horsehead?

No, Godfather.

A six-pack of energy drinks?

Yes! How'd you know?

Dots formed, then erased. Formed, then erased. She grinned at his confusion.

JK. I got an obnoxiously large
bouquet of happy white daisies.

Whew. You had me there for a minute. I was about to make an angry phone call to a certain florist. 😨

I had no idea what to expect when
you gave me that random code
to an Amazon Locker in Tyler,
but it was worth it.

She fingered one of the blooms.

I hope so. I wanted to say thank you.

She took a long sniff of the daisies before

replying. She hadn't received flowers in a long, long time.

> I don't really see what I did to help, but I appreciate the gesture.

Her dad had sent her flowers a few times during his travels. For her fifth-grade school play. Sixteenth birthday. Senior graduation. Then another memory infiltrated. Holding a rose at her mother's gravesite, years after the funeral she didn't remember. Her dad, wearing a dark coat, holding up one finger and telling her to "sit there and look pretty" while he finished a phone call. She remembered how the towering oak trees above the tombstones cast wavering shadows across his weary face.

That phrase became way too frequent over the years. Tugging her dad's hand for attention while he was talking with a client. *"Just sit there and look pretty, darling."* Offering to help in his office on a Saturday morning when he had no sitter. *"Sit there and look pretty."* Trying to be involved in the purchasing of her first car. *"No need, you sit there and look pretty."*

She jerked her attention back to the screen as StrongerMan99 typed.

I was able to take some first steps out of a bad situation last night, and you were part of my motivation to bite the bullet.

How so?

Knowing you were cheering me on helped a lot.

The dots popped up, then vanished again.

She held her breath, willing him to keep typing. He was getting more vulnerable, more . . . relationship-y. If that was a word. Not that she'd dare be the first to suggest something like that.

But she liked where this was going. Especially in the throes of that surprise chemistry she had with Jude. He was handsome, but StrongerMan99 was slowly stealing her heart, one sentence at a time. Attraction of the soul was much more powerful and lasting than physical attraction.

Besides, who was to say he wasn't incredibly good-looking too? And if not, who cared? Wasn't that why she was on the dating app to begin with — to be considered past her own appearance?

The memory of Jude's strong arm brushing hers in the food truck tingled through her stomach, and she shoved the thought away, focusing back on her laptop screen. She was on a date. With an incredibly kind man who had just sent her flowers — to a locker, of all things. Talk about creative. This guy had a heart of gold.

Jude, well . . . Jude was a prominent businessman with the accompanying distractions of wealth and status. He lived a totally different lifestyle from hers — one with strikingly opposite rules and etiquette. He hadn't even known Alton's name.

Thankfully, the last half of that disastrous second lesson had ended cordially enough. She'd gotten a quick gulp of fresh air, Grady had come back in her ear to finish coaching her through the taco shell prep, and she'd expertly erected a sturdy wall to prevent any more accidental fireworks — or embarrassing blunders.

This guy before her now deserved all her attention. She began to type.

I'm glad I could be there for you.

Remember that lesson I told you about? I made a big choice afterward. Of course, it could all blow up in my face and I should be freaking out, but right now I'm just excited I finally get to do something I love.

So what do you love?

Sharing my natural abilities with people who will actually appreciate them. It's going to be a dream come true.

I'm happy for you — and a little envious. That sounds amazing. I don't have that choice right now — too many people are depending on me.

She wasn't really in a place to take risks . . . like starting her own party-planning business or design shop on Etsy. Anything that took start-up funds or time away from Salsa Street was a poor idea for the indefinite future.

Do you want to know my suggestion?

Any kind of unbiased, outside counsel would be fantastic. Even Grady didn't quite get it. He was always teasingly nudging her to get a job she loved, but that was easy for him to say. He didn't have Hannah's security or the weight of a family legacy riding on his shoulders. If Rory took a risk and failed, people would get hurt. The last thing Hannah needed was more change after her mom's illness and passing. Besides, Grady was already working the job *he* loved. If she got rid of the food truck to pursue her own dreams — or spread herself too thin and let the business slip into bankruptcy — it would topple his goals.

She sent a thumbs-up emoji and waited as dots began to assemble. StrongerMan99 had proven to be incredibly wise so far. Would he throw some genius at her via Scripture or the ancient poets? Maybe offer to help prepare a business plan for a new venture in the future, just to have at the ready? Break down her budget and tell her to create a pie chart of risk calculations?

Eat Oreos.

She blinked at the screen. Oreos? She typed slowly.

> You mean all my problems will be solved by consuming cream-stuffed chocolate wafers?

Well, at least they're not a garnish.

A laugh escaped, and she pressed her fingers to her lips. Another *You've Got Mail* reference. This guy was perfect, even if he didn't have any real advice for her.

Somehow this was better. Someone to

listen. To understand, as much as they could — as much she'd let them. Someone to just . . . care.

I highly recommend. And I have some right here. I'd share, but you know. Rules. 😳 😌

The wink dipped her stomach a little, and she took a sip of cider.

Those pesky rules, indeed.

In that case, do you think we should meet?

Oh no.
She plucked a daisy from the vase and twirled it between her fingers. The idea swirled around her heart, setting off a cacophony of alarms. She wanted more with StrongerMan99 — but she also wanted this ideal flirty friendship. What if she couldn't have both?
It was too risky.

I'm guessing by your sudden paralysis, it's too soon.

She sucked in a gulp of air before stroking the keys.

I want to. But I feel like this isn't the

125

> best time. Not yet. You've got your
> new thing going on, and I've got . . .

She stopped typing. What did she have, other than a bunch of anxiety and fears about the Salsa Street business and change in general?

> I've got a big work-related event
> coming up that needs my full attention.

That was true, at least. The festival officially started in one week.

She held her breath. Hopefully, he'd understand. Please understand . . .

> I understand.

Her shoulders relaxed a fraction. Any man who would send daisies to an Amazon Locker and offer commiseration Oreos would understand. What they had was perfect.

But for how long?

A notification suddenly dinged. The Love at First Chat logo fluttered across her screen on Cupid wings. "IT'S TIME FOR PROGRESSION! TRY TEXTING?"

Oh no — again. She stared at the blasted flittering emoji as it dipped, twirled, and then flew off the screen.

She typed painstakingly.

> Did you see that too?

See what?

He added *JK* before she could respond. She took a deep breath.

> I think it's telling us to compromise.
> Too soon to meet . . . not too soon
> to text?

She could do that. Right? Progression was change — change was scary. But at the same time . . . this was safe. He was safe.

Do you need convincing? What if I found an old boom box and serenaded you under your window?

She grinned.

> Did you really write the word
> boom box?

Handheld stereo?

> Wow. You're ancient.

I'm twenty-nine.

So you didn't lie on your app.
Good to know.

I never lie.

She squinted.

You probably just did.

Touché. How about, I hate lying and try never to do it?

Perfect.

And that's what scared her the most — he really seemed to be.

She was foolish if she didn't take this opportunity for progression. Maybe she couldn't do anything risky with Salsa Street or her own business dreams right now, but she could give Stronger Man99 her phone number.

Before she changed her mind, she quickly typed the number sequence into their chat and hit Send.

Her phone immediately lit up beside her laptop. She glanced down at the displayed text from an unknown number and grinned at the words.

We've got to stop meeting like this.

Modest, Texas, might have a lot of quirks, but it also possessed a lot of charm.

Rory waved at Mr. Hardin as he arranged freshly baked baguettes on his outdoor display. He lifted a burly hand in reply. She sidestepped two giggling children playing tag and grinned at their weary-eyed mother, who trailed behind them. Rory felt a little like Belle every Saturday morning as she strolled through the farmers' market, holding her heavy-duty canvas basket and gleaning supplies for the truck. Homegrown tomatoes, ripe hot peppers, and — reluctantly — fresh cilantro.

As much as Rory didn't like to cook, she loved the market. Rich, bold colors neatly arranged in rows across planked wood. Blooming flowers provided bursts of inspiration on each tabletop. Pristine white awnings flapped invitingly in the wind. It was a sigh of relief for her soul.

Sort of like last night's "date" had been.

She smiled as she adjusted her hat — the wide-brimmed straw one she wore every summer on market days — and stopped at one of her favorite vendors as her phone rang. It was Grady, who was supposed to be opening the truck to prepare for the day.

He probably forgot to add something to the grocery list, which was longer this week because of prepping for the festival.

She shouldered her cell as she gestured to elderly Mrs. Johnson that she wanted six of the yellow peppers. "What's up?"

Grady's voice sounded over the phone. "Hey, hermana. I've got good news and bad news."

The joyful bubble lingering from last night threatened to burst. "Go ahead." She briefly closed her eyes in preparation, then opened them as someone jostled her, knocking her broad hat askew.

"Sorry about that." The owner of the deep baritone apologized but didn't step back from the close contact as he pushed forward to make his order. The brim of her hat prevented her from viewing anything above his chin.

She quickly stepped aside to avoid being smushed against his navy polo, frowning at the back of his ball cap. Rude. She struggled to hear Grady through the sketchy connection. "What's the bad news?"

"I think we should start with the good, don't you?" Grady's voice practically sing-songed. He must not be too upset about the bad, then.

Still . . . she hated surprises. "I'd rather

end with the good."

"But the bad won't make sense without the good first."

"Fine." She adjusted the basket on the crook of her elbow, all while trying to simultaneously frown into the phone and smile at Mrs. Johnson.

"You said twenty-six peppers, dear?" The woman's voice warbled over the wooden display between them as she pressed wrinkled hands against her floral apron pockets.

"Ooh, are you at the Johnson booth? Grab me a jar of her salsa while you're there. I'll pay you back." Grady practically drooled over the phone.

"This isn't the best time." Rory lowered her voice as she struggled to hold the phone with her shoulder and not get crowded out of the line by the polo guy.

Mrs. Johnson frowned over her glasses. "It's not? Am I holding you up, dear?"

"No, ma'am, not you." Her normally serene marketplace was turning into a circus. "Only *six* peppers, please."

Mrs. Johnson nodded, turning toward the brimming bins. "Twenty-six peppers."

"And the salsa," Grady begged.

"No! *Six!*" Rory closed her eyes. "Grady, forget the salsa. What's the news?" Anticipation was the worst. It was why she despised roller coasters. If she could walk right onto the thing, she'd be fine. But the waiting in line, the buildup — no thanks. Her nerves were far too shot, far too fast. Grady knew that, so why was he dragging this out?

He cleared his throat as pots clanged in the background. He had her on speaker again. "So the *good* news is, I just got word that Mayor Whitlow has turned the summer food festival into a competition between local trucks. I found the flyer for it between those two bills you were ignoring."

She ignored that part too. The bills could wait — hopefully. "A competition? How is that good news?"

"Because cash prize, baby!" She could hear Grady rub his calloused hands together with glee. Or, knowing him, more like a Disney villain.

She fumbled not to drop her basket as the polo guy bumped her again. She gritted her teeth at his lack of apology. "How much of a prize?" Any amount would be helpful right now — if they won, of course. But the locals loved Salsa Street, and their only real competition was possibly the fried dough truck that cranked out beignets and greasy elephant ears.

Grady chuckled. "How about enough to open a storefront?"

"What?" Her jaw dropped. "Did you sign us up?" Her mind whirled with all that needed to be done. Grady would have to cook for them, of course. And they'd have to pick the perfect recipe from Aunt Sophia's stash.

Her heart fluttered with excitement at the ways she could contribute. Like looking up plate presentation ideas and —

"I turned in our application via email about ten minutes ago. We almost missed the deadline."

She felt jump-started with hope for the first time in days. If they won — *when* they won — they would have enough to float the truck through the slower winter season. They could pad Hannah's account for her Unity Angels tuition. And Salsa Street could even entertain the idea of a storefront — expanding the business and her aunt's legacy all in one bold move. What could be better?

"So about the bad news."

Oh yeah. She inhaled sharply just as polo guy stepped backward, directly onto her foot. Rory hopped to get out of his way. He didn't even notice as he turned with his own canvas bag overflowing with bell peppers and onions.

Her aggravation — and anticipatory dread

over the next piece of news from Grady — flared along with her voice. "Come on, tell me already!"

Mrs. Johnson's white eyebrows dipped in concern as she held out the bag of yellow peppers to Rory. "But I already told you, dear. I said the total is eight forty-nine."

"Oh, not you, Mrs. Johnson." She fumbled in her back pocket for the cash she carried for market days. Her hat tilted again, and she fixed it with the hand still holding her phone before jerking her cell back to her ear. "What is it, Grady?"

Grady's voice hitched, his usual joy slightly diminished. "Rumor has it there's another truck that could mean trouble."

"Who? DoughBaby?" Rory shook her head as she pulled another dollar free from its denim trap. "No way. Too greasy. Locals like them, but a judge would never score those powdered heart attacks higher than your quesadillas."

"No, not DoughBaby. It's a new truck." Grady hesitated. "One that serves tacos."

Rory tugged on the rest of the crumpled bills, which were stuck on the hem of her pocket. "That's ridiculous. Who would start a taco truck when Salsa Street has held the monopoly in Modest for years?"

Grady fell into silence.

Uh-oh. He knew. "Who's the competition, Grady?" The wad of bills dropped to the ground, and she bent to grab it just as the man in the polo did the same.

Their gazes locked. She sucked in her breath at the familiar eyes beneath the brim of his ball cap. "Jude?"

Grady's sigh held both relief and surprise. "How'd you guess? And here I was trying to break it to you gently."

Jude's dark eyes crinkled as he squinted against the sun. "Rory, hey."

She snatched the bills from the ground as the reality of Grady's words assaulted her full force.

Jude.

Jude Worthington.

The man in the navy polo who couldn't maintain marketplace decency was the same lawyer who had taken cooking lessons from her — apparently to start his own food truck.

A competition truck.

A competition that *she* had to win.

Indignation flared, heating her chest like that time five years ago when Grady had goaded her into a pepper-eating contest. She slowly straightened as Jude did the same, an easy smile splitting his face. His conniving, manipulative face.

135

"How's it going?"

She glared back, never breaking eye contact. "Grady? I've got to go."

"Don't forget the salsa!"

She hung up on him and pointed. "You."

Modest, Texas, was anything but predictable. Here he was trying to buy fresh onions, one of the thousand overwhelming tasks he needed to complete over the next few days before he opened his truck for the festival next weekend, and Rory popped up out of nowhere, almost miniature under a hat that stretched wider than her shoulders.

Her smooth, pale shoulders, bare against the wide neckline of a blue top that did ridiculous things to her eyes. Eyes currently burning with something not quite . . . friendly. He inched back a step, glancing at the elderly booth owner in the flowered apron as if she could help clear up the confusion. No luck.

"Me." He repeated, half asking, half stating. What had he done? Besides bump into her a few times . . . Ah. That must be it. The crowd had thickened around the food stand, which he figured was a good sign of the vendor's quality of vegetables. "It's great to see you again. Look, I'm sorry for running into —"

"I should have known."

The fog of confusion thickened. "You should have known I'd bump into —"

"You're a lawyer, after all."

So the mood swings were back. He smiled, the good family smile, although he liked to think his wasn't as plastic as Warner's. "Technically — no. Not yet." What did being a lawyer have to do with anything?

"Yet?" Her pointed finger lowered an inch at his words.

"I haven't taken the bar." Because he'd started making tacos — and sort of never stopped.

"Passed it, you mean." She quirked one eyebrow at him in challenge.

He bristled. "As I said, I haven't *taken* it." In the past twenty-four hours, he had, however, taken out an application for a loan on his own credit, in his *own* name, and applied for a business license and created an LLC. All sans trust fund, which he was more than a little proud of.

None of which she needed to know, especially while he was on some sort of sudden, undeserved trial.

His chest tightened. He had errands to run, permits to finalize, and a fridge to stock. Whatever had changed in Rory during their last lesson to make her colder had

spiraled even further. She was downright
icy today, despite the warm summer sun
drenching the tents. Which was fine. Their
brief cooking partnership hadn't helped
nearly as much as he'd anticipated, and
while he'd enjoyed their time together in
the first lesson, the second had fallen flat
and left him feeling a little ripped off. Still,
he'd gleaned what he needed and made up
for the rest over the past few nights by
watching YouTube videos about tacos and
food trucks nonstop.

He needed to watch more of those — not
entertain more of *this drama.* "Is that all
you needed?"

Rory lifted her chin, her hazel eyes raking
over him, and a gust of wind lifted the hat
from her head. She grabbed at it, and a flash
of recognition surged through Jude's subconscious. His frustration at her unex-
plained mood temporarily fled.

"That's it!" He snapped his fingers. "I
can't believe I didn't see this sooner when
we were cooking together. Has anyone ever
told you that you look like Fiona —"

With an agitated sigh, she turned and
rushed away from him. He squinted as he
watched her. Was she running? Yes, sprint-
ing, really, her canvas basket bouncing
against her slim jean-clad hip as she wound

through the thickening crowd like a running back on Super Bowl Sunday.

He shook his head. Only in Texas.

A bony finger tapped his shoulder. He turned to find the older booth vendor smiling at him with smudged lipstick and holding out a mason jar. "Don't forget your complimentary jar of salsa for being a first-time customer."

Make that only in Modest.

SEVEN

Rory hadn't power walked since her favorite binge-worthy Netflix show had been canceled without warning last spring. And she hadn't full-out jogged since the evening of her first day of owning Salsa Street, the smell of cilantro in her nose and the burden of the turn her life had taken affecting every step.

But tonight — she ran. She ran because of the sudden new competition thrust in her face, dampening the only good news she'd had in weeks. She ran because everything seemed to be changing despite her best efforts to stop it.

And she ran because she hadn't talked to StrongerMan99 in forty-eight hours.

"Do you hate yourself? Or just me?" Nicole struggled to keep up, her messy blonde bun bouncing atop her head. "Slow down, sister!"

"You're like Grady with all that sister

140

talk." Rory adjusted her stride slightly, her feet pounding the pavement as she struggled to breathe evenly. Deep down, she liked the reference — really deep down, in the places where mushy stuff didn't make her want to run faster. "Thanks for coming with me. *Sis.*" There. That was about all she could offer. Sweat trickled from her eyebrow and down her nose, and she swiped at it with her forearm.

"I might disown you after this," Nicole panted. "And never mind my question. I'm pretty sure you hate both of us at this point."

Their feet pounded a rhythm on the sidewalk as they made the next turn a block away from Rory's townhouse. She wasn't sure which of her reasons to run bothered her most. They were all stressful, but StrongerMan99's silence and her own recognition of it grated on her. She cared. Dang it, she cared.

And they hadn't even met yet. When they did — *if* they did — how much more would her heart get entangled?

She pushed herself harder, feet churning, forcing Nicole to keep up. The summer evening wind washed their faces in warmth, and Rory's chest heaved as she struggled to breathe. Struggled to process all that was churning in her mind.

After Aunt Sophia passed, Rory saw a grief counselor, so she knew it was best to go ahead and feel the feelings rather than dismiss them. Emotions rarely got truly dismissed — they tended to get stuffed down and explode later, something akin to opening Pandora's box. She didn't want to do that and explode on Grady, Hannah, Nicole, or anyone else she cared about.

Like StrongerMan99.

Her throat tightened. Her shins ached. Her side hitched. But she ran, her long shadow chasing alongside, and allowed herself to feel the wave of anxiety over potential rejection. She was no stranger to it. From Thomas. From other ex-boyfriends.

She couldn't even get her own dad to stick around.

"Am I needy?" The question burst out on her next breath.

"Insane, maybe, for running in June, but not needy." Nicole's bun bounced askew, and she reached up with one hand to balance it. "Why? Trouble in online paradise?"

"We haven't talked in a couple of days. I'm thinking maybe he went silent because I said something wrong last time."

"Well, did you?"

Nicole was just like Grady. Blunt and to the point. Rory shook her head. "I don't know. He suggested meeting, and I said I wasn't ready yet. Maybe he thought that meant I wasn't interested."

Nicole slowed to a walk, and Rory automatically slowed with her. Her breath came in short rasps as her lungs struggled to catch up.

"Who is ever ready for anything? You've got to meet this guy and do this the real way. Fewer communication issues." Nicole planted her hands on her lower back and stretched.

Rory shrugged. "We communicate more than I used to with most of my ex-boyfriends. Being in a talking-only relationship makes you actually talk."

"Good point." Nicole wiggled her eyebrows. "Less distraction."

"That too." Rory felt a blush creep up her already-heated neck as she broke into a slow jog. The emotion wasn't burnt up yet. She had to keep going. "We did exchange phone numbers. And he said he was starting a new venture. Maybe he's just busy."

"Exactly. Everyone's busy." Nicole pushed to match Rory's pace. "That's probably it."

Rory focused on the rhythm of her footsteps. "I should forget about romance right now. It's not like I don't have bigger problems to deal with first." Like winning this contest to secure Salsa Street's future. "Tell me — how concerned is Grady *really* about this new competition?"

Nicole panted. "It's hard to tell. He's so laid-back — but I think it caught him off guard. Just because of who it is, you know?"

Exactly. Why in the world was Jude Worthington starting a food truck business in Modest? It wasn't fair. Women would flock to his truck simply to speak to him.

They rounded the paved curve in front of her townhouse. Nicole eased up on her pace, but Rory kept going. Her friend whimpered her protest. Rory ignored her as they carried on down the street. "It doesn't make sense. Jude and his family obviously don't need the cash. Do you think it's a publicity stunt?"

"With them, who knows. Anything is possible when you have that much money."

"Even their business hardly needs the marketing effort." Everyone in North Texas knew that if you wanted to win in court, you hired Hollis — if you could afford him.

The setting summer sun began its descent, finally coaxing Rory to slow down. She bent over, hands on her knees, heart pounding. "I should call Grady. Tweak recipes. Make sure he's ready to bring his A game."

"He'll be ready. He's always ready." Nicole sat down on the sidewalk and put her head between her knees. "Unless, of course, he's planning my funeral because you killed me."

"Breathe." Rory slowly straightened, wincing as her side caught, and then half collapsed on the grass next to her friend. She crossed her legs in a stretch and glanced at her townhouse up the street, the friendly turquoise front door a welcoming sight. Hannah had helped her paint it last summer.

Anxiety knocked, despite her current rush of endorphins. She couldn't disappoint Hannah and let Sophia's business fail, not after everything her aunt had put into it — and not after the grief Hannah had already been through this past year. If Rory could help it, Salsa Street would thrive. For Hannah's sake. For Sophia's. For Grady's. And somewhere down the line, for herself.

Jude slid an Oreo on a paper napkin across the expanse of his office desk and raised his eyebrows. "What about now?"

"Sir, I'm a part-time law firm runner who constantly debates whether to buy groceries or pay for Netflix. Do you really think cookies can bribe me?" Alton set his narrow jaw and raised his eyebrows.

Yikes. How much did the firm pay their runners? Clearly not enough. Jude stacked a second Double Stuf Oreo on top of the first and scooted the napkin closer toward Alton. "Yes, I do."

"Good call." Alton snatched both cookies and shoved one in his mouth. "So you said the pay would be the same, right? I just have to help you make tacos in a truck instead of doing all this stuff?" He gestured around Jude's office with the Oreo.

"Right." Jude ignored the kid's smacking — well, tried to. He averted his eyes as Alton peeled apart the second cookie and scraped the cream off with his bottom teeth. "And there'd be some free food along the way too. Leftovers and taste testing."

He nodded eagerly. "I'm in, Mr. Worthington."

Ugh. The closer he got to his goal of escaping the family legacy, the more he hated the power-name association. He'd have to deal with that part of his identity eventually. But not today. Today he had a thousand other things to do. Like find out why his bulk shipment of paper goods hadn't arrived yet and decide if he was going to include guacamole on the side of his orders, which seemed like a good idea in theory but was also yet another recipe to master . . .

He cleared his throat. "Please — call me Jude."

Alton swallowed his mouthful of cookie, crumbs dotting his chin. "Yes, sir."

"Jude," he reminded.

"Right. Jude." Alton's voice cracked when he said it, as if it was that foreign to do so. And it probably was. It wasn't as if Jude had even known the kid's name before he started taking lessons from Rory. That didn't bode well for his past approachability with the lower-level office staff.

Though Alton *was* willing to help him out, so that had to mean something. Either way, he didn't blame the kid for wanting to get out of the law office for a few weeks. Wasn't that his own goal — freedom?

After Jude had officially signed up for the contest, he'd been emailed a PDF of rules and guidelines from the mayor's office. The contest allowed one sous-chef for the duration, and Jude hadn't been too prideful to realize he would need a second set of hands — badly. He was already at a disadvantage, being new to the industry and new to his own truck. If he'd had more time, he could have hired someone who knew what they were doing. But the festival started Friday, the contest was Saturday, and he had to play the hand he was dealt.

He watched Alton pick a black speck from between his front teeth. Jude wasn't exactly working with a flush or full house here, but if he could be taught, so could Alton. He'd assign him a few YouTube videos to watch over the next week.

But first the kid needed to know the stakes.

He braced his hands on his desk and leveled his gaze at Alton. "I need to make sure you understand that we have to win." He hesitated. "In fact, you know one of our biggest competitors."

"That dessert truck? They have good stuff, man. I actually gave up Netflix one month to hit up those powdered doughnuts." Alton did a fist pump.

"No, not DoughBaby." Though, on second thought, if Alton's testimony held any merit, they might be more competition than Jude had first imagined. "Well, maybe. But I was talking about Salsa Street."

Alton's eyes widened. "You're competing against that hot — I mean, that really pretty brunette and her taco truck?"

Every ounce of him wanted to agree with the kid, but he let the slip pass. She was now — however unintentionally it had happened — the competition. The obstacle between him and his freedom. "No." Jude pointed at Alton. "*We* are."

Alton's face paled. "Right."

"Think you can handle it?" With all of Alton's Wednesday lunch runs for the firm, Jude had to make sure Rory hadn't pulled him into her lair of loyalty. He wouldn't blame him if she had. The woman ran so hot and cold, who knew what manipulative tricks she had up her sleeve?

Alton nodded slowly, eyeing the open package of Oreos on the desk. "Don't worry, I'm a contender. I played lacrosse in high school."

"So you're competitive." Good to know. Then he should be able to keep his head in the game.

"Definitely." Alton tilted his head, his blond hair falling across his face. "Like, I'd totally challenge you right now to an Oreo eating contest."

His phone chimed a text alert, and Jude's heart stammered. Maybe it was finally ColorMeTurquoise writing him back.

"No contest necessary. Knock yourself out." He slid the package to Alton, then quickly grabbed one last cookie for himself as the kid's eyes began to gleam.

Jude turned his attention to his phone. He'd texted her last night, hating that they

149

hadn't spoken in a few days, and explained he'd been caught up with his new project. He'd been a little concerned by her silence — after all, the last time they'd messaged, she'd turned down the opportunity to meet him in person. He'd been too busy the last few days to give her the attention he normally dedicated to their conversations — but what was her excuse?

They also didn't have "read" notifications on for each other, which felt like an entirely separate level of progression for the future.

He skimmed her long response, breathing a sigh of relief at the lighthearted tone, then went back to the beginning and began to read through it more carefully.

The fact that he'd been worried that her silence indicated she was upset with him tapped a nerve he really didn't want exposed. He could tell himself or his family this was a casual online friendship all day long, but the facts were starting to speak for themselves.

Sorry for my delay too! I didn't get your text until today — I crashed early last night. I went for some much-needed stress relief endorphins yesterday and got a few too many apparently. Also, I think I permanently injured my best friend in the process of obtaining said endorphins, so that position might be open for audition.

> Sign me up.

> You were already first on the list.

> Wait. Did I just get friend-zoned?

Dots formed, then erased. He grinned. He'd flustered her. Then his smile faded as no new dots formed on her side. What if she'd taken his teasing as too serious? Too pushy? He quickly added a wink emoji. Then grimaced after hitting Send. Now he just looked sleazy.

He let out a long sigh. This was getting complicated. And this wasn't even what he was supposed to be focusing on this afternoon. She finally responded with an *LOL,* and he relaxed a fraction. He wasn't nearly as good at this online stuff as he'd thought he'd be. But then again, he never expected anyone like her.

He took a deep breath.

> I'm sorry, but I really need to finish up some work. But let's talk later this evening.

It sounded so cold, so distant. But he

couldn't tell her the specifics of his pressing work goals without her knowing he was entering a food truck competition. How many of those could there possibly be around this area? She wanted to play by the rules and the app's suggested progression timeline, so he'd respect that. Even though part of him at this point just wanted to be able to knock on her door, shove flowers into her hands — daisies — and whisk her off on a romantic date. The old-fashioned way.

Sounds good.

He breathed a sigh of relief. At least she wasn't offended. He debated sending a smiley-face emoji, rejected the idea, and put his phone in his pocket. Then jumped a mile as Alton loudly wrangled the last Oreo from the package. Good grief. Jude had forgotten he was there.

"I won." Alton stuffed the last cookie in his mouth with a sheepish shrug. "Told ya I'm competitive."

ColorMeTurquoise:
I had a gut feeling you'd be on now.

StrongerMan99:
Bonus points for more *You've Got Mail* quotes.

Thank you, thank you. I try.

I still don't get it, you know.

Get what? My fantastic sense of humor?

Why you're on this app in the first place.

Probably because of my sense of humor.

You're sweet. Charming.

Ooh, tell me more.

Kind. Encouraging. Hilarious.

To give you a real answer and to stop blushing, I'll just say the anonymity of this app is a gift.

I can understand that.

Why are you? You're kind of sweet,

charming, kind, encouraging,
and hilarious yourself.

You forgot endearing and ruggedly masculine.

My bad.

Same reason, basically. Anonymity.

So, what are you, famous? Hang on.
Is this really Ryan Reynolds?

Do you *wish* I were Ryan Reynolds?

Probably no more than you wish
I were Blake Lively.

Okay, that's beside the point.

What is your point?

My point is . . . it felt funny when we didn't
talk for two days.

I agree. It made me worry that
we weren't okay.

I'm glad we're okay.

Me too. You're often the most
okay part of my day.

I want more.

More . . . Oreos?

That too. But mostly, more of this. Us.

I do too.

Is that weird? Too soon?

Yes. But I feel the same.

Yet for now . . .

For now. This. Us. Here.

I can appreciate that. And you.

We have seriously mastered the use
of pronouns in this conversation.

I'm telling you — power couple potential.

EIGHT

"You can't dump the rice and beans together like that."

"Oh, I'm sorry. I thought I'd been the chef here for the past year." Grady pointed his wooden spoon at her. "Please feel free to take over anytime you'd like."

"I meant for the contest." Rory turned her laptop around on the truck's counter and pointed. "See?" She'd been looking online at plate presentations for the past hour, trying to finalize their entry's look for the contest that weekend. They were going to be judged on a variety of points per topic, such as taste, creativity, and visual appeal. Every detail mattered. "If we want to beat Jude and his family name, then everything has to be perfect."

"You think the judges will vote for him simply because he's a local semicelebrity?" Grady shook his head. "I'm not nearly as worried as you are. We don't even know that he can cook."

Rory leveled him with a stare. "He can cook."

"Would you even know?"

She twisted her lips.

"Sorry." He held up both hands. "Not trying to rub it in, but seriously, would you even recognize —"

"Trust me. We're going to have to pull out all the stops. He made a mean taco." Not to mention his pretty-boy face would draw a crowd. If any of the judges were female, single, and aged twenty-one to forty-one, they were in trouble.

She tapped the laptop screen. "Look — this plate is downright artistic." She admired the straight edges where the two foods met but didn't overlap. The darkness of the beans against the stark white of the rice topped with green peppers and sprinkled with a dusting of chili powder provided a pop of color in all the right places. It made her want to host a fiesta-themed birthday party, complete with striped piñatas, hand-bunched fuchsia and burgundy crepe flowers, and turquoise pompoms dangling off canvas cacti —

"Well, whatever. The contest isn't here yet, so for today Jane Doe can deal with her rice and beans touching." Grady tucked in the lid of the to-go container and plopped it at the serving window, then turned back to stirring the giant pot of black beans.

Someone was grumpy. Which meant . . . "You and Nicole fighting?" Rory shut her laptop and leaned forward.

"What's there to fight about when she's always right?" His laugh morphed into a cough, which he directed into his elbow.

"Those words biting you back, huh?" Rory hid a smile. Nicole and Grady were the perfect couple in pretty much every way, but that didn't mean they didn't have their moments.

He winced. "Sorry. I don't know what my deal is. We're not fighting. I think I'm just tired — I didn't sleep well last night."

She could relate. She had stayed up DMing with StrongerMan99 for hours. It felt a little awkward at first — the elephant of their not meeting yet seemed to constantly lurk in the corner — but after a while, they had found their natural bantering rhythm again. She hadn't wanted it to end. Every time she signed off Love at First Chat, she feared what they had would evaporate before it had time to gel.

Great. Now she was thinking in food analogies. She'd been staring at plate presentations for far too long. But it was the least she could do since Grady had to handle everything else.

Plus, it was way more fun than attempting to help cook.

Grady quirked an eyebrow at her as he turned off the burner under the pot of beans. "You're going to make each plate a rainbow of peppers, aren't you?"

"Not a full rainbow." Rory grinned. "For instance, there's no blue or purple."

"But there'll be red, orange, yellow, green, and probably some kind of pink, won't there?"

He seemed resigned to his fate, so she nodded. "The last thing I'm worried about are the presentation points." That area came naturally to her, which was part of what made this contest finally seem exciting and less like something to dread — she was getting to contribute in tangible ways. This time, she wouldn't have to "sit and look pretty."

"Well, don't worry about the taste points either." Grady coughed again into his elbow. "Sorry about this tickle in my throat. Pour me some of that atole, will you?" He gestured toward a black coffee mug on the counter near her laptop. "I've been experimenting with how much brown sugar to add. This batch is my favorite so far."

She ladled the hot cinnamon-rich liquid from the slow burner into his cup. "Isn't this a winter drink?"

"It's a specialty. Trust me, it'll make a big splash with the judges. I doubt the other trucks will think about a bonus beverage."

"And that's why we're going to win." Rory held up her hand for a high five, but he was busy chugging back the atole.

He tilted his head in consideration. "Needs more cinnamon. Less vanilla extract."

Rory handed him the container of seasoning. "You're the boss."

"Be sure to tell Nicole that."

She opened her mouth to jokingly refuse when a knock on the serving window interrupted. "Hey, it's Alton." She slid the half-cracked window all the way open. A warm breeze ruffled the tendrils of hair that had escaped her hat, and she squinted down at him. "We didn't get a call-in order today — weren't sure if you were coming."

Alton's shirt was untucked, his smile genuine. "Today's my last day at the firm."

"Wow, congrats, man." Grady joined her at the window, bracing his arms against the frame. "Where to next?"

"Well, that's the interesting part." He rubbed the back of his neck. "But first, I'll need to order that taco salad for the *former* boss man."

"No quesadilla with extra cilantro today?"

Rory narrowed her eyes at Grady. "*No. Obviously.*"

Grady blinked in confusion. Then recognition lit his tired eyes. "Ah, right. That was Jude's order, wasn't it?"

"*Judas,* you mean."

Grady snorted. "Now, Rory, I hardly think this is on the same level as —"

Alton cleared his throat. "I'll take some street corn, if that's cool."

"Of course." Rory smiled at him and went to ladle the spicy corn concoction into a to-go bowl. She secured a lid over it while Grady pulled one of the premade salads from the fridge. "So what's next for you? More school? An internship somewhere?"

"Sort of. I'll be working with a chef." Alton busied himself with plucking paper napkins from the dispenser.

"A chef? I didn't know you were into cooking." Rory crossed her arms. Then the dots began connecting. "Wait. This wouldn't happen to be a new chef, would it?"

"I, uh —"

Her arms fell to her sides. Panic pitched her voice an octave higher. "A new *local* chef? With a new taco truck?"

"I — you know — tacos are —"

Grady slid the salad container across the serving counter. "Here you go, man." He darted a side glance at Rory, then leaned down and whispered to Alton, *"Run."*

Alton ducked his head. "See you guys at the festival." Then he was gone, shirttails waving in his wake.

Jude was such a traitor. Irritation heated her chest. "I can't believe that guy would hire Alton, of all people, after tricking me into teaching him how to cook." How arrogant. How selfish. Alton might be the firm's runner, but Jude was clearly using the kid. Probably baiting him with promises of more money or free food. Baiting him with more lies.

Like he had done to her.

Of all the times she'd felt used in her life, this one especially stung. She'd been duped, and now Jude was pulling Alton into it, when he hadn't even known the kid's name two weeks ago. Rory clearly cared more about him than Jude did.

It was wrong, all of it. Wrong that he was entering the contest in the first place. Wrong that he had tricked her into teaching her own competition how to cook.

Wrong that he kept stealing these pieces of her thoughts when she was supposed to be focusing on StrongerMan99 and saving her family's business.

The irritation turned into indignation tinged with fury. She grabbed the dish towel hanging on a hook by the sink. "We have to beat him. There's no other alternative."

"Hey, Rory?"

She wiped at the serving counter with the towel, the pressure of all that was riding on the competition mounting on her shoulders. The food truck. Her aunt's reputation and lifetime of success. She scrubbed harder. "He lied to me. It's completely inexcusable."

"Rory."

She finally looked at Grady, at the sweat beading his forehead and the bags beneath his eyes. He gingerly touched his throat. "I'm not feeling so hot."

Then he sagged against the counter.

"Mono?!"

Now it was Rory's turn to sag against the counter, except she was in her townhouse kitchen. Then she quickly stood upright, her cell dropping from her hand. Wasn't mono extremely contagious? But wait. After calling Nicole earlier to take Grady to the doctor, she'd closed the truck early and cleaned the entire vehicle from top to bottom. Hopefully that had done the trick. Her shoulders relaxed a fraction. She couldn't get sick now. Not with the contest —

The contest.

Her throat closed, and she quickly grabbed for her phone.

"I know, right?" Nicole prattled on, sounding strangely upbeat for this level of bad news. Probably trying to project positivity for Rory's sake. It's what Grady would have done. In fact, she'd have bet Salsa Street that he had told Nicole to do exactly that.

She forced out her friend's name. "Nicole . . ."

But she kept going. "I tested negative, thankfully. Now he's quarantined, and I'm sleeping in our guest room for the next week." She laughed. "At least I get a break from the snoring, right?"

"Nicole."

"Also, perk. My house has never been so clean. I must have used the entire bottle of bleach —"

"Nicole!"

Silence pulsed. "Hmm?" her friend finally asked, sounding at once naïve and completely in denial.

"The contest is Saturday."

She sighed. "Right."

Rory squeezed her eyes shut, then sank

onto the barstool at her kitchen island. She fiddled with the turquoise oven mitt she rarely used, spinning it around so the straight lines of the opening matched perfectly with the groove on the countertop. "How long will Grady be down?"

"The doctor said best case, two to four weeks." Nicole's tone dripped with sympathy.

Rory inhaled deeply as the ramifications of canceling their spot in the contest loomed before her — all of them dollar signs. And an image of her aunt's sweet face. What was wrong with Rory that she couldn't get herself together — hold the business together — the way Sophia had? Wasn't it in her blood?

Why couldn't she cook?

Since they wouldn't have the contest winnings now, maybe she could take a second job to help pull the truck through. She could be a barista at the local coffee haunt over on Clark Avenue — once again, working with food she didn't even particularly like. The noose tightened. "I'm a tea person, Nicole."

"I know. It's strange. Coffee is clearly superior."

Rory shook her head, forgetting Nicole hadn't followed on her runaway train of thought. "Listen — tell Grady to focus on getting well, and it'll be okay. I'll cancel the contest, and we'll figure something out." Like finding a tree with money growing on it.

A scuffle sounded over the phone, followed by the opening of a door and muffled voices. Then Nicole spoke. "Hang on. He wants to talk to you. But I told him he can't use my phone, so he'll call you in a sec."

"Nicole, wait —"

Too late. The call ended.

Her phone screen immediately lit with a new call. Rory hit the green button to accept as she wandered outside to her front porch. "Grady, you should be napping."

"Hermana, I feel fine. They gave me this steroid shot, and I offered to clean out the pantry for Nicole, but she refused." Grady scoffed. "Can you believe that? So now I'm cleaning out the guest closet. I just found the tennis racket I thought I lost."

"Grady! Get in bed." Crickets chirped from the bushes beside Rory's front door, providing an exclamation point to her command as she sat on the porch bench.

"You and Nicole are like the same person," he grumbled. A mattress squeaked, then he sighed with obvious relief. "Okay, yes, maybe this is better."

166

"I'm going to pull out of the contest, okay?" The words tried to stick in her throat, but she forced them out. This wasn't Grady's fault. She stared up at the stars starting to poke through the inky canopy above and tried to accept Salsa Street's fate. They wouldn't be able to cook in the festival either — the entire truck would have to shut down until Grady was back.

Losing the business . . . it felt a little like losing her aunt all over again.

She straightened her shoulders. "I don't want you to feel guilty. This is just one of those things."

"No way." His voice, tired but firm, left little room for argument. "You're doing this."

"Me?" She closed her eyes. "I burn things."

"You know the recipes."

Desperation clawed. "I mismeasure things."

"You've seen me cook a hundred times." His tone turned pleading. "You can do it."

"I don't have an assistant."

A long silence pulsed over the phone. Then . . . "Nicole! Come here!" His voice returned full volume. "I'm going to see if she'll get me a bell."

Rory smirked as she tucked her legs up

167

underneath her on the bench. Nicole would move into a hotel before she gave this man free rein with a bell.

"You rang?" She heard Nicole's dry tone over the line, sounding as if it were from a distance.

"See. It's like a prophecy!" He chuckled into the phone. Then his voice muffled again. "Go get your cell, babe. I'll conference you in."

A few minutes later, Grady announced to both women that Nicole would be Rory's helper for the contest.

A stunned silence followed. Finally, Rory cleared her throat. "Have you ever heard the phrase, 'The blind leading the blind'?"

"Hey!" Nicole feigned indignation. "I'm not that bad."

"Compared to who? *Me?*" Rory snorted. "You need a new yardstick."

"Ladies. Y'all can do this." Grady's voice, assertive moments ago, dipped with exhaustion. "You also don't have a choice. Salsa Street needs this."

Rory traced a line in the grain of wood on the bench's arm with her finger, unsure if she should hope Nicole would agree or not. But it wasn't just Salsa Street needing it, was it? It was Grady too. The truck had always been his baby. And she owed it to her "brother" to give this her best shot.

Nicole drew a long breath, laden with the same hesitancy Rory fought. "It's not that I don't want to help. I just don't know how much help I'd be."

"Come on. You're a rock star, remember? That's why I married you."

Nicole laughed. "I might actually have more luck on stage with a guitar than in a cooking contest."

"Maybe Grady's right." Rory's courage rallied a bit, and she leaned forward on the bench. "We just have to do it twice. One day for the festival and one day for the competition."

"So you're shooting for beginner's luck now?"

"Something like that." The thought of giving up before they even tried didn't sit right. Hadn't StrongerMan99 taken a leap of faith in his career? It was her turn to do the same. And just like she'd encouraged him, she could imagine him encouraging her forward. To do the hard thing, the risky thing.

Nicole's resigned sigh sounded over the line. "We're going to need matching aprons."

Rory sat up straight. Did that mean —

"Yes! That's my girl!" Grady whooped, then immediately coughed. "Okay, ow."

Relief flooded Rory and she grinned. "Aprons, yes. Tutus like every middle-aged female on televised cooking contests? Over my dead body."

"Deal." Nicole's voice projected a confidence Rory almost believed. They could do this.

She couldn't wait to tell StrongerMan99.

"I really appreciate you working me in last minute." Jude awkwardly lowered his neck back into the oversized sink and tried to relax. But the black cape around his throat felt like a noose. Hopefully that wasn't an omen for the upcoming weekend's big event. He had so much left to do.

"No problem at all." His brother's girlfriend, Maddison, pumped shampoo into her hands and then began to scrub, her fingers working up a thick lather. "You've got to look sharp for the festival."

"I'm normally more organized than this." He'd realized just that afternoon he hadn't ever rescheduled his regular haircut at his barber shop in Tyler after his barber canceled on him last week, and now there wasn't time to work in a trim before the festival. "It's really nice of you."

"So are you ready for the contest? Nervous?" She used the hose to rinse the suds out of his hair, her hands brisk and professional, her tone sweet and genuine. Not for the first time, Jude wondered what she was doing with someone like his brother. Apparently, opposites still attracted.

An image of Rory flickered to his mind, and he immediately removed it. That was different. He and ColorMeTurquoise had plenty of differences to keep things interesting, but also plenty of things in common to help avoid frequent fights. It was the perfect balance. He and Rory were more like oil and water. Or was it oil and vinegar? No, those went together on salad. He and Rory definitely didn't complement each other.

The awkward silence stretching out suddenly made him remember Maddison had asked a question. He racked his brain for what it had been about. Right, the contest. "I'm more eager than nervous, I think."

"That good ol' Worthington family confidence." Maddison chuckled as she began applying conditioner. The scent of lavender and honey filled his senses, and he closed his eyes. "I think your father patented it."

"That's one way to put it." Jude chuckled back, but it felt — and sounded — forced. He cleared his throat, and the cape pulled tighter. "If I win, I want to earn it."

"So you're not part of that famous cutthroat, win-at-all-cost mindset, then?" The hose turned on again, temporarily saving him from an answer.

Jude swallowed hard, debating how to respond. Everything he said could easily be repeated back to Warner. Maybe not intentionally used against him, but as kind as she was, Maddison would be loyal to his brother first. He opened his eyes. "Let's just say lawyering isn't really in my blood."

She snorted, tossing her long side-swept bangs out of her eyes. "And here I always thought Worthingtons didn't have a choice." She shut off the water, helped Jude sit up slowly, and draped a towel over his shoulders.

Jude grasped the towel. "That's exactly what I'm trying to win."

Their gazes locked. Defense cloaked Maddison's gaze, until she finally looked away. "Warner is a good guy," she whispered, almost as if trying to convince herself. "He gets . . . passionate, you know?"

"I know." Jude didn't have the heart to tell her exactly how well he knew.

"Your father has a lot of influence over him, but I think the longer we're together, the more Warner sees potential."

Water dripped down Jude's forehead, and

he dabbed it with the towel. "Potential for what?"

Maddison glanced sideways, as if Warner — or maybe Hollis — could appear in the salon at any minute. Knowing them, it wasn't impossible or even all that unlikely. She bent down closer to where he sat. "For other things."

Like Jude was trying to carve out for himself. Did Warner have a secret ambition outside the law firm? Or was Maddison talking in general — maybe about their relationship?

Either way . . .

"We all have to make our own decisions." Jude held her gaze to let the double meaning sink in. "Regardless of the risks."

Like he'd done with taking out a loan and purchasing this truck that was supposed to be delivered tomorrow. If Warner wanted to do something and was holding back because of the risk, well, the odds were that he wasn't going to do it. Not without Hollis's full permission. It was how his brother operated. Always had, always would.

Maddison shrugged. "Well, I'm not exactly risky, but Warner chose me. He could have any girl in Modest — or Texas, for that matter — yet I'm his girlfriend." She shook her head, as if she still couldn't believe it.

But she didn't look as happy as she should have at the thought. Jude frowned, lowering his voice as another client took the shampoo chair next to them. "Do me a favor. Don't put him on a pedestal, okay? You're not beneath him."

A flicker crossed her face, then her features steeled back into her usual smile before Jude could decipher it. "I know what it looks like, but don't worry. Warner will make the right decision when the time comes."

"What decision?"

Instead of answering, she popped the recliner portion of the chair upright. Jude's feet hit the floor, and she gestured him toward her styling chair, the moment — and the conversation — over.

NINE

"If you can eat, you can cook."

Jude stood back from assessing the new-to-him truck parked in his driveway and glanced at Alton, who mimicked his stance, hands planted on his skinny hips. "Say what?"

"That's what my granny used to say, God rest her soul." Alton dipped his head for a moment until Jude felt compelled to do the same. Before he could, Alton abruptly straightened, his long blond hair flopping back over his forehead. "But I think she got tired of getting up to make me more ramen."

Perfect. His much-needed sous-chef was an expert on the world's cheapest noodles.

Jude slid his hand down over his chin as he took deep breaths. The longer-than-usual stubble on his face scrubbed against his palm. He should have had Maddison give him a shave while she was at it yesterday.

Now he needed to shave before tomorrow . . . he needed to do a *lot* before tomorrow. For now, though, the truck was here, gassed up, and ready to go. The fridge was stocked. The recipe was written down — mostly for Alton's sake but also in case Jude got flustered during the rush tomorrow.

Please let there be a rush.

"I like the cover. The skin — whatever you call it." Alton tilted his head, studying the truck. "Pretty rad."

The words *Nacho Taco* covered the bulk of the side of the truck, minus the space taken by the large serving window, in vibrant primary colors. With bold bubble letters, it intentionally resembled graffiti. At first Jude hadn't been sure about it, but the designer he'd hired *was* working with a last-minute rush order — and swore it would bring in the attention Jude needed as a newcomer.

It stood out, he'd give him that.

"You think people will try to order nachos?" Alton squinted.

Jude shook his head. "The menu on the side points out we only sell tacos." Beef, chicken, or pork. The sides they offered were refried beans, Mexican rice, and chips with salsa. Pretty simple.

Hopefully.

"But it says —"

"It's a play on words. Like, this isn't your taco." Jude demonstrated holding a taco, as if somehow pantomiming would communicate his point better.

Alton imitated the taco-hold gesture. "Not your taco."

"Exactly."

"Not *yo* taco."

"Yep."

Alton examined the fake taco in his hands. "Shouldn't we have painted Not Your Taco on the truck, then?"

"The point is the pun, Alton."

He nodded eagerly. "Right. That's why it's confusing."

Jude's hands fell to his sides. "It'll be fine." He took a deep breath. Thankfully, the good news remained — no matter how hard this turned out to be or how terrifically he failed, he was working for himself. No longer did he report to his father. No more did he have to dance around Warner and avoid petty challenges, sarcastic comments, and demeaning one-liners. No more shuffling paper and pandering to his father's clients and making forced small talk at board meetings. He was free.

For now.

"So, what's next, boss?" Alton rubbed his

hands together, anticipation lighting his boyish face. "I like calling you 'boss.' "

"I was already your — never mind." Jude forced a smile. "I think we're set. Why don't you go home and get a good night's sleep before the big day?" He hadn't had a good run in forever, but tonight he might go for a few laps. Something to work off these pre-show nerves.

Alton nodded. "Cool. I am pretty hungry. I might go heat up some beef ramen."

"You do that."

A half hour later, after Jude had laced up the running shoes he hadn't worn in several weeks, he made steady progress out of his gated neighborhood and toward downtown Modest, which was only about two miles away. His feet steadily tapped the pavement, the familiar rhythm bringing a measure of peace to his chaotic thoughts.

He was really doing this. The festival was tomorrow. Tomorrow his meager offerings would be judged by the public for the first time. And if he didn't get booed off the stage, so to speak, he'd be participating in the contest on Saturday. He drew deep breaths — in through his nose, out through his mouth — as he leveled his pace.

Tomorrow he'd get his first hint as to what

his future would hold.

He turned onto Spruce Street, picking up speed as he passed the Worthington firm. No need to linger there. Though — wait — was that Mayor Whit leaving the building? After hours? His dad and Warner never stayed late for anyone, but maybe there was some business with a paralegal Whit had to tie up.

Jude slowed, lifting a hand to wave, but Whit abruptly reached up and scratched the side of his head, blocking his view of Jude with his hand.

Oh well. He really didn't want to chat right now anyway. Jude resumed his pace and directed his attention to the window of the closed hair salon across the street, remembering his cryptic conversation with Maddison the day before. Which only reminded him of his dad and the crazy plan to launch Warner into local politics if Whit didn't cave to channeling the family's funding in the direction Hollis demanded. Was that what Maddison meant about Warner making decisions?

And had his dad always been that domineering over others, or had it gotten worse over the years? Maybe his dad hadn't changed. Maybe Jude had.

Maybe Jude was finally seeing what used

to be normal for what it really was — unfair. He ran faster as he turned off Spruce and onto Maple. Too bad he couldn't outrun his DNA.

Ding.

His phone.

He jerked his pace back to a fast walk and opened the text. His previously sinking heart leapt.

I suppose I should be sending you daisies.

He slowed more, grinning as he typed back.

What did I do to deserve the friendliest of flowers?

Motivated me. I took a big leap of faith at work. My coworker needed me to step in for him, in a position I would normally not be comfortable with at all, but something about all our recent talks made me believe maybe I can do it.

There was a pause. Dots.

You're contagious.

Jude's smile broadened, and he narrowly

avoided running into one of the black lamp-posts lining Maple Street. He darted around it at the last second as he responded.

Great job!

He wanted to suggest a leap of faith in meeting him, but he couldn't — wouldn't — push that again. That ball was bouncing around her court now, and as much as he hated watching basketball, he was fully invested in waiting her out. He typed again.

You won't regret it.

I hope not. It's a sink-or-swim situation. People are counting on me.

Well, I'm leaping with you. Same boat, different metaphor.

She sent a laughing emoji, and he smiled back at it, as if she could see him. As if he could see her. But couldn't he? More and more so with every conversation.

He slipped his phone into his pocket and resumed his jog, still grinning like a fool when a shadow caught his eye across the street. Another jogger, clad in gray sweats and . . . a familiar ball cap. The long dark hair sticking through the back was also familiar.

Rory.

As if sensing his presence, she slid her phone into her sweatpants pocket and met his gaze. Her eyes widened beneath the hat brim, then she jerked her head back to face forward.

Jude's good mood soured. Maybe jogging was her stress reliever too. But what in the world would she have to be worried about? She could probably man the truck with one hand and sell out in half a day. Probably impress the judges with one simple plate. He needed this way more than she did. Salsa Street was already a household name in Modest.

Waves of frustration propelled him forward. Frustration at his family, for putting this kind of pressure on him to succeed and leaving him no plan B, but also frustration at Rory, for turning what could have been a decent, industry-related friendship into melodrama. He still had no idea what bee had flown into that worn hat of hers, and the fact that she wouldn't tell him made him press even harder with his strides. And now she was pretending like he wasn't running right across the street.

He darted a glance back at her, certain

he'd left her in the dust. But she was running parallel with him on the other side of the street, matching his pace stride for stride as they turned off Maple and onto Main.

The two-story courthouse flew past his peripheral vision as they continued. Man, she was quick. His side hitched, and he forced deep breaths through the next several steps. He couldn't allow this new business venture to get him out of shape. He hadn't run a 5K in a while, and with his pace tonight, he certainly wouldn't be winning one anytime soon. He hated losing.

He was beginning to think Rory did too.

He surged forward, ignoring the warning cramp aching up his shin. When Jude was little, Warner would tease him about how he always tried to predict future events based on the environment around him. *"If the next two cars that drive down the street are blue, I'll win my Little League game tonight. If the mail comes before two p.m., Sarah Mesquite will ask me to the Sadie Hawkins dance."*

He cast a sideways glance across the road. It was ridiculous, but he couldn't help it.

If I beat Rory to the end of Clark Avenue, I'll win the cooking contest.

They rounded the next block onto Clark. He tucked his head down. A sidelong glance showed her in a similar form. Her long legs were a churning gray blur, her ponytail swinging erratically. They approached the coffee shop, with its red awning, then sped past. Clark Avenue ended at a gazebo before splitting into two opposite-facing one-way streets. They were almost there.

He poured all his fears into his stride. Breath steady, head straight, shoulders back, eyes focused straight ahead . . .

And Rory pounded past the gazebo first.

Jude pulled up short and bent over, hands on his knees as he sucked in painful breaths. Disappointment fisted in his stomach. He didn't know why she was running tonight, but he was running to prove himself.

And Rory might have just proven him wrong.

Rory's attempt at a peaceful "burn the stress off" evening jog had turned into a full-fledged sprint away from anxiety.

Rory stopped pacing her townhouse and sat down next to her coffee table, where her laptop waited. She paused to take a deep breath of the calming lavender-scented candle that so far wasn't lending any effect.

She'd started to vent in a text to StrongerMan99 a dozen times on her walk home, but she immediately erased everything she typed. She couldn't get into why it upset

184

her that she saw Jude tonight without explaining who Jude was — and she couldn't talk about the contest or the festival. What if StrongerMan99 pieced info together and sought her out there? They both knew Love at First Chat only matched up people within sixty miles of their registered addresses.

She wasn't ready to meet. Especially not like that — unaware, unprepared.

Rory took a sip of her cooling tea. When she'd first seen Jude jogging downtown, she'd tried to pretend she hadn't. Then she'd noticed him running faster, as if he were silently challenging her to a race. She couldn't figure out why it mattered so much to her that she beat him, but as her legs ate up the sidewalk and she pushed herself harder than she had in a long time, all she knew was that it did matter.

Something about the way Jude had snuck into her life and her food truck and then betrayed her stirred up her urge to put him in his place. He didn't need this festival or this contest. He didn't even need an income! The man was infamously wealthy.

And yet, for some reason, he was trying to take away everything that mattered to Rory. Encroaching on her heritage, her family's specialty foods . . . and for what — a new hobby? It wasn't right.

Too much wasn't fair lately, and somehow Jude had become the face of all those things.

How's your evening going?

Sweet guy. Ever since their two-day hiatus from chatting, he'd been diligent to check on her regularly.

I've been better.

She hesitated. Maybe there was something she could say to explain.

Tonight I expected to see someone
I trusted, and I met the enemy instead.

Hopefully the *You've Got Mail* reference would explain what she couldn't.

I'm sorry. What happened?

The "trusted friend" = my favorite
stress-relief hobby. But it got
interrupted by someone who has
recently started threatening my career.

Disgruntled coworker? Or annoying boss?
Been there — with both.

More like a brush with Mr. F-O-X.

Competition, huh? Is this for your work?

It is. Part of the new step I told you
I was taking. 😜 Funny how much my
life is starting to mirror my favorite
movie in the not-so-great ways too
.

I had kind of a weird night too. I'm glad to
be home.

Home. She wondered what that looked
like for him. Where did he sit when they
chatted? With a laptop in a bachelor's
leather recliner, feet propped up with black
coffee in reach? Or did he sit at a desk or
table, tea bag steeping nearby? Was his hair
gelled and spiked up or long and casual?
Did he have a beard? Five-o'clock shadow?
Blue eyes? Brown? Was he dressed in a
baggy sweatshirt, like her, or a sporty polo?
Graphic tee with Captain America?

She needed answers. She desperately
wanted to envision him, to connect on a
different level.

What are you wearing?

Then her eyes widened. Oh no. Not that

level. She typed feverishly as heat flooded her cheeks.

NOT LIKE THAT.

😂 😂 😂 😂 😂

I DIDN'T MEAN IT THAT WAY.
I'm so sorry.

I think I get it. You want to "see" me.

Humiliation performed a tap dance in her stomach. She couldn't bring herself to confirm.

Green athletic T-shirt. Leather couch. Iced coffee with sweet cream, which I'll most likely regret drinking this late.

She stared at the words, soaking in the closest hint to a visual she'd had yet and somehow still forming a thousand questions in response. What color green, exactly? Was the coffee roast blonde or bitter? Was it from the local diner, or did he make it himself?

Oh yeah. It was her turn.

Sweatshirt. Water bottle.
Lavender candle.

This is interesting.

A pause.

Food Network. My left sock has a hole in the toe.

She snorted, then glanced around the room.

> Blue floral rug (covering a stain
> on the carpet). Origami swan
> courtesy of my cousin.

And just like that, her blunder was forgotten, and their usual banter was firmly in place for the next fifteen minutes. But Nicole's admonition from the other day kept tapping Rory on the shoulder. "You've got to meet this guy and do this the real way. Fewer communication issues," she'd said. And her friend was right. There was plenty of wisdom in her advice.

But there was also a lot of fear wrapped up in that scenario. If she met StrongerMan99 and something went south . . . if they didn't click . . . or worse, if only *one* of them clicked . . if she were to lose her friendship with StrongerMan99, she was afraid her label of loneliness would start to stick a little too tightly.

Grady and Nicole had each other. Hannah had her life at Unity Angels. Aunt Sophia was gone, and Rory's father was rarely even in the US — and showed zero interest in having anything to do with her outside of the occasional pity gift and obligatory phone call.

She swallowed. When had her world gotten so small?

She eyed the keyboard. Aunt Sophia's words rang in her head, her soft voice humming as she rolled out dough, eyes sparkling as she whispered about soul joy. *Gozo del alma.*

Rory took a fortifying breath and then a tentative step — toward joy. She typed, *After my work situation has calmed down in a few weeks, I'd really like to see you in person.* She hit Send before she could change her mind. Or throw up.

His response was immediate.

I can't wait — but I will. I have a feeling it will be worth it.

TEN

This was going much better than he'd imagined.

"Order up!" Jude turned and slapped a Styrofoam to-go box into Alton's outstretched hands. He said it because he wanted to, and because he could. The first time, Alton had rolled his eyes. The third time, Alton had mouthed it along with him. The sixth time, Alton played along, making up names of greasy diner dishes and giving each of their walk-up customers imaginary order numbers that meant nothing.

It was the first day of the food festival, and they were really cooking. Jude smirked at his own pun as he sprinkled an extra dash of paprika into the taco meat. He felt confident today. In the evenings, when he wasn't chatting with ColorMeTurquoise or experimenting with seasonings to tweak Maria's recipe, he spent all his free time immersed in YouTube videos on food truck management, cooking in bulk, and customer service in the food industry. He had even bribed Alton with another package of Double Stuf Oreos to watch a few of the same courses and had fallen asleep most nights while reading his way through an authentic Mexican cookbook.

He was as ready as he could be.

Outside the truck, on the festival grounds set up in the empty parking lot behind the courthouse, kids shouted and laughed while weary parents called after them. The festival committee had set up a giant bouncy house nearby, while rows of sprinklers offered a respite for anyone desperate enough to cool off from the blinding Texas sun. The giant parking lot spilled over into the public park on Main Street, blossoming with carefully tended flowers that provided pops of color around the playground equipment. The landscaping was courtesy of Hollis's donation two years ago. A plaque announced as much on one of the swing sets.

He briefly wondered what beautification project his dad and Mayor Whitlow weren't seeing eye to eye on this year, but as the meat sizzled, he decided it wasn't the time or place to guess. He couldn't afford any distractions right now.

He called over his shoulder to Alton as he

removed the meat from the fire. "How many?"

"Customer nine wants six." Alton twisted the long tie of his apron and then stilled. "I mean, customer six wants nine."

"Which is it?" He stirred the meat one more time. Perfectly browned and ready for the next batch. They probably needed to chop more onions soon.

Alton looked at his palm, smeared with black ink, and nodded confidently. "Customer nine wants six chicken tacos." He squinted. "Unless I wrote upside down?"

Jude pointed with his spatula. "Go put on gloves."

He shook his head with a grin as Alton complied. Regardless of the kid's random numbers, he knew for a fact they'd served more than nine customers today, and the festival had only officially started an hour ago. Nacho Taco was a hit. The instant success — and what that meant for his future — created a bubbling joy inside that made Jude want to celebrate and buy everyone a round of tacos.

But it might be a *little* too early for that. He tried to keep his focus on cooking and not on the expression Warner would surely have once Jude was announced as the winner of tomorrow's contest.

He lowered the heat on the pot of beans. Everything was going exactly as planned. Even their last customer requesting no cilantro couldn't put a damper on the day. At this rate, the contest would go seamlessly and he'd be officially free of the Worthington Family Law Firm forever.

It was almost too good to be true.

"There's a dude outside who wants to see you." Alton snapped the band of the plastic glove around his wrist. "And he said he wants free stuff."

"What?" Jude craned his head and stooped to see out the serving window just as Cody leaned inside and waved.

He should have known. "Here." Jude handed Alton the spatula. "Trade me. Box up those six tacos — and don't forget the rice and beans."

"Aye, aye, Captain Crisp." Alton began loading a box with steaming golden tacos as Jude took his spot at the window.

Wait. Jude held up one finger at Cody and turned back to Alton. He raised his eyebrows. "Captain Crisp?"

"You know, like Captain Crunch. Crunchy." Alton held up a taco. "But that's taken, sooo . . ."

"No."

Jude turned back to Cody, squinting

against the sun. At least ten people were lined up behind him — two older gentlemen in fishing shirts, a family of six, and . . . Mayor Whitlow.

Maddison stood next to the mayor on the lawn, laughing as she gestured to her perfectly curled dark hair, then pointed at Whit's head. He patted his hair cautiously as he responded. She laughed again, then leaned in a little closer and showed him something on her phone.

Jude tore his eyes away from the exchange. "You're a paying customer, right?" He fist-bumped his friend through the open window, enjoying the ruffle of wind that eased inside. The truck was stifling in the midday heat.

"Of course. Hit me with some nachos, extra jalapeños." Cody riffed a drumroll on the tray mounted outside the serving window. "And none of that green weed you like so much."

Jude swiped his brow with the shoulder of his T-shirt, thinking he'd need to grab a second fan for the truck tomorrow. "No can do. Only tacos here. Crunchy or soft. And we have refried beans, Mexican rice, or chips and salsa."

"But your truck says nachos." Cody pointed.

Alton must have put him up to that. Funny. "Soft or crunchy?"

"Four soft. No rice. Extra beans."

"And *that's* why you're single." Jude ignored Cody's protest as he turned to call to Alton. "Customer thirty-two wants four!"

Straight-faced, Alton shook his head. "He's forty-nine."

"I most certainly am not." Cody feigned offense. Or maybe he meant it.

Jude stifled a laugh. "Fine. Customer thirty-five wants four."

"You realize we're the same age."

"But do we look it?" Jude gestured between them as Alton began prepping Cody's order.

Cody grunted. "Maybe quit the comedy routine and stick to your new taco situation here."

"That's the plan, man. Trust me."

"Order up!" Alton bellowed as he turned with a box of tacos.

Cody narrowed his eyes at Jude as he accepted his box. "These better be good."

"Fifteen dollars."

He handed over a twenty. "Keep the change."

Jude raised his eyebrows. "Thanks man, that's —"

"You can buy me a beer with it later." He

tossed a grin over his shoulder as he exited the line. Jude rolled his eyes.

"Nice guy." Alton handed over the spatula. "Trade ya, Captain."

This was going much worse than she'd imagined.

She'd scorched an entire batch of black beans, forgotten some apparently important ingredient in the rice mixture, and her customers' wait times averaged approximately ten minutes each.

And now Nicole was missing. *Missing.* She'd turned around after serving Judge Dawson's redheaded teen triplets three very different orders, and her friend — her sanity — had vanished.

Rory was about one broken taco shell away from an all-out anxiety attack.

She rolled up the short sleeves of her turquoise T-shirt and took a deep breath of the stuffy truck air. Even with two fans, the summer heat and crowd lining up outside the window — not to mention the sun beating directly down in the festival parking lot — threatened her two applications of deodorant. Her shot nerves were probably making it worse.

Perspiration dotted her forehead under her hat as she fought the urge to crawl into the fetal position on the truck floor. Instead, she numbly tossed together a taco salad into a to-go box. *Just do the next thing . . . then the next . . .*

She scooped jalapeños into a mini container. What would Aunt Sophia think if she could see her beloved truck now? She'd see Rory, with lettuce on her shoes and salsa stains on her apron, barely holding things together while people piled outside like ants converging on a picnic blanket, each waiting a ridiculous amount of time for her to serve them what was surely Modest's worst food imaginable.

The contest was tomorrow.

She was going to fail.

What was wrong with her? Why couldn't she do this?

Nicole opened the truck door and stepped inside, carrying a paper plate. A water bottle was tucked under each arm. Her cheeks, stuffed like a chipmunk, sported powdered sugar like extra freckles.

"Where have you been?" The words hissed through Rory's lips, much like Nagini stalking Voldemort's next victim. She slid a taco salad to a waiting customer, then faced Nicole with her arms crossed.

"I told you I had to go the bathroom. You were boxing up the triplets' order."

"They're giving away dessert at the port-a-potties?" Rory hiked an eyebrow and gestured toward the half-eaten dessert.

Nicole shrugged. "I was getting light-headed, so I swung by —"

"DoughBaby?" Rory sucked in a breath. "Nicole!"

"What? They're so good." She held out the plate and wiggled it. "Try it."

Rory recoiled. "They're our competition." Which equated to the enemy. That'd be like someone advising her to go try one of Jude's tacos.

The thought sent a lingering growl through her stomach, and she pressed her hand against the front of her apron to quiet the hungry roar. Nicole had had a friend of hers monogram tacos on the front of the aprons the night before.

Dressed in tutus.

"We're way behind, and the line keeps growing." Rory pointed to the front of the truck. "I've got half a mind to call Grady and tell him to shoot back an energy drink so he can get down here to salvage this mess."

"Well, as fun as a major health code violation would be, I don't think that's our best choice." Nicole set the bottles of water on the counter and grinned. Then she must have registered Rory's rising panic because she immediately sobered. "Calm down, hermana. We can do this."

"Stop it. Why are you speaking Spanish?" Rory's question pitched into a half wail she barely recognized as her own voice. "We don't need Spanish. We need a Mexican. We need *Grady.*" She planted her back against the fridge and slid to the ground, hands pressed against her cheeks as her voice fell to a resigned whisper. "I'm too white to do this food any justice."

Nicole, still holding the plate, squatted in front of her. "He's only half Mexican." Her consoling tone, much like a mother comforting an irrational toddler who'd dropped her ice cream, wrested a strangled half cry, half laugh from Rory's chest.

"And I'm only a quarter." She hated this feeling — the overwhelmed sky-is-falling feeling that flapped on anxiety's shoulders like a villain's cape. Grady was always able to talk her through it. In the truck during lunchtime rush hour. At the desk when paying overdue bills.

In the hospital waiting room during Aunt Sophia's worst days.

As much as Rory joked about the hermana bit, Grady was absolutely her brother and Nicole 100 percent her sister. And if she couldn't pull herself together, she was going to let them down.

Let Hannah down. Aunt Sophia.

The entire community who assumed she knew what she was doing.

Nicole dropped fully beside her, her legs crisscross applesauce. "Cooking Sophia's authentic Mexican food isn't about being white or being Mexican — it's about cooking with heart, like she always did. With *joy.*" She hesitated. "And right now, your stomach is louder than your heart. You're hangry. Take a break, get some food."

Rory cut her eyes sideways to Nicole. "And who will run things here? You and your doughnut?" She jabbed her thumb toward the powdered concoction on Nicole's plate, biting off the word like it tasted bad. But it didn't. It sort of tasted as amazing as that dessert looked.

"It's actually an elephant ear." Nicole reached to set her plate on the stove top, then stood and hauled Rory to her feet with a grunt.

A sudden knock sounded at the half-open window. A dark-haired guy in a plaid shirt waved for their attention with a handful of cash.

Rory gestured for him to hold on, pinching the bridge of her nose as she adjusted to

201

the standing position and the accompanying wave of light-headedness. Her stomach growled. "I'll be okay. We've got to get back to work."

"Eat this." Nicole tore off a significant hunk of sugar dough and held it out. "People don't share these, Rory. This is a true gesture of friendship."

"I don't need friendship right now. I need —" Rory shoved her hands into her hair, forgetting she had on a ball cap. It hit the floor behind her with a flop, taking her loose ponytail holder with it. Her hair splayed across her shoulders.

Plaid Shirt's eyes sparked with sudden interest. "Hey, has anyone told you that you look like —"

Nicole lurched forward and slammed the serving window shut. She spun around, hands braced against the counter and eyes wide as she blocked his view of Rory. "He didn't say that."

"I know what he was going to say."

"He was going to tell you that you look hungry. Go get some food."

Mounting pressure knotted into her shoulders, and she rotated her neck from side to side in a futile stretch as she worked her hair back into a ponytail. She didn't need food. She needed ibuprofen. And a winning lottery ticket.

No, she needed to be capable, and at the end of the day, she was proving herself very much the opposite. What if her father was right? What if she *was* just a pretty face?

The truck tilted again and she swallowed. "Nicole —"

"Look." Nicole held up both hands in surrender, mimicking Rory's Nagini hiss from earlier. "You're no good to me if you pass out. I know you didn't eat breakfast because of how early we got started here. So please go. I got this."

"Got this? You essentially slammed the door in the face of our next customer."

"It'll be fine. Watch." She plastered on a smile, adjusted her blonde bun under her thin hairnet, and opened the window, her voice a dozen times more patient now and twice as sweet. "I'm sorry about that, sir. There was a bee. What can I get for you?"

Rory squeezed her eyes shut. Fine. She'd get food. Take a break — a *short* one. Shoot StrongerMan99 a text. And maybe they could avoid any more fires that day.

She opened her eyes to grab her hat and froze. The paper plate of half-eaten funnel cake was steadily burning, orange flames on top of the stove.

Fire.

She opened her mouth to scream just as Nicole turned around and saw the same. She gasped. "FIRE!"

They both grabbed for the bottles of water Nicole had purchased. Rory doused the burning plate while Nicole shrieked and — missed. Half her bottle wound up down the front of Rory's shirt, while the soggy remains of burnt funnel cake sat somberly atop a black, smoking plate. Rory quickly turned off the burner.

The guys in line at the window started a slow clap. Nicole turned and bowed. Rory tugged the brim of her cap down low, grabbed her wallet, and left. Right in time to hear Plaid Shirt make an awed declaration.

"Man, they *totally* got that bee."

During the afternoon lull, Jude stood outside his truck in the shade cast by the awning, sipping a jumbo lemonade and nibbling a fried Oreo from DoughBaby. He hated to support the competition, but since the contest didn't officially start until tomorrow, he figured he'd better err on the side of comfort food while he could. Besides, this gave him the opportunity to view his truck from a customer's perspective.

So far, they were holding their own.

Jude swiped his hair off his forehead with his forearm, appreciating the breeze that swept through the sleeve of his polo with the motion. Two children chased each other past the truck, melting sno-cones in hand. Purple syrup trailed down their arms as they giggled their way across the lot toward the park. A tired-looking mom pushing a baby stroller followed at a much slower pace. He offered an encouraging nod as she passed.

DoughBaby's truck, two down from his, had peddled funnel cakes almost nonstop all day, and even now, while the lunch-catering trucks' business slowed, a line of cell-phone-obsessed teens, bouncing kids, and sweaty parents created a new rush for the dessert truck. In his concern over beating Salsa Street, he'd almost forgotten how popular DoughBaby was.

He turned. Speaking of Salsa Street, five trucks down in the other direction, they'd kept up steady business all afternoon too. He couldn't help but notice a large majority of their customers had been men between the ages of eighteen and forty.

Though, come to think of it, he'd sold quite a few tacos to females in that same age bracket. Two napkins had slid back across the serving counter with phone numbers on them. Alton had assumed they were for him, and Jude had gladly let him tuck the strips of paper into his back pocket without comment. The only female support he wanted was from ColorMeTurquoise — he couldn't wait to tell her about this weekend in detail. Soon.

Hopefully.

The sun glinted off the tin roof of his new baby, casting shadows on the bold Nacho Taco design. Two other people had tried to order nachos after Cody, and he wondered now if his friend had put them up to it. Their menu was so obvious, it had to be a joke. Leave it to Cody to provide initiation hazing.

Jude slurped the last of his lemonade and strolled a few yards away to a nearby trash can. From this vantage point, he watched as Alton half danced, half wiped at the empty counter with a rag. Strains of a popular rock song filtered through the open truck door over the whirring of the fan. The kid had been a big help today, and tomorrow felt equally as promising. Jude hadn't figured out the official sales total yet, but no one had returned with a complaint, so that had to count for something, right? Besides, the festival technically wasn't over for another several hours.

His back hurt. His feet ached. But his

heart was as full as his belly, and he was happy. He was doing his own thing and doing it well.

The fact that his dad and brother hadn't come by to notice brought equal parts relief and disappointment.

A petite figure walked up and hesitated in front of his truck before ringing the little bell he'd put on the serving window — make that a familiar figure.

Jude crushed the cup in his hand. After the attitude Rory had given him lately, what was she doing — coming to gloat about sales? Talk smack about tomorrow's contest? He tossed the trash into the garbage can and headed to the truck, just in time to hear Rory's equally petite voice order nachos.

"Very funny." He sidled up next to Rory, crossing his arms over his chest. "Want an ice cream sandwich too while you're at it? Or sushi?"

"What are you talking about?" She flicked a weary gaze at him before returning her attention to Alton. Her eyes softened as he shimmied to whatever hip-hop tune he had blaring from a portable speaker. "Hold the cilantro, if there is any."

Well, now she was being antagonistic. He reached up and deftly slid the partition shut.

"Hey!" Rory turned, her eyes now sparking with indignation instead of fatigue. "What is this? Reserving the right to refuse service?"

He squared off to face her. "I'd be happy to sell you a *taco.*"

She frowned. "I wanted *nachos.* After the day I've had, melted cheese sounds amazing."

Oh. "So you weren't joking?" His ire faded, and he suddenly remembered he held a fried Oreo in his hand. He tried to hide it behind his back.

"Why would I joke?" She glared at him. "Your truck says *nachos* in giant letters."

Jude breathed in. She smelled like smoke. And her eyes were red-rimmed. Had she been crying? He sniffed deeper. Or had there been a —

Alton slid the window open, oblivious to their battle. "I heard there was a fire."

"A fire?" Jude raised his eyebrows.

Rory closed her eyes and sighed. "Word travels fast."

"It *is* Modest." Alton shrugged, as if that explained everything.

Jude braced one hand on the serving window, the other hand still concealing his dessert. "What happened?"

Alton gestured with his hand. "There was a bee, and —"

"There was *not* a bee." Rory planted her hands on her hips as she looked back and forth between them. "There was, however, a host of other problems, so if you could just give me my nachos, I'll be on my way." Her voice pitched, like when someone was attempting to hold back tears and was failing.

Something tight loosened in Jude's chest. "We don't have nachos."

"You know what? Forget it." Rory jabbed her finger toward him, much as she had that day at the farmers' market. "Nicole told me to go get some food, and I thought I'd see how you were doing. My *protégé*." She rolled her eyes. "I guess I'm not welcome."

"No, really, we only sell tacos . . ."

Alton's protest muffled as Jude slid the window shut again. This time for privacy. He took Rory's elbow and led her a few steps away. "I don't think you realize you were the one who had an attitude with me first. Remember? The farmers' market?"

"You mean the day I found out you had used me?"

"Excuse me?"

She crossed her arms, mimicking his former position. "Asking for cooking lessons from your number one competition? Ring a bell?"

He exhaled loudly. So that's what that had been about. "Rory, I didn't —"

Her eyes dropped to his hand. "Is that a giant Oreo?"

"Yeah. Fried." He lifted his chin, as if there was any dignity left to save.

Her gaze shifted to DoughBaby's truck. She clearly wanted one.

He hadn't used her. But right now, she'd never believe it. There was only one thing to do. He held out the cookie. "Truce."

She hesitated, wariness spreading across her face. He understood, and he felt the same pause. But honestly, he didn't need the distraction. And somehow, knowing his pretty — irrelevant, however factual — competition down the row hated his guts was distracting.

"I don't know."

He shrugged. "I think you need something sweet."

The wariness fled, replaced by defense. "Why, because I'm being so b—"

"Because you're probably experiencing a blood sugar crash." He waved the Oreo in front of her. "That's why I went and got one a little while ago. I'd barely eaten all day. I had a turkey leg too." No need to mention the Cajun fries. "Take it. I'm full."

She gingerly took it from his hand, as if

making sure not to brush his fingers with hers. Good plan. She'd apparently already dealt with one fire today, and that annoying spark they'd initially shared in the truck still sizzled. He didn't want to fan anything into flame with anyone.

Well, he did. Just not with her.

Jude waved to get Alton's attention. The window slid open. "One soft taco, please." He glanced back at Rory, remembering her nacho woes. "Make that extra cheese."

"You got it, Captain." Alton turned and began assembling.

Rory pulled her wallet from her back pocket, and Jude pushed it aside. "It's on the house."

"Thank you." Her guard had finally dropped, and instead of a fireball, there was now only a weary, smoky woman eating the last of his Oreo. She looked up at him, cookie crumbs dotting her cheek. It took everything in him not to brush them off despite his recent resolve not to touch her. Besides, she clearly despised him. She'd probably slap him. But for the moment . . . what the heck.

He brushed off the crumbs and her eyes widened. "You're being nice to me."

"Well, we are in the South."

She tilted her head at him as she bit off

another hunk of Oreo. "So you're a gentleman by default?"

He'd never felt so microexamined as he did under her full gaze. He straightened. "I'd like to think so."

"Jury's still out." A grin teased the corner of her lips.

Alton produced the taco, and Jude passed it over, warm and wrapped in a napkin. Excess cheese poured out the ends. "Here. Pretend it's nachos."

"I will." She licked her lips, studying him. "This isn't over, you know."

But it needed to be. Staring down at her this close, the urge to hug away her bad day suddenly draped over him like a suffocating cloak. He took a step back. That obviously wasn't what she meant. She meant she was still ticked at him.

He nodded. "Duly noted."

She nodded back, satisfied, then held up her taco as she walked backward a few steps. "Thanks again."

"Watch out for bees!" Alton called helpfully from the truck.

Rory waved her acknowledgment over her shoulder without slowing her pace.

ColorMeTurquoise:
Do you ever feel weak and
hate yourself for it?

StrongerMan99:
Unpack that.

It's too heavy.

But my handle is StrongerMan.

 True.

Try me.

Today at work, I was in a situation
that needed strength. Clarity.
Perspective. And I failed. I got
overwhelmed and irrational, and it's
like — it's like I couldn't turn myself
off even though I knew I was
overreacting. Everything seemed
bigger than life and impossible.
And it makes me . . . mean.

Mean? I doubt that.

No, it really does. I don't come off
the way I do in my mind. In my head,
I make sense at the time, but to
other people, I probably
just seem like a jerk.

Sounds like anxiety taking over.

You've been there?

Not exactly. But I know what's it like to wish you could be different in certain areas of your life or personality — and feel help-less to accomplish it.

What do you do when that happens?

I'll let you know when I figure it out. 😉

So you're not actually perfect? 😆

Far from it.

Prove it.

I think Golden Oreos are a counterfeit from Satan.

😂 Okay, so you're not perfect.

Close enough, though?

Close enough. 🐦 Thanks for being there. Again.

Try and stop me.

ELEVEN

"This is happening." Nicole gripped Rory's shoulders between her hands and shook her slightly. "The contest is today, and you're not in the fetal position. Nothing is even on fire!"

"I know." Rory laughed as she eased away from her overly eager friend. She turned off the burner under the taco meat and raised her eyebrows as she reached for a bowl. "Your point?"

"My point is, we are going to celebrate small victories." She pointed at Rory with an oven mitt. "Maybe not with DoughBaby again, because, you know. Competition. But we're going to celebrate later at the Silent Spade. You're doing great!"

Had yesterday been *that* bad? Rory winced. Yes. It had. She took a solidifying breath and squared her shoulders. Today would be different. The panel of judges would be coming by within the hour to sample their entry, and so far, everything was going as smoothly as it could. Maybe they'd gotten all their mistakes out of the way yesterday.

"Did you say DoughBaby *again*?" Grady's voice, tiny through the speaker on Nicole's cell, chirped from its stand on the counter where Nicole had parked it.

"Yes, dear," Nicole cooed as she edged closer to the phone. "That funnel cake was to die for."

"Was it worth *losing* for?"

"Yes," Nicole immediately said.

"What do you mean?" Rory and Grady asked simultaneously.

Nicole and Rory locked eyes.

"The contest winner is partially determined by who has the most sales over the weekend." Grady's tone was weary. "Did you guys not read the fine print?"

Uh-oh.

"It was one funnel cake." Nicole dusted off her apron and shrugged. "I regret nothing."

Rory's stomach tightened. *And* one taco — except, wait. Jude hadn't charged her for it, had he? Did that mean he hadn't read the fine print either? Or was he . . . being nice?

"You guys have to submit all your sales

from yesterday when they come by to judge." Grady's voice broke through her thoughts. "And has anyone stirred the beans in the last ten minutes?"

"On it, honey." Nicole pranced to the stove, her voice singsongy. "We got this."

"Got it like yesterday — when you bought food from the enemy and started a fire?" Grady let out a tired sigh, followed by a trail of Spanish.

"I heard that." Nicole snorted.

Rory shot a look toward the phone as she dipped a ladle into the slow cooker full of atole. She hadn't even stopped to think what missing this festival and contest meant for him — stuck in bed with saltines and chicken soup instead of bantering with customers and chasing Rory around with cilantro.

Her throat knotted. "We're going to make you proud, Grady."

"I know that tone." Nicole whipped around, pointing the slotted spoon at Rory. Her eyes widened with mock panic. "Rory's having feelings. You know she's not used to those!" She raised her voice toward the cell phone. "Grady, back off with all that. I can't have her collapsing on me again under the pressure." She shook her head and mumbled in Spanish.

"I heard *that,"* Grady said.

"You guys, I'm fine. I'm not collapsing." Rory took a deep breath, the memory of last night's conversation with Stronger Man99 calming her building nerves. She didn't have to give in to anxiety. She could dislike something about herself, or her circumstances, and not overreact. The judges were coming soon, like it or not, and she and Nicole had done the best they could. Soon this would all be over — and out of her hands.

She poured atole into a mug for a taste test. "I'm realizing how much Grady must miss this, is all." Her voice flexed again.

"You're right, wife." Grady's voice turned firm. "She's getting emotional. That's not good for anyone — especially the tacos."

Rory paused, her cup raised halfway to her mouth as their previous words fully registered. "Wait. You guys really believe I don't have feelings regularly?"

Nicole held out her hand in protest. "No one said that."

"Actually, that's exactly what you said," Grady pointed out.

Nicole scowled at the phone. "Not helping!"

"Rory, we know you have feelings."

"Thank you." Rory nodded. If someone

were to ask her, she'd say she had too many of them. Hence the anxiety and her new effort to recognize her faults and accept them rather than let them overtake her.

Grady continued breezily. "You just don't like to admit it. Or talk about them. Or let other people see them."

He wasn't wrong. However . . . "Guys, can we psychoanalyze me later? Like when there isn't a contest about to happen?"

Nicole clapped twice. "Come on, we need to focus. Is the plate ready for the judges?"

"It will be. I wanted to keep it warm until they get here." Rory sipped the atole, and all her previous protests vanished. "Oh, wow, that's good. Grady, you have officially perfected this drink recipe."

"You think so?" He sounded as if he was trying to act surprised, but the attempt fell flat, even through the phone. "Okay, okay. I know. It's pretty awesome."

"Enough of that. You need to go rest," Nicole barked toward the cell. "And we need to get those receipts together from yesterday. We'll call you if we need you."

"I'm not tired," Grady argued, but a yawn broke up his word.

"If you turn off that game show, you'll be asleep in five minutes and you know it."

The background noise from the other side

of the line muted. "I guess you're right."

"As usual," Nicole mouthed to Rory, who grinned. "Bye, honey," she said sweetly to Grady.

"Don't forget to dice the bell pepper really small. Like I do it."

"Will do." Nicole pursed her lips. "Sweet dreams."

"And don't forget that dash of cayenne pepper in the rice. It's crucial."

"We would *never.*" Nicole made a face and frantically pointed to the pepper canister. Rory grabbed it and sprinkled it over the rice.

"And don't forget to butter the —"

"Byeee." Nicole clicked the phone off. "Whose idea was it to put him on speaker again?"

Rory grinned. "The rice is ready now, at least." She'd dish it up and serve it with colorful strips of pepper crisscrossed across the top. She took another contemplative sip from her cup of atole. They really were doing this — and she was staying calm, despite the emotional analysis Grady had given her. She was proud of herself.

Or maybe the calm meant she'd given up? Accepted their failure-laden fate? Or maybe she'd finally started to believe in herself a bit.

"How's the local gentry?" A familiar voice sounded at the open serving window.

Mayor Whitlow.

Rory waved, stashing her half-full mug behind her with her free hand. She wanted the judges to be surprised when they realized Salsa Street had created a bonus drink for them. Each contestant was only required to submit one entrée and one side for the contest. But the atole would complement their entry's color-coordinated presentation perfectly. "Is it that time, Mayor?"

Nicole shot Rory a wide-eyed look as she riffled through the receipt book from yesterday. Ready or not.

"Indeed, it is, Ms. Perez. Mrs. Moser."

"Please, it's Rory," she said. With their age gap, they'd never been exactly friends, but she remembered watching him star in the local community theater productions while on field trips in elementary school. He did a mean Shakespeare dialogue.

Mayor Whit nodded as he fiddled with his watch. "Rory Ann." He tilted his head toward Nicole. "Nicole Louise."

"Louise?" Rory mouthed to Nicole, who rolled her eyes in return. She turned back to Mayor Whit. "Wait. You know the whole town's middle names?"

His thin eyebrows furrowed, as if perplexed. "I'm the mayor."

And that explained it?

Nicole leaned forward against the serving counter, offering her best smile as she crushed the receipt book against her apron. "Are you part of the judges panel?"

"Unfortunately, no. I'd love to taste all these delicious concoctions, but I'm afraid it wouldn't be fair. I might not be impartial." He grinned.

"Well, if you're partial toward us, then I highly recommend you judging after all." Nicole winked.

Mayor Whit laughed. Then his face sobered. "You know I can't do that, right? That wasn't a bribe, was it? I'm supposed to report —"

"Of course not." Rory hip checked Nicole out of the way of the window. Whit's hair, askew from the wind, formed a little tunnel down his forehead that reminded her of Danny Zuko from *Grease*. In fact, she remembered seeing him in that play too. But he'd played Putzie. "She was joking."

"I was joking." Nicole nodded her confirmation, mouthing to Rory, "Was I, though?"

Rory smiled at Whit. "If you're not judging, what can we get you? Maybe a quesadilla, or a tostada?" Hopefully not a burrito. For the life of her, she still couldn't figure out how Grady folded them so that they stayed so perfectly intact.

"I'm here for yesterday's receipts. We've got to tally sales for the judges to factor into their decision." Whit hesitated, his gaze nervously darting from Rory to the worn grass at his feet. He lowered his voice. "You know, I —"

He stopped as Nicole suddenly leaned out the window to hand him the records. "Here's a carbon copy of everything from yesterday."

The pile looked thinner to Rory than what it seemed like it should have, after how busy and hectic yesterday had felt. But it would have to do. She put on a brave smile as Nicole disappeared back inside the truck.

"What were you going to say?"

Whit shook his head. He looked exhausted, as if he'd single-handedly put on the festival. And maybe he had. No one loved Modest more than Whit. But beneath the tired lurked something a little more wary. Not pride from achievement. More like — anxiety.

She recognized it because, well, how many times had she wished someone had seen her silent struggle and reached out? She made an impulsive decision and chose to pour Whit a fresh mug of atole. "Here. On the house. And don't worry — it's not a bribe."

He accepted the steaming mug. "Sort of like Christmas in July." He took a sip. "Mmm. That's oddly comforting."

"Isn't it?" Rory smiled. "Even in the heat of summer, this drink is somehow just right." She'd done it. It'd been Grady's recipe, but she'd executed it well.

"It really is. Thank you." The crinkles around his eyes relaxed a bit, and something warmed inside Rory that went far deeper than the hot cinnamon-laden liquid. She had connected with someone who shared her same struggle and had managed to ease their burden.

It made her own feel a little more manageable.

"There's one more thing." Whit took another gulp from the mug, as if fortifying himself. "The contest is being extended."

"What?" Nicole was back at Rory's side. "Extended?"

Whit looked sheepish. "There's been a small change of plans, due to extenuating circumstances —"

"Afternoon, ladies." Warner from the Worthington Family Law Firm strode up with a straight white smile, looking perfectly pressed in a starched button-up and linen slacks despite the sweltering heat. He held up a briefcase. "I'm going to need a few signatures."

Rory shot a look at Whit, who let out a sigh and resumed his examination of the grass under his scuffed loafers before offering Rory a feeble shrug.

Looked like she was going to need another cup of that atole for herself.

Jude honestly couldn't tell if the blonde judge in the red tank top would rather have another taco — or nibble on him. He stepped behind Alton, who stood to the side of the truck in the sun, his hands shoved in the pockets of his cargo shorts as the three judges tasted their entry of soft tacos and beans. Hopefully the simplicity of Maria's recipe would speak for itself.

And hopefully that one judge would stop eyeing him like he was dessert.

Alton leaned in close to whisper. "I almost forgot to tell you — the mayor came by while you were at the port-a-potties. He needed yesterday's receipts."

Jude raised his eyebrows. "Did you find the receipt book we kept yesterday?" Sales had been better than he'd expected, and he'd been proud of their haul by the end of the day. He didn't know to what extent their sales factored into the judges' final tally, but hopefully they had earned enough to aid a win.

Alton crossed his scrawny arms over his chest. "Yeah, I gave it to him. Easy peasy." He paused, then frowned. "Hey, is that blonde lady okay?"

Jude stifled a laugh, taking another half step behind Alton as the female judge attempted to maintain eye contact while shoveling in forkfuls of beans. "I sure hope so." Maybe she'd eventually switch her focus to Alton instead. After all, he was young. Single.

Jude was — well, not really either of those anymore. He held back a smile. Man, he wished ColorMeTurquoise was here. Wished she could share the anticipation of the results with him.

Wished her shoulder was pressing into him instead of Alton's sweaty one.

He'd texted her earlier but hadn't gotten a reply yet. She must be swamped today too.

The judges mumbled to themselves, marking on scoresheets. Red Tank shot him another sultry look. Jude sighed. He didn't want to win that way. Surely the other two judges — one an older male in suspenders, the other a middle-aged woman sporting a T-shirt that looked as if it'd been hand-painted by young grandkids — wouldn't let her get away with that.

Alton slurped the soda he'd purchased earlier from the fried chicken truck — claiming it was the only one that offered Dr Pepper — and held up one finger at Jude. "Your family came by too."

"Really?" Jude hadn't heard from his brother or dad since the start of the festival. He'd expected them to show up for appearance's sake at some point, make a round through the tents and trucks, smile at a few babies, and pass out a few business cards — but so far, there'd been no sign of them. Of course, this morning he'd been so busy filling orders and finalizing his entry for the judges that he could have missed their arrival.

"Yeah, it was mad awkward." Alton nodded enthusiastically.

He could imagine. "What'd they want?"

Alton raised one T-shirt-clad shoulder. Since leaving the firm, Jude had yet to see him in anything besides clothes one step up from pajamas. "I don't really know. Something about the contest being extended?"

"Extended?" Jude echoed, voice raised with surprise. "What do they even have to do with the contest?"

The judges looked their way from the serving window they were using as a table,

227

and Jude lowered his tone to a whisper, angling toward Alton but also a little afraid to turn his back completely on Red Tank. "What do you mean?"

"There's some new bonus prize or something involved now. I didn't really pay that much attention. They just wanted signatures saying we agreed to whatever they were going on about. It was a bunch of legal jargon, and then Kimmy Peters started waving to me from the Cluck Truck, so you know . . . ." Alton wiggled his eyebrows and shimmied a little dance with his soda.

Jude briefly closed his eyes. He should have known his family would be up to something. But how in the world had his father managed to commandeer the contest? Was it an attempt at sabotage?

His heart thudded. At least he hadn't been there to sign. Whatever it was, it wasn't too late to figure it out and undo if needed. "Are they coming back to go over it with me?"

"Nah, dude. Don't worry. I signed your name." Alton clapped him on the shoulder. "If I've learned one thing from working at the Worthington Family Law Firm, it's not to bother the bosses with petty stuff." He smiled with pride.

Oh, man. Jude sucked in a tight breath. His dad and brother knew a forged signature wasn't valid. So why would they have accepted the signature from Alton?

The judges began to stack their empty plates and forks into a pile, preparing to move on as Jude and Alton headed back inside the truck. Jude forced a smile he didn't feel and thanked them through the open window as they mumbled vague praises. Red Tank wiggled her painted fingernails at him and nodded her head toward the napkin she left behind next to her plate. Thankfully, Alton was obliviously scooping it up as he gathered the trash.

"You okay?" The kid frowned, arms loaded with paperware. "Is this about the signature? I might have messed up doing that. Because Kimmy had on this new dress, and dude, I stopped listening because you know how your brother can be, and she's like, really pretty today."

"It's fine. You didn't know." He *should* have known — but they could deal with that later. Besides, Jude knew exactly how manipulative and conniving his family could be. The fact that they even led Alton to believe his signature counted proved they were up to something.

Jude cast a panicked look out the open side door of the truck, hoping to see two familiar figures on the horizon. Maybe he could catch them and undo Alton's mistake and see what they were allegedly agreeing to.

But the grounds around the food trucks were clearing as the crowds began congregating closer to the courthouse, on their way to make one last bathroom trip and snag seats before the mayor announced the winner. If he still was doing that. Surely someone would announce *something* if there had been an extension.

Then Jude's eyes widened as the truth registered. That was it. His dad and brother didn't need a real signature. They needed to stall.

And, thanks to Alton, Hollis and Warner had just bought themselves the time they needed to make whatever they were planning happen.

TWELVE

So many red and white balloons were tied to the makeshift stage on the courthouse lawn, Jude was tempted to find a dart.

He stood in front of a folding chair in the second row, which was reserved for the contestants of the competition, and crossed his arms over his chest as he scanned the perimeter, searching for his dad or brother. The wicking material of his athletic polo hadn't done much good today in the food truck. He needed a shower. He needed a nap.

He needed *answers.*

Chairs with a balloon tied to each of their backs lined the stage, part of that small-town charm that was both tacky and endearing. Modest tried. But the question was, if the contest had changed, why still proceed with all this pomp and circumstance in the first place? If there wasn't going to be a winner yet — what *was* going to be announced?

What did his future hold?

"Is this seat taken?" a tired voice sounded behind him.

He turned and saw Rory — and a much shorter brunette, with wide cheeks and sparkling narrow eyes.

Rory must have recognized him the moment he turned, as her expression drooped. "Oh. It's you."

"Hey, yourself." He briefly debated being offended, then decided he didn't have time. Instead, he supplied a grand gesture toward the empty chairs on the far side of his. "It's all yours. Both of them."

He went back to combing the stage as they sat down next to him. Mayor Whit stood by the podium, covering the mic with one hand as he spoke with a city council member wearing dark slacks and a blazer. He must be sweltering. No sign of Jude's family. But that wasn't surprising. Whatever they were scheming, they wouldn't show their faces yet. Even in court, Hollis made a production of breezing in at the last possible second.

Jude spun around, searching the crowd of people pressing in for seats behind the reserved rows, but they wouldn't be there. Nor would they be at any of the food trucks.

He ran a frustrated hand down his face,

and sweat dripped from his chin. Alton had allegedly gone to get them both some bottled waters, but if he'd gone to that chicken truck to see Kimmy, well, Jude might dehydrate before the kid made it back.

Defeated, he sank into the chair next to Rory.

She shot him a sidelong look. "The truce is still on for today, right?"

"It's hard to keep up, but I'm pretty sure that was the deal." He looked farther down the row of chairs now filling with other contestants. "Where's your cooking buddy?"

"Nicole went home to check on Grady." She perched on the edge of the chair, shoulders tense. Her dark hair, always in that high ponytail, poured out from under a creased ball cap. This one, a gray trucker's hat, boasted the word *PLANNER* on the front in a shade of greenish-blue. "This is my cousin Hannah."

"Pleasure." He extended his hand. Hannah gave it a firm shake before returning her hands to the sequined blue purse draped across her legs. She kept darting her gaze between him and Rory. Rory, either oblivious or pretending not to notice, kept her expression trained straight ahead.

"What's wrong?" He blurted out the

words before he realized she probably wouldn't tell him anyway.

Her hazel gaze caught and held his. "Are you asking to scope out the enemy's weaknesses? Or are you asking because of the truce?"

"I'm asking because your shoulders are up to your ears." He cast a glance at her lap, where her hands gripped a paper Salsa Street menu. "And you've creased that thing so perfectly down the middle a dozen times now, it's halfway to becoming a paper airplane."

She immediately flexed her fingers, dropping the menu into her lap.

Well, that hadn't helped. It seemed their truce had vulnerability limits.

"I want to try." Hannah eagerly grabbed for the folded menu, a childlike innocence lighting her expression. She moved her arm in broad arcs, flying the "plane." A row of kids behind them immediately pressed in close to watch.

Rory didn't want to talk shop? Fine with him. He'd keep it surface level while he continued his stakeout for his brother. If he so much as caught a single whiff of Armani cologne . . . "So, what do you plan?"

Rory cast him a confused look as Hannah

234

adjusted the fold on the paper. "Excuse me?"

"Your hat." He gestured to it.

She looked up, as if she could see past her own brim, then recognition dawned. "Oh, Nicole got me this a few months ago. Allegedly as a compliment to my obsessive organizing skills."

She didn't recognize a compliment when she got one? Not even from her own friend? "Allegedly?"

She ignored the question. "Right now I'm planning menus." She rolled her eyes. "And apparently mayhem."

He hid a smile. "Today go that well, huh?"

Hannah made *zooming* noises now, the menu fully resembling a plane. Rory ducked before it caught in her ponytail. "You haven't heard?"

"No." He hadn't even thought to ask Rory what the big announcement was. Of course. He shifted eagerly to face her. "Have you?"

Her eyes, full of suspicion, squinted. "Is all this somehow because of you? It was your brother, after all, bringing those papers around . . ." Her voice trailed off. "Wait. Are you trying to rig the contest by —"

"But what did the papers actually —"

Music blared from the speakers, interrupting their interruption of each other. Jude whipped back to face the stage. Warner and Hollis strode into view to a cheerful big-band tune, joining the mayor and council members at the line of chairs. Hollis, in his designer golf shirt and belt that were probably worth the cost of Alton's first semester of community college, looked ridiculous perched amid a hundred balloons when he took his seat.

Why in the world were they on stage? And better yet — why was his father catering to this cheesy show? And Warner — he wanted to be back in Dallas. Surely this was all a joke to him.

But what was the punch line?

Mayor Whit tapped the mic, reeled slightly at the feedback, then grinned. "How's my local gentry?"

The gathered crowd clapped and whistled. Behind Jude, a toddler whined. He could relate. Jude sat up straight, piercing Warner with a glare that should have blasted his profile with fire. But Warner's fake smile didn't flinch. In fact, it almost seemed like he was intentionally not looking back at Jude.

Hollis, however, boldly met Jude's gaze.

Whit attempted to adjust the height of the microphone before giving up and stooping slightly toward the podium. "We've had an exciting change of plans — as the contestants already know."

All but one, anyway. Jude crossed his arms. Out of the corner of his eye, he saw Rory glaring at him. He refused to give her the satisfaction of a look. He wasn't going to feel guilty about something he didn't even know was happening.

Alton ducked into the aisle seat saved next to Jude and handed him a water bottle wrapped in a napkin from Cluck Truck. Figured. "Sorry it took so long. What'd I miss?"

"Nothing yet." Just the answer to whatever was agreed to in those papers Alton had signed on Jude's behalf. He eased back as Alton leaned forward and offered a wave to Rory and her cousin. Rory's expression softened as she returned the wave. Hannah's joy never dimmed as she waved enthusiastically, the paper airplane still gripped in her other hand.

"Thanks to these generous gentlemen here, all contest applications have now been officially signed and notarized — courtesy of the Worthington Family Law Firm." Whit gestured to Hollis and Warner, who gave what everyone else would take as humble nods.

Jude unscrewed the lid of his water while

simultaneously trying to get a grip on his frustration. So they'd muscled their way into the contest by volunteering to revise the legal paperwork for free. But what was in it for them?

He took a long sip, pondering for a deliciously delirious moment whether he should chuck the bottle at his dad on stage. Or better yet, find a few tomatoes to toss.

Instead, he recapped the bottle with the cool, calm demeanor his family had instilled in him, starting with Grandmother. He'd get through this, appearances intact. Then he'd deal with his family. It couldn't be that bad.

But his stomach — and precedent — disagreed.

"Which brings me to my announcement for the rest of the crowd." The mayor attempted a dramatic removal of the mic from its stand, but feedback screeched again. He quickly repositioned the mic on the holder. "As outlined in the new contracts signed today, the contest has been extended. Today we're announcing the three finalists from the festival, who will then go on to compete against each other for the grand prize — and now, in addition, a bonus prize."

If he still had a chance at the grand prize, and if there was a secondary award with it

— well, that didn't sound so bad. But what did any of that have to do with his family?

His shoulders relaxed a notch. Maybe they had finally taken him seriously about their floundering reputation and were simply milking the spotlight by offering to legally change the applications.

Not that *his* had been a legal change. His neck tensed again. There had to be more to this.

"I'd like to announce the three finalists from this weekend's contest, who will go on to compete in a final round next weekend with their themed entries."

His stomach threatened to expel his hastily eaten lunch. He had to be one of the names called. *Had* to be.

"In no particular order, the three contestants who will proceed to the themed round are . . ." Whit's voice trailed off, and he looked around. The crowd started a half-hearted drumroll attempt, but it sounded more like fifty people trying to spit at the same time. "Salsa Street!"

Hannah leapt to her feet and cheered. Rory's face flushed and she nodded, keeping her seat. One down. He tugged at his polo collar and tried to take a deep breath.

"Cluck Truck."

Uh-oh. DoughBaby couldn't take the last

239

spot! Two down. He held his breath. This didn't bode well. If he wasn't called next, it was over. Freedom was over. He'd be back at the law firm, back under his dad's heavy thumb and Warner's designer boot.

Would he even be able to look at tacos again?

The crowd fell silent, waiting for the mayor to continue. Whit grinned, clearly enjoying the suspense. "And, last but not least . . ." He paused.

Say it. Say it.

"Nacho Taco!"

Jude exhaled a year of his life away as Alton jumped up, water sloshing from his open bottle and splashing onto Jude's neck. "We did it! And we didn't even use nachos!"

Jude opened his mouth, then shut it. Not worth the correction. His eyes darted to his father, whose expression remained pleasantly detached. Not surprising — he was in crowd mode. He'd perfected his poker face decades ago.

Beside Jude, a stiff Rory reluctantly held out her hand. "Well done."

He shook it absently, his thoughts racing. "Same to you." Then a tingle shot up his arm into his shoulder, and he quickly removed his grip, flexing his fingers wide. At the same time, Rory rubbed her upper arm. Their eyes met and held.

Jude looked away first, just in time to see Hannah watching their hands, a grin teasing her cheeks. His face burned, and not from the afternoon sun.

"Will the final three contestants please come to the stage for the bonus prize announcement?" Mayor Whit gestured to the open space to his right. "Come on, now. Don't be shy."

It definitely wasn't about being shy. It was about not getting within a certain parameter of his dad and brother. At this rate, his dad might push him off the stage to try to render him incapable of cooking. Jude trailed behind Rory as they made their way to the short steps leading up to the platform. He whispered toward her hat. "Do you know what the bonus prize is?"

She frowned over her shoulder. "Why would I?"

Maybe because she'd actually read the paper she'd signed? But he couldn't explain that now. Not that it would matter. She'd already written him off as the bad guy. She believed the extension was his doing.

Jude nodded at his father and brother as he shuffled past, ignoring Warner's sarcastic "congrats," and took his place between Rory and "Farmer" Peters, owner of Cluck Truck.

Everyone in town knew he wasn't a real farmer, but ever since he'd created an amazing fried chicken seasoning, he ignored that minor detail, wore overalls daily, and always had an answer on upcoming weather stats from the *Farmers' Almanac.*

Mayor Whit led the crowd in one more round of applause. "Now, here's the exciting finale, folks."

Jude couldn't help but steal a glance at his father, whose face remained trained in a neutral expression. Warner hadn't mastered that look yet, however — he fidgeted with his cuff link, one shoe bouncing a rhythm against the platform floor.

Jude turned his gaze back to the crowd of sunburned and sugared-up community members. The older lady from the farmers' market who'd given him free salsa sat to the right, her hands folded primly in her lap. One of the middle-aged paralegals from the firm was situated to the left, looking weary — she'd probably been the one to prepare, print, and deliver the adjusted applications at the last minute. And Maddison sat toward the front, her dark curls brushing her cheeks as she beamed at Warner on stage. Poor girl. Hopefully she'd wise up to his brother soon and realize there were other fish — with much smaller teeth — in the sea.

"Now, along with the original cash prize and bragging rights, the grand prize winner next weekend will also win the honor of catering this summer's biggest society engagement party!" The mayor held up one hand, urging the murmuring crowd to silence. "Might I be the first to offer a hearty congratulations to Modest's very own Warner Worthington and Maddison Bussey!"

Jude's gasp stuck in the back of his throat. Engaged? He covered his mouth with his fist and coughed hard, eyes watering. Thankfully, his cough was drowned out by clapping and whistling as Maddison bounced up from her seat and began hurrying to the stage, all smiles. Jude turned to the row of chairs behind him — just in time to see Warner's graciously raised hand, his father's proud clap on the back . . . and something far less than happy lurking behind the mayor's pained smile.

THIRTEEN

There must have been a sale on balloons. She'd never seen such a gaudy sight in her life, even for Modest. In fact, there were several things she'd have done differently had she been in charge of planning the event.

Rory stood with her hands on her hips, surveying the now-deserted courthouse lawn. Paper cups and Styrofoam plates blew across the grass, while two coverall-clad men from the parks and rec department began to stack the abandoned chairs. Slow-moving families with toddlers carrying sagging balloons meandered to their cars.

But in her mind's eye, she could see the festival the way it had been — and how it could have been. The port-a-potties, for example, should have been closer to the bounce house, for families with multiple kids to have the chance to keep an eye on everyone during bathroom breaks. The lineup of food trucks should have been shifted to the side of the lot adjacent to the park, where all the kids naturally wanted to migrate after obtaining fried or sugary snacks. That would have allowed moms pushing strollers or tired grandparents chasing grandkids to have a shorter walk across the hot parking lot.

These were all thoughts that proved a lovely distraction from the fact that she was once again going to have to cook to save Salsa Street.

She'd called to tell Nicole and Grady the good news about their being finalists. Grady's enthusiasm had been sincere, of course, while Nicole's sounded more like Rory's — happy to still be in the running for the prize they desperately needed, yet discouraged at the thought of having to pretend they knew what they were doing through another round. They'd been lucky so far. Besides the fire and a few other minor mishaps, they'd survived the weekend by sticking to the recipes and babysitting each other in the kitchen with Grady on virtual standby. But they'd only expected to have to do so for two days — the duration of the festival and the contest. Now an entire second weekend loomed ahead.

And now they were supposed to come up

with a theme?

Rory had to admit, Nicole had pulled more than her weight in the truck the last two days. Rory had basically stirred, set timers, parroted Grady's instructions, and served food on color-coordinated, aesthetically pleasing plates — the one element that she'd been able to contribute with complete confidence and joy.

This was all Jude's fault. If that meddling Worthington family hadn't stepped in at the last minute to change things up, this could have been over. She plucked a clover from the ground and twirled it between her fingers. This had to be rigged somehow in Jude's favor. Why else would his family be involved?

Rory held one hand up against the afternoon sun and squinted across the grounds. She and Hannah had been heading to her car to drive back to Unity Angels when her cousin had seen a huge patch of wildflowers growing across the grounds by the park. She'd insisted on picking a bouquet to take back to the campus — and going by herself.

Despite the heat and current lack of chairs, Rory didn't mind waiting for her cousin. She liked when Hannah was able to exert her independence in little ways. Plus, they might as well kill time since Rory didn't want to leave until Nicole brought Grady's truck back to haul Salsa Street home.

She sank onto a patch of warm grass. Across the park, Hannah bent to gather a fistful of yellow flowers, carefully adding them to the bouquet forming in her other hand. Rory smiled, her heart tugging with love and protection and all the things she couldn't control for her sweet cousin.

And regrets for the ones she should have.

Like her ex-boyfriend, Thomas, who had weaseled his way into Rory's heart last year by telling her about all the things he'd done for Hannah — having lunch with her frequently at Unity Angels, donating to the facility for updates, etc. The truth? He'd dropped off McDonald's *once* — and gotten Hannah's order wrong on top of that — and donated a measly twenty-five-dollar check from his company's account. It had all been lies, all manipulation.

The worst was when he'd promised to be Hannah's date to the annual spring dance at the care center but stood her up after he and Rory broke up a few days before. No phone call, no acknowledgment of the change of plans, no offer to send someone else in his place. Zero consideration for Hannah's innocence in their breakup. That was when the truth of all his "efforts" finally came out, and Rory realized it'd been a ploy. She'd been played — and Hannah had been used.

Her phone buzzed, breaking into her runaway thoughts.

On my way.

She sent a confirmation text to Nicole and leaned back on her palms to wait, grateful for the interruption. She'd spent enough time wallowing in regret. Hannah wasn't any worse for wear, but Rory was determined to make sure nothing like that would happen again.

A muffled exclamation sounded from the parking lot to her left. Jude was wrestling with something under the hood of his food truck, muttering things that weren't quite curse words.

She tried to look shorter, to blend into the grass and disappear, but . . . nope. He saw her. He jogged toward her, his polo shirt clinging to his broad chest and gripping his biceps in a sweaty vise.

Not that she was noticing. It was just hot outside. Her own shirt could be wrung out at this point. She stood and crossed her arms.

"Can I borrow your cell phone? My battery died about half an hour ago."

She raised her eyebrows, slowly pulling her phone from her back pocket. "Truck trouble?"

Jude took the phone from her. "Apparently that battery died too." He hesitated. "Do you have jumper cables?"

"I do, but my car won't jump that giant thing."

His face fell. "Guess I better call my brother." But he just stared at the phone still in his hand, as if considering all his options and deciding that was the worst one. "Or maybe roadside assistance."

Rory debated if she had it in her today to be a Good Samaritan. She would technically be aiding and abetting the enemy, but she couldn't leave him stranded. Plus, he was holding her phone hostage.

She checked her watch. "Look, Nicole should be back with Grady's truck to haul Salsa Street home any minute. She'll have cables. Save yourself the roadside expense."

"That'd be great." He relinquished the phone, and she slid it back into her pocket.

Maybe it was the heat of the day affecting her or the exhausted lines crinkling his forehead, but a sliver of her ire slipped away and was replaced with something akin to . . . sympathy? She grabbed her keys. "It's too hot out here. Follow me."

Within minutes, they were settled in the front seat of her car, AC on full blast.

"You don't have to wait." Jude adjusted the vent to blow straight on his face. "But I do appreciate the gesture."

Rory pointed toward the park, where Hannah was carefully considering each wildflower before either passing it over or picking it for her bouquet. She smiled. "I'm waiting for other things too."

He followed her line of vision. "I see." A gentle smile cured the tired lines near his eyes momentarily, and his expression relaxed.

Seeing him look at her cousin — *her* Hannah — with such compassion almost made her forget he was the enemy.

"I didn't know." His voice, low and nearly monotone, made her jump.

She gripped both hands on the steering wheel. "What do you mean?"

"About the contest change. I know you were assuming. That's why you're mad, isn't it?"

"I'm not mad. It's truce day, remember?"

He leveled his gaze at her. "You're mad."

She swallowed and looked away. "It looks shady, you have to admit. *Your* dad and brother show up with their fancy pens and notary stamps, and suddenly everything changes."

"Exactly. That's why they didn't even bother to get my signature." He ran a hand over his jaw, then let out a defeated chuckle. "They got Alton's."

Understanding dawned. "So your application change isn't legal." Technically, that could be grounds for elimination from round two. But all he'd have to do is sign a new one before next weekend and it wouldn't matter. Nobody would care.

Besides, she didn't want to win by playing dirty. That sounded more like a move from the Worthington rule book.

"No, it's not, but we'll fix it. They needed to buy time and knew I wouldn't agree if I were approached directly." He shifted slightly in the passenger seat to face her, the draft from the AC blowing around loose strands of his normally gelled and perfected hair. "Why did you sign?"

"Because I knew everyone else would." She lifted one shoulder in a shrug. "And, to be honest, the appeal of the bonus prize." Then his previous statement registered. "What do you mean, buy time?"

Across the field, Hannah straightened with her finished bouquet, a proud smile lighting

251

her round face. She looked around, caught sight of Rory's car, and began heading their way.

"I think they have a scheme going. But I don't know what." Jude shrugged. "I didn't even know my brother was engaged."

Rory's gaze collided with his. "Are you serious?" Another ping of sympathy ricocheted off the defensive wall she'd erected. She exhaled slowly. "Wow."

"Yeah. That about sums up my family — wow." Jude stared out the window as Hannah drew nearer. "You have no idea."

Maybe there was more to her enemy — frenemy — than she'd initially thought. But that wouldn't do. She needed her wall. After all, he'd come to her for cooking lessons just to turn around and open a competitive business. Then he literally competed against her, endangering her chances of saving Salsa Street.

A truck engine revved, and a black Dodge Ram pulled into the space next to them. Rory drew in a deep breath. "There's Nicole." She wasn't sure if she felt relieved . . . or disappointed. She hadn't hated their conversation. It'd been enlightening.

But maybe a little too much.

"And here comes Hannah. Thanks for letting me borrow your AC." He reached for the door handle. "I guess that means the truce is over?" His expression mirrored the conflict she felt.

She responded with a hesitant nod. "Truce over."

Yet, deep down, she couldn't shake the feeling that none of this was over.

Jude drank maybe one beer a month, and that one was happening tonight.

He leaned across the slightly sticky bar at the Silent Spade and ordered a Guinness. Warner had always turned his nose up at bars that also served cheese fries, which was precisely why Jude had gone to one that did tonight. He didn't want to run into his family if they decided to celebrate Warner's big news.

The news his own brother hadn't bothered to tell him before announcing it publicly.

He accepted his foaming beer, thanked the bartender, and stashed a five in the tip jar. The weekend crowd was in full swing, but the only thing Jude wanted to do was relax after a long day of cooking, truck trouble, and family drama. He didn't know if he should take the high road and call his brother or give in to the obvious slight and continue to ignore him.

He'd decide later. Right now, he would

try to find a private table in the corner and process the day while texting ColorMeTurquoise. At this point, he was about one sip away from blurting out everything he felt — rules or not. Lately, she was the only one who seemed to understand him. Somehow she had cut through the surface-layer mess and seen to his core, even if she'd never seen his face.

How was it possible to miss someone he'd never met?

The laughing crowd of college-aged kids gathered around the jukebox parted long enough for Jude to glimpse his ideal table — already occupied.

Mayor Whit sat with his head propped on one palm, bow tie askew as he dragged a pretzel around a pile of ketchup, looking as if he'd already had a few too many drinks.

Jude headed that direction. "How's the local gentry?"

His attempt at humor fell flat. Whit acknowledged him with a half grin that looked more like a grimace. "Been better. Have a seat."

"Let me order you a coffee, man." Jude nudged the mayor's almost-empty glass, which still contained a sliver of lime in the bottom. "I think you've had plenty." The last thing the mayor needed right now was rumors flying about being drunk in public.

He shrugged. "I've only had three."

"Three beers?" Jude winced. Hopefully not anything stronger. Still . . .

"No, club sodas." He tilted the glass for Jude to see the clear, bubbly liquid against the remnants of ice. "See?"

Good ol' Whit. He should have known. Jude relaxed. "Sorry I assumed, man. You seem so down over here in the corner."

"Well, there is that." He went back to his pretzel/condiment routine. "But drinking would make me feel worse."

Smart man. In fact, Jude should probably not drink either. He glanced at his Guinness, sighed, and set it aside. The bartender caught his eye, and he held up two fingers. "Club sodas with lime."

Whit attempted to straighten his bow tie. "You're a gentleman."

That soggy pretzel was going to make him barf. Jude gingerly scooted it out of the way, then leaned toward Whit and lowered his voice. "What's going on?"

Whit unbuckled his Swatch, then buckled it again — but didn't speak.

Jude waited. The festival had seemed like a hit. And now, with the extension, the publicity for local businesses was going to boom even longer — all of which looked good during the mayor's political term. What could be so bad? "I've got all night."

Whit started to grab for the pretzel again, then withdrew his hand. Thank goodness. Jude shoved a clean napkin at him, which Whit immediately began to shred into bits. He glanced up at Jude. "They didn't get your signature, did they?"

Jude shook his head.

"I figured you didn't know. You looked really surprised." Whit tore the napkin faster. "I truly didn't mean for it to go down like that."

For what to go down? Had Jude missed some back-alley exchange?

"You're confused." Whit nodded emphatically. "I understand."

Good, because he didn't.

"Remember when I said I owed your dad a favor? Well, he cashed in. We sort of made an exchange." Whit pursed his lips. "At least he compromised on the statue."

"Statue?"

"Of himself."

Jude breathed in through his nose. "My father wanted to use his yearly donation to put a statue of himself in the town square?"

"Are you surprised?" Whit grimaced. "Sorry, that was rude. But really, are you surprised?"

No. "What was the exchange then?"

Whit hesitated, as if choosing his words carefully. "He agreed to let the statue go and not to put Warner in the next election if I extended the contest."

Jude frowned, leaning back in his seat as the bartender set their drinks before them. "Why would he care about the contest going another weekend?"

Whit averted his eyes. "I don't know. Maybe he wanted the spotlight on Warner's engagement? He said something about it being good PR." He took a sip of his clear soda.

Baloney. His dad clearly didn't care about that — at least he hadn't when Jude had presented the idea before. Had he changed his mind? Or was this still part of a larger scheme Jude didn't have all the puzzle pieces to yet?

"He said he'd handle the paperwork and all the red tape." Whit began to stack the torn pieces on top of each other. "Plus, he . . ."

"Plus?"

Whit widened his eyes. "What? There's no plus."

Jude stirred his drink. One thing still didn't add up. "So you're sitting here in the corner of a bar downing club soda because

257

you're upset that the contest is extended?"

Something flickered across Whit's expression, then vanished before Jude could identify it. "No, I think that part is actually a good benefit for everyone."

"So it's a win-win."

"No."

Jude briefly closed his eyes. "You've lost me again. Why are you down?"

Whit braced his elbows on the table, lowering his voice until Jude could barely hear him over the sudden laughter coming from the bar. "I'm bummed because I played the political game and failed. I couldn't stand up to your dad."

Ah. Jude let out a long breath.

He took a sip of his drink, the slightly sour bubbles fizzing in his mouth. "Don't worry, man. It wasn't your fault. You did what you had to do." Jude laid another ten by his half-full glass and stood, shoving his chair backward against the table. He just wanted to go home, chat with ColorMeTurquoise, and forget this mess of a day. "We'll fix the signature on the application, and it'll all be alright. No harm, no foul."

"I hope so." Whit kept his gaze trained on the napkin tower he'd created. "But I'm pretty sure you're wrong."

"About the foul?" Not surprising. That's

how his dad played all games.

Whit crunched a piece of ice and finally met his gaze, his eyes full of worry. "About the harm."

FOURTEEN

She needed a theme.

Rory tapped Nicole's napkin with a cheese fry to get her attention. "Focus. We have to figure this out."

The Silver Spade was in full swing tonight, making it hard for them to hear each other. After Nicole had hauled the food trailer home and brought Grady dinner, she'd met Rory at their favorite hangout and treated them both to appetizers and Coke. They were supposed to be planning the next round of the competition, but the line dancing that had broken out by the jukebox was more than a little distracting.

"I'm asking Grady his thoughts." Nicole finished sending her text and set her phone down before snagging a fry from its cheesy prison. "Why do they always put bacon on these things?"

"Because bacon makes everything better." Rory tried unsuccessfully to keep the "duh" out of her voice. "We could make bacon tacos."

"Blasphemy." Nicole's phone screen lit up, and she craned her head to see against the glare of the overhead bar lights. "Grady thinks we should keep it simple and do a fiesta theme."

Rory's fry lodged in her throat and she coughed. "But that's . . . boring." She ran through her mental checklist of ideas. The thought of being that limited on something this important irked her creative side. "We can do better than that."

"Can we, though?" Nicole arched an eyebrow.

"I didn't say we could *cook* a better theme. But we can at least come up with one." One problem at a time. "Besides, what if Jude and Nacho Taco do fiesta too? Then we're at a disadvantage."

Her friend smirked. "He should do a nacho theme — blow everyone's mind."

Rory couldn't help but grin. "The truck name is a little confusing." And his graffiti-print truck skin was a little obnoxious. But to each their own. She loved the skin she'd designed for Salsa Street — it seemed like one Aunt Sophia would have loved, with its classy, bright colors and elegant tomato vines growing up the side. Too bad she never

261

got to see it.

And no one ever would if they didn't win the contest and get the money to have it printed and installed.

"Hey, you're not grimacing when you talk about Jude anymore." Nicole sipped her soda, a teasing spark lighting her tired eyes. "That's progress."

"Is it, though?" Rory retorted, mimicking Nicole's previous statement.

"Touché." Nicole held up both hands in surrender. "I'm just saying, you don't hate him."

"I never hated him. The Bible says not to."

"It also says not to lie."

"Touché." Rory dropped her fry back into the basket. "I think I'm done."

"With the conversation or with carbs?"

"Both." Rory leaned back from the table. "This is all a bit overwhelming. I didn't see this extension coming." And that was when the anger began to simmer again. Well, not anger. And not hate. More like . . . extreme frustration.

Though the look on Jude's face when his brother announced his engagement had not been one of pride or haughtiness. It hadn't been the look of someone whose master plan was going swimmingly either. He'd denied knowing, and she believed him.

So where did that leave them?

Nicole nodded. "No one saw it coming."

"Not even Jude." Rory whispered the admission.

"What? But isn't his own family's law firm —"

"He didn't even know his brother was engaged."

"Ouch." Nicole blanched. "I guess he can't be to blame for any of this, then."

Rory clutched at the remainder of her disintegrating protective wall. "Well, he's still to blame for hiring me to teach him how to cook and then starting a competition truck ten minutes later." There. That was one trusty brick in her wall no one could break.

Nicole pointed a bacon-less fry at Rory. "So he misled you, which could have been unintentional . . ."

"That's assuming a lot."

"But you quite intentionally misled *him* into thinking you could cook in the first place."

And poof, there went her last brick. Rory opened her mouth, then shut it. "That's different."

"Is it, though?" A smile threatened Nicole's lips.

It wasn't. But she needed it to be, because otherwise . . . "You're like a female Grady — all wise and stuff." Rory licked her dry lips before sucking down a long sip of her Coke. At this point, all the carbs in the world couldn't comfort her. "I see your point."

"I'm only saying, maybe he isn't so untrustworthy." Nicole shrugged. "Maybe he just likes to cook tacos."

"You're only saying — right, with zero agenda, I'm sure." She knew that glimmer in her friend's eye — the one that made Cupid grab his bow and suit up.

"Well, he's not hard to look at, Rory."

"I'm taken, if you don't remember."

Nicole tossed a fry in her direction. "By a computer screen."

"He's real." More real than any of the men she'd sat across from at a dozen restaurants over the years. "We have a chat date scheduled for later tonight."

"How romantic," Nicole said.

She forced a smile. "Look, I'd much rather argue with you about the theme for next weekend." *Hint, hint.*

"Fine. Why don't we give it a day or two to decide? We don't have to choose a theme right now. We have a week, right?" Nicole plucked a piece of bacon off her fry and set it on her napkin.

Rory popped the rejected scrap into her mouth. "Less than that. We have to shop for whatever we decide to make, remember?"

"Oh, right." Nicole wrinkled her nose. "Details."

Rory twirled a fry between her fingers, watching as the dancing crowd of laughing young adults and feisty senior citizens began to attempt the Cupid Shuffle. "What are the chances of Grady getting better by next weekend?"

Nicole rolled her eyes. "Slim to none."

"What are the chances of Grady not being mad at us if we go with a totally different theme than the fiesta?"

"Even *slimmer*." Nicole started rapping the lyrics to "The Real Slim Shady."

Rory held up one hand. "I get it. No need to prove it."

Nicole laughed, then her expression sobered as her eyes shifted to something over Rory's shoulder. "I need you to remember something for me."

Rory finished her Coke. "What's that?"

"Remember when you said you didn't hate Jude?"

"Yeah?" She poked the ice in her cup with her straw.

"Keep that in mind." Nicole pointed.

Rory glanced over her shoulder and saw Jude near a private, back-corner table with none other than Mayor Whit.

A new brick settled into place as she turned back to Nicole. "Trustworthy and innocent, huh?"

He'd talked Whit off one ledge and had somehow ended up balancing precariously on his own.

Jude wound through the maze of tables to the exit. "Excuse me," he muttered under his breath, wondering if maybe his brother was onto something when it came to avoiding these crowded, sticky places. Yeah, sure. And maybe his brother had a good reason for not telling him about his own engagement too. And maybe his father had a good reason for campaigning for a statue of his own pretentious mug in the town square.

He squeezed around a raucous table for two, then stopped short as a brunette blur darted in front of him, blocking his path.

Rory.

He exhaled, unsure if she would be in friend or foe mode after their earlier conversation in her car. "Hey, how's it —"

"So the second the truce is off, you're seen in cahoots with the mayor?" She crossed her arms over her chest. "Planning the next secret bomb to drop on us?"

Foe it was. He squinted, shifting his keys to his other hand. "What are you talking about?"

She shook her head. "After all I've done for you?"

"All you've done —"

"Teaching you how to cook." She began ticking off points on her fingers. "Visiting your food truck during the festival. Jump-starting said truck."

"Easy there, hermana." Nicole appeared over Rory's shoulder, linking her arm through Rory's. "It's late. Everyone's tired."

A staying hand landed on his own shoulder. He glanced behind him. Whit. Great. He and Rory had officially reached the "hold me back" part of their archenemy status. Why was she even in foe mode to begin with? He thought they'd connected a few hours ago in her car. Unless that'd simply been the exhausted, too-tired-to-fight Rory. This Rory looked downright feisty.

"What seems to be the problem, ladies?" Whit cleared his throat. "And gent."

Jude pinched the bridge of his nose. "I was just leaving."

"That's probably a good idea." Rory's eyes narrowed.

Okay, that was it. He'd had enough of her hot-and-cold attitude, her cheap drama, her mood swings . . . enough of everyone keeping secrets from him. Enough manipulation and lies from everyone in his life. He wanted nothing more than to go home, chat with ColorMeTurquoise, and watch someone *else* cook something on the Food Network. But now he had three emotional nuts separating him from his goal.

He began to tick off his own points on his free hand. "One, you didn't teach me much more than I already knew. Two, I told you that you didn't have to wait around today for the jumper cables, and *you* chose to. And three, I'm not in *cahoots* with anyone." He held up a fourth finger. "And the 1800s called. They want their vocabulary back."

She gasped. Nicole snickered, then coughed. Whit's hand tightened on Jude's shoulder. "We were talking about some family matters." Whit lowered his voice, leaning in closer to Rory as though confiding something dark. "All Jude did was buy me another club soda."

Something flickered in Rory's hazel eyes, something that looked a little like regret, before quickly vanishing. "Family matters, as in, the contest extension? You have to admit, *gentlemen,* this isn't great timing to

268

be seen lurking in dark corners."

"Oh, that bulb is out. Don't worry, I reported it." Whit's expression turned serious.

Nicole rolled her eyes. "Rory, you're reaching."

"I am not." Her expression tightened. "I have every right to be suspicious of everyone at this point."

"You're *really* reaching. Reaching like that stretchy mom-chick in *The Incredibles*." Nicole tugged on her arm. "They were just talking."

"Talking or scheming?" Her eyes flashed. "They're making everything harder."

Jude's stomach clenched. She knew nothing. And, speaking of harder, his frustration was becoming nearly impossible to hold back. He attempted to rein in his volume as he pointed to his chest. "*I'm* making everything harder?"

"Well, I'm certainly not the one whose family is pulling strings behind the scenes. All to win a contest you don't even need to win."

Didn't need to — that was it. What did she think this was to him, some big game? He narrowed his eyes. "Have you even thought for a single second that I could be in the same boat you are?"

Rory scoffed, flipping back her ponytail. "Oh, yes, you poor multimillionaire. Let me help you row."

Jude sucked in his breath and reeled backward.

Nicole and Whit exchanged a look.

Rory hesitated, and he saw something akin to an apology dancing in her eyes, but it never quite made it to her lips.

"Right, then." He nodded, then swallowed hard. "May the best truck win." He pulled free of Whit, sidestepped the women, and stormed out of the bar.

Rory tugged her sweatpants-clad knees closer to her chest, cradling her phone on her shoulder as she attempted to sip from her full mug of tea. Her laptop sat open to a DM window with StrongerMan99, but her father had called, and with those occasions as rare as they were, she'd accepted the call.

And was starting to regret it. She didn't need anything else emotionally draining tonight after that run-in with Jude, and her father was in his usual downer mood.

"Where are you again?" She squinted, as if that could help her hear better over the background noise.

"Tokyo."

Last time they'd talked, he'd been in Dubai. She set down her tea and glanced at her phone display before putting it back to her ear. "What time is it there?"

"Tomorrow, I think." He sounded tired.

"Did you sleep last night?"

"Enough."

Which meant not really. Because of bars and foreign nightlife? Or because of tucking himself away, all hermit-like, in whatever condo his oil and gas company had put him up in this time?

Rory plucked at a loose thread on her sweatpants, wishing she were still young enough to ask for presents, simply for something to say.

As if reading her mind, he chuckled a little and asked, "Need some monogrammed chopsticks?"

"Always." Rory relaxed slightly, glad to hear the lighthearted pitch to his tone. He'd been spiraling downward lately, but with him so far away and so focused on his work, it was hard to tell if it was depression or simply the result of his being a workaholic.

Awkward silence filled the line. Then her dad coughed. It was the same cough he always used before getting off the phone — once they'd exhausted all possible conversation points. She glanced quickly at the phone screen. Tonight they'd accomplished that in approximately six minutes.

He sighed. "Well, I guess I better —"

"I met someone." She blurted out the words before she could retract them and then winced. She hadn't planned on telling him yet — especially not before she and StrongerMan99 had even met. Would he be bummed at the reminder of marriage and all he'd lost? Or happy for her?

"Really?"

She frowned at the surprise in his voice.

"What's his name?"

And this was why she'd spoken too soon. She darted a glance at her open laptop, then closed her eyes. "We haven't gotten that far yet."

Silence reigned.

She spoke fast. "I met him online, but we've been talking for about a month now, and we've really hit it off —"

"You haven't met in person?" His voice dipped with disapproval. Or maybe pity. She wasn't sure which she hated more.

She bit her lower lip. "No."

"Rory, maybe it's time to get out of Modest."

She opened her eyes.

"You could come travel with me. Sell Sophia's business and see the world for a

272

while with your old man."

"And what would I do while you were at work all the time?" But she already knew, could hear the words echoing in her head.

"Whatever you wanted. Shop, hang out — have all the local boys follow you around. The usual." He laughed — not in a condescending way, but in a genuine way, which felt worse. He had no idea he'd demeaned her down to that surface level of an existence. That's what it'd always been about, and with him, that's all it would ever be. No matter what she accomplished, that's the only thing that would ever matter in his eyes. His pretty daughter. The one he could set on a shelf and visit only when it suited him.

Rory shook her head even though he couldn't see her. "That's okay, Dad. I have a life here." *And you could too if you'd quit running away from all your pain.*

The memory from Disney World popped back up, the one she'd shared with StrongerMan99 a few weeks ago during their "first memories" conversation. Two years after Rory's mom passed away, Sophia talked her dad into coming to Disney World with her, Rory, and Hannah. Rory didn't remember her mother's funeral, but she remembered that Disney trip. Remembered her dad's constant sadness in the "happiest place on earth." Remembered the way his knees folded to fit into the spinning pink teacup in the Magic Kingdom. She remembered the joy on Sophia's and Hannah's faces as they spun past her in a purple cup. Remembered the bleak expression on her dad's face and the anxiety building in her own stomach.

Remembered wondering why they were the only ones not having fun.

He'd never stopped running from it. From her mother's death, from the reminder Rory must surely be for him. From truly living. Maybe this offer was his way of reaching out to her, of including her after years of hiding.

But she wasn't a little kid at Disney World anymore. And she had more to offer than a pretty face, whether he wanted to admit it or not. Winning this cooking contest could prove that. For the first time, she had a chance to be successful at something without Aunt Sophia or Grady taking the much-deserved credit for it.

Maybe then her dad would acknowledge her worth.

He cleared his throat. "Well, if you change your mind, all you have to do is call. I can have you on a flight in no time."

Sure — to wherever he happened to be at the moment, in whatever random time zone. "I know, Dad." One day maybe he'd be able to make a genuine gesture that she could accept without uprooting her entire life.

Or did he know that she wouldn't, and that's why he made it?

This time she didn't try to fill the silence that followed, and when he coughed next, they said their goodbyes and hung up.

FIFTEEN

"We need to talk." Jude didn't wait for an invitation but strode purposefully into his dad's office on Monday morning and shut the heavy oak door behind him.

Hollis leaned back in his desk chair, the wheels squeaking under the sudden shift of his weight. "Well, well, the prodigal returns."

Like his father ever read the Bible. If not for Grandmother's influence in that department during Jude's childhood, he probably wouldn't have ever done so either.

Jude lifted his chin, hoping his strumming heartbeat wasn't evident under his collared shirt. "You and Warner are up to something, and I demand to know what it is."

"Wow. Too bad you aren't more concerned with channeling this demanding presence of yours into a future in the courtroom." Hollis laughed.

Jude stood his ground, breath steady, feet planted wide. Holding his gaze. Waiting. The grandfather clock behind his dad's desk ticked down the standoff.

One, two, three . . .

Hollis tossed a pen across his desk. "Alright, son, you win."

Hardly. His dad never lost. This was simply more plot unfolding before him. Jude tensed, bracing for whatever might be next.

"You look exhausted." Hollis gestured to the armchair. "Take a seat."

He sniffed. "I'll stand, thank you."

Something hard glinted in his father's eyes. "This is my office, and I'm telling you to sit."

Fine. He'd concede this one battle to win the bigger war. Jude perched on the edge of the seat and rested an elbow on one of the chair's arms, resisting the urge to relax fully against the imported leather. The fake potted plant to his right grazed his arm beneath his rolled-up sleeve. "And by the way, you don't look so chipper yourself."

Hollis raised his thick eyebrows at Jude, reaching over to adjust a stack of papers under his gold paperweight. "Maybe that's because I'm doing the work of two men now."

False. More like he'd been eating fast food nonstop again. "I sincerely doubt that. You have Warner and the paralegals. You're not

277

lifting a finger more than necessary around here, and you know it."

A spark lit in his dad's eye — was that respect? But it disappeared before Jude could tell for certain. "You sure seem to know a lot for someone who hasn't been around."

Jude shrugged. "I've been working."

"You mean cooking." Hollis wrinkled his nose.

"That's my job."

"For now." He steepled his fingers and peered at Jude over the top of them. "Don't forget, this isn't over yet. I wouldn't go putting all your *tacos* in one basket." He smirked.

The door creaked open before Jude could respond, sending in a fresh rush of air-conditioning. He swiveled in his seat.

Warner.

His brother shut the door behind him and took the chair next to Jude without being told. As if it'd been planned.

As if they'd known Jude was coming.

"Speaking of it not being over yet — apparently there's a consent form I need to sign." Jude held Warner's stare until his brother sheepishly looked away. "I'd hate for someone to sue you guys."

Hollis grinned. "You're in luck. I believe I

278

have that particular document right here." He reached into his in-box and slid the revised form across his desk to Jude.

Luck, indeed. That was one thing to call it. Jude skimmed the document before scrawling his signature across the bottom. "Well played, by the way."

"You don't get to my level of success without a few tricks up your sleeve."

"*Our* level," Warner protested.

Hollis ignored him. "I knew you'd sign it anyway."

"Yeah, after I didn't have a choice." He shoved the paper back across the desk. "There."

Hollis slid the form under a paperweight. "Why wouldn't you want the contest to go into round two?"

"Yeah, why wouldn't you want to win the honor of catering a party for your big brother?" Warner chuckled.

Jude cut his eyes at him. "That, for the record, was a low blow."

"What, off to up the ante on the grand prize and help out a hardworking citizen of the community at the same time?" Warner's eyes widened in exaggerated innocence.

"Is that the story for the media?" Jude shook his head. That was an even bigger spin than he'd imagined. "Nice."

"I thought so."

"Why didn't you tell me you'd proposed to Maddison?"

The charade slipped a little then, and something more authentic — and tired — landed on Warner's face. It was hard work keeping up with their father's games. Jude would almost feel sorry for his brother if he wasn't . . . well, his brother.

Hollis answered before Warner could. "It's about leverage, son."

There was that word again. Why couldn't anything ever be about doing the right thing? Jude rubbed his hand down his face. "How so?"

Hollis and Warner exchanged a glance.

"Oh, stop the theatrics. I've already talked to Mayor Whitlow. He said you were trying to coerce him into putting up a statue of yourself in the town square."

Warner snorted, hands raised. "That was all Dad."

"You gave in with the condition to extend the contest." Jude shifted in his chair, thinking.

Hollis and Warner shared a second glance.

Jude continued talking it out, halfway to himself at this point. "But you didn't ever want a statue, did you? It was only leverage, as you say."

Hollis eagerly leaned forward in his seat, as if silently urging Jude to keep going.

"So you made a trade. Told the mayor you wouldn't pressure him with the statue anymore, and you'd take the threat of Warner running for office away if he did you this favor with the extension instead. But why?"

The grandfather clock ticked away his rush of internal guesses. Then realization hit, confirmed only by Warner's eye roll. "You're extending the contest to delay it." Dismay spread through Jude's stomach. He shook his head, as if he could push away what was now so obvious. "You're hoping that putting off the grand prize would make me drop out or be more likely to lose."

"See?" Hollis slapped his hand on his desk with glee as he looked at Warner. "I told you he'd be a good lawyer."

"You're betting against me." That shouldn't have been a surprise. It wasn't a surprise. But . . . "You saw I actually had a chance to win and panicked, didn't you?"

That got their attention.

Warner's eyes shot to their father, whose poker face didn't falter, though he paled slightly. Warner schooled his features to match. "We got wind after the first day of the festival that business was booming.

Turns out you were one of the leading contenders. Dad didn't want to risk it."

"So you openly admit you're trying to sabotage me."

"Not sabotage. Challenge," Hollis said. "We'll see if you were lucky or if you can really earn the win."

Jude bit back his first response, which wasn't respectful. "I'll take the fact that I'm a threat to you as a compliment. But why *this*? Why the engagement party?"

"Mayor Whit hasn't been as cooperative lately as he's been in years past." Hollis tapped his pen against his desk. "He needed a gentle reminder of who exactly is in charge around here."

Threats, bribes, coercion. He'd hate to see a nongentle reminder at this point. "I'm sure you were all too happy to help."

"He made it easy." Hollis lifted one burly, suit-clad shoulder. "Especially after Coined Bank & Trust backed out of their sponsorship."

Something cold and hard filled Jude's stomach. "What do you mean, they backed out?"

Hollis waved one hand flippantly through the air. "Something about expense freezes while they're undergoing corporate consulting."

"Yeah, if Dad hadn't saved the day, your little contest would have been postponed until next year — if it got rescheduled at all." Warner smirked.

"Wait. You're the sponsor now?" He stared at his dad, but it was like viewing his and Warner's matching smiles in a fun-house mirror. Everything felt distorted yet, somehow, unfortunately, all too clear.

"Well, technically, the Worthington Family Law Firm is." Hollis spread his hands with faux humility.

"You're funding the contest you didn't want me to enter."

The ticking of the grandfather clock was all the confirmation he needed.

But one thing didn't make sense. His father's callousness and manipulation made all the sense in the world, but there was one factor . . .

Jude leaned forward in his chair. "Why not let it get canceled? What's in it for you to keep it going?" If there hadn't been a contest to enter, there wouldn't be a contest to win. Wasn't *that* what Hollis had wanted all along — Jude out of the food truck and back in his office, studying for the bar?

"Come on, now. Everyone loves a local hero." Warner clapped Jude on the back. "Dad is ours."

"Plus, I knew you'd just find another way." Hollis dropped the pen on his calendar and leaned back in his chair, the leather squeaking in protest. "We had a deal. Worthingtons keep their word."

Jude's jaw tightened as he filled in the blanks his dad didn't have to. Now it was obvious.

Being this involved in the contest was the easiest way for Hollis to control the outcome.

Anger crept up Jude's stomach and into his chest. He leveled a stare at his father. "So is that the deal with Maddison too? Warner proposed to let you keep your foot on Whit's back? Like you're keeping your foot on mine?" Jude turned his glare to Warner, not bothering to wait for an answer. "How romantic. You're truly every woman's dream." That was next-level low, even for Warner. Poor Maddison.

"No." Warner bit off the word. "It's time. We've been dating for a while, and our firm needs —"

"The positive PR?" Jude jerked forward in his seat, nearly upsetting the fake fern. "So you believe me now about our reputation? Because you sure didn't when I brought up this whole food festival in the first place." If they had listened to Jude and done this PR thing the way he'd suggested, they could have avoided all these layers of deceit and manipulation.

He swallowed back the anger that was slowly morphing into rage. But no, they couldn't do that, because that'd be boring. His family thrived on games played at the expense of others. Warner was transforming into an exact replica of their dad, and it made Jude sick.

"We do not have a bad reputation in Modest." Hollis spoke firmly, as if his authoritative tone could simply dictate reality. "But it'd be foolish to write off a natural opportunity to boost public opinion. Presenting the community with a more approachable side of the firm — especially with one of us potentially running for office in the future — is wise."

False again. "What's *natural* about any of this? You schemed the entire thing! And Maddison — she's an innocent pawn in all these small-town political games. How's that starting off a marriage on the right foot?"

"That's enough!" Warner stood abruptly, his chair rocking precariously behind him. "If you were actually a part of this firm — and this family, for that matter — you might understand that's exactly what it's doing."

Jude jumped up, going toe-to-toe with Warner. His brother was only half an inch shorter than him, but Jude straightened to his full height advantage and lowered his voice. "You're using your wife before you're even married."

"Shows how much you know." He poked at Jude's shoulder. "What are you going to do about it?"

Jude clenched his jaw, resisting the urge to punch his brother square in the face. "I'm going to tell her exactly what you're doing. And we'll let her decide."

"What I'm *doing* is setting us up for success." Warner scowled as he poked him a second time. "Something you'll never understand with your pathetic little online relationships."

And, just like that, further resistance was futile.

ColorMeTurquoise:
You punched your brother?

StrongerMan99:
I'm waiting to feel bad about it, but so far — I got nothing.

I don't have any siblings, but I figure that can't be all that uncommon.

It is for us. We were never the playful fighting type growing up.

So you skipped that part and went straight to the for-real fighting type.

That's one way to look at it.

I'm a glass-half-full kind of gal.

Just one of the many things I adore about you.

"Try not to stir the meat too much — only occasionally." The polished blonde with a pristine apron smiled into the TV camera as she wielded her spatula — proving that she, indeed, wasn't stirring too much.

Whatever *too much* entailed.

"It's like half of cooking is pure instinct." Defeated, Rory grabbed for the remote, which was tucked into the side of the chair next to her. "How is anyone supposed to have a chance?"

"Don't change it yet." From her seat on Rory's sofa, Nicole tossed a piece of popcorn in Rory's general direction. It fell forlornly to the carpet. "We've already learned you need to heat the pan before browning meat so you don't accidentally steam it."

"You two are hopeless." Grady's face, still tired but slowly looking more and more like his old healthy self, filled Rory's phone via FaceTime on the coffee table. "I've told you to heat the skillet first literally ten times. Minimum."

"But you didn't wear an apron while talking sternly into a camera." Nicole shrugged. "Less impact."

Rory clicked off the TV and rubbed her temples. "I'm trying, you guys. I've been watching nothing but the Food Network for days. And so far, all I've learned is that I have a severe shortage of custom aprons, I never salt my pasta water, and I'm absolutely terrified of the bossy guy in the chef hat on that one reality cooking show." She let out a little shudder. She'd actually had a nightmare about him the night before — him chasing her around a burning food truck, waving a rubber chicken, and yelling that she was a failure.

"He is a little scary." Nicole shoveled another handful of popcorn into her mouth. "That's legit."

Rory peered at Grady on the phone. "Did you know you're supposed to store ginger root in the freezer?"

He pursed his lips.

288

"See? You're learning more than you realize." Nicole applauded, dropping popcorn onto the couch cushions. "Oops."

"But we don't even cook with ginger. It's useless knowledge." Rory stood and arched her back. She'd been so motivated to cook after the run-in with Jude at the Silent Spade and telling conversation with her father. So eager to go into round two strong. But here it was Tuesday, and they still didn't have a theme picked out for Saturday's contest. "I'm doomed. Again."

Maybe if she had more time. Say, six months to really invest in cooking courses, overcome her fears, and get a few successes in the kitchen under her belt. But if she had six months, there wouldn't be a problem. Grady's mono would be long since healed, and he'd be back in the kitchen where he belonged.

Where she most certainly didn't.

Nicole tilted her head. "What was it that little Disney rat always said? Anyone can cook?"

Rory and Grady groaned simultaneously.

"Maybe that's our theme. Ratatouille." Nicole grinned.

"Right. Or maybe we should pick another animated classic and go all out Under the Sea or Into the Unknown."

Grady snorted. "You guys are overthinking this. As usual."

"Has he gotten grumpier since he's been sick?" Rory raised her eyebrows at Nicole.

"Nah." She smiled sweetly at Grady. Then, as he turned his head to cough, she widened her eyes and nodded an exaggerated "yes" back at Rory.

"Speaking of grumpy — what's the deal with Jude? Nicole said you told him off the other night." The camera zoomed in closer on Grady's face. "It's only a contest, Ror. Not life or death."

She leaned in closer to the phone. "Maybe not *your* life or death. But it could be Salsa Street's."

"I get that there are stakes. But maybe it's not worth creating enemies over. Everyone is trying to do their best here."

Rory rocked back on her heels. "You're defending him?"

"I'm not defending anyone. But hey, *he* didn't verbally assault you in a bar." Grady shrugged as he adjusted the pillow behind his head. "I'm just saying."

A blush heated her cheeks. "Well, Nicole must not have given you a fully accurate report."

"Oh, I did." Nicole scooted forward on the couch, closer to the phone. "Rory was

290

in full MMA fighter mode." She flexed a bicep.

Rory rolled her eyes. "Right. That's not exaggerated at all." The fighting reference reminded her of StrongerMan99's confession last night — he'd hit his brother in a recent argument. Maybe there was something in the air lately. It was the heat of summer — tempers were boiling. She might not have hit Jude, but she'd verbally assaulted him, as Grady pointed out. And that wasn't any classier of an action. That wasn't who she wanted to be — definitely not how Aunt Sophia had raised her.

Something about Jude just brought out all her panicked fight-or-flight tendencies. Why did she keep presenting herself this way? She felt caught in some weird tornado of protection and loyalty to her family — and attraction toward the enemy that made no sense at all. She didn't hate Jude. She was threatened by him.

And that was a lot scarier for her heart — and her business.

Grady coughed again. "I think you two are more capable of all this than you realize. Do your best. It'll work out."

"Doing our best won't matter without a theme." Nicole pointed at Rory. "Let's put our creative energy there instead of toward creating insults for the next time you see Jude."

"Did you two really do that?" Grady's voice pitched higher in disbelief.

A blush crept down Rory's neck. "It was only a few one-liners while we made the popcorn." She tossed a pillow at Nicole. "Hush."

"What about a circus theme?" Nicole tossed it back to her and grinned. "It's a reflection of our lives lately, at least."

"I wish I could be more help." Grady sighed. "I feel like I'm letting you down."

Rory hugged the pillow in her lap. "You're not, Grady. None of this is your fault." It was her own fault, if anyone's. For keeping up the charade for so long. For letting their business finances get to the point of needing this win so badly.

For not saving Salsa Street long ago, the way her aunt would have.

"Just keep learning all you can." The screen dipped as Grady shifted against his pillows. "I can help with that part, at least. I'll try to find you some more cooking tutorials online and —"

A message notification chimed, indicating Rory had a DM. Her heart skittered in her chest. "Oh, that's StrongerMan99. I need to go." She'd almost forgotten they had a chat date planned.

"Wait!" Grady's face filled the screen as he brought the phone closer.

The message notification chimed again. Rory bit back her impatience, finger hovering over the disconnect button. "What?"

"Remember — always slice beef *against* the grain. And don't open the oven to check food unless it's absolutely necessary. Oh! And it's always faster to boil water with the lid on —"

She hung up and clicked on her DM.

"Good decision." Nicole nodded solemnly. "He probably had ten more of those."

She couldn't read StrongerMan99's message fast enough.

I had a gut feeling you'd be on now.

She smirked as she typed.

Don't go stealing my line, now.

Hmm. Technically, we're both stealing Tom's.

So, gut feeling or just remembering we had a date scheduled for 8:00 p.m.?

Dots formed. Paused. Formed.

293

Is this a date?

Her breath hitched, and she bit her bottom lip before responding.

                    Close enough, huh?

We need a real one.

"Man, you've got it bad, don't you?"

Rory jerked. She had almost forgotten Nicole was still sitting on the couch, watching her as she watched her phone. She swallowed. "We're . . ."

"Flirting." Nicole smirked. "Don't worry, it's cute."

Rory redirected her focus to the screen, her heart still stammering and her pulse still racing.

I'm not rushing you — I'm eager.

So was she. Eager and somewhat nauseous too. She just had to get past prepping for round two of the contest and figure out what they were going to cook —

                    When we finally meet, it'll
                    be like Christmas.

Christmas. She sucked in her breath and

looked at Nicole. Adrenaline flooded her veins and she grinned. "I think I figured out our theme."

Sixteen

She'd never been to the rec center community kitchen alone before.

Rory hitched her bag of ingredients higher
on her shoulder as she stepped inside,
slowly easing off the heavy metal door to
keep it from slamming behind her. Fluores-
cent lights buzzed above gleaming stainless-
steel counters, all scrubbed and prepped
and waiting for a masterpiece to be created.

Rory dumped out the contents of her bag
onto the counter and started opening the
Tupperware containing her ingredients,
fighting the usual wave of self-doubt that
sprung up every time she found herself
about to cook. Maybe if she convinced
herself she was still only an assistant, her
body would relax and she could pull this
off. She'd reserved the room tonight to start
experimenting with the Christmas in July
menu she'd brainstormed the night before.
Nicole had planned to meet her but backed

out at the last minute, stating she needed to make a grocery and med run for Grady instead.

Rory pulled out a thick foil-wrapped slab of pork, a garlic clove, and a fresh tomato, then set her bag aside. Maybe Nicole's absence was for the best. After all, Rory finally had a chance to use her recent self-taught knowledge of cooking, and better yet — no one was there to see her try.

She popped the lid off a can of hominy and dumped the contents into a pot. When she had told Grady earlier that morning that she was going to attempt a traditional Mexican pozole as a side for the contest, he probably assumed she was going to use raw hominy and cook it herself, like he would have done. *Ha.* She knew her limits. At this point, she'd be doing well if she could get the seeds out of the guajillo chiles without losing a finger. She still needed to nail down a main course, but if she could get the soup right, that would help her determine what to pair with it.

The silence of the kitchen weighed against her shoulders, tensing her neck as she preheated a skillet for the pork. No wonder Grady always liked to cook with music playing in the background. She quickly pulled up a playlist on her cell phone, propped the phone against the tile backsplash by the sink, and began to hum along to Cyndi Lauper's "Girls Just Want to Have Fun."

The longer she chopped lettuce and prepped the vegetables for the soup, the more she relaxed. By the time her playlist reached Bryan Adams's "Summer of '69," she was almost enjoying herself. She swayed a little as she tossed the garlic into the skillet, reached back for the onions, and executed a little twirl. This wasn't so bad. Of course, it helped that nothing had burned or exploded yet.

She turned from adding salt and pepper to the browning pork, right in the middle of belting out Heart's ballad "Alone," and suddenly realized . . . she wasn't. Jude stood just inside the doorway, arms crossed, a giant grin spreading across his face.

Speaking of burning up.

She futilely fought the blush rising in her cheeks, cloaking her neck and chest in heat. Her pale skin never let her get away with hiding any strong emotion. "What are you doing here? This room is reserved." She cleared her throat, as if that's all she'd been doing when he walked in — rather than singing into a guajillo pepper. She clutched it behind her back.

He strode farther inside. "I know. I reserved it." Still grinning, he set a giant tote bag on the counter. "I didn't realize I'd rented a concert hall."

The heat in her face scorched upward a few degrees. "Clearly the community center double-booked. And I was here first."

The teasing light faded from his eyes, and he let out a long exhale. "So that's how it's going to be? We're back to that?"

She set the pepper on the counter. "What do you mean, back to that? We agreed the truce was off." Maybe they'd had a brief understanding in her car that day, but it didn't excuse the rest of it. He was the enemy. She had to remember that.

Even if he did smell like a musky forest.

"Can we form a new truce, just for tonight?" Jude gestured around the room. "This is a huge kitchen. Big enough for even the two of us."

She rolled in the corner of her lip. He had a point. It would be legitimately bratty of her to insist he leave.

"I promise I won't watch you or steal any cooking tips." He held up both hands.

"You mean, steal them *again*?"

"As I recall, I paid for the last ones." He slowly crossed his arms, dipping his chin pointedly toward her.

True. But . . . "Under false pretenses."

"Is that what you think?"

"That's what you *did*."

He shook his head, studying her with eyes dark and rich like her favorite box-mix hot chocolate. "I'm not going to convince you otherwise, am I?"

She dipped her chin back at him.

He sighed. "Fine. May I stay, at least?"

She matched his sigh, then gestured with her spatula. "You take that side of the room."

"Gracias."

She flicked her gaze to him but didn't reply as he began unloading his bag. She pulled a knife and cutting board from their designated spots on the counter and watched from the corner of her eye as he unpacked several fresh ingredients and what looked to be a container full of . . . cilantro? Figured.

The last thing he removed from the bag was a package of Oreos. She snorted as she began preparing to slice her first guajillo chile. "Fancy dessert you got there."

"These are my favorite." He ripped open the package and pulled one free.

"My boy—" She swallowed back the rest of the word, tightening her grip on her knife. Was StrongerMan99 her boyfriend? Maybe unofficially. But it also felt inaccurate

300

to simply say "my friend." She slowly cut the pepper in half. "I know someone who really loves those."

"Smart person." He grinned and shoved a whole cookie in his mouth as he began lining up his ingredients on the counter, assembly-line style.

Wait. Jude was . . . organized?

He lined everything up perfectly straight, seemingly in the order he was going to use them, with all the labels facing inward. Rory couldn't look away. For some reason, she'd pegged him as the type of guy to create a giant mess while he cooked.

"I thought we weren't going to watch each other."

She jerked her attention back to her pepper, intaking a sharp breath. Busted. She shrugged. "I'm just surprised you're not messy, is all."

"Why? Do I look messy?" He stepped back, motioning to his khaki shorts and dark polo shirt. Not a wrinkle or blemish in sight. Only . . . muscles.

Ugh.

"Forget it." She sliced into the next pepper, then carefully began removing all the seeds. She scraped them into the trash, then repeated the process with the next two peppers — trying not to look at him again.

Jude suddenly stood upright and lifted his chin. He sniffed. "Do you smell something burning?"

"My pork!" She dropped the pepper and the knife, spinning toward the stove so quickly her sneaker slipped on pepper seeds that had fallen to the tile floor. She caught herself against the counter with a thud, her wrist bumping the skillet handle and over-turning the pan full of pork — burned pork — onto the floor. She jumped backward. The stench of scorched seasonings filled the kitchen, along with a cloud of smoke.

Jude waved a dish towel and coughed as she turned off the burner. "You okay?" He strode toward her, then gently grasped her arm and helped her straighten.

"I think so." Mortified, though. She gently flexed her wrist where she'd landed. A little sore but probably not sprained.

He held her gaze and her elbow as a flash of something — pity — flickered across his face. And there it was — she'd failed. Again. And in front of her competition, no less.

She briefly closed her eyes. Jude must have taken that to mean she was in pain, because he dropped the towel on the counter and gingerly slid his grip from her elbow down to her wrist. "Does this hurt?"

Now his brown eyes were merely inches

away, peering down at her as he gently flexed her wrist. She tried to remember the question. "No."

"What about this way?" He carefully flexed her fingers backward with his own, as if he were about to hold her hand. Her fingers weren't hurt — but they were automatically trying to grasp his. What was wrong with her? You'd think she'd have hit her head instead.

"I'm fine, really. Thank you." She tugged her hand free, reaching up to swipe a strand of loose hair that had fallen across her eye.

The realization of what she'd just done simmered, matching the slow boil of pain spreading across her eye. Oh no. She inhaled deeply, and then the scorching waves built into a crescendo.

Pepper juice.

"Ow, ow, ow!" She automatically reached to press her fingers against her stinging eye, then stopped just in time as tears flowed down her cheeks. She flapped her hands frantically against the sting.

"The peppers! Oh no." Jude pressed his own hand against his eyes in sympathy, then his mouth gaped and his cheeks flushed. "It must have gotten on my hands too when I touched yours." He blinked rapidly, sucking in a tight breath. "Where's that towel?"

Squinting through the blur of tears, Rory reached for the dish towel on the counter at the same time Jude did, and they collided. She bounced hard off his firm chest, and he grabbed for her before she could slip again on the pork. But his hand grasped her wrist — her sore one — and she yelped.

"I'm sorry! Wrong hand." His face bright red, Jude grabbed the towel and held it out. "Here. Ladies first."

She shook her head, blinking hard. "No, you first. It's my fault the pepper juice got on you too."

"Together, then." He extended half the towel to her and, standing inches apart, they dabbed their eyes with the clean rag.

The worst of the pain past, Rory blinked up at Jude. His watery gaze blinked back. The scent of forest mixed with spice wafted over her. The emotional toil of the day struck hard, and she found herself wanting to simultaneously fall into a hug and run screaming from him. But his magnetic gaze held her steady, until the sting lessened and all she could think about was his proximity.

"It's really hot."

She drew a ragged breath. "Excuse me?"

"The skillet." He used the towel to grab the scorched skillet and move it into the industrial sink, and Rory exhaled a big sigh of . . . relief? Disappointment? She didn't know. She took advantage of his turned back to compose herself, holding her wrist against her chest. The residual pain and the adrenaline of the accidents — both of them — was what had her heart racing, not the chemistry between her and Jude.

Jude used the sink's attached hose to spray water on the scorched pan, and more smoke billowed. She grimaced at the reminder of her epic mistake. He lowered the water pressure and kept it running as he looked back at her, slinging the towel over his shoulder. The pork lay between them on the floor.

"I usually take my meat medium-rare, but I guess well-done isn't so bad." He nudged it with his toe.

She grabbed a wad of paper towels to protect her hands — which she still needed to wash with soap before being totally cleared of the pepper oil — squatted down, and scooped the charred mess into the garbage can. "I should have known better."

Sympathy lit his face as he shut off the water. "Did you forget to oil the pan?"

Oy — yes. But that wasn't what she meant. She should have known better than to attempt something like this on her own. Mexican pozole? It was a leap, regardless of how many YouTube videos she'd watched.

She was like Charlie Brown in *A Charlie Brown Thanksgiving* when he listed the things he knew how to cook — "cold cereal and maybe toast."

She'd gotten distracted — and hurt. Twice. The main ingredient for her soup was in the trash. The contest was in three days, and now she'd wasted the entire night's worth of practice.

"Why are you doing this?" The emotion in her voice throbbed louder than the ache in her wrist and the leftover sting in her eyes.

"Doing what? Dishes?" He laid the skillet on the drying rack.

She shook her head.

"Cooking tacos?"

Wordlessly, she stared at him.

"I need some context here, Ror."

The nickname rolled off his lips way more naturally than it should have. She narrowed her eyes, hating what the sound of him saying her name did to her insides. She was taken, in the emotional sense. She had no business responding to him this way.

Her insecurity and frustration — and leftover embarrassment — combined into a mix that threatened to run over. She shouldered past him to wash her hands with soap. "Why are you in this contest?"

"I have my reasons." A sudden guard

hooded Jude's expression as he shifted his stance by the sink.

But she didn't buy it. She ripped off a paper towel and dried her hands before facing him. "You're a wealthy white man. You have everything you could possibly need already, and yet you chose tacos."

"I'm a *what*?"

She should have stopped but didn't. Couldn't. Because she was right. And he was going to take everything from her if he won. "You dove into the one genre of food that means nothing to your heritage or to your family — and means everything to mine."

He had no idea about her culture, about Aunt Sophia, about family. Just look at his. He didn't have a clue about carrying on a legacy that everyone expected you to manage — one that *deserved* to be carried. Zero idea what kind of pressure that was for her proud lineage. If she lost the truck, there would be nothing left of Aunt Sophia. Of Grady's hard work. Of Hannah's inheritance.

It went beyond business. It would mean Rory would have failed her entire family.

Jude stared at her, speechless, and looked as surprised to hear what she was saying as she was to finally be saying it to his face.

"Aunt Sophia was a *legend* in Modest. It's a lot of pressure to follow in her foot-steps, under the best of circumstances — and may I add that entering a contest with someone who tried to steal her recipes and open a competing food truck is *not* the best of circumstances." Tears pressed, begging her to shut her mouth, but she couldn't resist the final blow. "So, seriously, if you want to cook so badly, why don't you just go open a hamburger stand or something?"

That did it. Now that the dam had opened, the tears flowed freely, chasing each other down her cheeks in winding tracks as she frantically tried to wipe them away. Un-like the tears caused by the peppers, these felt endless and carried a lot more pain.

Jude continued to watch her, silent. Fi-nally, he pulled the towel off his shoulder and tossed it onto the counter. She braced herself for a torrent of harsh words — ones she deserved — but instead, he stepped toward her and looped one arm around her shoulder. "Come here."

He walked her five steps back toward the island, where his forgotten food waited for his attention. He pulled two cookies from the package and shoved them into her hand.

She let out a garbled sound, something between a choking snort and a huff of disbelief. "I just told you off, and you're feeding me?"

"You need it. And I figure if your mouth is full, you'll be more likely to listen." He smiled to soften his words — a courtesy she hadn't provided.

Chagrined, she shoved an Oreo in her mouth and waited.

Jude leaned one hand against the counter, picking up the closed container of cilantro and slowly turning it over in his hands. "You're right. I grew up spoiled and entitled. Pretty sure that's what's wrong with my brother.

"But we had this housekeeper, Maria." Fondness filled his eyes. "She was full-blooded Mexican. She cared for the house and cooked for us, but more than that, she parented me when my dad was . . . well, my dad." He ran a hand over his hair. "She was the only mom I ever knew."

Rory's mouth went dry. Numbly, she started eating the second cookie.

"All my favorite childhood memories are wrapped up in Maria teaching me how to make her authentic family taco recipe." He smiled, eyes distant as if picturing himself back in those days. "I'd kneel on a stool so I could reach all the ingredients she lined up on the island."

He gestured with the container of cilantro. "Dad and Warner were usually off doing their own thing — golf or whatever. We'd simply cook." He shrugged. "Those moments with her were peaceful — pretty much the opposite of how things went once my family got home."

Rory swallowed.

"She gave me this passion for cooking, and it's what I want to do. You could say she was my Aunt Sophia." Jude set the container down and reached for his own Oreo. "I don't want to be a lawyer anymore. I want to do what brings me inner peace. Long story short, winning this contest would let me do that."

"How? Why can't you just open a truck and not compete?"

He held her gaze, a debate pulsing in his eyes — clearly, he was deciding whether to trust her. Rory waited. Honestly, she wouldn't if the roles were reversed. But miraculously, he continued.

"I have a deal with my dad. I'm free and clear of the family obligation if I win."

Rory blinked. "Isn't that . . . blackmail?"

"More like coercion, but regardless, it's the only deal on the table. I have to take it if I want out." He shrugged. "I know you think I don't need the money, but in this

310

sense, I do. I have a lot on the line too."

Ignoring the cookie crumbs that were surely stuck in her teeth, Rory found her voice. "I owe you an apology."

He waved it off. "I appreciate it, but I get it. This is all pretty stressful." He cut her a sidelong glance. "Remember that boat I was talking about?"

That hadn't been her shiniest moment either. "I'm sorry for what I said in the bar too." Something about Jude brought out her inner attack mode. She didn't have this same level of resentment toward Cluck Truck . . . but that was why, wasn't it? Jude wasn't just competition — he was direct competition against everything she stood for, everything she identified with.

It'd always been him, from the moment he first asked for cooking lessons. Jude threatened her heart in a way that went way beyond the contest. But now that she knew the truth — the details of what drove him — well, it changed things. And that was pretty scary too.

His dark eyes turned wary — and hopeful. "Can we . . . maybe row together?"

A mixture of relief and fear rose in her chest. Jude wasn't a monster in a suit trying to steal her business. After that speech about Maria, she couldn't even declare him an enemy to dominate. They might be different in a lot of ways, but he was just a guy with a goal and a dream, born of his own desperation.

A desperation quite like her own.

And on top of that, he just wanted to cook — it was what brought him joy. Aunt Sophia would only applaud that. Rory had this backward. She'd been trying to take him down rather than make room at the proverbial table.

She still had a lot to learn from Aunt Sophia.

Rory hesitantly held out her hand, which probably smelled like pork. "Permanent truce?"

He immediately shook it. "Done."

She nodded and pulled her hand free, mentally blaming the action on her sore wrist but unable to deny the tremors that shot through her fingers at his contact.

His brow furrowed. "One more thing."

Uh-oh. Had he felt it too? She put on a casual smile to mask her panic. "What's that?"

He grinned. "You have Oreo in your teeth."

ColorMeTurquoise:
"Do you ever feel you've become

the worst version of yourself?
Someone provokes you, and
instead of smiling and moving
on, you zing them?"

StrongerMan99:
Not at all. I'm perfect in every interaction.

That's probably true.

I'm kidding. Nice quote usage by the way.
What happened?

I was wrong about someone.

Been there. In my former career, it was
bound to happen. Either you believed
someone to be truthful and they weren't
— or you believed them to be wrong and
they were right.

I feel bad about it.

Did you make it right?

I think so. I apologized.

That's all you can do.

I wish I had better discernment about people.

That's an art form. Takes practice.

Well, I'd like to learn faster.

Want to practice on me? 😉

😊 I think I have you pegged already.

I feel like I should warn you before we meet — I do have faults.

Like what?

I leave the toilet seat up.

You're a man living alone — why wouldn't you?

I'm incredibly picky about my toothpaste brand.

Understandable.

I pretend my laundry hamper is the basketball hoop, and my T-shirts are the winning point.

That can be unlearned.

Your turn.

If I don't put mascara on my
right eye first, I can't function
the rest of the day.

Whoa. Are you trying to scare me off?

Is it working?

Never.

Seventeen

"Dude. I can only fit six Hershey Kisses, five Starbursts, four Laffy Taffys, and two packs of Skittles in here."

Jude turned from his kitchen island, where he was experimenting with homemade pico de gallo, just in time to see Alton peering deep into the stomach of a llama piñata. "Don't forget the partridge in a pear tree."

"Huh?" Alton set the piñata on the table next to its fiesta-colored twin and frowned. Cody, straddling a chair across from him, snatched a leftover piece of candy and grinned.

Before Jude could clarify, Alton stared into the hole again. "I can do this. It's like that online game where you have to stack the blocks just right to get them to fit."

"Okay, wait." Cody dropped the Starburst he'd nabbed and leaned forward, his chair legs hitting the kitchen floor. "You mean you're old enough to know Tetris but not old enough to recognize the phrase 'a partridge in a pear tree'?"

"I know, that game is ancient, right?" Alton snorted as he rearranged the piñata contents. "Hand me a Kiss, will ya?"

Cody blew a figurative one at him, Alton's eyes widened, and Jude shook his head as he continued to chop onions. He wasn't entirely sure how his post-dinner-rush evening had ended with his home turning into a weird frat party. All he knew was he'd locked up the taco truck for the night after an exhausting day of steady sales and mentioned going home to plan out the details of their fiesta theme for the competition. Suddenly, Alton was ringing his doorbell, Cody coincidentally right behind him carrying a large pizza.

"The piñata is for the competition?" Cody tore open a mini package of Skittles and poured the candy directly into his mouth. "Who's going to hit it open?"

"It's supposed to be decoration for the contest, but Alton likes to take things literally."

"Oh yeah. It's going down." Alton nodded intently as he pulled the colorful pieces of Laffy Taffy from the llama's belly and exchanged them for Skittles packages.

Cody rocked his chair back on its legs.

"Speaking of hitting things with sticks — I heard Warner has a black eye."

"Does he?" Jude focused on dicing.

Cody chomped his candy, grinning. "No judgment here, man. What'd he do?"

Jude shifted his grip on the knife. "How would I know? I'm not my brother's keep—"

"Careful, now." Cody held up one hand. "That line didn't work out so well last time."

Jude scraped the onion into the bowl with the chopped tomatoes and moved on to the jalapeño. "He pushed me too far. I shouldn't have done it." Yet the regret didn't go too deep. At this point, if it hadn't been for his proper grandmother and sweet Maria's influence over the years, his father might have one too.

"Did he hit back?"

He grimaced. "I ducked."

Warner had never been much of a fighter. His reactive swing had been wild and easy to dodge. Hollis had immediately interceded, threatening to call security on them both if they didn't sit down and shut up. So Jude had thrown out the most heartfelt apology he could muster and left the office, while Warner demanded his father's secretary bring him ice. He hadn't seen or spoken to them since and didn't plan to.

The betrayal of his dad's involvement in the contest lingered.

"This is working better," Alton announced from the depths of the llama, as if that was the main concern of the conversation.

Jude ignored him. "It was a low moment."

"I'm sure he had it coming. I wouldn't feel bad if I were you."

He did a little. But mostly he felt bad about his interaction with Rory in the community kitchen last night — in a totally different way. He didn't know which was worse — her being rude to him because he was the competition or her letting down that hostile guard and being vulnerable.

One was frustrating, but the other felt downright dangerous.

The jalapeño, now diced, joined the other vegetables in the bowl. It'd add a much-needed kick to the tomato and onion mixture. Sort of like Rory. All spicy — but probably sweet underneath if she'd ever let anyone get there.

But it wasn't his job to try. He had a romantic interest elsewhere, and Rory — well, they clearly weren't meant to be.

"You think Warner will seek revenge?" Cody downed another Starburst.

Jude cut a lime into several wedges. "I think Warner will do whatever my dad tells him to." He squeezed the juice over the chopped vegetables. "So, basically, there's no telling." Depending on which game his father was playing on any given day — that could go either way.

"Oh, he totally will." Alton looked up from the piñata, his eyes serious as he continued fisting candy into the cardboard animal. "You remember that paralegal Warner overheard mocking him in the bathroom stall that one time? The dude got canned five minutes later." Alton's eyes widened. "Canned. Oh, man, I just put that together. The irony." He slapped his leg at his own joke.

"Well, he can't fire you — you already quit," Cody pointed out with a smirk.

Jude rinsed lime juice off his hands at the kitchen sink. "No, but he'll think of something to get to me." That was the problem. What would it be? He had no way to predict.

"Got it." Alton squeezed the plug into the bottom of the llama and held it triumphantly in the air. Then the plug plopped out and candy poured into his lap.

Jude smirked. At least some things were still entirely predictable.

"I feel tricked." Nicole panted as she collapsed onto the bench on Rory's front

320

porch. "You said there'd be ice cream."

"There is — inside my freezer." Rory bent over beside the bench, stretching to touch her toes, then reached upward, exhaling deeply. "Running gets easier the more you do it."

"Maybe. You have to remember, though — I don't have *all* the emotions driving me forward." Nicole swiped sweat off her forehead with her shirt. "You've got anger, regret, and fear — plus good ol' fashioned anxiety. You're like a human propeller right now."

"I'm not — well, okay, yes. I'm anxious about this weekend." Rory sank onto the other end of the bench, tilting her head up to the warm evening breeze drifting under the porch overhang. "I'm feeling better now that we have a theme and a menu picked out, though." She hadn't told Nicole about the burned pork incident last night. Or about her connection with Jude in the kitchen.

Somehow voicing it would make it too real.

"*And* it's a good menu, at that." Nicole offered a high five, then sniffed and winced. "Scratch that. No lifting of the arms."

"Tamales won't be the easiest, but if we can pull off my aunt's recipe, they'll have

321

the most impact on the judges." Rory pulled one knee up to her chest in a stretch, then rotated her ankle.

"Since the judges are letting contestants prep food the day before, we should be golden." Nicole rubbed her hands together in anticipation. "Golden like a corn husk."

"Those are some of my favorite Christmas memories — making homemade tamales with Aunt Sophia and Hannah." Soaking the corn husks. Mashing the masa. Putting the tamales together in an assembly line. Back then, cooking had been optional, something to do while spending time with her family. Zero pressure, zero obligation. If she failed — as she always did, be it dropping husks on the floor or wrapping the tamales too loosely — it was something to giggle about. Sophia never made her feel less than, and she never made her sit there and look pretty. She just handed over paper towels to clean the mess or patiently repeated her instructions on how to do it the right way.

Rory missed her.

"Did Sophia ever sell tamales in the truck?" Nicole stretched her legs in front of her. "I don't remember Grady ever talking about them."

"No." Rory hesitated. "Do you think she'd

care that I start now?"

"I think she'd tell you to follow your instincts and trust your gut."

That did sound like something her aunt would have said.

"So, if you're feeling a little better about Saturday, what's with the human propeller act?" Nicole nudged her in the side. "Wait. Get the ice cream. Then answer."

Rory returned a few moments later with a pint of cookies 'n cream and two spoons. The crushed cookies reminded her of Jude . . . but wait. Weren't they supposed to remind her of StrongerMan99 first? He was the Oreo fanatic.

She groaned, then immediately recognized her mistake as Nicole sat up straight. "I know that sound." Her friend dug her spoon into the pint. "Spill it." She pointed. "And don't think this means you're getting away with not answering my original question too."

"It's all kind of the same issue." Rory scooped up some ice cream and nibbled a bite off the edge of her spoon. "I'm starting to think it might be time to meet Stronger-Man99."

For multiple reasons, all of which she wasn't sure she could vocalize — even to her best friend. How could she admit that she was still attracted to Jude, despite his current status as the competition? His letting his guard down in the community kitchen had shown her a side of him she'd so far been able to pretend didn't exist. Now she had proof it did. He wasn't the enemy anymore.

She and Jude would never work, even if StrongerMan99 wasn't in the picture — which he very much was. And it was time to make that relationship more of a priority.

She took a deep breath. "I think I'm ready."

"Finally!" Nicole cheered. She dug out a piece of cookie from the carton. "You should do it."

"After the contest, I'll make it happen." Probably. Yes. She would. Most likely.

"*Before.*" Nicole's tone left little room for arguing.

Rory tried anyway. "I don't need the distraction while trying to cook." She glanced at her watch. "Plus, that's only two days away. That'd be impossible."

"Hardly impossible! What better time than tomorrow night? Friday night . . . date night. You could grab a pizza or something low-key. Get your mind off the competition for a bit."

Rory's stomach dipped, and it wasn't from

the sugar rush. "That makes me want to run again."

"I know. That's why you need to do it." Nicole gestured with her spoon. "Face your fears. Plus, you know you're going to hit it off great. Meeting at this point is a formality, right?"

Maybe. Rory scooped one more big bite, then relinquished the pint to Nicole. What if it wasn't? What if they didn't click in person? What if she didn't have the same chemistry with him that she did with Jude? "I don't know . . ."

"Think about it this way." Nicole shifted on the bench to face her. "Wouldn't you rather have the support of an actual boyfriend while you're cooking on Saturday? Rather than stressing over your undetermined relationship status . . . and Jude?"

Rory choked on her ice cream. "Jude?"

"I know you're attracted to him."

"I am not —"

"A good liar," Nicole finished. "Agreed."

"What does Jude have to do with anything?" She reached to take the ice cream back.

"Right now, I think he has to do with everything." Nicole shrugged as she surrendered the carton. "You tell me, hermana. You're already telling stories to yourself."

"Fine." Rory set down her spoon and shared the connection she'd had with Jude last night in the community kitchen. The burned pork incident. The way he'd taken care of her injury. The pepper fiasco. The way he'd stayed to help her mop the scorched seasoning off the floor. "Turns out, he's not so much of a monster, after all."

"Villains rarely are. Everyone has their side of the story." Nicole reached over and scraped the bottom of the carton with her spoon. "Perspective can change a lot."

"It was easier when he was the enemy."

"Because now you're not immune to his charm anymore, are you?" Her friend winked.

"Sure, crack your jokes, old married lady." Rory rolled her eyes. "This is all easy for you to say." She hesitated. "What if Stronger-Man99 doesn't like me in person?"

"Then he's a fool."

"Also easy for you to say."

Nicole shrugged. "Doesn't make me less right."

"The app hasn't even prompted us yet to this particular progression. That's got to mean something."

Nicole rolled her eyes. "It means you're two adults who can plan your own love lives.

What's the next prompt?"

"Photo swap."

She snorted. "Skip that one. You'll accomplish two steps at once if you just go ahead and meet already."

Rory stood, nervous energy flowing through her exhausted muscles. "I'd be risking everything if we met tomorrow. Like losing an amazing friendship right when I need it most."

"You'll be risking everything whether you take this step tomorrow or in three weeks. Besides, you're also risking gaining an amazing *relationship,*" Nicole said. She stood too, then grimaced, pulling her leg into a stretch. "No pain, no gain, right? Or does that only apply to running?"

Good point. "I hate it when you're right."

"So does Grady." Nicole switched legs and grinned. "Yet here we are."

Rory pulled her phone from her yoga pants' pocket and opened her texts. No new messages. They were supposed to chat later tonight, but if she didn't send this now, she'd chicken out without Nicole's boldness driving her forward.

"Do it! Do it!" Nicole chanted as she bounced on the balls of her feet.

Rory typed a quick text, then hesitated. Her finger hovered over the Send button.

"Are you sure?"

"Are *you* sure?" Nicole crossed her arms over her sweaty tank. The breeze stirred again, ruffling loose tendrils of hair that had escaped from her ponytail. "Let me tell you one little fact. One day, years ago, I woke up and didn't even know Grady. And the next day, I woke up and did know him."

"Talk about a good night's sleep."

Nicole stifled a laugh. "My point is — things happen quickly. One day you didn't know this guy and the next you did. It's time for another step. Because what if the one after that is something more permanent — but you never let yourself get there?"

Another good point. A dozen thoughts and emotions flowed like adrenaline through her limbs — those dreaded feelings she was constantly getting blamed for avoiding. Because she hated messy. She liked straight lines and things that added up and made sense and blended aesthetically. Right now, nothing was blending except her nerves and anxiety. It was much easier to avoid her feelings.

Run from them.

But no. She had to fight through them, or she'd never grow in this part of her life.

"It's scary."

The vulnerable words hovered between

them, and despite her earlier declaration, Nicole lifted her arm and wrapped it around Rory's shoulders. "Trust me." Nicole's voice lowered to a whisper. "He's not going to reject you."

A montage of her and StrongerMan99's conversations floated through Rory's head. All the inside jokes. The encouragement. The deep connection. The flirting. Rory slowly nodded. "You're right." She hit Send and sucked in a deep breath. "I hope."

ColorMeTurquoise:
I'm ready.

StrongerMan99:
For . . . some football?

😆 As long as it's on TV and comes with cheese dip, sure.

I knew I liked you.

I meant I'm ready for us to meet. 😛

I know. You're just so fun to tease. Plus, I really like watching football.

I really like cheese dip.

Match made in heaven. When do you have this meeting in mind?

Tomorrow night?

Friday night? Whoa. Are you asking me on a date?

Hardly. I'm agreeing to the date you already asked me on.

Well played. And also — accurate. What about 7:00 p.m. at Pizza Butler?

That depends. Am I going to have to watch you consume pineapple on your pizza? That might be a deal breaker.

Don't knock it 'til you've tried it.

Some things are instinctive.

I agree. Which is why I can't wait to see you tomorrow.

EIGHTEEN

"You're meeting him tonight?" Hannah's voice didn't hold nearly as much shock as Rory would have anticipated.

Rory turned to face her from the rec center kitchen counter, wooden spoon in hand. "You're not surprised?"

Hannah shrugged and put her hands on the island, where she sat on a barstool sorting corn husks for the tamales. "I think you should have met him already."

"You're not the only one. You and Nicole should start a club." Rory sprinkled cumin into the meat mixture simmering on the stove. Nicole had volunteered to work the truck solo while Rory and Hannah started prepping Sophia's tamale recipe for tomorrow's contest.

It was gearing up to be a big weekend, in every way. She still couldn't believe she'd initiated meeting tonight — ahead of the app, no less. But if Nicole and Hannah —

and StrongerMan99, for that matter —
thought it was the perfect time, well, maybe
they knew something she and her fears
didn't.

As if reading her mind, Hannah piped up.
"I wish I could be there at Pizza Butler."

Rory laughed. "I'll do much better without
an audience, trust me." Nerves flitted
through her stomach, and she wondered if
she'd even be able to eat. Nicole's pep talk
last night echoed through her thoughts.
"He's not going to reject you."

If only that was her sole concern.

"Oh, I didn't mean for you. You'll be fine."
Hannah grinned mischievously as she carefully stacked the dry husks. "I just want
pizza."

"If I survive tonight, I'll take you to get
some next weekend, after all this contest
stuff is over." She added some pepper,
considered a moment, then tossed in a dash
of onion powder.

"You're pretty good at that now."

Rory glanced over her shoulder, waving
one hand against the thin cloud of steam
wafting from the pot. "At what?"

"Cooking. You're getting instincts."

Rory snorted. "Don't tell me we need to
take you for an eye exam."

"I have great vision. Twenty-twenty."

Hannah's serious gaze met Rory's, unblinking.

"You're right — about your eyes. Maybe not about my ability, though." Rory stirred the bubbling mixture and turned the burner down another notch.

"You've only looked at the recipe a handful of times." Hannah pointed to the note cards lined up on the counter by Rory. They were filled with Sophia's familiar cursive. "And I saw you experimenting with the seasonings earlier."

Rory turned to face her cousin, hands fisted on her hips in mock defense. "What's your endgame here?"

"It's not a game, Rory. I think it's more serious than that."

Yikes. She set the wooden spoon on the spoon rest, then took a seat at the island next to Hannah. "That's too bad. Tamales shouldn't be serious." She kept her tone light, not wanting to get into anything heavy — not with tonight's date looming.

"You've been reading recipe books. You've been watching cooking videos. And you've been doing more and more with Mom's truck without Grady's help." Hannah set another husk on her growing pile.

She clearly didn't know about the pork incident from the other night. Though Hannah would probably just say it had been an accident . . . and *los accidentes ocurren* — accidents happened. "So?"

"*So*, you're cooking, cousin." Hannah offered a little shrug. "I think maybe the problem isn't that you can't cook. It's that you don't want to."

"I don't want to because I can't," Rory argued. She stood abruptly and headed to the industrial fridge, where her bowl of mixed masa harina and chicken broth waited for the rest of the dry ingredients to be added. "You have it backward."

She searched the counter for the rest of the seasonings and began to sprinkle them into the bowl, fighting back the thoughts demanding precedence. She didn't want to evaluate Hannah's theories. Right now, she needed to focus on the salt. And the chili powder. Where was the pork lard?

Hannah appeared at her elbow and held out the lard, a small grin tugging her lips. "That excuse about not being able to cook won't work anymore. It's no longer true."

Was she right? Rory looked at the contents of the bowl. A couple weeks ago, she'd have had no idea where to start with homemade tamales — recipe or no recipe. She hadn't known the difference between kneading and folding. She still made mistakes, but her common protest of "I can't even make a grilled cheese" didn't ring true to her defense anymore.

She should be proud. Sophia would be proud. Grady *was* proud. Why didn't this realization give her joy?

"I don't know, Hannah." It was too much to dissect right now. She needed to focus on her date and the giant leap of faith she was taking — bigger even than Joe Fox's and Kathleen Kelly's.

Rory dropped the lard into the bowl and began to stir. The recipe said to mix with an electric beater, but it felt good to take her frustration out on something tangible. Hannah didn't know what she was stirring up, but it certainly wasn't tamale dough.

It felt an awful lot like grief.

Like failure.

Like letting down the people she loved the most.

Hannah's hand on Rory's arm stilled her erratic whipping. Rory forced herself to meet her cousin's gentle gaze, hoping the pain she fought wasn't evident in her eyes.

Hannah's were bright and clear — and wise. "Maybe you didn't want Mom's truck at first because you couldn't cook. But now you can. So there's only one question left to be asked."

Rory swallowed, looking at the partially mixed batter dripping off the spoon. "What's that?"

"Why don't you want the truck now?"

Jude checked his watch as he strode toward the community kitchen door. Ten thirty. The lunch rush would be hitting in the next half hour, and he'd left Alton alone at the truck to come grab the quart-sized Tupperware he'd left the other night. Hopefully he could sneak in and snag it without disturbing anyone who might be renting the space today.

The sun warmed his bare arms and sweat was already gathered under the brim of his hat. It would be another East Texas scorcher today, but the humidity was lower than usual. Perfect competition weather if it stayed like this through the weekend. Hopefully the projected rain would hold off that evening too. Then he and ColorMeTurquoise could sit outside on the patio at Pizza Butler. It'd be less formal that way, which would probably be more comforting for her — she had to be nervous.

Heck, he was nervous, and he'd been trying to meet her now for weeks.

He eased the door open, squinting to make out two shadow-shrouded figures in the corner of the room as his eyes struggled to adjust from the brilliant sunlight. Someone was stirring a giant stockpot on the stove, while someone else was hunched over the counter table, rolling out . . . something. He cleared his throat to alert them of his presence. "Don't mind me, I'm only grabbing something I forgot."

"No problem." The figure sitting at the table offered a beaming smile, teeth white against the shadows in the room. His eyes came further into focus, and he recognized the chin-length hair. Rory's cousin Hannah. Which meant —

"Morning." Rory turned from the stove, her smile forced and her voice tight.

Not good.

"I'm just here to get my bowl." Jude held up both hands and slowly entered the room, as if approaching a wild tiger. Of all the days for Rory to reserve the kitchen again. He'd assumed she'd be manning her truck today. "I need it for tomorrow."

Hannah pointed to the industrial sink, where a few dishes lay stacked inside. "Help yourself."

He tentatively crossed the room and fetched his missing plasticware. The last thing his and Rory's fledgling acquaintanceship needed was her gathering ammo to accuse him of spying or some other ridiculous thing. They were in truce mode as of Wednesday, and he wanted to keep it that way.

"I'm not looking, I'm not looking." He half joked, pretending to cover his eyes with his hands as he started back across the room.

But as his gaze caught Hannah's and she offered a sweet and genuine smile, his steps slowed. How many people in her life breezed past her without true contact? "Whatcha got there?" He gestured to her project on the table.

She beamed and held up a strip of thin dough. "We're making tamales."

Rory coughed suddenly, hard and sharp. Hannah frowned. "If you're not feeling good, Rory, you shouldn't be cooking." Her matter-of-fact tone made Jude duck his head to hide his smile.

"I'm fine, Hannah." Rory's voice softened toward her cousin, then her eyes narrowed as she looked back at Jude. "I meant the tamales were supposed to be a secret until tomorrow. Remember, he's the competition."

Hannah covered her mouth with both hands. "Oops."

Uh-oh. He was about to be in trouble and

get her in trouble too. He sniffed appreciatively, hoping to ease the tension rolling off Rory in waves. He hadn't come to spy — surely she knew that. "They sure smell amazing." Whatever she had boiling in that stockpot — he'd guess the meat, judging by the seasonings stacked on the counter — wafted through the kitchen on delicious waves of cumin and garlic and . . . something spicy. Red pepper? Cayenne?

He realized then that he'd stopped on his trek back to the door and was literally sniffing the air while Rory stared at him, eyebrows arched. "You done?"

"Sorry." He released a sheepish smile. "I'm leaving now."

Rory glanced at the door before resuming stirring. Hint, hint. "See you tomorrow."

She was using her manners, but it was obvious he'd come at a bad time. Something had already stressed her out, and his presence was going to be the boiling point if he didn't leave.

"See you tomorrow." He nodded and reached back for the door handle, disappointment and relief mingling in his chest. He hated their lingering awkwardness, especially after their positive connection in this same kitchen just a few nights ago, but it was apparently for the best. For many reasons.

One of whom he was meeting tonight at seven. He didn't need any distractions. And while Rory ran hot and cold toward him with her assumptions and judgments, there was that soft and vulnerable part of herself she'd revealed enough times for him to see past the tough shell. She was much more bark than bite, and her desire to protect her family's legacy was honorable. Admirable, even.

Bottom line, she had the potential to be a big distraction. But his developing relationship with ColorMeTurquoise had to come first.

"Wait." Hannah jumped up, plucking something from the table, and half jogged after him. She stood before him, forthright and unashamed. "You're the competition."

"It appears I am." He stood motionless beneath her scrutiny, her scrunched eyes studying what felt like his every pore.

Across the room, Rory cleared her throat. "Hannah, he's got to go."

Jude cast an uneasy look between the two cousins, unsure who to listen to. But something in Hannah's pure gaze held him still. He opened his mouth, then shut it.

"You might be the enemy, but I still want to say good luck." She reached out and pressed something white and papery into his hand. "The Bible says to love our enemies."

Rory stiffened but didn't protest further as Jude gently accepted the gift.

"Thank you." He unfolded his fingers. A tiny, perfectly folded origami swan. "Wow. This is amazing."

She nodded as if she already knew the quality of it and was agreeing with his accurate assessment. He wished for one ounce of that self-confidence. Maybe then he'd have stood up to his dad years ago. Speaking of enemies.

He recoiled slightly at the realization. They'd always had a tumultuous relationship, but when had his father turned into an actual foe in his mind?

Hannah drifted back to the corn-husk-covered counter and resumed her work, seemingly unaware of the moral bomb she'd dropped in his heart. Jude lifted his hand in a wave, then quickly exited before he could do any more damage.

The door slammed behind him, then Rory burst through it.

Too late.

"I've seen some pretty low-down things in my lifetime, but that one really took the cake." Rory crossed her arms, her eyebrows scrunched into an angry line across her forehead. Her eyes were already red-rimmed and flashing fire.

"What are you talking about?" He opted for some humor to douse her lit fuse. "I don't even like cake. I'm more of a cookie kind of guy. Remember? Oreos?"

Didn't work. Her glare darkened. "You were pumping my cousin for information."

Wait. What? Jude shifted his weight, cradling the swan protectively in his hand. "I just wanted my Tupperware. I had no idea you'd even be here today."

"That didn't stop you from taking advantage of Hannah's honesty."

Whoa. "You think I was —"

"I'm not stupid *or* blind."

Jude coughed into his fist, partially to buy a moment of time and partially to hide the shock spreading through him that she could think that poorly of him. After everything that had been said the other night, she still thought him capable of something like that? "Rory, I would never. I was just making conversation."

"You just did. I saw you. I *heard* you."

He reeled back. "So you're accusing me of cheating?"

She faltered. "Not *cheating*. Just . . . .

you're not the first to try to use her to get to me."

He frowned, confused. "But I'm not using her, or trying to get to you, for that matter." If anything, he was trying to get *away* from her at this point.

She lifted her chin, her tight expression wavering. "I meant get information *about* me. About the contest."

His struggling patience dissipated. Always a roller coaster with Rory. He thought he'd seen a different side of her the other night, but now he wondered. Maybe he'd given her too much credit. "Why don't you say what you mean then?"

Her eyes flashed. "Fine. How about this? Stay away from my cousin!" She turned with a flip of her long ponytail as she strode back inside the kitchen. The door banged behind her.

Of all the nerve. Jude inhaled a deep breath in an effort to gain control over his growing frustration. He started to make a fist, then remembered the swan just in time.

He studied the bird's folded wings as he headed for his truck, the little gift enveloping him with a strange sense of peace. Hannah was talented. In fact, she could even sell these if she —

Something familiar washed over him, then

— a sudden shower of memory. His steps slowed. The sun caught the white paper and beamed off the crisp beak. Origami swan. Where had he seen that recently?

Wait. Hannah had been creating these guys that day he met Rory at the truck and asked for cooking lessons. That was it. He held it carefully as he unlocked his truck and slid inside. He perched the swan on his dashboard and smiled. Hannah had a unique gift. To be able to look past the surface and see the core of what really mattered — wishing him good luck despite being the main competition against her angry, paranoid cousin . . .

Her cousin.

Another memory tapped on his shoulder. He squinted at the paper bird. There was something else. Something more recent.

He racked his brain, unsure why it mattered, but equally sure it would bother him until he figured it out. Had he seen Hannah with more swans — maybe at the competition last weekend? No, this memory wasn't in person. This was a text. He could almost make out the words in his mind's eye.

Words on a screen.

ColorMeTurquoise.

"Blue floral rug (covering a stain on the carpet). Origami swan courtesy of my cousin."

That was it. He sucked in his breath and looked back toward the rec center, his pulse drumming a hard rhythm in his ears. No. There were lots of people who made origami.

In the small town of Modest?

Who were cousins with someone in his life?

The sun inched behind a cloud. Outside, birds chirped and a squirrel darted across the parking lot. The world continued spinning, but his had stopped abruptly on its axis.

It couldn't be.

But everything in his heart screamed that it was.

The smell of pepperoni would be forever burned into this memory.

Rory took a sip of her lemon water, then cleared her throat and began folding her straw into an accordion to keep herself from staring at the door. From her vantage point in the back corner of Pizza Butler, she could view every patron who entered or exited. And every time the door opened, adrenaline surged through her veins and her heart stammered.

Since it was a busy Friday night, she was fairly certain she'd be going into some form of cardiac arrest soon.

The scent of bubbling cheese and spicy meat drifted from the kitchen to her left. Rory inhaled deeply. This moment could be one of the most important in her entire life. If the date went as well as she hoped — and as well as Grady and Nicole expected it to — this could be her last first date ever. Her stomach flipped. It could be the date she told her future grandkids about.

"Still waiting?" The waiter hesitated by her table, water pitcher in hand, and hiked an eyebrow in doubt.

That is, if he showed up.

"Yes. He's just running late." She glanced at her watch. Only by nine minutes. That could easily be accounted for with traffic or a string of red lights.

The waiter topped off her water. "Let me know if you decide to order without him."

"I won't." Rory met his gaze directly. "He'll be here."

The waiter's smirky expression immediately dissipated. The pitcher lowered to his side. "Has anyone ever told you that you look like —"

"On second thought, why don't you get us a bowl of those breadstick bites?" Rory tapped the picture on the menu. "Extra marinara."

"Right away, miss."

A few minutes later, the bowl of breadstick bites appeared in front of her, along with two cups of marinara. She thanked the waiter, who wisely remained silent, and accepted the extra napkins before he vanished again.

Seventeen minutes.

She opened a game app on her phone, but the colorful squares blurred before her despite the game's promise to help players "escape reality." She'd wanted to escape tonight. Escape the fact that the contest and her fate hinged on the next twenty-four hours. Escape the fact that once again, someone in her life was using her — worse yet, using the people she loved. She couldn't believe Jude had scouted the kitchen that way, looking for hints of what they were cooking. And then he hit up Hannah, of all people — sweet, innocent, trusting Hannah — for information when it didn't work.

Just like her ex, Thomas.

Jude had proven to be untrustworthy time and again, and eventually she would need to trust her instincts. Jude was a Worthington lawyer, after all. Maybe that whole sob story he'd told about not knowing his brother was engaged was all made up. A tall tale to buy her trust, get her guard down.

347

After all — didn't he admit that because of the deal with his dad, he had as much to lose in this contest as she did? Why should she expect him to play fair when he'd been trained his whole life to do the opposite?

The door opened again, and her breath hitched. Nope. Just a middle-aged couple who immediately started arguing over whether to get thin crust.

Twenty-two minutes.

The waiter appeared beside her again, his expression neutral. "Still want to wait to order?"

Rory popped a breadstick bite in her mouth. "Yes. He'll be here."

He replenished her water, which she had barely touched since the last time he'd filled it, his eyes darting back and forth from the pitcher to Rory. "You're way too pretty to get stood up. We all agreed." He gestured over his shoulder to a woman he'd whispered with earlier and another, younger waiter, who shot her a double thumbs-up.

Rory groaned. "I'm not getting stood up."

"Traffic?" He nodded knowingly. "That's what he'll say, anyway. If he comes."

She swallowed.

"Oh, he'll show up." Doubt flickered across his expression. "But, hey, if it doesn't work out . . . . I have a girlfriend, but my buddy in the kitchen over there is single and said he'd totally —"

"Thin crust pepperoni, please. With bell pepper. And sausage."

"Onions?"

"No, thanks."

His grin reappeared. "Still holding out hope. That's the spirit." He grabbed her menu and headed to the kitchen.

Rory checked her phone for the tenth time. No texts. She checked her DMs. Nothing.

Twenty-eight minutes.

This was not the part of *You've Got Mail* they were supposed to imitate.

The door opened, and a man walked inside, head down, eyes on his phone. Her chest tightened. She dabbed the corner of her mouth to remove any rogue marinara sauce. Was that him? Tall. Dark-haired.

He looked up.

Jude, his expression shuttered and dark.

Rory slunk down in her seat to avoid being seen. But he saw her — and headed her way.

She straightened and lifted her chin. Whatever he wanted, he'd better not linger. Though she couldn't imagine what he'd have to say to her after how she had gone off on him earlier.

She felt a flicker of regret but shook it off. How many truces could she form before enough was enough? Still . . . what if she was wrong? What if she'd misinterpreted his interaction with Hannah earlier today? It wouldn't be the first time she'd been overly protective of her cousin.

He paused in front of her table, one hand reaching up to rub the scruffy shadow on his chin. "Is this seat taken?"

She looked away from how his blue athletic shirt lit his tan complexion. "It is. I'm expecting someone."

He sat down anyway. His eyes looked different than earlier. Shielded. Not that she blamed him. "I'm not staying."

Rory stiffened. "Good, because I don't —"

He popped a mini breadstick in his mouth. "These are much better with cheese dip than pizza sauce."

"They are not —"

He tilted his head. "We don't agree on anything, do we?" The guarded look was transitioning into something else. Something weary and half amused and . . . angry?

"I'm sorry?" She shook her head, trying to keep up but not entirely sure she wanted to. Why was her heart pounding like she'd just run a marathon? He wasn't who she was waiting for. He was the competition.

The competition who now knew exactly what she was cooking tomorrow and had plenty of time to use that information against her. The competition who maybe had a beating heart of his own but also an agenda. Simply put, despite their previous connections, he couldn't be fully trusted.

Jude rocked his chair back on two legs, his expression tight. "Who are you waiting for?"

"A . . . friend."

He squinted. "Are you being stood up?"

Her heart dropped into her stomach. *"No."*

The waiter swooped in, another menu in hand. "You made it! See, I told you he'd be here." He handed one to Jude with a relieved smile.

Rory reached to snatch it. "He isn't staying." She fixed her gaze on Jude. "You're not staying."

The waiter darted between them as they played tug-of-war with the menu, his hands fluttering above theirs as he tried to grab the laminated board.

Jude won. "When he gets here, I'll leave. In the meantime, maybe just a brief perusal." He studied the page of pizzas with exaggerated intent.

"So do I bring you a water or . . . ?" The

waiter's lips quirked to the side.

Jude shook his head. Rory wilted a little with relief.

"Coke will be fine."

Ugh.

"Coming right up." The waiter leaned down as he passed Rory's chair. "Y'all make a cute couple, even if he isn't Mr. Right. And hey, he's here, so that's saying something."

Heat burned her face at his departure.

"He makes a good point." Jude shrugged.

She snapped her gaze to his. "What, that we make a cute couple?"

"*No*. That you're still here. Why are you still waiting?"

"Because I know him. He'll be here." Doubt tap-danced across her heart, but she immediately kicked it aside. StrongerMan99 was her safe place. He'd proven himself over and over in a positive way, unlike Jude. They were exact opposites. Jude knew nothing of her date's character.

"First date?" Jude tilted his head. "Wait. Let me guess. *Blind* date. That's why you were staring at the door so hard when I came in." He leaned back slightly. "In fact . . . I bet you don't even know what he looks like, do you?"

How in the world did he figure all that

352

out so quickly? Rory tossed her folded straw at him. "Absolutely none of that is your business."

"Maybe not, but it's interesting."

Anger and something akin to sadness meshed into a lumpy ball in her stomach. She hated his cocky posture but fully realized she'd earned it with her verbal attack on him. When had she started bringing out the worst in people? Her aunt would be ashamed.

She lowered her voice. "I think the real question is, why are *you* here?"

"Well, it's not for the marinara, I can tell you that." He popped another plain breadstick bite in his mouth. "Don't worry, this bowl is on me."

Frustration welled up and over at how flippant he was acting. "How generous of you." She slapped her hands on the table. "If it's so easy to throw your money around, why are you even in this stupid contest anyway?"

Jude smirked. "I'm offering to cover breadsticks, not college tuition."

Okay, that was it. She'd tried. "Get out."

"Oh, come on." He dragged a breadstick through the red sauce. "If I leave, who will keep your man's seat warm?"

If she could have physically hauled him

from the chair and shoved him outside, she would have. Despite having never been his biggest fan, this wasn't the Jude she knew. This wasn't the Jude who'd laughed with her in the food truck, tended to her injured wrist, and helped her scrub pork off the floor.

But maybe she hadn't ever known him at all.

She leaned forward, her voice hissing through clenched lips. "Everything's a joke to you, isn't it?"

He bit into the breadstick. "Trust me, it's either laugh or cry at this point."

She narrowed her eyes. "What are you talking about?"

"You have no idea."

"Then why don't you say what you mean?" She threw his words from earlier that day back at him, pointing her chin to drive the inflection home. "Isn't that what you like to advise? Mr. Lawyer Man?"

"Mr. Lawyer Man?" He snorted.

"I'm holding back. I'm trying to be nice."

"Right. Like you were earlier today?"

Rory pointed at him. "That's on you. You were manipulating my cousin for your own gain."

"I wasn't. *She* approached *me*."

"After you asked what she was doing.

354

She's trusting and vulnerable." Rory's throat tightened. "And she's been used before."

"So you said. But guess what? Not by me. When are you going to stop making me pay for someone else's mistakes?"

"You *did* use me. With the cooking lessons."

"And we're back to that." Jude sighed and tossed the partially eaten breadstick on a napkin. "You're like a broken record."

"You're one to talk. All this sappy stuff about how awful your father and brother are, and how different you are." Rory rolled her eyes. "Maybe one particular apple didn't fall as far away from the tree as you think."

Jude flinched as if he'd been sucker punched. Remorse started a slow burn in her pounding heart. Too far. She opened her mouth, unsure how to fix it, but he interrupted before she could try.

"Do me a favor." He pulled out his phone and gave it a few abrupt taps. A notification dinged. Then he held out his hand. "May I see your phone?"

She recoiled. "I don't think —"

Jude leaned forward in his chair, his gaze serious. "This is important."

She shouldn't trust him. But she'd also just said something pretty horrible, and he

355

didn't look like a man bent on revenge. In fact, he just looked . . . sad. Rory opened her phone via facial recognition, then reluctantly dropped it into his waiting palm. "I don't know what's happening right now."

"You're about to." He made a few swipes until another ding sounded — this time from her phone. "Here. You have a notification."

He handed her cell back over, his eyes riveted to her face. She glanced back and forth from her phone to his somber stare. "What . . ." The Love at First Chat app was open and had prompted her to accept a photo swap.

StrongerMan99 had already accepted from his end. Why would he . . . where *was* he . . . Her thoughts jumbled together, clawing for clarity until she couldn't process a single one of them. She shook her head to clear it. Had StrongerMan99 backed out? Did her appearance matter that much to him, after all? He had to make sure she was worth meeting?

She began to shake.

Jude reached around her trembling outstretched hand before she could protest and hit the Accept button on her display. She reeled backward. "What do you think you're —"

Jude's face filled her screen.

Rory sucked in her breath, staring, but the picture didn't fade. Instead, it matched the one sitting directly across from her. Her eyes darted between the duplicate images. He was even wearing the same shirt.

Jude shoved back from the table, his eyes downcast. "Goodbye, Rory." He tossed a twenty-dollar bill into the breadstick basket and walked out the door.

He didn't look back.

NINETEEN

How had so much changed in only twenty-four hours?

Jude sprinkled cilantro over the top of an open soft taco with gloved hands and cast a quick glance at his watch. The lunch rush would hit momentarily, and the contest would take place later that afternoon once the trucks closed for the day around 1:00 p.m., allowing them a few hours of prep time in between. He had so much to do, he couldn't think straight. And the thoughts he had were wavy and circular and somehow all centered on ColorMe Turquoise.

Rory.

The same person.

Whom he hurt last night.

Rory sort of deserved it — maybe.

ColorMeTurquoise didn't.

But they were the same person.

"Dude, I know you're into cilantro, but that's probably enough." Cody quirked an eyebrow at Jude from his stance outside the truck window.

Jude jerked his hand away from the piling tower of cilantro he'd built on Cody's taco. "Sorry, man." He brushed off half. Cody pursed his lips and gestured with a wave of his hand to remove more.

"You could always order no cilantro." Jude boxed the taco with the others.

"Or you could put a normal amount on there." Cody accepted his lunch through the serving window and slid a ten-dollar bill across the counter. "What's the deal, bro? Stressing over the contest?" He nudged the piñata sitting on the counter and grinned. "You could always crack open one of these bad boys. I'm surprised Alton hasn't yet."

Speaking of, where was his helper? He stooped down and peered out the open window across the festival grounds, where the community milled about, killing time before the contest by ordering lunch, letting their kids play on the playground, and gossiping from colorful lawn chairs.

No sign of Alton. At this point, Jude wouldn't be surprised if his dad or brother had kidnapped him to keep him from helping Jude. What else were they capable of?

"Okay, what gives?" Cody leaned his forearms against the serving counter.

Jude averted his eyes. "Have you seen Alton?"

"I saw him chatting up the Cluck Truck girl on my way over." Cody bit into a taco. "Hey, these are really good."

"I'd hope so by now." Jude scooped the spilled cilantro into the catch tray off the side of the counter. He'd empty that after the lunch rush.

Was ColorMeTurquoise okay?

She was Rory. It kept blowing his mind. As much as he tried to mesh the two of them together, he couldn't. He'd think of Rory and get angry. He'd think of ColorMeTurquoise and feel sad. He'd think of them being the same and become . . . confused. Weary?

Hopeless.

"You finally met her, didn't you?"

Cody wouldn't let up. Jude released a sigh, tugged off his gloves, and bent down, resting his arms on the counter and mimicking his friend's stance. "Sort of."

Cody flicked a stray piece of shredded cheese off his takeout box and onto the grass. "You know, looks don't have to be the most —"

"Spare me." Jude frowned. "A, I'm not like that — you are. And B, she's gorgeous."

"Fair enough." Cody shrugged and took

another dripping bite of his food. "So you *did* meet her."

Jude scanned the festival grounds — no sign of his main competition — but lowered his voice anyway. "It's Rory."

"Where?" Cody took another cheesy bite and turned, glancing over his shoulder.

"My online girl . . . my online . . . whatever she is . . . *was* . . . it's Rory."

Cody brought his fist up over his mouth, cheeks bulging, eyes wide. "ColorMeTurquoise is Rory?" He coughed, swallowed, then coughed again. "Rory, like — competition Rory? Salsa Street Rory?"

"One and the same."

Cody shook his head slowly, then changed it to a nod. "You got the gorgeous part right."

"*That's* your main takeaway?" Jude crossed his arms.

"Remember your point A?" Cody shrugged.

"This is serious."

"I agree. Rory is seriously good-looking."

Jude briefly closed his eyes. "I'm going to slap you in the face with a taco."

"Would I get a discount then?" Cody grinned. "I'm kidding, man. Trying to lighten the mood. You need some Oreos or something."

A teen girl approached the truck with what must have been her kid brother, and Cody scooted out of the way to let them order. Then Alton reappeared with a big grin, going on and on about Kimmy at the chicken truck, to the point that Jude didn't get a chance to lecture him on abandoning Nacho Taco right before the lunch rush. The following two hours blurred into a series of prepping orders, seasoning beans he'd forgotten to salt, cleaning counters, and convincing Alton not to smash the piñata yet.

When Jude finally stilled and chugged back half a bottle of water, he had two hours before the contest began. Two hours to create a fiesta for the judges. Two hours to secure his future.

Two hours to try to figure out what in the world to say when he saw Rory.

"StrongerMan99 is Jude?" Nicole stopped abruptly, causing the plastic tub of Christmas decorations to bump into Rory's shins. "Jude Worthington?"

Rory snorted and adjusted her grip on her end of the heavy tote. "I think I'd rather he'd have been the Unabomber." To say the least.

"The *what* now?"

She shook her head, to both dismiss Nicole's confusion and shake off the tears that permanently threatened to escape. "Never mind. Keep going."

Nicole shook her head as she resumed slowly walking backward toward the food truck on their trek across the parking lot. They'd stashed the tub of décor in Nicole's truck until their break before the judging began. "I just can't believe it. I'm in shock."

Rory hoisted her end of the tub higher in her sweaty grasp. "*You* are? I'm the one who put myself out there for nothing." The look on Jude's face when he'd handed back her phone . . . it was pure grief.

He was disappointed.

With her.

Nicole picked up her pace as they neared the food truck. "Maybe this isn't a bad thing."

"Of course it's a bad thing." Rory's grip slipped. She set the tub on the ground and swiped her hands down the front of her apron. The full impact of last night's pizza parlor reveal hit once again, and her voice wavered. This was why she tried to avoid feelings. It wasn't worth it. When did it ever pay off? Caring about Aunt Sophia had left her in grief. Caring about her father had left her dealing with endless rejection. Caring about Thomas had left her duped.

And caring about StrongerMan99 had left her betrayed and alone.

"I actually would have rather had him stand me up than him be Jude." Of all people in a sixty-mile radius of Modest. She pressed her fingers against the bridge of her nose. How had she not seen the signs before? She had never thought about Jude's middle name — not that that would have been enough to put it together. Jude Strong Worthington. StrongerMan99 was a runner . . . he used to run 5Ks, train for marathons. It was an athlete's reference. She'd thought so, anyway.

What else did she have wrong?

F-O-X.

It seemed so obvious now.

The Oreos . . . the dysfunctional family relationships . . . the new venture at work. So many clues, clicking rapid-fire into place. "I feel like an idiot." They hoisted the tub inside with them, then Nicole shut the truck door while Rory began pulling out string lights.

"You're not an idiot." Nicole's voice, soft and compassionate, threatened the dam holding back Rory's tears. "There was no way you could have known. How did he find out?"

Rory drew a deep breath as she began working through a tangle in the strands. "Let's just say our conversation didn't get that far." And it really didn't need to take up her mental space right now, limited as that space was. She had to focus on their final to-do list. She and Hannah had finished the food prep yesterday at the community kitchen, with Nicole's last-minute help and Grady's advice via FaceTime. It was crunch time. This final round was happening, ready or not.

She looked up from the Christmas lights, avoiding meeting Nicole's sympathetic gaze. "Is the steamer ready to go?"

Nicole stood and checked the device on the counter. "Yep. Grady said they'll only take about fifteen minutes to steam when we're ready, so we need to set a timer." She pulled out her phone and began tapping. "Thirty-minute window before judging?"

"That should work." Rory set the strand of lights aside and reached back inside the tub for a box of miniature ornaments.

Nicole crossed her arms. "Are you sure you don't want to talk —"

"Why don't you stir the pozole? Then we can hang the lights."

"Okay, but this is a lot to process. If you need to —"

"I'll start working on the mini tree."

Christmas in July. It'd been such a fun idea at first. Now everything seemed dull. And whenever she thought about Stronger Man99 not being on the other side of her screen to vent to later that evening, well . . . A tear slipped through the barrier and dripped down her cheek.

A knock sounded on the shut serving window.

Rory shoved away the rogue tear with her sleeve and looked up from her cross-legged position on the floor.

Jude.

She dropped the ornaments as she stood, sending a plastic ball rolling across the floor. "Are you kidding me?"

He pointed to the end of the truck where the door was and pantomimed knocking again.

Rory shook her head. No way. Not an hour before the contest. This was the last thing she needed to —

"You guys have to talk." Nicole started for the door.

"No! Not right now."

"Rory, you can't hide from him. Wouldn't it be better to deal with this before you see him in front of a crowd?"

Nicole opened the door without waiting

for Rory's confirmation or denial, and Jude suddenly stepped inside. His presence filled the small space, a mix of spicy cologne and taco seasoning drifting in with him. Rory's heart stammered a wail of protest.

"Ladies, sorry to interrupt, but I really need a few tomatoes."

Tomatoes.

They both stared at him. He stared back. Somewhere, a cricket chirped.

"Um, you know what? There's still one box of decorations left in the truck. I'm going to go get it." Nicole patted the keys in her apron pocket and nodded to herself. "Yep. Off I go."

The door slammed behind her. And if Nicole could have turned the lock, Rory would have bet the entire business that her friend would have locked them inside together.

"Tomatoes?" Rory met his gaze briefly, then turned to scoot the tub of Christmas décor out of the way. Tomatoes. So that's how it was going to be. Fine with her.

At least he had the decency to look as uncomfortable as she felt.

"I'll buy them from you, if you have any extra."

Rory whipped around, partially annoyed and partially relieved he was avoiding the elephant in the room — truck — but she hadn't expected him to be standing that close. She sucked in her breath as she looked up from his broad chest, clad in a hunter-green shirt, and eased away a step until her backside collided with the counter. "How — how many?"

Jude closed the slight distance between them. "How many do you have?"

She had no idea. He was standing too close. She tried to think of the contents of her vegetable bin and not the emotions brimming beneath the surface. She wanted to fall into StrongerMan99's arms now that he was here, in the flesh. But she also wanted to run far away from Jude, who was also here, in the flesh. It was an unnerving contradiction. She struggled to focus. "Maybe five?"

"I was hoping for a dozen. Let's just say Alton had a mishap." He shook his head.

She shrugged. "I have five. Take it or leave it."

"Sold." Jude reached up, his hand hesitating in midair, then gently swiped at a lock of hair that hadn't made it into her ponytail. "Better watch out. Health hazard."

She snapped back. "Don't."

"I'm sorry." He lowered his hand.

"For?" She crossed her arms in challenge — and defense. Unsure which made her feel safer. Right now, nothing about Jude provided any measure of security.

"I shouldn't have clued you in that way last night. It was rude. I was so shocked when I found out earlier that same day, and you were angry at me over Hannah . . . I handled it poorly."

Yes, he had. But regret reminded her that she had also.

"How did you find out?"

"The origami. You'd mentioned online about your cousin making paper art, and then when Hannah kept showing up with it . . ." He shrugged. "It just clicked. And then it seemed so obvious."

Obvious. Maybe it should have been to her too, but she'd remained blissfully oblivious. Regardless, the bubble had been popped, and now there was a mess to clean up. She took a deep breath, preparing her next words in her mind. "I shouldn't have yelled at you at the community kitchen. I'm sorry for that."

"Do you still think I used Hannah?"

"I don't know what to think." Rory tried to wrap her mind around the fact that her former reluctant attraction to Jude in person — and her current digital attraction to StrongerMan99 — were morphing into one. Like Nicole said, it was a lot to process.

And nearly impossible to reconcile the two men together. In most dating relationships, there was a slow progression of seeing the best and worst parts of someone. But with Stronger Man99 and Jude, she'd been exposed to each, separately, in two extremes.

But hadn't she done the same to him? Revealed her best character online while letting her insecurities and fear make her rude and paranoid in person?

He pressed on. "You've got to believe me. I would never do that to you. Or her."

"In my experience, people often do what they think they never will. Like betray a —"

"A what?" He lifted his chin, his turn to challenge. "What are we, Rory?"

She swallowed, her arms slowly lowering to her sides. "You mean, what *were* we."

Something indistinguishable filtered through his gaze, and he nodded slowly. "I see."

"No, you don't." She should tell him she wasn't on trial, and she sure as heck didn't need a lawyer. But her ability to explain further seemed more akin to pudding at the moment and she stared, watching the brown of his eyes turn from milk chocolate to something darker, stronger. Espresso.

She looked away. "Take the tomatoes. On the house. Consider it an honorary ribbon for losing later." She tried to smile to show she was teasing, but it probably didn't make it to her lips. And maybe she wasn't teasing. She *had* to win today. She couldn't let Jude take one more thing from her.

"Touché." Jude didn't back away. But she knew without a doubt he would have if she gave any indication that she wanted him to.

So why wasn't she giving any indication?

"Tell me this is all past tense, Rory." He reached up and skimmed the same lock of hair again, tucking it behind her ear. The back of his fingers grazed down her arm, past the end of her short sleeve, all the way to her wrist. Chills immediately broke out across her skin. "Tell me, and I'll stop."

She opened her mouth, but her lips were void of all words.

"Tell me." His voice, urgent now, almost seemed as if he were hoping she would stop him. But she couldn't.

He was going to kiss her.

He leaned in, eyes seeking permission. She had no idea what her eyes were saying back, but it apparently wasn't no. Heat flooded her chest and poured down her limbs, replacing the chills with a rush of adrenaline she thought might lift her feet from the floor. She clutched his arms to stay grounded, the athletic material of his shirt silky beneath her fingers. She hung on for dear life.

Another inch closer. His breath warm and fresh like cinnamon gum. Her stomach clenched. She was supposed to be mad at him, but for the life of her, she couldn't remember why.

StrongerMan99.

Wait. That was why. She wanted a kiss from *him* — not from this traitor who threatened her heart and her business and all the things she held dear.

This wasn't right. They were the same person, and yet, in her heart, they weren't.

She turned her head at the last minute, Jude's breath grazing her temple. "I can't." She forced her fingers to release his biceps and dropped her hands to her side, immediately missing the contact.

He hesitated, inching back just enough to meet her eyes. "Rory, I'm not . . . this isn't about —"

She pushed against his chest, and he immediately backed up two steps, giving her room to breathe. Room to regret.

And room to imagine.

"The tomatoes are in the drawer in the fridge." Surely her no-nonsense tone would cover the contradiction still spinning in her weary heart.

Jude held her gaze for a long moment, his chest rising and falling in the same rhythm as hers. The rhythm they weren't supposed to have. She wanted that kiss.

But there was someone else's she wanted more.

TWENTY

He'd gone to beg or barter for a dozen tomatoes and somehow came back with only five and a stone in his chest.

She'd rejected him.

And he deserved it.

Jude slipped back inside his truck and dropped the tomatoes on the counter. Alton was gone again, but this time, he didn't care. He needed a minute.

He grabbed a cutting board and knife and lined up the tomatoes on the counter, then began dicing the red fruit for the double-decker tacos he was making, his heart thumping an unsteady rhythm laced with adrenaline and confusion. He was wasting time mulling this over right now — the clock was ticking, his helper was MIA again, which maybe was for the best after his tomato-dropping incident, and — *whoa!* He moved his finger just in time. He was about to add his own blood to the recipe if he didn't pay attention.

Jude set the knife down, leaned over the cutting board, and took a deep breath. He shouldn't have tried to kiss her. But those big hazel eyes staring up at him during his apology had diluted his wisdom and common sense. His own shock and frustration last night at Pizza Butler was no excuse for the way he'd carelessly mishandled her heart. He walked into the room knowing a lot more than she did and having all the puzzle pieces securely in place, whereas she'd simply been waiting to meet someone she cared about.

He'd ruined it all. He hadn't allowed her the time to process the realization that he'd had all day to work through. Just now, in her food truck, he'd wanted to make up for it. Wanted to make her feel less rejected.

Instead, she'd rejected him.

He shook his head. The irony of it all was that she wanted nothing to do with him now that he was free and clear to reveal his entire life to ColorMeTurquoise.

He'd messed up — big time.

The door opened and Alton stepped inside, his expression sheepish. "I cleaned up the tomatoes I smashed earlier. Oh, cool, you found some more."

He began chopping again, more carefully

375

this time. "Salsa Street gave me some."

"That was nice of them." Alton scraped his shoe against the floor, his eyes not quite meeting Jude's despite Jude's frequent glances.

"So, where have you been? Hot date at Cluck Truck?"

Alton rubbed the back of his neck. "Yeah, I went to chat with Kimmy again after I finished cleaning. You know, wish her dad good luck and all that. And hey, I scored a free bucket of chicken wings if you want some." He held out a striped bucket with a few crispy pieces of chicken nestled inside.

"No thanks." Jude looked up again, then did a double take. "You spilled something on your shirt."

"Weird." Alton averted his gaze and brushed at the red powder covering his graphic tee. "Maybe it's from the tomato situation."

Situation was one way to put it. Alton had tripped earlier while carrying a plate of tomatoes across the truck, and while he managed to catch his balance at the last minute, the tomatoes were unfortunate casualties under his clumsy feet.

But it'd given Jude an excuse to see Rory. His chest tightened, and he stopped dicing to scoop the tomatoes into a bowl. He couldn't start remembering the way she'd felt in his arms, however briefly, or else he'd never be able to finish getting their contest submission ready. That was the last time he'd be doing that with her. The memory would have to last.

Alton set the bucket of leftover chicken on the counter near Jude. "Kimmy said hello."

He started dicing the last tomato. "So you're fraternizing with the enemy now?"

Alton frowned. "I don't know for sure what fraternizing means, but aren't you doing that too with the girl from Salsa Street?"

Not anymore. Jude cracked his neck to the side. "I was kidding." He scraped the last of the diced tomato into the bowl and began working on grating some cheese. "Look, we've got about an hour until we need to get everything moved over to the festival grounds. So why don't you —"

"Actually, I think we only have thirty minutes." Alton held up his phone, which displayed a neon alarm clock slowly ticking down. "Kimmy and her dad are already putting their displays out in front of the courthouse. Rory too, and that nice blonde lady who works with her."

No way. Jude checked his own watch, and sure enough, he'd been daydreaming about

Rory for much longer than he'd thought.

He grated faster. "You take the decorations to our table and start setting up the fiesta. Then I'll bring the salsa, queso, and double-decker tacos over in a minute."

They were allowed one entrée and two sides for the presentation, though the entrée would factor most heavily into their score. He scanned the crowded truck to make sure he wasn't forgetting anything, then quickly looked back at the cheese before he grated his knuckles.

"Will do. Then I can smash the piñata?" Alton turned hopeful eyes toward the stuffed llama in the window.

"You can smash whichever ones the judges don't want to smash for themselves." Jude pulled a plastic container full of fresh pico into easy reach, then began stuffing crunchy shells with taco meat. He gestured with his elbow toward the oven, which was keeping the chips they'd baked warm. "Take that big bowl of chips down when you go."

"Aye aye, Captain." Alton draped a festive tablecloth around his shoulders like a cape, tucked a piñata under each arm, and grabbed the bowl. He hesitated at the door. "And hey, man — I'm really sorry."

"For what?" Jude reached over to stir the slow cooker full of homemade queso. "Being late? It'll be fine. We don't want to submit cold food anyway." He also didn't want to be rushing around like this, but Alton had a crush. He remembered how it felt.

Make that *knew* how it felt — present tense.

"Yeah, being late. That's what I meant." Alton nudged the door open with his foot. "See you down there."

"If you run into Cody, get him to help you set up!" Jude hollered before the door shut behind Alton. At this point, they'd need all the help they could get.

He sprinkled grated cheese onto a warm tortilla, then wrapped the soft taco around the crunchy shell of one already stuffed. Alton was acting a little weird — but weirder than usual? Hard to say. He was a good kid. Hopefully Kimmy treated him right.

He wished he would have had the chance to treat Rory right. Maybe, once the shock wore off, like it had for him, they could talk things out. See if they still fit together. Their timing was horrible at best, but maybe . . .

He unplugged the slow cooker, finished packing up the contest supplies, and cast one more look around the truck. Then his heart sank. *Maybe* didn't exist. Because even if Rory got over the shock, even if she gave him another chance to win her heart . . . he was heading to a contest for which only one winner would be announced.

Within the hour, he would either kill her dream or she'd kill his.

"Are you serious?" Nicole leaned back in her chair and whistled, drawing more than a few curious stares from the crowd gathered by the judges' tables in front of the courthouse. The same makeshift stage from last weekend had been set back up, this time with fewer balloons. It finally looked less like a political rally and more like a festival. "I can't wait to tell Grady."

Rory gripped Nicole's arm, sinking slightly down in her folding chair in the front row, where the contestants were instructed to wait during the live judging. "Hush. Don't make me regret telling you."

"The only regret you should have is *not* kissing that man." Nicole tugged her arm free and waved her hand in the air.

"Nicole." Rory fought to keep her own voice down now. "It's *Jude.*"

"It's also StrongerMan99."

"That's the problem. It's both."

"You sort of wanted both at one point, if I recall." Nicole raised her eyebrows.

Rory looked away. "It's different now."
She shouldn't have said anything. Now she
wasn't any closer to getting Jude out of her
head than she had been an hour ago.

After he'd left the truck with the tomatoes,
she'd immediately started hauling their
Christmas decorations to the judging station near the courthouse, where Nicole had
joined her. They'd strung Christmas lights,
set up the mini tree, and plated the heated
tamales while having a hastily whispered
conversation about the near-kiss.

Now they were waiting on the judges, who
were perched at a table piled high with
Mexican food, colorful paper plates, Christmas decorations, and fried chicken stacked
inside a miniature cardboard food truck.

Jude strolled into view, pausing to take a
seat, wearing a pinched expression as he
settled into a chair at the far end of the row
they sat in, next to Alton. Rory swallowed
hard and leaned back in her seat, out of his
line of sight.

Her eyes darted to the chairs on the stage,
where the town council members sat chatting with Mr. Worthington and Jude's
brother, Warner. Maybe if she just stared
straight ahead, she could get through this
whole event with her heart — and sanity —
intact. But that depended on the outcome

of the contest.

"We're going to talk more about that non-kiss later, you know." Nicole leaned over, thankfully remembering to whisper this time.

"Fine. Later." Rory sucked in a tight breath. "Are you nervous?"

Nicole shrugged. "I think we have this in the bag, honestly. Those tamales came out fantastic, your pozole was perfect when we taste tested it this morning, and I'm pretty proud of those buñuelos Grady talked me into making."

Maybe she was right. The sweet cinnamon sugar bread Nicole had made at the last minute as their optional second side dish was sure to score them bonus points. It was another favorite holiday recipe of Aunt Sophia's, and — surprisingly — Nicole had nailed it.

Maybe they did have this in the bag.

Thankfully, the judges began lining up to take their places, and Mayor Whit headed to the microphone on stage. Rory's internal torture was almost over.

Feedback squealed through the mic, and Whit tapped it twice. "Sorry about that." He pulled it from its stand and gestured to the three judges. "Our team here is getting ready to sample all of these delicious goodies, but first, I wanted to give a round of applause to our contestants for presenting such a delightful display."

The crowd began a slow clap, and Rory's stomach twisted. This was it. Finally.

"And I'd like to give an extra show of appreciation for the contest's last-minute sponsor, the Worthington Family Law Firm." Whit led the clapping for that round, then continued talking over the din. "Without their generosity, the contest would have been indefinitely postponed."

And there was Jude's family, back in the middle of another sudden change. Was the entire contest rigged? If she had doubted it before, she knew now. She was dodging a bullet. How could Jude be trusted?

Rory watched as the judges were reintroduced to the crowd. She was unable to remember their names but recognized the same features from the previous weekend — suspenders on the male judge, cleavage on the second, and a tie-dye T-shirt featuring multiple grandkids' names on the third.

The judges took their places in a huddle around Cluck Truck's table first, and Rory sighed in relief. She hadn't wanted Salsa Street to be first.

They slowly made marks on clipboards, whispered among themselves, and bit into each item with as much concentration as a college student taking the MCAT.

Mayor Whit read from a note card as the judges continued working their way down the row of tables. Salsa Street would be last. "What's a tree's favorite drink?" He grinned at the audience as he turned the card over. "Root beer."

Everyone groaned on cue.

Rory craned her neck to try to interpret the look on the female judge's face as she sampled a taco from Jude's table. Her eyes closed. In bliss? Focus? The male judge frowned as he shoveled a big bite of a queso-covered chip into his mouth. So did Rory. What did that mean?

"You've got to calm down." Nicole slapped Rory's hand, which was gripping her arm. She hadn't even realized she'd been digging her nails into her friend's skin.

Rory pulled her hand back. "Sorry. I'm ready for this to be done."

"Why do bees have sticky hair?" Mayor Whit asked.

Nicole smirked as she whispered, "I'm ready for *that* to be done."

"Because they use a honeycomb!" an older kid shouted from the back row.

Mayor Whit's eyes widened. "Hey, you must have eaten that popsicle too."

The judges finished at Nacho Taco's table with a few more scribbles, then stopped in front of Salsa Street's station.

This was it. Rory sat up straight and fought the urge to cover her eyes. A warm breeze flapped the edge of their red tablecloth draped in Christmas lights. Thankfully, the mini tree was heavy enough to withstand the gust.

Everything was as perfect as they could have made it. With Hannah's help, the tamales had come out even better than Rory had expected — which only proved the point Hannah had made in the kitchen yesterday. Rory could cook.

She still wasn't sure what she was going to do with that information.

"Where do books sleep?" Mayor Whit didn't wait long enough for someone to steal his glory this time. "Under their covers!"

Nicole groaned. The crowd snickered. Rory studied the judges, who were slowly unwrapping tamales, taking cautious bites, and pouring pozole into soup mugs. The middle-aged judge in the tie-dye shirt bit into a buñuelo, nodding eagerly as she marked on her board.

All good signs. A bit of tension rolled off Rory's shoulders. She took a deep breath as the others finished sampling, chugged water, conferred with each other, and finally gave a thumbs-up to the mayor.

"Looks like they're ready to announce the winner!" Mayor Whit extended the wireless mic toward the row of judges as they joined him on the makeshift stage.

The blonde judge squared her shoulders and smiled. Rory half expected her to launch into a speech on world peace. "We want each chef to know this was a tough decision, and we're so proud of their hard work and remarkable entries."

Now Nicole was the one squeezing Rory's arm. Rory gripped her friend's hand with her free one, and they held on.

"Like Tonya here said, it was a mighty close call. That was possibly the best fried chicken I've ever had." The male judge grinned. "And those taters! Whew!" He slapped the leg of his jeans.

"The tacos from Nacho Taco were especially top-notch," the blonde added.

"One entry in particular was too spicy for our liking." The male judge shrugged as he leaned closer to the mic. "Make that a *lot* too spicy." He snapped his suspenders in emphasis.

"I didn't use anything spicy." Rory's hopes lifted. That eliminated one of the other contestants.

The woman in tie-dye leaned into the mic. "Personally, I was a big fan of the buñuelo. I felt like Goldilocks — it wasn't too sweet, and it wasn't too dry. It was just right."

Nicole held out her hand, and Rory slapped it in a high five. Her spirits soared into the "dare to hope" stratosphere. This could be it. Her ticket to providing Salsa Street with enough cash to get ahead — maybe even open a storefront. Grow the business. Stabilize Grady's career and protect Hannah's future. Prove she could contribute something worthwhile to her family's legacy and heritage — even if it didn't bring her soul joy.

The blonde judge handed their verdict to Mayor Whit. "Here you go. The first-place winner!"

"Thank you very much." Whit pressed the card against his chest. "Instead of reading this myself, I'd like Warner here from the Worthington Family Law Firm to do the honors. After all, whoever's name is on this card will be catering your engagement dinner." He chuckled and gestured for Warner to step up. But something didn't read genuine about the mayor's laugh — and Warner's smile looked downright catty as he accepted the mic.

"With pleasure, Mayor." He cleared his throat, then held out his hand for the card.

"Get on with it." Nicole practically squealed under her breath. "Man, I really don't like that guy."

Rory didn't either, but at this point she couldn't think straight or remember exactly why. She wiped her sweaty palms down the front of her apron, which she'd forgotten to take off.

Mayor Whit hesitated, then glanced at the card as he handed it over to Warner. Then his eyes locked directly with Rory's.

Rory's breath caught in her chest, and her mouth went dry. They'd done it. Why else would he have given her that look? With a win for Salsa Street, everyone Rory cared about won.

Except her. But all that mattered was that Aunt Sophia's legacy would remain intact.

"The official winner of the food truck festival cook-off and the recipient of the catering gig and the grand cash prize *is . . .*" Warner's voice trailed off, and his cagey smile shone over the waiting crowd. "Nacho Taco."

TWENTY-ONE

The next few minutes blurred as chaos erupted. The crowd clapped, the noise droning in Rory's ears like a mosquito she couldn't escape.

Vaguely, she became aware of Nicole's hand warming her shoulder through the sleeve of her shirt. Absently, as if removed from her own body, she observed Mr. Worthington take hold of Mayor Whit's elbow and lean over to whisper in his ear. Sudden motion caught her peripheral vision and jolted her back — Alton taking a stick and smashing a piñata dangling from a stand above Nacho Taco's table. Candy began to rain to the ground. Kids shouted and charged, shoving each other as they grabbed fistfuls of treats. The table wobbled under the sudden attack. Parents hollered instructions about sharing as Alton grinned from the middle of the huddle.

Nicole's grip tightened on her arm. "Um,

what's happening?"

But Rory couldn't respond. Couldn't take in a full breath of air. She could only stare as Jude hesitantly took the stage, his gait faltering on the riser steps, his cheeks fiery red as he accepted the mini trophy Mayor Whit held out.

He'd beaten her.

"Speech! Speech!" the crowd chanted. Somewhere behind her, a baby cried, and Rory wanted to yell along with it.

The timing of all this felt so shady. Jude knowing who she was before he let her in on the secret . . . the way he handled things at Pizza Butler . . . the attempted kiss in the food truck. And now securing the competition he'd entered at the last minute — the one his own family had commandeered along the way.

Had he known the truth of her identity longer than he'd let on?

Her thoughts raced, swirling into a chaotic, clanging mess. She'd been used, all right — in more ways than she'd ever anticipated.

She refused to let her gaze linger on Jude, even as he stared down at her from the stage. Refused to listen to whatever impulsive speech he was stumbling over as his eyes tried to send a message she refused to absorb, refused to interpret. He'd gotten what he'd wanted all along.

He'd won it all.

And she'd lost.

A congratulatory crowd pressed in on Jude, separating him from the only person he wanted to reach — Rory. It was all he could do to force a smile at the well-meaning community offering him their praise.

"Guess you found your calling, after all." Cody gave Jude a high five, seemingly oblivious to the fact that everything had just crashed down hard around him. He'd won.

Rory had lost.

How would he ever recover from that?

"Good job, man."

Before he could respond, someone else pressed up against his elbow. "Very impressive. Your tacos are even better than my mother's." Mrs. Johnson, the elderly owner of the vegetable stand at the farmers' market, squeezed his arm with strong but bony fingers.

He tried to focus on her sweet smile. "That's high praise."

"But don't tell her." Her grip tightened. "God rest her soul."

"Um, I won't." He cleared his throat. "Thank you, Mrs. Johnson. That's very kind." And creepy.

He peered over her puffy white head at Warner, who stood talking with their dad, the mayor, and the rest of the council. The judges lingered nearby. The one in suspenders had snagged a handful of the piñata candy and was munching away. Unfortunately, the blonde judge — Tonya? — looked up at the same time and caught his eye. He quickly averted his gaze, but he wasn't fast enough.

He cast a desperate glance at his friend and spoke fast. "Cody, when I give the signal — it means help."

Cody frowned, crossing his arms over his chest. "Wait. What signal?"

No time to answer. Tonya was immediately on Jude's arm, the one Mrs. Johnson had just vacated. This time, a red manicured grip held his bicep hostage instead of arthritic fingers.

"Congratulations." He was certain she was attempting to purr, but the word rolled out more like a hoarse Italian. She coughed at the end.

He pulled his arm free. "Thanks. I know everyone tried their best."

"Some more than others." She flipped shaggy bangs out of her eyes and cast him a sultry look.

Cody looked back and forth between them, obviously waiting for the signal Jude hadn't specified. He tried to think of something to say that would clue Cody in on taking over the conversation. He didn't want to talk to Tonya — or anyone, for that matter. He wanted to get to Rory. Fix what he'd damaged. Panic rose in his chest. What must she be thinking right now?

"Cluck Truck did good, but there's only so much you can do to impress with chicken, you know what I mean? And good grief, that one side dish from Salsa Street was so incredibly spicy." She stuck out her tongue, probably thinking it made her look cute rather than ridiculous. "I thought poor Maggie was going to drink that whole pitcher of water afterward."

He hesitated, tuning in to her monologue. Salsa Street — spicy? Rory didn't even like spicy food.

Tonya trailed one finger down his shirt sleeve. "I like *some* things spicy, though." She peered up at him.

Cody's eyes widened. Yeah, now he was getting it.

Jude sidestepped out of her touch and shot Cody a clear look. "Tag."

If that wasn't obvious enough for Cody to pick up that he was being passed the baton named Tonya, he didn't know what was — and no longer cared.

"I'm Cody." His friend held out his hand and flashed a smile.

From his peripheral vision, Jude caught Tonya's confused look, then she shrugged and turned her charm toward his frat brother. "Nice to meet you. I'm Tonya."

Good luck, Cody. Jude pushed past a lingering crowd of teenagers clutching skateboards and made his way to the stage. Maybe if he got somewhere higher, he'd be able to see where Rory went. See how she was handling the loss. Mayor Whit started to intercept him with a smile, but Jude just lifted one hand in a wave and didn't slow his pace. He waved off the judge in tie-dye — Maggie, he guessed — with a forced smile, nodded at the candy-eating judge in suspenders, and briefly thanked another townsperson who shouted congrats, all without hesitating. He had to see where Rory went.

Then suddenly, his dad and Warner stood before him. He stopped short.

"Congrats." Warner's face, neutral for the crowd's sake, couldn't disguise the disdain in his voice. "Well done."

"I'm sure you think so." Jude wasn't in the mood for his brother's games. But one fleeting thought registered over the aggravation and the desperate urge to find Rory — he'd done it.

He was free.

He temporarily faltered in his search.

"Now, boys." Hollis's firm voice rose over Jude's — the one that used to leave Jude cowering in his room as a child and still caused anxiety to shoot through his stomach as an adult. "Play nice."

"I don't think I have to anymore, *Dad.*" Jude used the term more to irk his father than as an endearment. To attempt to maybe, just maybe, remind him that they were family. But Hollis and Warner didn't seem to care about any of that anymore. It was only ever about what they could do for themselves. But they'd lost this one, and he'd won. "I'm a free man."

Warner scoffed. "You'll be back. You think you'll actually make a living doing this?"

"Boys, remember where you are and *who* you are." Hollis shot them a firm look. "This isn't the time or place."

"You can't just say congratulations, can you?" Jude tilted his head toward his father. "You have no idea how to handle something not going your way."

Warner snorted. "Shows how much you —"

395

"That's enough!" Hollis's firm tone still worked on Warner at least. He shot Warner a glance. "Save it for later."

"Still worried about that positive family reputation, huh, Dad?" Jude jerked his head toward the small knot of people pressing closer, obviously eavesdropping on their escalating conversation.

Hollis's face immediately transformed into a faux grin as he headed in the group's direction, arms extended wide like he was about to hug them all. "Ladies and gents, can you believe my good fortune? My own son — a cooking champion." He wrapped his arms around the two men nearest him and started slowly herding them away from Warner and Jude, like Jude knew he would.

He turned back to Warner, lowering his voice. "What do you mean, shows how much I know?" They were still up to something. They had been all along, and nothing had changed. He could read it in Warner's eyes.

"You'll find out." Warner shrugged, his face cold and callous as he stared into the crowd somewhere over Jude's shoulder.

"Why do you hate me?" The words slipped out before Jude could censor himself, before he could weigh the pros and cons of uttering them. Raw honesty, brother to brother.

"What in the world did I do? If anything, I figured you'd be ushering me out the law firm door, not hoping I lost the bet or scheming with Dad behind my back. I don't get it."

Then the mask slipped, and suddenly, Jude was standing before his brother. Not a potential politician, not a manipulative lawyer, but the same big brother who used to sneak into Jude's room at night during thunderstorms and deny it the next morning. "Because you're the golden child, Jude. You've always been."

He reeled back. "The *what*?"

"I have to work twice as hard to win Dad's approval. He's always had extra patience for you and been more lenient with you. You're the baby of the family — you get away with whatever you want."

"Hardly. I'm the one living in your shadow." He couldn't believe what he was hearing.

Warner lifted one shoulder in a dejected shrug. "Maybe you're in my shadow, but you always manage to find a spotlight. Like with this taco truck."

Jude raked his fingers through his hair. "You're *jealous*?"

Warner sighed, crossing his arms, then immediately brushed at the crease in his jacket sleeve. "When I saw your name on that slip of paper, after everything Dad and I did —" He coughed. "After everything that had been said between us and Dad . . . . you don't know how it feels. You *won*. You always win at everything."

"Warner, you're engaged. You love your job. You have Dad's favor at work. What do I have that you want so badly?"

"You have it all, Jude." Warner set his jaw. "And I end up with the leftovers."

"That doesn't make any sense."

"You're even successful in online dating, of all things." He scowled.

ColorMeTurquoise. Rory. Jude's eyes scanned the straggling crowd still loitering on the courthouse grounds. Warner's eyes narrowed. "Of course, that could all be past tense now."

Jude's gaze collided hard with his. "What do you mean? What do you know?"

Warner loosened the knot of his tie, his tone rising in pitch. "It's a small town, Jude. It's not that hard to find the truth if you're looking for it." He smirked. "Though Rory might argue with that. Poor girl."

"What?" Impossible. Warner hadn't been at Pizza Butler. How could he have put two and two together so quickly?

"Let's just say you really should log out of

your personal apps on the work computers when you're done using them."

Indignation began a slow boil in Jude's stomach. "You read my DMs —"

"You're also not very aware of your surroundings. Maybe it's a good thing you're a chef now and not a spy."

So he *had* been at Pizza Butler. Which meant Hollis had put him up to it, no doubt. "You were spying —"

"Rory deserves better than that, you know. She's a nice girl. In fact, there she is now." Warner pointed toward the edge of the parking lot, where Rory stood with her co-chef, deep in conversation. Her arms were crossed as if holding herself up, and even then her slim figure slouched.

Because of him, no doubt. Regret flooded him, dousing the anger firing through his body. He had to make it right with Rory — with ColorMeTurquoise. Would she ever let him?

Warner's cat-ate-the-canary grin made him 100 percent lucky they were still in public and Jude couldn't physically take him down. The slow boil began to roll as Warner took a few steps in Rory's direction. "I might have a proposition for her."

A muscle in Jude's jaw began to twitch. "Stay away from her."

Warner eased backward a few more steps, his hands raised in exaggerated surrender. "Of the two of us, I don't think I'm the one she most wants to avoid right now."

Jude watched helplessly as Warner pulled off his jacket, hooked it over his shoulder with one finger, and waved cockily before loping across the lot toward Rory.

"I'm following you home. I've got to talk to Grady." Rory's head spun as the sun beat down on her and Nicole in the parking lot near the courthouse. Her arms felt so heavy and fatigued, she could barely heft her purse onto her shoulder.

She set her jaw in determination. "I'll stand six feet back if he's still contagious. I'll bring chicken soup. Whatever it takes." She didn't care about mono. She just needed her brother — in person. Needed to see for herself that he was okay. That this news hadn't devastated him. That he somehow had a plan to save Salsa Street.

That he didn't think she was the ultimate failure.

Nicole rested her hip against Rory's car door and crossed her arms. A warm breeze ruffled her blonde hair. "He's upset — but not because we lost. He's worried about *you*. When I told him Jude won, and who Jude was . . . well, he started muttering in Spanish." She wrinkled her nose. "I only caught half of it, and half of *that* wasn't repeatable."

"He's got to be so disappointed. He was counting on this prize money." They all were. Rory swallowed hard as the ramifications of everything that had happened in the last twenty-four hours continued to press down on her shoulders. She couldn't even decide which burden felt the heaviest. Jude. Her aunt's legacy. Salsa Street.

They weren't in danger of shutting their doors just yet, but even with the uptick in sales from the festival, they wouldn't last much longer. Especially not with Nacho Taco stealing part of their business. Modest was too small for two successful Mexican food trucks. And the votes had been cast.

"I don't know what we made that was so spicy." Nicole shook her head. "I don't get it. We tasted everything before we submitted it. Do you think they were talking about Cluck Truck?"

"It had to be us. I remember seeing the judges chugging water after tasting our entries." A heavy rock settled in her stomach. Rory pressed her hand against her waist. "I'm sure I screwed something up."

What if her dad was right? What if she had nothing worthy to contribute?

Nicole suddenly dipped her head in warning. Her eyes narrowed. "Don't look now, but here comes trouble in Armani."

Rory turned to see Warner striding toward them across the emptying parking lot, jacket slung over his shoulder like he was about to pose for a magazine. Despite the climbing afternoon temp, not a single bead of sweat dotted his brow. His hair wasn't even mussed.

She stiffened as he drew nearer, not returning his easy smile.

"Ladies." Warner's grin wavered momentarily as they kept their straight-faced, silent stares in response. He recovered quickly and moved his jacket to the crook of his arm. "Nice job out there today."

Nicole didn't respond. Rory's heart stuttered in her chest, and all the fatigue she'd felt moments ago morphed into a fresh surge of adrenaline. "Not nice enough."

"Well, there can only be one winner." Warner shifted his weight on what looked to be brand-new leather loafers. "Unfortunately."

"Are you here to spout arbitrary facts, or do you have a point?" Nicole said, her head cocked to the side.

Rory stifled a snort of surprise at Nicole's comment.

Warner's smile didn't falter this time. "I was actually here to see Rory. I have a proposition for you."

"Not interested." She twisted around, reaching for her car door handle. Nicole sidestepped out of the way as Rory tugged the door open.

"It pays well."

Her hand stilled, but she kept her back to him. As much as she wanted nothing to do with any of the Worthingtons, the offer of a job from the wealthiest man in town might merit hearing out under the current circumstances. She felt Nicole's warning stare drill into the side of her head before she slowly turned to face him. "What's that?"

"You might not be catering our engagement party, but I've heard you're a natural at event planning." Warner shrugged. "Interested?"

She narrowed her eyes. "How'd you know that?"

Warner adjusted the folds of his jacket. "You were in the paper last year for a big party you hosted for Unity Angels." He raised his eyebrows. "I believe you have family there, right?"

Was he a lawyer or James Bond? The fact he knew all that made her even more uncomfortable. Had Jude been talking to him?

What else had he blabbed about their relationship or her personal life?

Had he been laughing at her all along?

Regardless, nothing had changed. She didn't want to attend Warner's party, much less plan it — but she had to know one thing before she walked away. "How much?"

Warner's smile returned. "You tell me."

Rory inhaled sharply through her nose. Nicole offered a warning grunt, but she ignored it. Dollar signs spun. She was being given a second chance. Maybe she could prove herself this time. Earn her place in her family tree. Make Aunt Sophia proud. Make her dad notice.

And have a distraction to get over losing StrongerMan99.

Warner slipped a business card into her hand. "Let me know your bottom line by tomorrow afternoon. We're under a bit of a time crunch, since we were waiting to see who won the contest before hiring this out. The party is in two weeks." He nodded at Nicole, then strode away.

The second he was out of earshot, Nicole grabbed her arm. "Why in the world did you do that?"

Her friend was right to be concerned. Rory was crazy to be getting mixed up in anything else that family did. The corners of the card bit into her palm as she stared after Warner, a dozen answers vying for first place in her mind. Salsa Street needed the money. She needed the victory. But one thought rang louder than the others.

"You know what they say — the enemy of my enemy is my friend."

Rory leaned forward from her perch in the worn recliner and craned her neck to see Grady's eyes. "You don't have to hold a pillow in front of your face. Didn't the doctor say you shouldn't be contagious anymore?"

"Doc said *probably* not contagious anymore." Grady's words were muffled behind the yellow-striped cushion from his position on the couch across the room. "And since it's weird enough that I got mono as an adult in the first place, I don't want to take chances and spread this to you or Hannah. Then who will run the truck?"

"Not it!" Nicole teased as she set a plate of chocolate chip cookies on the coffee table and settled onto the paisley-patterned armchair next to Grady. He rolled his eyes above the stripes. Hannah lunged forward from the straight chair they'd pulled up nearby and grabbed a cookie. "Please and thank you," she mumbled before taking a big bite.

"It seems like the issue of anyone running the truck at all might not be a problem much longer." Rory pulled in her lower lip. She'd settled on a price to present to Warner, but even if he agreed to pay it — which she had to admit was on the high end of fair — it would only be yet another bandage on a hemorrhaging wound. Salsa Street needed a long-term solution, especially now with permanent, award-winning competition in the area. How long could Rory survive under the stress of keeping multiple people — and an entire business — living paycheck to paycheck?

Grady tossed the pillow to the other end of the couch. He looked more like his old self, finally — with significantly more facial hair. Nicole had threatened more than once to shave it while he slept. "I have a bigger concern right now."

"Like the damage Jude did to Rory's heart?" Nicole quirked an eyebrow as she reached for a cookie.

Grady's eyes narrowed. "That will also be dealt with when my strength is back."

She beamed at her husband. "Good man."

"I'm glad I wasn't there yesterday." Hannah talked around her cookie, a smear of chocolate dotting the corner of her lips. "It wasn't right what he did to Rory. I would have told him that."

"You guys, I don't need anyone to scold or beat up Jude. I just want him to go away." She wanted all of it to go away — the whole horrific, mortifying turn of events. But the unfortunate fact was that she *would* be seeing Jude in the future. If not at Warner's party, then whenever she bumped into him around town. At all the food truck festivals and community events, for however long Salsa Street hung on. At the farmers' market. Everywhere.

She had to find a way to cope — with the hurt and betrayal that wouldn't leave, with the indignation that burned on the regular, and most importantly, with the deep ache of loss.

"What I meant was — Rory, you don't want Salsa Street."

She jerked her gaze to meet Grady's slightly puffy eyes. "What do you mean?"

"Face it. You're tired of Mexican food, you hate cooking, and you'd rather dig a hole than smell cilantro. It's not a good long-term fit for you. It was never supposed to be."

It wasn't that easy. Rory scrubbed her palms down the leg of her jeans. "But Aunt Sophia —"

"I think she'd agree."

Maybe. Aunt Sophia was all about family. "I wish we could know for sure." But if Aunt Sophia were still here, none of these problems would exist in the first place.

A slow look of understanding brightened Grady's face. "Nicole? Do me a favor?" He motioned for his wife to come closer, then whispered something in her ear.

She smiled and nodded. "Great idea. Be right back."

Rory frowned. "What's she going to get? A séance candle?"

Grady snorted. "You'll see."

"Ooh, a secret." Hannah bounced in her chair with a grin. "May I have another cookie?"

Rory nodded, and her cousin eagerly took another one. "Grady, what is going —"

"It's time." Grady's voice was soft but confident.

"Time for *what*?"

"The letter." Nicole strolled back into the room and pressed a sealed envelope into Rory's hands.

She stared at her name scrawled across the front. No address, just *Rory* — in Aunt Sophia's unmistakable cursive. Tears immediately pressed the back of her eyes. "What is this?"

"It was in the settlement of her will. I haven't read it." Grady held up both hands. "I have no idea what it says. My instructions were to hang on to it until the right time."

A little vague, and charmingly cryptic. Just like Sophia. Rory shook her head and smiled through the tears as she slid her finger under the flap.

My dearest Rory,
It's so cliché to write this line, since my life isn't exactly a big blockbuster movie, but I'm going to do it anyway: if you're reading this letter, it's because I'm gone.

Rory pressed her fingers against her lips. A tear dripped onto the page. She took a deep breath and kept reading out loud.

Now, stop crying.

She hiccupped-laughed. Hannah grinned wide.

I hope Grady was able to interpret what this letter was intended for, and that it is, indeed, the right time. I'm trusting the Lord to work out those details. He's perfect with his timing, even when it seems so strange to us here.

I want you to understand something. You were such a big help to me, working in the truck with Grady and keeping the business running as this sickness took up more and more of my time. You served us well, Rory. I appreciate it more than you could ever know.

I left the truck to you because it should be yours. You're "next in line" in the family name, and family takes care of family. I knew if I left the business to Grady, you'd always wonder. Wonder if you had what it took, wonder why I didn't leave it to you, wonder all sorts of dark things about your worth and value and place in the Perez family tree. While Grady is very much like a son to me, you, dear, are my daughter. Maybe a niece in blood but daughter of the heart.

But I also knew that if you chose not to keep the truck, because of your loyalty, it would be the hardest decision you ever made. Loyalty is a gift, my dear — don't turn it into a curse. I figured that you needed a season of obligation to determine where your heart really lies. That's why I instructed for this letter not to be delivered to you until you had experienced it first.

411

So now you have a decision to make. I'm sorry I can't be there to walk you through it. But hear me, sweet girl. You're a blessing to the Perez name — whether you sell the truck and start your own life or jump in with both feet and become a world-renowned chef (or somewhere in-between, which would probably involve a city-wide sweep of cilantro).

So there's only one thing left to ask. What gives you *gozo del alma*?

Rory slowly folded the letter, smoothing the creases with her thumbs. Soul joy.

What made her deeply happy these days? StrongerMan99 had. Her heart throbbed. But that was over. Her life felt like a blank slate now, and she hadn't the slightest idea what to scribble on it. And, according to Aunt Sophia, she had a choice. To fly and leave the familiar behind to someone else — someone not with the Perez name — or stick to family and duty. To loyalty and heritage and do what she'd been doing.

She needed chocolate. She grabbed a cookie.

"Sophia's right." Nicole's gentle voice eased Rory back into the living room. "This is *your* decision."

"Mother knows best." Hannah nodded somberly. "Trust me. I knew her the most."

Emotion welled in Rory's throat, and she reached across the chair to squeeze Hannah's hand. "You did. And she loved you the most."

The room fell silent, thick with memories and the sweetness of the past and the bitterness of the present.

Grady reached to adjust the pillow behind his back. "Honestly, I think losing the contest was a blessing in disguise."

Rory snorted. "Leave it to you, Grady. Sometimes the glass really is half-empty, okay?"

Nicole turned apologetic eyes to Rory. "He's still on some meds."

"I'm not doped up." He grabbed for his own cookie. "Think about it. You're good at event planning, Rory. You love it."

She nodded as she chewed. She did love it. Planning the Christmas in July theme and the decorations for the second round of the contest had been the best part of the entire event.

"And now, thanks to Worthington brother number two, you have an opportunity to plan a major society event and get back in the papers like you did last year with Unity Angels."

Rory paused.

"Look." Grady shot Nicole a cautious look. "Why don't you let me and Nicole handle Salsa Street for a bit? I'll get clearance from my doctor, or if I need to hire some help for a few days until I can get back in the truck with Nicole, we'll figure that out. You focus on the party planning for now. Give this your best shot. Then you'll be able to make a permanent decision."

The wise words sank in, along with the effect of the chocolate, and a bit of the weight she'd been carrying lifted from her shoulders. She had a chance to make a new venture work. If she gave Warner's party her all and it was a hit, she'd get the publicity and credit for it. That could be enough right there to get her career rolling in Modest and possibly beyond.

"But what about Warner?" Nicole asked.

Grady wiped chocolate from the corners of his mouth. "What about him?"

"There's no way he actually saw my article last year and thinks I'd be the best fit." Rory brushed crumbs off her jeans. "He could hire the best of the best from Dallas for this big of a party. I know he's using me to get back at Jude or something."

"So use the user." Grady shrugged.

Nicole grinned. "I like it." She reached

over and patted Grady's shoulder. "You just earned yourself your beard with that one, honey. No more shaving threats."

Grady smiled at Nicole, then turned his attention to Rory. "Who cares what his motive is?" Grady explained. "That's between him and Jude, which no longer concerns you."

Ouch. Rory winced. The truth still stung. Would it ever stop? She missed him so bad. But every time she remembered who he really was, the betrayal overrode the hurt and the cycle of emotions started all over again.

"Do the job, take the money and the glory, and move on," Grady said.

And in the meantime, she could organize and plan to her heart's content.

She pulled Warner's card from her pocket, ran her finger over the number, and took a deep breath. This was her chance. Jude probably wouldn't like her working for his brother. Which was now all the more reason to go for what she wanted. She'd invested enough of herself into that dead end.

It was time to take another leap of faith.

She drew a fortifying breath. "Okay. I'll do it."

Sunday — his day off. He wished his racing

thoughts and pounding head would get the memo.

Jude leaned down and touched his toes, his tight hamstrings protesting. One downside — perhaps the only one — to starting his own business was that he didn't have nearly as much time for his regular jogs anymore. His world had gone from incredibly structured and routine to somewhat chaotic. But it was the best chaos he could have ever imagined . . . because it was his.

He stood, then stretched his back, the words from that morning's sermon at church echoing over the incessant replay of yesterday's events. Coincidentally, the sermon had been about the same words Hannah had spoken to him on Friday morning. *"The Bible says to love your enemies."*

Or maybe it wasn't a coincidence.

The front door opened behind him, and Cody emerged from Jude's house, coffee mug in hand. He'd come over after church, offering to let Jude vent so long as they could order sushi from his favorite place. They'd eaten fried rice and salmon rolls and commiserated over women and family drama. After an hour of channel surfing, Jude couldn't stand it anymore. He had to jog. Had to release the emotions flooding his body with regret and adrenaline and helplessness.

"I still can't believe you're going to cater your brother's party." Cody took a sip from his mug.

Jude lifted his heel behind him and held it to stretch his quad. "I'm doing it solely because Nacho Taco needs the continued publicity, and if I didn't cater the party, there'd be no way to explain to the community why." What would he say? *I turned down part of the grand prize because I'm too good for it?*

His dad and brother had put him between a rock and a hard place — their favorite position to stick him. Worst part was, they knew it. He'd won the contest, and he *still* wasn't totally free and clear of their influence. It was maddening, at best.

And it'd cost him Rory.

He squeezed his eyes shut against the wave of ache that threatened to envelop him and cracked his neck. Much better — a pain he could control. "At least this thing will be over in a couple weeks, and I won't have to see either of them again until Warner's actual wedding."

Cody set his mug on the porch table. "When is that?"

"I didn't even know they were engaged,

417

so I'm guessing at this rate I'll get a sticky note delivery from the firm's runner the morning of." Which was fine with him. If it wasn't for Maddison, he wouldn't even go. But the sweet young woman deserved all the moral support she could get before officially joining ranks with his family.

Love your enemies . . .

Easier said than done. Jude planted both feet on the porch and bounced up on his toes. Maybe if he kept moving, the conviction would move along too. "Ready to go?"

Cody held up a finger and took one last drag of coffee. Gross. Jude tapped his foot as he waited. And suddenly, he didn't want to jog anymore. He'd been running long enough. He wanted to do something truly productive.

He wanted to show love.

Not to Warner. Not yet. Maybe he'd never be that mature. But he could do something for the one who had advised him to do so. For now, that would have to be enough.

Jude snatched the mug from Cody's hand. "Grab your keys. We're taking a detour."

Knock, knock.

Rory sat up straight in her armchair, blinking fast. She must have dozed off. Her novel was propped open on the floor, as if

418

it'd slipped from her fingers, and a quick sip confirmed that the remainder of her tea on the end table was cold. She shuddered at the taste.

Knock, knock, knock.

So she hadn't imagined it. She stood, feet tangled in the teal throw blanket she'd been using, and attempted to smooth the frizzy sides of her messy bun. It was probably Nicole stopping by for another pep talk, knowing Rory had officially accepted Warner's offer. She shoved up the sleeves of her baggy sweatshirt and opened the door.

Mayor Whit stood before her, wearing a somber expression and holding a single — and slightly crumpled — pink rose.

Rory braced one arm against the doorframe. "Mayor?" She squinted. Sometimes drinking lavender tea late at night gave her weird dreams. Maybe she was still asleep.

"Good evening." He shuffled his feet against her porch mat, and the sound grated in her ears. Nope, he was really standing there, dressed in a short-sleeve button-down that looked as if the wrinkles had been ironed directly into the material, his trademark Swatch perched above the hand clutching the stem of the flower.

"This is a surprise." She waited, assuming he'd reveal the reason for his impulsive visit.

Instead, he nodded. "It is for me too."

Rory tilted her head, and Whit twirled the flower between his fingers. Seconds ticked by. She hesitated, then finally took a step backward. "Do you want to come in?"

He nodded, head down, and stepped inside. He stood in the corner as if afraid his shoes might contaminate her needing-to-be-swept-anyway floors. She shut the door, then turned and leaned against it, crossing her arms over her sweatshirt. Maybe this was something else about the contest. But why the flower?

Regardless, he didn't seem ready to talk yet. "Would you like some tea? I was about to reheat mine."

"No thanks." He shifted his weight awkwardly. "I came to ask a question."

"Okay." She straightened a little. "Shoot."

"Well, I did shoot, and I missed."

Rory raised her eyebrows.

"This is for you." He shoved the flower toward her and she reached for it. Then he took a step back, nearly bumping into her foyer bench. He sat down quickly, as if that had been his intention the whole time.

"Thank you." To make him feel better, she joined him on the bench, holding the rose. The pale petals were lovely and soft beneath her touch, though already a little wilted. The flower looked like it'd been through a lot — and so did Whit, for that matter. His mussed hair seemed as if it'd survived multiple rakings over the last hour, and his socks didn't match.

She pasted on a smile that hopefully hid her confusion and exhaustion. It'd been the world's longest weekend, and she didn't have the emotional energy for guessing games. "What's the occasion?"

Whit bounced his knee up and down. "Does pink mean friendship?"

"I'm not fluent in flower color meanings, but I think so." Rory shrugged. "Or maybe it means gratitude."

"I'm in love."

Rory's eyes widened, and the rose suddenly felt like fire in her hands. She resisted the urge to toss it back at him and swallowed hard. "That would be a red rose."

"Not with you."

She let out a breath she didn't know she'd been holding. "Oh." She stopped the words *thank goodness* from leaving her lips and instead waited for further explanation.

"Would you go with me to Warner's engagement party?"

Further explanation was apparently not coming.

Whit looked at the rose, then gave a firm

nod. "Yes, I think pink means grateful. Because I'd be really grateful if you went."

Rory laid the rose in her lap and held up both hands. "Whit, I was napping when you knocked, so I don't know if I'm a little dazed still or what but —"

"I'm so sorry I woke you." He stood so fast, the bench wobbled and the rose rolled off her lap and onto the floor. "I shouldn't have come."

Rory grabbed the flower as she stood next to him and gently touched his shoulder. He flinched like he'd been shot. Oh, man. Whit was quirky, but this level of anxiety and nervousness was high — even for him.

She put aside her own issues and held his searching gaze, willing him to calm. "I'm going to make you that tea, okay? And then we can talk."

He looked from side to side, as if spies were lurking in her living room, then slowly nodded. His gaze turned hopeful. "Peppermint?"

She let out a sigh of relief. "Coming right up."

"Do you see her?" Jude stuck his head into the colorful media room at Unity Angels and then pulled back into the stark white hallway, raising his eyebrows at Cody.

"I don't know who we're looking for," Cody stage-whispered back, pressing in close to Jude as he pretended to comb the room with exaggeration. "That might help."

Oh yeah. Cody and Hannah had never met. He scanned the room again, his eyes flitting over the tables where several young adults played various board games, past the big-screen TV where a video game character hopped and collected coins, and over a bank of computers with mini partitions in between until he finally caught sight of a familiar figure bent over a stack of brightly colored paper at a table in the back. "There she is."

He hitched his laptop bag higher on his shoulder and started toward her, but Cody grabbed his arm and held him back. "Are you ever going to tell me what we're doing here?"

"You'll see." He motioned for his friend to follow, then strode toward Hannah, earning a few curious stares from a table of puzzle workers.

Hannah didn't look up as they approached, just continued folding the thin, colorful sheets into intricate designs. A tiny turtle, goat, and rabbit already sat perched by her stack of paper.

"Hey." Jude smiled, waiting for her to look

up, but she didn't. *Fold, fold, crease.* "Remember me?"

Cody nudged him in the side. Jude shifted his weight. "This is my friend Cody. Cody, this is Hannah."

She looked up then, pausing to reach over and matter-of-factly shake Cody's hand. "Nice to meet you." Then she went back to work.

Fold, fold, crease.

Cody raised his eyebrows at Jude, and Jude shrugged back. He'd assumed he was interrupting her train of thought, but something about the rigid line in the young woman's shoulders made him consider there was more to it than that.

"I had an idea I wanted to share with you." Jude pulled out the chair next to her, and Cody took the one across the table.

She stiffened a little but kept folding.

He set his laptop bag on the table. "Do you want to hear it?"

Finally, she set the sheet of paper down and looked at him, tucking her hair behind her ears. "You hurt my cousin's feelings."

Ah. There it was. He nodded slowly. Hannah was a straight shooter, so he would be too. "I did. I'm sorry."

"Have you told her that?"

"I tried."

424

She began folding again, her tone growing more patronizing. "Should you try again?"

Cody smirked, then immediately rubbed his chin as if yawning. Jude shot him a glare before answering. "I don't think she wants to talk to me right now."

She paused midcrease. "That part is her fault, then."

Hannah was a wise woman. And he really wanted to help her, no matter what Rory thought or did. "Do *you* forgive me?"

She nodded. *Fold, fold, crease.* "I have to."

"Because you want to, or is it part of that love your enemies command?"

Hannah tilted her head, as if considering. The video game bleeped in the background as he awaited her verdict. It really mattered to him, and not because of her connection to Rory. It mattered because she was a kind woman with more depth than most, and she'd already taught him a lesson he'd been a long time in learning. He wanted her to think well of him. Wanted her to understand his side and his motivations.

He couldn't get into all of that, obviously, but somehow, he knew if anyone could sense the truth, it was Hannah.

She finally nodded. "Both."

He breathed a sigh of relief. "I'll take it." If Hannah could forgive him, could Rory?

It wasn't nearly as simple or direct with her. The betrayal went deep. But maybe Hannah would talk to her for him . . .

No. One look at the row of origami animals popping up before them, and Jude knew he needed to stick to his original mission. It wasn't fair to put Hannah in the middle by asking her to sway Rory on his behalf. He refused to use either of them that way.

"It's not your fault you won the contest." She pointed out the obvious as she kept folding.

"I'm not sure Rory sees it that way. My family's involvement . . . it looks iffy, at best, I'm sure."

"Your timing with Rory has been the worst," Hannah said. "And that's not her fault."

Was it really this clear-cut for her? If so, he needed lessons in how to think likewise. All he could see was a muddled mess. "I don't think she'll forgive me for threatening her family's business."

"You might be surprised." *Fold, fold, crease.*

It almost sounded like she thought he just wasn't trying hard enough. "I tried to talk to her before the contest. I apologized for how rude I was when I let her know who I was at the pizza restaurant on Friday night."

At this point, Cody was looking back and forth between them like he was watching a tennis match. "Go on." He grinned.

Jude rolled his eyes.

Hannah watched him, her serious expression reminding him this wasn't a joke, even if it was to Cody. "How did you apologize?"

"He tried to kiss her," Cody said.

Jude popped his friend's shoulder with the back of his hand. "It wasn't like that."

"Maybe it was like that to Rory," Hannah offered.

He opened his mouth, then shut it. He couldn't exactly explain that she'd almost kissed him back.

Thankfully, Hannah prevented him from answering. "I know that if I felt betrayed and used, I would want someone to tell me they didn't mean it and do what they could to fix it."

He'd tried that. She hadn't wanted to talk it through any further. She'd made that clear by her rejection in the food truck. She wasn't ready. And after he beat her at the contest, she'd never be. She'd assumed the worst about him before he'd ever had a chance.

He let out a short breath. "If only it were that simple."

Hannah quirked an eyebrow. "People think I'm simple. But I think they just make things complicated that aren't."

"Hey, man, this lady is wise." Cody pointed at Hannah. "I'd listen to her."

"Thank you. You may pick one." She shot Cody a wide smile, and *there* was the Hannah that Jude had expected when he first approached — the sweet grin, the generous spirit, the reserved enthusiasm lighting her narrow brown eyes as she gestured to the paper wares.

"Cool." Cody plucked the turtle from the table.

Jude leaned in a little closer. "Can I tell you about my idea now?"

"Yes, you *may*. Just remember, visiting hours are over in forty-five minutes."

A stickler for the rules. He could work with that. Jude briskly rubbed his hands together in anticipation. "Great. Cody, my laptop, please."

Cody made a show of sliding the bag Jude could have reached for himself across the table.

Jude unzipped it, then hesitated. "We might need to get one of the staff members to help."

"That's fine. But first . . ." She handed him her latest creation — a heart.

428

With a jagged folded line down the middle.

Cody's eyes widened.

Jude accepted it carefully, unsure if he should admire the crisp lines or be worried about its meaning. "What's this?"

"A reminder about Rory." Hannah pointed at him. "For you to try harder."

Whit stirred his tea with a candy cane Rory had dug out from her leftover Christmas candy stash in the junk drawer. "So, will you go with me to Warner and Maddison's party?" His face suddenly crumpled a little, and he coughed into his elbow.

"I'm actually going to be there as part of the staff." Rory ran her finger over the edge of her teacup.

"Staff? Are you cooking, after all?" Whit looked as confused as she must have when he showed up at her door with a "friendship" flower, which was currently lying on the table between them. "Don't tell me you and Jude are pairing up to cater together."

Rory nearly sprayed her tea. She pressed her fingers against her mouth, swallowed, then shook her head. "Warner asked me to plan the event."

"That's fresh." Whit stared into his cup. "Of course he did."

429

Her heart stammered. "What do you mean?"

"I'm in love with Maddison." He lifted his gaze, and the sincerity pouring from his eyes was like something from a classic romantic movie.

"Oh, Whit." She leaned over and touched his hand, her worry about the party disintegrating. "I'm so sorry." Poor guy. No wonder he'd been stumbling all over the place lately — and no wonder he'd looked like he was about to burst into tears when he said Maddison's name.

"That's what I meant by I've already shot and missed. I missed my chance, and now it's too late."

"Have you told her how you feel?" Rory asked.

He averted his eyes. "Yes and no."

"So mostly no."

"Yeah, mostly." He shook his head. "But she's cut my hair for years. We'd gotten pretty close — as much as you can during a twenty-minute haircut, anyway." Then he closed his eyes, and Rory half expected a montage of salon visits set to a soundtrack to suddenly appear on her kitchen wall. "I was eventually going every week instead of every other week because I needed the excuse to see her."

430

"That's really sweet."

"So you have to be my date." His eyes flew open and locked with hers. "I can't go to her engagement party alone and watch her on Warner's arm. And I don't know of anyone else in this town who would be willing to be a fake date." He lifted his shoulders in a sheepish shrug.

A fake date sounded fantastic compared to a real one. And showing up alone to a party where Jude was also on staff, well . . . that sounded much worse than the alternative of going with Whit.

Rory nibbled on her lower lip, then smiled. "I'll do it."

Whit lit up. "Are you sure?" He sobered. "Because you can keep the flower either way."

Rory snorted back a laugh. "I'm sure." A rush of empathy swelled in her chest. She understood the feeling of love unrequited. And, most recently, of love betrayed. Maybe it'd be a good distraction for them both.

She gave him a comforting tap on his forearm. "For the record, Maddison doesn't know what she's missing. You're the sweetest, most considerate guy I've ever met."

Whit's expression grew guarded. "Thanks, Rory, but remember, that rose wasn't red."

He tapped one of the petals. "Gratitude only."

She hid her grin with her teacup. "Right, right. I won't forget." Apparently, his self-esteem wasn't as bad as hers.

"We'll have fun at the party." He stood, scooting his chair in against the table. "Just don't fall in love with me. I doubt I'll ever get over Maddison."

"Thanks for the warning." Rory walked her new friend to the door, not even protesting when he got into his car still holding her teacup, and stood on the porch as she waved goodbye.

And it was only after he'd already driven away and she'd locked the front door that she realized he'd never explained what he meant when he said, "Of course Warner did."

TWENTY-THREE

Neat rows of tombstones stretched across the rolling cemetery grounds. Rory hung back a few paces while Hannah carried a fresh bouquet to her mother's gravesite.

SOPHIA PEREZ — WORLD'S BEST MOM. That'd been Hannah's choice of engraving, and she hadn't been wrong.

Rory blinked back the burn of tears as Hannah crouched in the short grass and began chatting with Sophia as if she were still there and could hear her. Rory and Hannah had talked often in the last year about where they believed Sophia's spirit was — namely, that it wasn't in a wooden box six feet below. Hannah understood heaven, understood her mother's faith that she'd made her own as an adult — but she told Rory she just liked to talk to her, sort of like a phone call if she'd still been alive. It made her feel better.

It made Rory feel better too. She'd treasure that last letter from her aunt for the rest of her life.

Rory turned her face up to the afternoon sun and half listened as Hannah chatted about her latest drawings. Despite the July humidity, a gentle breeze wafted through the low-hanging branches of a nearby tree, which offered a patchy respite of shade. But the sun warmed her bare arms and made her feel lighter than she had all week. She gravitated toward it.

It'd been six days since Whit showed up at her front door. Six days since she'd agreed to plan Warner and Maddison's engagement party. Six days of endless scrolling, pinning, and sketching table centerpieces. Everything was coming together seamlessly. She couldn't be happier.

Except for the lingering reminder that she was alone. No more DMs. No more text messages. No more giddy, late-night chats surrounded by daisies and twinkle lights.

". . . turns out Jude's a pretty good guy."

Rory jerked her attention back to Hannah, who was continuing on with her "phone call." Had she said Jude's name, or was Rory somehow hearing her own thoughts?

"He came by Unity Angels the other day. It made me happy."

Jude had gone to Unity Angels? Was that another step in his scheme to get to her through her cousin? After all, he'd been mentored by the best in manipulation.

She started to interrupt Hannah for answers, then shut her mouth when she noticed the delight in Hannah's eyes and her animated gestures as she continued to verbally process the last few weeks. Jude was Rory's problem, not Hannah's. It wasn't Hannah's issue to get mixed up in, and honestly, until the big engagement party was over, Rory didn't know if she could handle any more negative truth.

So she stepped into the shade, crossed her arms over her chest, and sat on a patch of grass.

Alone.

Jude laid a single yellow tulip on the headstone marked EMMA L. WORTHINGTON and ducked his head for a moment. Hollis paid for regular professional flower deliveries to the gravesite, but as far as Jude knew, his dad hadn't been by in years to visit personally. The landscaping was neatly kept, the mounted black-iron bouquet holder filled with fresh daisies.

Daisies. *The friendliest of flowers.* Best he could remember, Grandmother had always liked them too. Though as a self-proclaimed green thumb, she loved most flowers that offered color and required sunshine. He couldn't stand the thought of no one putting a personal touch on her grave marker periodically, so he tried to come by every few months.

Sometimes the urge to talk to her welled up inside, but he felt foolish. He knew she wasn't there. But he still longed to feel connected to a member of his family who wasn't totally selfish and conniving. He wished he'd had more years to know her — more years for her influence to rub off on Warner and Hollis. Grandmother might have been born of the same stoic, unaffectionate, overly dignified Worthington stock, but she'd had faith. Integrity. And character.

She'd have liked Rory.

The thought hit him hard, and he blinked rapidly as he stared at the tulip lying on the headstone. "I messed up." He swallowed, realizing the futility of talking to a granite marker. But saying the words out loud — be it to himself, to a gravestone, or via prayer — made him feel better. "I lost one of the greatest women I've ever met."

He hadn't known Grandmother well enough to understand what she'd advise if she were still alive or if she'd even listen to his sob story. More than likely, she'd have put him to work in the flower bed. Jude knelt by her tombstone, feeling the warm, sun-soaked grass through the thin knees of his faded jeans, and began to pull rogue leaves from the stalks that the landscaper had missed.

"Pretty sure she's still mad at me too. I didn't take Hannah's advice to try harder yet. You'd probably tell me I'm being a coward if you were here." He plucked a stray weed growing by the tombstone next to Grandmother's, then surveyed the mass of dry leaves in his hands. Crumbled. Broken. He sighed, then dusted it all back into the grass.

"But I just have this sense that Rory isn't ready. The Rory I knew online was so hesitant to change, so slow to trust. This isn't going to be something she bounces back from fast. I can't rush her."

He'd rushed her to meet. If he'd waited, would anything have been different? He still wanted to kick himself every time he thought about the way he'd accepted the photo swap notification and practically shoved the truth in her face.

So many what-ifs. And now he'd never know.

What was he even doing anymore?

He rocked back on his heels. His own family schemed against him at every turn. He was about to cater an engagement party for his brother, whom he'd recently punched in the face. And he had won enough of a cash prize to consider opening a storefront or investing in some major truck renovations — via money his own father had funded with the original intention of making sure he lost.

Now, without his favorite confidante and cheerleader — Color MeTurquoise — rooting him on, it felt meaningless. What was the point of success if it couldn't also come with the joy of knowing she was only a text away?

Without the hope that one day, she'd be only a couch cushion away?

Sudden female voices broke the stillness of the cemetery. He twisted around, still kneeling, and caught sight of a familiar pair walking up the hill to his right. Hannah and Rory.

Panic rose in his chest, along with a mix of elation and fear. Part of him wanted to jump up and wave — she'd *have* to talk to him now — and the other part wanted to duck down low and hide behind the granite marker.

Hannah saw him first, her smile big and

genuine. Rory's steps faltered, and her expression matched the mass of feelings rushing through his body. Which one would win out?

He slowly stood, smiling at them both, hoping it wasn't as wobbly as it felt. "Afternoon, ladies."

Hannah hurried up and gave him a side hug. "We were visiting my mom."

"I was visiting my grandmother." He gestured to the tombstone.

Hannah's face immediately sobered with respect. "I'm sorry for your loss."

"I'm sorry for yours." They shared a smile.

Rory silently hung back — out of reach — her slim arms crossed over the front of a loose blue tank. Turquoise. He met her gaze, and she immediately looked away.

A million words and explanations pressed to the surface, demanding vocalization, but he couldn't decide which to start with. He also didn't know if she'd want to discuss any of it in front of Hannah.

Yet this was his big chance. Rory was standing directly in front of him, where she'd *have* to hear him out. He'd be a fool to let the opportunity pass him by.

He opened his mouth, then hesitated. *I'm sorry I handled this in the rudest way possible. I'm sorry my incredibly dysfunctional family made all this worse.*

Nothing felt adequate.

And, by the firm clench of her jaw, she didn't seem to be in a place to hear anything. His instincts had been correct.

"Be right back." Hannah darted in the direction they'd come from. Rory called after her, but the determined young woman kept marching forward as if she were on a mission, hair swinging around her chin.

Rory reluctantly faced him, rubbing the grass with the toe of her white Converse. "How's business?"

So they were going straight to that. Jude shifted his weight, keeping his gaze on a tombstone instead of Rory's rigid posture. "It's solid. We've been really busy since the contest." He swallowed hard, unsure if the next part would go badly or not. "You?"

"I'm on a break from Salsa Street this week. Nicole and Grady are handling the truck."

"Grady's back?"

"Finally." She looked at him, then away. "I've been working on some event planning."

"That's great." A sudden burst of hope filled Jude's chest. If Rory was leaving the food industry and starting a new project, could that mean there was a chance she'd

440

forgive him after all? Maybe her losing the competition opened a new path — one she'd love even more. Hadn't they had so many conversations about that online? A bubble of pride rose to the surface. She was going for a new dream. That took guts. "What are you planning?"

She lifted her chin. "Your brother's engagement party."

The words punched his stomach with all the effect of a solid right hook. "Warner's party?"

"He asked me last weekend."

So that's why his brother had rushed to Rory in the parking lot after the judging. All Jude's planned apologies fled his thoughts. "And you're going to do it?" He wasn't sure if he was more surprised or angry. Betrayed. All three. Why would Rory do anything for his family after she knew all they'd done to him? When she knew how untrustworthy they were?

"Are you still catering?" She cast him a pointed look.

"That's different. I'm obligated after the win." He hated to remind her of her loss, but he couldn't believe she thought it was the same thing. "The community expects me to be there. They wouldn't understand me just not showing up."

"How incredibly selfless of you." Rory rolled her eyes.

He started to remind her about Maddison, about not being willing to abandon her when she was innocent in all these family ploys, but then Hannah appeared, huffing back up the hill, her round cheeks pink.

Rory glanced at her, then back at Jude. "Not all of us have the luxury of ignoring a trail of dollar signs."

He stabbed his hand through his hair in frustration. "It's not about the money."

"Maybe not for you." Tears coated her eyes, and she blinked twice. "You had your reasons for needing this win, and I had mine. But your problems are solved — you're a free man, assuming any of that stuff you told me was true. My freedom is a little more costly."

Jude hesitated. "Your freedom? You're not going to keep Salsa Street?"

"Salsa Street might not give me a choice. Sales are down, largely thanks to you."

Jude flinched.

"If the only way out of this mess is to help your brother, well, at least he's offering help." Rory sniffed. "I would appreciate it if you didn't judge my choices when I have so few of them." His burst of anger fled, leaving behind an aching, gaping hole that once again reminded him that his ColorMeTurquoise — his *Rory* — wouldn't be there for him later. And never would again.

Her voice cut cold and hard across the distance between them. "Was any of it even real?"

He wanted to reach for her but knew how well that'd go over. His arms ached to hug her, to start over, to somehow go back and redo the chain reaction of his mistakes. And yet some of their obstacles weren't his fault, as Hannah had pointed out. He wanted to explain, but the words twisted and died on his tongue.

"It wasn't my fault I won." He winced. Great. Of all the choices that existed, those were the words that came out? He held up his finger at her sharply raised eyebrows. "I just mean, the contest wasn't rigged, if that's what you're thinking."

She shook her head. "You don't want to know what I'm thinking."

"I do." His voice softened, and against all his better judgment, he reached for her hand. "It's all I want."

"Don't. Don't be compassionate and sweet. Don't be like StrongerMan—" Her voice broke.

The pain doubled. "Rory, I —"

She shot him a look as Hannah drew

nearer, effectively shutting him up. "Not right now."

He watched with a lump in his throat as Hannah stooped over and laid a rose on his grandmother's grave, next to the flower he'd brought. "There." She dusted her hands with pride. "Now the tulip isn't lonely."

Well, that made one of them.

TWENTY-FOUR

Rory grimaced as the spike of yet another miniature cactus found a new home in the pad of her thumb. The centerpieces were coming together perfectly, though — as long as she didn't accidentally draw blood and drip it on the white tablecloths.

The late-afternoon sun spilled her shadow across the table as she straightened it, tucking the LED battery pack out of sight under the edge of the cloth. So far, her intended design was blooming to life as vividly as the tiny blossoms on the cacti. The fiesta-themed party — with an elegant twist — had to be just right. Because, once again, her entire future career rested on perfecting the details of a single event.

How did she keep getting herself into these situations? Oh yeah — money.

Even after reading Sophia's letter, she still wasn't sure what to do. Knowing she had Sophia's blessing to choose was one burden lifted — but that didn't make the decision itself any less risky. What if she chose to stay in the food truck industry and regretted it? What if she branched out and sought her own career and failed? And what would Grady do if she sold Salsa Street — or it went bankrupt?

There was still so much to work out in her mind, and it all seemed to depend on the success of this one party.

She shook off the negative thoughts. For now, she just wanted to enjoy this space, this chance to work hard at something she truly liked and see the fruit of it grow before her.

And inhale air most definitely not tainted by cilantro. She breathed in appreciation.

"This looks so wonderful." A soft voice sounded behind her.

Rory turned, one arm draped with the next strand of twinkle lights ready to go on the adjoining table, and smiled her gratitude at Maddison. "Well, that's a relief to hear — since your opinion is the only one that matters today."

"Actually, that's probably Warner's. He paid for it all." Maddison wrinkled her nose as she crossed her arms over her pink zip-front hoodie. She'd already done her hair up in loosely pinned curls for the party, which would be starting in about two hours. Rory cast a quick look around the expansively landscaped backyard at everything that was left to do.

"I won't keep you," Maddison said. "I just wanted to say thank you for all your hard work."

"I'm happy to help."

Maddison was sweet. And she was marrying Warner — whose opinion tonight *did* matter, despite Rory's contrary words to the bride-to-be. Except it mattered for entirely different reasons, though there was no need to get into that.

Or into how in the world Maddison was about to marry a guy as spoiled and conniving as a Worthington.

Rory winced. Although hadn't she come a little too close for comfort herself? She glanced across the yard to the wrought iron gate that led to the front circular driveway, where Nacho Taco had parked about an hour ago. Where Jude cooked even now, preparing the catered menu for that night.

She sniffed. Maybe she did smell cilantro.

Maddison lingered, as if there was more she wanted to say. Rory waited quietly, arranging the next strand of lights and fluffing the peach tulle around the centerpiece until it looked the way she'd envisioned.

"You have a gift." Maddison ran her finger carefully over the tablecloth. "This is better than anything I could have imagined. It's like a fairy tale in the desert."

"Thank you." Rory stepped back to admire the table beside her. "That's a great way to put it — desert fairy tale." The mint-green-and-peach color scheme went perfectly against the white tablecloths. She'd done it.

Well, almost. She glanced at her watch. She still had to get home and shower and change before Whit picked her up for their nondate.

Seemingly oblivious to her time crunch, Maddison continued to ramble. "Jude has a gift too. His tacos are amazing — I think it's some old family recipe of theirs."

Rory's stomach tightened. "Actually, it's an old recipe of their former housekeeper."

"Oh, really?" Surprise dotted Maddison's face. "Warner said it was a family recipe. He must have been confused."

Or, more likely, trying to take some level of credit for something he hadn't been involved in. Rory bit back the accusation. It didn't matter.

Maddison suddenly pressed her fingers against her lips. "I'm sorry. I didn't even think about pointing out Jude's talent." A sudden pink flush tinged her cheeks. "You're just so good at this" — she gestured to the tables around them — "I forget you were a chef before too. I forgot he was your competition."

"Don't worry about it." If only Rory could forget the entire last couple of months. She'd thought Thomas had hurt her last year, but that was nothing compared to the wound Jude had inflicted.

She rolled in her lower lip, allowing herself to feel what she rarely took time to acknowledge — and even more rarely was willing to admit. Two emotion-filled facts.

One, she'd never loved Thomas.

Two, she'd completely fallen for Stronger-Man99.

An image of him filled her mind — his flirty text messages and banter, the daisies in an Amazon Locker, the encouragement and support in all his DMs. The way he sought her advice, reciprocated with his own, and pursued her heart.

But if she was going to remember those things about Stronger Man99, she also had to remember the way *Jude* had betrayed her. The way he'd used her and then tried to use Hannah to get to her. The way she couldn't quite trust him. The way he'd acted with her heart that night at Pizza Butler.

The way he seemed to have no idea what it was like to live in a world that wasn't already paid for.

Rory took a deep breath and forced a smile at Maddison as she finished the table's finishing touches. This was why it was better to keep her feelings stuffed neatly away, like candy inside a piñata.

She couldn't afford to break.

People in Modest really liked tacos.

Jude handed off yet another plated taco setup to Alton, who placed it on the giant serving tray and paused to straighten his plaid bow tie. "How do I look?"

Like Mayor Whit. Jude smiled. "Dapper. Now go, before those get cold."

Jude stirred the new vat of salsa he'd made, then paused to take a deep breath. The truck air, stuffy and laden with the scent of garlic and onions, was stifling in the evening humidity.

They'd been at it for hours already, prepping, cooking, serving. While a hired waitstaff doted on guests, refilled drinks, and kept appetizer trays of nachos (Alton's suggestion) circulating, Alton had taken it upon himself to dress up in slacks (that were an inch too short for his gangly legs) and a dress shirt, complete with bow tie, to try to look the part as he ran trays back and forth from the truck to the backyard party.

It felt weird to be catering a party in the backyard of the expansive, ultramodern two-story home Jude had grown up in. Like a kind of backward prodigal situation, he was on the outside seeking his own path while his family partied inside without him. He knew in one sense, if he changed his mind and came back to the law firm, his dad would welcome him with more than one figurative fattened calf — though considering his dad's poor diet lately, there might be a literal one too.

But despite the ache in Jude's lower back and the steady throb in his feet, he had never felt so accomplished. Feeding the masses, working for himself, producing something physical with his hands that benefited people and getting paid to do it — with zero games and manipulation along the way — was worth every sore muscle and Epsom salt bath it took.

Not all law offices operated in shady ways, but the Worthington Family Law Firm did. And even if for some reason Jude lost the truck tomorrow, he wouldn't go back. Couldn't. Not now that he'd tasted freedom and seen the full extent of the lengths his family would go to in order to get their way.

How were they treating clients if this is how they treated their own flesh and blood?

He didn't want anything to do with any of it. Which made his big decision yesterday especially difficult to make. But the worst part was, he couldn't talk it over with ColorMeTurquoise — with *Rory* — anymore.

Alton returned with the empty tray just as Jude finished prepping the next several plates. Jude needed fresh air. And if he was being honest, he needed to see Rory. Wanted, needed. Same thing.

Working to keep his expression casual for Alton's sake, Jude reached for the tray. "I'll trade you this time. Why don't you box up the next few plates, and I'll deliver these?"

"You're the boss." Alton scooted aside to make room for Jude and the wide tray to exit the truck door. "Besides, I owe you."

Jude hesitated at the bottom of the truck stairs, the tray balanced on his shoulder, and turned back to look at Alton. "What do you mean, you owe me?"

Alton's eyes widened, and he immediately began to spoon rice onto a taco-filled plate. "You know, for letting me work for you. I'm sure Mr. Worthington would have fired me by now. I was a bad runner."

"I'm glad you're here." Jude shifted under

the weight of the tray. He genuinely meant it. The kid was a big help — when he wasn't flirting with Kimmy from Cluck Truck, anyway. "You're doing a great job."

Alton didn't inflate at the compliment as Jude had expected he would, but he did nod briefly as he continued to hyper-concentrate on the food in front of him. Weird. But that was Alton.

Jude toted the tray through the gate and into the backyard, where the party rocked in full swing, and stopped short at his first glance of the event. He'd been stuck in the truck for the past several hours and had no idea what Rory had managed to create.

She was an artist.

Sheer peach and mint-green fabric draped over white tablecloths, with miniature cacti and tiny floating candles forming graceful centerpieces. Tiny golden piñatas were tucked among the material, and a smattering of gold sequins dotted each table. Balloons in the same color scheme were tied in bunches near the slightly raised stage, where a dusky-rose carpet hosted the instruments for one of Warner's favorite bands from Dallas. The bar provided mixed drinks, a giant bowl of gold punch, bottles of sparkling water, and several multitiered stands of cupcakes — complete with mint-green frosting and edible flowers.

It looked like an autumn desert had blossomed to life and offered to host an elegant gathering.

He started toward the bar draped in twinkle lights to set down the tray and pass off the plates to one of the servers, but Maddison, looking very bride-to-be in a sleeveless white dress, immediately intercepted him.

"Warner's not here." Her eyes were wide and her makeup slightly smeared like she'd been tearing up.

"What do you mean, he's not here?" Jude set the tray on the bar and scanned the crowd as if his brother would magically appear. Surely he'd just stepped away for a minute, schmoozing a potential client or touching up his hair in the guest bath. But then, had he even seen Warner's BMW pull up outside yet? Jude frowned. At this point, he couldn't remember seeing his father either.

Despite the warm evening air, Maddison rubbed her hands up and down her bare arms. "He's late. He was supposed to be here forty-five minutes ago."

"Knowing Warner, his favorite suit was wrinkled." Jude touched Maddison's elbow. "He'll be here. Get some punch and wait it out." He gestured to the bartender, who poured her a glass, popped an umbrella in it, and then passed it over the bar.

"If you say so." Maddison accepted the cup, her brow furrowed.

"I know Warner. There's no way he'd miss this." Mostly because he'd paid for it, and because Warner never missed the opportunity to be in the spotlight or receive credit for something. "I better get back to the truck."

He turned, and then, like a cheesy romance movie, the crowd parted to reveal Rory, beaming and beautiful, a proud smile on her lips as she surveyed the party around her. Her long dark hair, usually in a ball cap, flowed down her back and over the strappy shoulders of her — he swallowed hard — *turquoise* jumpsuit. Cream-colored heels made her taller than usual, almost as tall as . . . Mayor Whit?

He blinked, but the image of Rory with her arm through Whit's and her head tilted back and laughing, shiny earrings swinging, didn't change.

Jealousy created a slow burn in his stomach. When had that happened? How could he . . . How could *she* . . .

No. He had no one to blame but himself.

Maddison suddenly gripped his arm. He

glanced at her just in time to see her face wash white. "There's Warner."

Jude sighed in relief. One crisis averted. He patted her hand. "See? I told you he'd —"

"Time to pa-aa-aa-rty!" Warner, hair mussed and sport coat wrinkled, lifted his beer bottle in a toast as he strode through the crowd. The people nearest him cheered.

"Let's do this!" He pointed to the band, who broke into a rousing song on cue.

"Be drunk?" Maddison finished Jude's sentence.

If it'd been in any other circumstance, Jude would have started streaming live for social media to see prim and proper Warner completely undone. But he wouldn't do that to Maddison, and besides, Warner was embarrassing himself enough for everyone. Jude grimaced as Warner took the mic from the lead singer and pointed to Maddison.

"We're getting married," he said, slurring his words.

Maddison lifted one hand in an awkward wave as everyone rallied around her, raising their glasses and chanting, "To the bride and groom!"

Rory caught Jude's eye across the yard, and his breath hitched. He started to mouth a compliment to her about the party, but she looked away, missing it. He clenched the tray, unsure what to do first — go to her or get his drunk brother off the stage. The crowd seemed to be enjoying this looser side of Warner Worthington, though, and the taunts and cheers kept coming.

Rory's gesture of tipping her head toward Warner decided for him, and he quickly handed the tray off to Maddison. "Be right back."

"Stop!" Warner yelled, and Jude halted in his tracks halfway to the stage.

"In the na-aa-ame of love . . ."

Jude rubbed his palm down his face, cast Maddison a helpless glance, then looked back at Rory. Her unease was tangible, practically pulsing in the air around her, but the rest of the gathered group of friends and community were singing along.

"Let it go." Maddison's cool grip on his forearm stopped any further attempt. "He would rather embarrass himself this way than us make a scene."

Jude was pretty sure Warner's off-key wails qualified as making a scene, but he resisted arguing, using Alton's line instead. "You're the boss."

He shrugged at Rory, who briefly closed her eyes, then plastered back on her public smile. She tilted her head up to whisper to

457

Whit, and Jude's chest constricted as Whit tilted his head down to listen.

Apparently, there were now *two* scenes he wouldn't be making.

Twenty-Five

Jude tried to get Alton to take the next round of plates to the party, but the kid had found his groove in the food truck, timing himself as he raced to plate tacos and chop more onions and tomatoes. "I've got this, boss."

That made Jude the delivery boy. But he didn't want to see Rory again, not on Whit's arm. Not looking so beautiful and happy — without him.

Jude set the full tray on the bar and kept his eyes downcast as he started to line up the plates for the waitstaff. Music pulsed in the background, the bass drum thumping a rhythm in his chest. He wouldn't look at anyone, and hopefully he just could pass the tacos over to the servers without running into Rory or —

Mayor Whit materialized at his elbow. "I'm in love."

Jude tried to school his features into

something that looked like he was happy for Whit, despite the fact that his fists clenched and his heart cracked. He crossed his arms over his chest. "Are you, now?" His heartbeat roared in his ears. That seemed soon. *Really* soon. How many dates had they even squeezed into the last week?

But how long had it taken *him* to fall for Rory? Both in person and online?

She made it possible.

Whit turned to the bar, bracing his arms on the tall counter. He raised his voice over the music. "I should have said something sooner."

Or not at all. Jude tried to say congratulations, but all he could think to ask was, "Do you know her favorite color?"

Whit tilted his head, as if considering. "I think pink."

Wrong. "It's turquoise, man." He tried again as the crack fissured deeper. "Do you know her preferred flavor of tea?"

The mayor pointed his finger like a gun at Jude and grinned. "Trick question. She *loves* coffee — caramel lattes." He squinted, then nodded with confidence. "No whip."

Glasses clinked as the bartender cleared the counter near them. Jude shook his head. "Wrong again. Green tea. And sometimes she drinks lavender in the evenings." Like when she used to sit around and chat with him on DM. Thinking back to those quiet conversations and now being able to visually place Rory on the other side of the monitor twisted Jude's heart into a hundred coils.

"Tea? Really?" Whit looked genuinely confused, which gave Jude a rush of both hope and frustration. If he didn't even know the basics of Rory's favorite things, how invested could he really be?

Whit scooted slightly closer to Jude, making room for two of the paralegals from the law firm to approach the bartender. "The last time she cut my hair, she was drinking a large caramel latte. I'm sure of it."

"She cut your hair?" Jude frowned. Why? Whit went to Maddison like most of the rest of Modest. The thought of Rory running her fingers through Whit's mop of hair made him want to systematically throw all the glasses in the bartender's portable sink against the side of his dad's house.

Whit waved off the offer from the lady to his left to get him a drink, keeping his attention riveted to Jude. "Of course. She has for a long time."

Now it was Jude's turn to be confused. He shifted his weight and gestured to Whit. "You're in love with . . ."

"I know, I know. Saying it out loud makes it worse." Whit groaned, reaching up to rub the back of his neck. "She's your brother's fiancée, after all."

"My brother's —" Jude swallowed, the words choking and dying in his throat.

Whit wasn't in love with Rory. He was in love with Maddison.

Relief performed a tap dance through his stomach, loosening the anxiety-ridden knot and leaving him with a burst of adrenaline he didn't know what to do with.

But Whit looked downright miserable as he twisted around, placing his back against the bar. "I understand if you need to deck me — for your brother's honor."

Jude held up both hands and chuckled, a deep laugh born of being suddenly freed of a thousand pounds. "First of all, this isn't the Wild West, and secondly, my brother wouldn't know *honor* if it bit him in the —"

"Look at him. He doesn't deserve her." Whit pointed to the stage. Jude turned, but watching his brother and Maddison play tug-of-war with the microphone wasn't registering on his list of priorities. If his brother wanted to make a fool of himself at his own engagement party, that was on him.

Jude only had one clarification on his mind.

"So you're saying you're not here with Rory?" He had to make sure.

Whit looked back from the stage. "Well, technically, I'm here with her. As in, I drove her. And she's technically near me, which is with me, I guess." Whit looked around, then shrugged. "She was, anyway. But no, we're not here together. Together in the sense that *you* mean together, I mean. We're together as in, I'm her ride home."

Jude clamped his hand on Whit's shoulder. "Maybe not for long."

Heart pounding, he released the mayor with a promise to be right back. He'd have to address the whole "being in love with Maddison" thing — after all, Whit was a friend, and his friend was obviously hurting and in a bad place. But there was something that had to be done first.

Something he'd started to do weeks ago.

Something that couldn't wait a minute longer. He might have lost his first chance with Rory — and his second — but he wasn't going to wait around and watch someone else find theirs.

He pushed through the throng of people, darting around a woman in a purple blouse who was gesturing with her champagne glass, and nearly smacked into a serving tray laden with nachos. He dodged the makeshift

463

dance floor near the stage, craning his head for a flash of turquoise.

Then he found it. Found her.

Rory stood away from the crowd near the back row of empty tables, her arms crossed, tapping one high-heeled foot in time to the music as she surveyed her handiwork. A slight smile played around the edges of her lips. She was proud of herself. And she should be.

He was proud of her.

He closed the remaining space between them with a few long strides, his breath as heavy as if he'd just navigated a raging river current. He stopped directly in front of her. "I have three things to say to you."

A guarded expression immediately spread across her face. "Oh?"

Upon review, that probably wasn't the most romantic way to start, but here he was. He cleared his throat. There was no going back. "One — you did an amazing job tonight. The place looks fantastic."

The rigid line of her shoulders eased a little. "Thank you."

Deep breath. "Two — I know you're not here with Whit."

Rory's crossed arms fell to her sides and her eyes widened. "Technically, I'm —"

"Three." He tucked his hands on both sides of her face and kissed her.

Fireworks shot through the sky, but Rory hadn't ordered any.

She kissed him back. Time stopped. Colors exploded.

Despite her wedge heels, she pressed up on her tiptoes to get closer, her hands gripping Jude's biceps as if he alone were responsible for keeping gravity in effect. Jude's thumbs grazed her cheekbones before he slid his hands into her hair, cupping her neck, and pulling her closer as his mouth danced with hers. Just the way she'd always imagined with StrongerMan99 — and just the way she'd never quite let herself imagine with Jude.

She wasn't sure if she broke for a breath first or if he did, but then they were kissing again, his arms guiding her three steps backward until her hips rested against a round table. His hands skimmed her shoulders, ran through her loose hair, then trailed down her arms as he continued to kiss her. Her hands splayed across the width of his broad back, and she dug her fingers into his dress shirt, inhaling his now-familiar and comforting scent of spicy cologne and tacos.

All the reasons she knew this was a bad

idea fled her mind as he paused to graze a kiss across her jaw and up her cheek. Jude was the enemy. But StrongerMan99 wasn't. He was *hers.* And she found his lips again and kissed him like there was no going back.

Because in her heart, she knew there wasn't.

Her cell rang from the pocket of her jump-suit.

The melody jolted her, and she pulled back, breathless, her heart stammering an unsteady rhythm as the chiming notes continued. She pressed her tingling lips together as she fumbled for her phone, unable to look away from the spark lighting Jude's eyes. The one she was certain her own gaze reflected right back.

She glanced at the caller ID, then shot him an apologetic wince. "It's Hannah. I have to make sure she's okay."

"Of course." Jude gestured. "Go ahead." He took a breath and raked his fingers through his hair as if composing himself.

She knew the feeling. She smiled and stepped aside, holding one finger up to Jude. Her legs shook like she was entering another portal of time and space. She wanted to go back to the other realm. The one where only she and StrongerMan99 existed.

She smoothed back her hair and swiped the answer button. "Hannah?"

"Great news, cousin!" Hannah's excited voice filled Rory's ears, bringing immediate relief that it wasn't an emergency.

But now she had nothing to distract her from Jude's careful gaze, the way his riveted attention held her captive despite his respectfully stepping a few yards back to give her privacy. Her cheeks flushed, and she gripped the phone tighter, turning slightly away to focus on Hannah. Her stomach tingled, and she tried to focus. "The admin staff said *what*?"

"They said the next full year of my tuition has . . ."

Her cousin's voice was lost in the din around her. Rory pressed her free hand to her ear to drown out the party and walked a few more steps away. "One more time. Talk loud."

Hannah dramatically overenunciated. "I can stay for two more years. For *free.*"

Rory turned her back to the party and hunched over the phone. "For free? Are you sure you didn't misunderstand —"

"Someone paid it," Hannah said. "The staff said they were anonymous."

Joy and confusion battled for top bidding

as Rory's thoughts raced. Who would have —

She whipped around. Her eyes met Jude's. He smiled, oblivious to the tumble of her heart.

No. Not him. But who else could have afforded it? And he *had* just been to the facility . . .

But why?

It was a pity move. It had to be. She squeezed her eyes shut. No, he cared. That kiss . . . She touched her lips. He had meant it. This wasn't a gesture of "poor you." This was a gesture toward Rory. To show that he cared.

Then why did it make her so uncomfortable?

Rory shook her head, feeling suddenly like she was on a carnival ride that wouldn't stop. Too many ups and downs. The last three minutes hadn't felt real, and this didn't either. She struggled for clarity. "The staff didn't say anything else about it?"

Hannah hummed in the back of her throat. "Something about the donor mentioning that it was all for a pretty girl?"

Rory glanced back at Jude across the expansive yard, over the sea of happy guests and half-empty champagne glasses and tables littered with taco crumbs. Nausea rose in her stomach.

He'd been trying to win her back.

He caught her eye and mouthed the words *everything okay?*

She only offered a wobbly smile, unsure of her answer. A pretty girl. Was that all she was to him now? Just like Thomas. Just like before.

No. Jude was different.

Then why was *that* his confessed motivation for leaving the donation for Hannah? He was using her family — again. He hadn't donated out of love or care for Hannah, for Hannah's sake. Only to get to Rory.

Always being used. Always the pretty face. *"Sit there and look pretty."*

But she'd done so much more tonight. She'd created this entire desert fairy tale with nothing but her own ideas and Warner's credit card. She'd given the guests a night to remember and the soon-to-be bride and groom an elegant masterpiece of a party. She'd proven herself.

Would it *ever* be enough?

Hannah was still talking, but Rory hadn't heard the last twenty seconds of it. She tried to tune back in, something about a website . . . Rory nodded, even though her cousin obviously couldn't see her, and swallowed back a round of tears. She couldn't pretend any longer. "Hannah? I'm sorry, I've got to go. Something came up. I'll call you later."

Her cousin cheerfully said goodbye and disconnected the call.

Rory slid her cell back into her pocket, trying to compose herself as her mind sprinted into marathon mode. She widened her eyes to stop the sting of building tears and took a deep breath. But the negative tidal wave wouldn't stop.

The microphone squealed with feedback. Rory's gaze jolted to the stage, just as Warner started hopping up and down to a rousing rendition of the Backstreet Boys' "Bye Bye Bye."

Rory dragged her fingers under her eyes for any remnants of smudged mascara. She'd have to wait and confront Jude later — she couldn't make a scene at the party. Maddison clearly had enough on her plate.

TWENTY-SIX

Rory had vanished.

Jude turned a slow circle by the table, but Rory's familiar turquoise was nowhere to be seen. He'd been looking right at her, soaking her in, relishing the memory of her in his arms and willing her to come back so they could talk out the details. Fill in any remaining holes between them that needed to be addressed, then move forward — preferably with more kissing.

But Warner's pitchy rendition of "Bye Bye Bye" had distracted him, and now she'd disappeared. Hopefully Hannah was okay. If it'd been an emergency, surely Rory would have called or texted him. He checked his phone one more time to be sure. No missed messages. Maybe she'd darted for the stage to do damage control, which honestly, he should probably be doing too.

He was just so tired of constantly trying

471

to make his family appear better than they were.

Speaking of control, where in the world was his dad? No way would Hollis Worthington stand by while his son humiliated "the family name" with bad karaoke. Jude turned and searched the crowd the other way. He was probably hiding in a corner somewhere, eating Jude's tacos where he didn't have to admit he liked them.

"You've got to do something." A strong, slightly clammy hand gripped his arm.

Jude sighed. Speak of the —

"Your brother is humiliating the family." Hollis's thick brows furrowed over his nose in indignation.

Jude crossed his arms, aggravated that the joy Rory had left in her wake was already being doused. "Well, why don't you join him, Dad? Make it a Worthington family tradition." That'd be the day.

"Not a bad idea." Hollis's dark eyes narrowed. "Not me, of course. You." He nudged Jude toward the stage. "Get up there and salvage this."

"Not a chance." Jude braced against the push, then stepped aside. "Besides, Maddison can handle it."

Apparently at some point after Warner and Maddison's earlier mic scuffle, the band had

472

given way to a DJ and karaoke. Warner now had his own lapel mic, which meant he didn't have to keep fighting Maddison for the real one. But that also gave him more confidence — and freed both his hands to hold more alcohol. Not good.

"I wouldn't be so sure about that." Hollis pointed to Maddison's downcast expression as she flipped through a laminated leaflet of karaoke choices. She wasn't having fun. Maybe he *should* step in . . .

No. That was just what his dad wanted. Besides, if Jude intercepted a drunk Warner, it'd cause a much bigger scene than the one his brother was creating for himself. Warner would never allow Jude to give him orders in public.

Jude pulled an empty chair out from the table near them and gestured for his dad to sit. "Where've you been, anyway?"

"I know you're trying to change the subject." Hollis adjusted his tie and frowned, ignoring the chair. His face, partially shadowed under the strings of twinkle lights and tiki torches, waxed pale. "I've been around."

Sure he had. Drinking? Eating nachos against his doctor's orders? Jude narrowed his eyes. He was hiding something, whether it was yet another shady secret or a pocket full of cupcakes.

"You need to go get your brother." Hollis was using his lawyer voice now, but it wasn't as firm or as loud as usual. Of course, that could be because of the new song beginning — "Bohemian Rhapsody."

Jude bit back a groan. "Warner is responsible for Warner." He cast a pointed glance at the stage as Warner tripped over the words. "If he's doing something you don't like, you know you can always fix it yourself."

"It'll look more natural if you do it." Before Jude could protest, Hollis steered him a few yards closer to the chaos.

Then they both stopped short as Warner's angry voice rose over the music. "If you don't know the words, don't bother singing." He scowled at Maddison.

She lifted her chin, speaking quietly, her hand covering the mic.

Warner didn't give her the same courtesy. He shoved past her toward the stairs, nearly knocking her off-balance in her high heels. "Forget it! I'm out of here," he slurred as the music abruptly stopped. "Just sing a solo, since you're so perfect."

Jude stepped past Hollis and hurried to intercept his brother. Warner stumbled down the risers, barely catching himself as he strode toward the bar. Jude grabbed his arm, keeping his voice low. Several guests averted their eyes and gave them a wide berth. The bartender wisely poured a club soda and passed it to Warner as the DJ started playing a new song — sans karaoke.

Ignoring the fizzy water, Warner perched on a barstool and rubbed his hand down his face. "I knew that song. She messed me up."

"Forget the song, Warner. What's going on? You never drink this much." He assumed. He actually didn't know much about what his brother did on his own time away from the law firm, but he'd never seen Warner lose control like this. The Warner he knew would never let himself be embarrassed or caught looking less than perfect in front of a crowd.

"I'm not drunk. I'm relaxed." His words slurred again.

Jude nudged the soda closer. "Drink that."

"You're so bossy." Warner belligerently crossed his arms. "Just like Dad."

Jude snorted. "I'm nothing like Dad."

"You're right." Warner picked up the soda. It sloshed over the side of his glass, and he cursed as he dabbed at his wet slacks. "You're not like Dad. I'm like Dad."

He couldn't tell if Warner was being

sarcastic or serious — or if he was bragging or commiserating. "I'm going to need more context."

"Me and Dad. We're never wrong, you know." His brother plucked the lime wedge from his glass and chomped into it. Jude winced, but Warner didn't even seem to notice the sudden burst of sour. "These lemons are bad."

"It's a lime, Warner."

"That's what I said." He shook his head and slammed down the cup. "Now what was I saying?"

"How you're never wrong."

"Right. We're never wrong. But you're perfect. And we're not perfect."

Jude sighed. "No one's perfect, Warner." He wasn't. One only had to look at how he'd handled things with Rory to know that. Not to mention how he'd handled things with his own family over the years. If he'd taken the steps to secure his future before this, he wouldn't have needed the contest or the bet or any of the things that had hurt Rory. They could have been on the same team much sooner rather than stuck in this endless competition.

Even now, post-kiss, he didn't know where they stood or where she had gone. Was the kiss enough to fix all the gaps between them? Or was it merely a blissful distraction from the inevitable?

Movement by the stage caught his attention — a group of Maddison's friends gathered around her, casting furtive glances toward Warner. He was going to be in big trouble after that immature exit — and Warner deserved every bit of it.

Jude jerked his attention back to his brother before Warner could flick the now juiceless lime wedge at the bartender. "Why were you being such a jerk just now — and why were you drinking before the party even started?"

Warner let out a long sigh. "I needed to relax. I was nervous."

Feedback from a mic squealed through the speakers at the stage. Warner barely seemed to notice. Jude moved the club soda out of his brother's way. "About what?"

Warner tapped his fingers on the bar, a little of the buzz fading from his eyes and leaving weariness in its wake. He propped his head in his hand. "Getting married."

So that was it. Jude twisted on his barstool to fully face his brother. "Maddison's good for you, Warner. She's sweet and really cares about you. She'll be a great wife."

Warner scoffed. "She's also ditzy and small town."

Jude briefly closed his eyes. "Warner."

"What? Not everyone is cut out for life in *Modest,* Texas." Warner slung the word like it was a curse. "Some of us might be destined for bigger and better things."

Jude sighed, ignoring the bartender rapidly gesturing at them. This wasn't the time for a refill. "And are you? Destined?"

"I'll never know, if I'm stuck here." He scowled. "Like you can relate. You're free and clear to sell your stupid tacos now. You won the contest, despite everything we —" He stopped.

A cold, hard fist pressed against Jude's chest. "Despite what?"

Feedback squealed again from the stage, and the crowd moaned. Warner lifted his chin. "Despite Dad talking Alton into sabotaging your final entry."

Sudden silence fell over the party.

Jude's heart thundered in his ears. "He *what*?"

Dad . . . Alton . . . he couldn't wrap his mind around which betrayal to process first. Sabotage how? With what? He'd won. Obviously, whatever plan they'd come up with hadn't worked. But what —

"Hey, man." The bartender draped his arms over the bar in front of Warner, his eyebrows furrowed. "Been trying to tell you — your mic is still on."

Rory had never fully understood the expression "could have heard a pin drop" until the moment Warner confessed over his lapel mic to a party of roughly fifty-five people that his fiancée was ditzy, he was too good for his own small town, and their father had stacked the odds against Jude.

"What?!" Warner's shocked voice filled the mic, followed by a muffled scuffle.

Rory stilled alongside the throng of people as all eyes shifted to the stage. The DJ yanked a cord from the control board, and the erratic sound of Warner's panic abruptly ceased. Whispers and pointing fingers led everyone's attention to the bar, where Warner slowly stood from a stool, clutching the counter with one hand. Jude stood next to him, his face grim.

Everyone stared. Rory's heart thumped hard against her rib cage. What had Alton done? And how could he do that to Jude — his own partner? Or had he . . . Jude had won, after all.

Nothing made sense.

She caught Jude's eye across the yard, saw the pain reflected in his gaze, and for a moment he was StrongerMan99 again, confiding in her over a screen.

"I know what's it like to wish you could be different in certain areas of your life or personality — and feel helpless to accomplish it."

"I feel like I should warn you before we meet — I do have faults."

Her heart twisted as time seemed to still, as if it were as stunned as the party guests. StrongerMan99 and Jude were still very much two different people in her head and in her heart. And, apparently, in real life. Who was the real Jude Worthington? The one she'd encountered a hundred times over text and chats? Or the one who followed in his family footsteps and used people to get what he wanted?

To get her.

Silence pulsed another millisecond. Then pandemonium erupted.

"I object!" Hollis's loud voice filled the shocked silence as he strode through the crowd toward the bar, shoving chairs out of his way. One was overturned onto the plush grass, knocking a centerpiece off-kilter on its descent. The jar with the floating candle tipped over and spilled onto the fabric Rory had so carefully arranged. "That didn't happen!"

The DJ took that moment to blare a new song, something hard rock Rory didn't recognize. But it was too late. The damage had been done.

Maddison, who'd been standing near the risers leading to the stage, was blushing a deep red against the white of her dress. Rory automatically reached out toward her, as if she could offer any form of comfort from yards away. A young redheaded woman standing near her touched her arm, but Maddison shook her off, head high, as she walked stiffly toward the front gate, her back a rigid line.

Warner called after her, his voice slurred and frustrated. Jude grabbed his arm to stop him.

Mayor Whit whipped off his bow tie and tossed it to the ground, then took off in a jog after Maddison.

And Hollis, halfway to the bar and face purpled with rage, took two more steps and collapsed.

TWENTY-SEVEN

"No update yet." Jude shoved his hair back as he paced the worn floor between the waiting room and the nurses' desk. Despite the steady flow of air-conditioning from the vents above, the hospital felt suffocating. His *shirt* felt suffocating. He undid the top button and took a deep breath.

Warner didn't open his eyes as he grunted acknowledgment from a plastic chair in the waiting area, his hem untucked, legs sprawled askew.

The longer Jude watched him, the angrier he became. All this was his brother's fault. And he was going to sit there and let it play out without any concern for their own father? After the commotion at the party . . . the ambulance and the sirens . . . the whirl of flashing lights the whole way to the hospital in Tyler.

Jude kicked the leg of his brother's chair.

Warner's eyes flew open. "I'm dealing with

a slight headache here, do you mind?" He squinted, his eyes red-rimmed and weary.

"I've been dealing with a very particular pain in my rear for a long time now because of you, so let's call it even." Jude kicked the leg again, harder. "Do you even care that Dad very likely just had a heart attack?"

Some of the color drained from Warner's face, and he slowly sat upright. "Of course I care."

Jude sank into the mint-green plastic chair next to Warner, his anger deflating. The last thing they needed was to get kicked out of the waiting room for fighting. "I don't understand."

"I do. Dad eats horribly." Warner shuddered.

"Not the heart attack." Jude reached over and used the remote to mute the TV mounted by the ceiling. The sudden silence after the blare of an eczema cream advertisement was bliss to Jude's over-stimulated ears. And he wanted Warner's full attention for this. "Us."

"What do you mean?"

"Our family. Dad can't be happy for me — he has to use my own employee against me to sabotage my chance at winning?" When he said it out loud, it sounded even worse than it felt. "And it was winning a bet that *he* made, no less."

"You know Dad never makes a bet he can't win."

He did know. Or should have known. That was why Hollis was such a sought-after lawyer across the entire state of Texas — he never lost. Except this time. "But he didn't win."

"Not because he didn't try."

Which led Jude to his next question. "What did Alton do?"

Warner blew out a breath, then winced, reaching up to pinch the bridge of his nose. He had to have a killer migraine after all that booze. If Jude had been a better person, he'd probably have brought him coffee.

Right now, he was not that person.

"Dad told him to put some ground ghost pepper in your entrée. Make it too spicy to eat."

Spicy . . . Jude sucked in his breath as the memories of that afternoon resurfaced. Of the judges chugging water. The one judge pointing out something was almost too hot to eat. The one side dish that pushed his entry into the winning position. "Rory."

"Yeah, apparently Alton screwed it up and somehow got it in hers instead." Warner snorted. "Which is typical. That kid never could manage to file a memo in the right folder."

Jude gripped the arms of his plastic chair, clenching his jaw as he fought to control his anger. Did Alton really try to go through with it? He couldn't imagine loyal, hard-working Alton stooping to that level of wrong. Alton was clumsy at times and had his distracted, teen-boy-in-love moments with the chicken truck girl, but overall, there was no way. Something else had to have happened.

Though Alton had been acting a little strange the past few days — apologizing like crazy, changing the subject, working extra hard in the truck.

Like he owed Jude something.

Jude swallowed back a wave of disappointment. It was true. Somehow, Hollis had gotten in the guy's head. But that wasn't even the worst part. "Do you even realize the irony? If Dad had left well enough alone, Salsa Street could have won. Him trying to hurt me backfired and contributed to my winning — and to Salsa Street losing."

"Definitely ironic." Warner smirked. "Shame."

It was more than a shame. It was Rory's livelihood. It was her family's business. The anger boiled up and over, streaking adrenaline through his veins. He clenched his fists and ground his teeth. "You two are the worst."

"Me? What did I do?"

Jude exploded from his chair, standing over Warner. He barely remembered to keep his voice down. "You didn't stop him. In fact, you probably helped him brainstorm it."

Warner sniffed. "I did not."

Jude couldn't tell if the pink tint on Warner's cheeks was from lying or sweating out alcohol. "Should I keep going on with what you *did* do? You showed up late and drunk, publicly humiliated yourself, and bashed your fiancée at your own engagement party."

"Sure, fine, I made some mistakes." Warner sat up straight, his red eyes narrowed. "Maybe I'm not Mr. Perfect, but at least Dad is on my side on this one."

"Right, *your* side. How accurate. It's always been you two against me, hasn't it?" Jude stood, pacing the area in front of the wide coffee table. He wanted to scream. Wanted to get out of there. Wanted to stop caring about it all.

But on some deep level, beneath all the hurt, he also really wanted to know his dad was okay.

"I, um, thought you two could use some coffee."

Jude whipped around. Rory stood at the edge of the waiting room, still in that silky turquoise outfit, dark hair pouring over her back. She held a small carrier with two lidded containers, her expression hesitant.

A million emotions jumped to the surface, but the one that won top bidding was a heavy roar of guilt. His family had ruined things for her — and there was nothing he could do to fix it. Nothing he could say to explain it.

Nothing he could do to earn back her heart.

"Thank you. I can't believe you drove all the way here." He accepted the coffee, briefly debating throwing Warner's cup at his hungover head, then settled for shoving the cup into his hand.

Rory shifted her weight in her heels. "It's no problem. I figured you guys were a little scattered and could use the caffeine."

Was that the only reason? Was she simply being a good community member, a caring friend . . . or something more? The cup warmed Jude's hands, and he couldn't do anything but stare at her and wonder.

"Any update on how he is?" She glanced down the hall, as if somehow that could answer her question about Hollis's condition.

Jude shook off his self-inflicted trance and took a sip of his coffee, appreciating the slightly bitter taste — and the reality check — as it slid down his throat. "Not yet. They were running a bunch of tests. We know he's stable for now but have no idea what really happened yet or why."

She nodded, her gaze darting from his eyes to Warner to the cardboard carrier in her hands. Jude took it from her and set it on the table, but now she looked more awkward, running her hands up her forearms as if unsure where else to put them.

He knew where he wanted her to put them — around him. Every portion of his body ached to enfold her into a hug, breathe in the scent of her hair, absorb the comfort of the woman he'd poured his heart out to piece by vulnerable piece over the past several months.

But that woman had been betrayed. Of all the times she'd assumed wrong about him in the past, this was one betrayal he couldn't deny.

Warner slumped back in his chair with his coffee, grabbing the remote on the way and turning the volume back on. The sudden blare of a cheesy sitcom grabbed Rory's attention, and Jude took the quick opportunity to memorize the curve of her jaw, the sweep of her long lashes against her cheekbones, the way her hazel eyes set off every inch of her skin and hair.

But more than that — more than the second-glance, head-turning beauty she so often tried to hide — was the woman he'd fallen for online day by day. The caring, considerate, insecure, understanding, clever woman who had brought him more comfort, more laughs, and more connection in these last few months than he'd had in a lifetime of relationships.

Now there'd be no more turquoise sightings. No more kisses. She would never forgive him — or his family — once she knew the details of what his dad had done and how it had backfired on her. With their off-again, on-again truce history and current unstable trust status, he was already coming in at a negative. No way she'd believe he was innocent in all of it.

He hated the anticipation. He wanted to get it over with, rip off the Band-Aid.

Jude stepped a few feet forward, ushering Rory toward the far end of the room at the front of the hospital. A nurse in red scrubs scurried past, clipboard in hand, followed by another pushing a cart full of medical equipment. "I'm sure you heard Warner's . . . confession . . . at the party."

Rory nodded, rolling in her bottom lip. "I think everyone did."

He hesitated. "Is Maddison okay?"

"I couldn't find her, and I didn't see her car." Rory shrugged. "I took care of a few things, then came here to check on you . . . on your dad." She cleared her throat. "Your father's housekeeper said he'd handle cleaning up and locking the gate once everyone left."

"Thank you for seeing to that."

Rory nodded stiffly. "That's my job."

Silence pulsed between them, almost as tangible as the chemistry still demanding Jude sweep her up.

"Look, about the kiss —"

"There's something you need to know —"

They broke the awkward silence at the same time, making the situation even more awkward. Rory gestured to him with a slight laugh that sounded forced. "You first."

Time to rip off that Band-Aid. Jude fortified himself with a sip of coffee. "The part Warner said about Alton sabotaging . . ."

Rory raised her eyebrows.

"He was supposed to put ghost pepper in my entry." Jude tightened his grip on his coffee cup. "But he put it in yours."

Rory's expression blanked. "In mine?"

"The judges mentioned how one of the entries was too spicy to eat. Whatever my father told him to do . . . it backfired."

He stepped back as a doctor in a white coat bustled past.

Nothing. No response. He still couldn't read her expression. Maybe she wasn't understanding him. "Rory, you lost the contest because of me. Because of my family."

A flicker then, in her eyes. A tightening of her jaw. She got it now.

Another doctor with a bristly beard and wire-rimmed glasses hustled up to Jude. "Mr. Worthington? Your father would like to see you and your brother."

Warner jumped up, joining them. At the same time, the nearby emergency room doors slung open, and several paramedics rushed a gurney into the room. Rory stepped back, away from Jude, and pressed against the wall as the harried team passed through a set of automatic double doors.

"This way, please." The doctor gestured with a kind but abrupt hand and motioned for them to follow in the opposite direction.

Rory stayed out of the way, giving Warner and Jude space to follow the physician down the beige linoleum hall. Jude allowed himself one painful backward glance as he rushed after the doctor's long strides.

She was gone.

There wasn't enough lavender tea in the world to come down from this night.

Rory pressed her fingertips against her temples, staring at the blinking cursor of the DM she'd been composing and deleting, composing and deleting for the past forty-five minutes. She could have texted, but sending a DM reminded her of their original starting place. Back where their relationship still felt safe and familiar.

She'd driven home from the hospital in Tyler in a blessed state of numbness, which had lasted all the way up through showering, tossing aside the beautiful outfit she'd probably never wear again, and pulling on her most comfortable pj's and fuzzy knee-high socks.

And then the numb wore off, and a deep ache rose in her chest that had yet to subside.

Jude's — StrongerMan99's — words echoed in her head from a long-ago conversation, when she'd only thought things were complicated and confusing.

"Either you believed someone to be true and they weren't — or you believed them to be

wrong and they were right."

She didn't know which it was with Jude. With StrongerMan99. Rory groaned. She knew two parts of one person, and they had yet to fully connect in her head, or in her heart. Maybe that was the entire problem — this permanent sense of disorientation that had clung to her ever since Jude's identity was revealed.

She loved him. But she wasn't sure if the "him" was a true person or parts of a whole man that didn't quite add up in reality.

The cursor continued to blink, mocking her with a blank box that demanded words. Jude deserved something from her, some form of acknowledgment after that spine-tingling kiss at the party.

If Hannah hadn't called at that exact moment, what might have happened? Would they have shared a slow dance next? Talked at a back table for hours? Would the enchantment of the evening have swept Rory away, as his kiss had threatened to do, and somehow dissolved all the standing issues between them?

But the phone *had* rung, and Rory *had* answered. And things *had* shifted for the worse with the admission of his donation. No matter where she turned, she kept getting faced with his less-than-ideal motivations toward her. The awkward encounter at the hospital afterward made it a dozen times worse. She shouldn't have brought the coffee — she'd been in the way. But it seemed wrong to not make a gesture of some sort after the emergency with his dad. She owed StrongerMan99 that much.

Did she owe Jude anything?

Maybe that's where she needed to start — addressing the difference.

She began to type.

"All this nothing has meant more to me than so many somethings . . ." The past few months with you online has been better than I could have ever imagined. I've never felt so cared for, so seen, so understood. Trying to reconcile that man with the man I keep encountering in person is still a work in progress for me. I can't make the two halves into a whole. And with the strikes piling up against us, I can't help but wonder if the fact that we can't seem to make our timing work is for a reason.

"People are always telling you that change is a good thing. But all they're saying is that something you didn't

want to happen at all . . .
has happened." (Kathleen Kelly)

Our friendship has changed. It changed with discovering who we really are, it changed with the contest, and it changed with that kiss. Honestly, I don't think I know you fully. Things keep coming up that make me question your motivations and make the man I know in person seem like a stranger when held against the man I knew online. It's confusing, and my heart is weary. I really need to figure out my business and my career before I can afford the liberty of figuring out my personal life.

I understand you're dealing with a lot right now with your father in the hospital, and with Warner and Maddison, and I want to be here for you. It just can't be in the way we once thought it might be.

But please know . . . *"I wanted it to be you. I wanted it to be you so badly."*

She hit Send, clicked off the living room lamp, and cried herself to sleep.

Twenty-Eight

"Unstable angina?" Warner looked back and forth from Hollis to Jude as he leaned over in the bedside chair, forearms braced on his knees. "What is that?"

"Blockage in my arteries, basically." Hollis shifted against the pillows that were propping him up in his hospital bed. "The doctor said I don't need surgery at this point. Only medication."

"*And* changes to your diet." Jude crossed his arms over his chest. "We talked to him too, so don't think you're getting out of that part."

Hollis winced. "Guilty as charged."

Was that a joke — from his dad? Jude leaned against the wall by the bed, careful not to bump any of the IV tubes flowing fluids into his father. Warner had taken the only chair in the room, which was fine, because with the current amount of adrenaline coursing through Jude's veins, he probably could have filled his own IV bag. Now that he knew his dad was okay, the inevitable conversation they needed to have danced before him, taunting him with a dozen what-ifs and spiking his blood pressure. But it had to be done.

Talk about bad timing. What was Rory thinking? Did she leave to be considerate and give them space or did she leave because of the bomb he had dropped about the contest?

He might never know.

"We should probably talk about that party." Hollis reached with an unsteady hand for the plastic cup of water on the bedside tray.

"Agreed." Jude cleared his throat.

Warner handed the cup to Hollis, his eyes averted. "I think Jude and I have talked plenty."

"Well, *we* haven't." Hollis's normally firm tone was lost to a dry cough, and he winced and took a sip. "There's something you need to know."

Warner rolled his eyes. "Trust me, Dad, Jude lectured me plenty. I doubt I'll ever drink again."

Jude snorted. That'd be the day.

Hollis set his cup back on the table. "It's not that. It's —"

A young nurse in red scrubs strode in with a smile. "Just checking your vitals, Mr. Worthington." She glanced at the machines and made a note on her clipboard, murmuring something about his blood pressure looking better. Hollis mumbled under his breath about all this being nonsense.

As she turned, politely ignoring Hollis's muttering, her gaze caught Warner's and her smile grew in wattage. "Oh, congratulations!"

Warner looked blank, then his eyebrows rose. "On the engagement?"

"That too." The nurse waved one hand in the air. "I meant your running for office."

"My *what*?" Warner sat up straighter in the chair and looked at Jude.

Hollis went strangely quiet.

The nurse tucked her clipboard under her arm and patted her scrub pockets before removing a crumpled sheet of paper. She unfolded it and held it up. "Isn't this you?"

Jude craned his neck to see. A red-and-blue background featured a headshot of Warner — which looked like a far cry from the exhausted, hungover version sitting in front of him. WORTHINGTON FOR MAYOR was clearly printed in block letters at the bottom of the flyer.

No way.

Warner went pale. "That's me." His voice broke, and he cleared his throat, searching Jude's face as if he could possibly have an explanation.

He didn't.

Warner turned to Hollis, who kept his eyes down as he fumbled again for his water glass.

The nurse returned the flyer to her pocket, brow slightly furrowed as she glanced at each of their faces. "I'm sorry. They're posted all over downtown Modest. My friend brought this to me — she knows I've always had a crush on . . ." Her voice trailed off, and she flushed. "She thought I might be interested."

Warner's cheeks had the courtesy to tint red. He opened his mouth, but no words emerged. That was probably for the best.

"Thank you." Jude smiled at the confused young woman, attempting to defuse the situation for her sake and her sake only. "It's been a rough night — we're all a little scattered, as you can imagine." He gestured toward his dad.

"Of course." She nodded, clutching her clipboard to her chest. "We're going to try to get you out of here in the morning, Mr. Worthington. For tonight, you rest." She ducked her head and slipped out the door.

It closed with a quiet click behind her.

Seconds pulsing with silence ticked by. Jude closed his eyes. Here it came.

Three . . . two . . .

"MAYOR?" Warner stood up, then seemed to remember that he was yelling at his father sitting in a hospital bed and dropped back down. Either that, or his legs gave out. He ran both hands over his already rumpled hair, his eyes wide. "Were you ever planning to tell me you made me an official nominee?"

Hollis only stared at him, stoic, as if waiting for the storm to pass before he bothered popping open an umbrella.

Warner wasn't done. "I can't be mayor. We agreed that was for leverage. I don't *want* to be mayor." He stood, paced the slight expanse of floor in front of the bed, and alternated running his hands over his jaw and through his hair. "How did you even do that without my signature?"

Jude watched from his position against the wall, almost feeling sorry for his brother. Almost. He raised his hand. "Let me guess. Did Alton sign it?"

Hollis chuckled as he reached for the remote to adjust the bed, slowly sitting more upright. "I have your signature on file, Warner. Give me some credit. That part

500

wasn't difficult."

"You used my signature for something this important without my permission?" Warner's red-glazed eyes narrowed to threatening slits. But his overall wrinkled, exhausted appearance took away any potential sharp edge he might have had otherwise.

Hollis smirked. "What are you going to do? Sue me?"

"I can't believe this," Warner said.

The puzzle pieces began to slide into place. Jude pointed at their father. "That's why you were so adamant about Warner getting offstage while he was acting a fool. The stakes for family embarrassment had suddenly gotten a little higher, hadn't they?"

Hollis scowled at Warner. "What were the odds that the one night you decide to get publicly wasted was the night my team posted your flyers all over town?"

"Anybody want to talk about the odds of one getting nominated to run for a government position they didn't actually choose?" Warner raised his hand.

Jude shook his head. "I don't get it. Why did you tell Mayor Whit you weren't going to have Warner run?"

"Oldest trick in the book." Hollis shrugged. "It's called hiding in plain sight."

"No, Dad, that's called *lying.*" Was there a

way to be emancipated as an adult? He was done with this. Had been for a long time. But, even for Dad, this was a new low. And it was directed at Warner, of all people.

It was a nice break, to be honest.

His brother shot him a desperate look.

Jude mouthed his only advice. *"Stand up."*

Warner slowly began to stand, his brow furrowed.

Jude rolled his eyes. *"Figuratively."*

His brother sat back on the chair. "Why did you do it, Dad?"

This should be good. Jude waited.

Hollis almost seemed flustered under their simultaneous scrutiny. The intimidating Worthington stare he'd taught them so well had rarely been aimed directly at him. He cleared his throat. "One of y'all find me a Coke."

"Dad." Warner's tone held a warning Jude had never heard directed at their father before. Jude wanted to applaud him.

Hollis sighed, more irritated than contrite. "Fine. You want to pester an old man in the hospital, have it your way."

Warner waited, unblinking. Jude raised his hand to cover his grin. Nice try.

"When Jude won the contest . . . well, I realized I was losing him."

Jude's grin faded.

Warner shot Jude a look. "And?"

"All you've done the past six months is gripe about wanting to move to Dallas permanently." Hollis suddenly looked exactly like what he was — an old man in a hospital bed. "I thought maybe getting you officially engaged to Maddison would be enough to keep you here, but it didn't seem like it helped much. I was out of tricks."

"What do you mean, getting him?" Jude asked.

Hollis fidgeted with the bed adjustment remote, then sighed. His tired gaze landed squarely on Warner. "I might have . . . encouraged the proposal."

Jude sucked in his breath.

"Encouraged? Try *badgered."* Warner stood up now, the literal matching the figurative as he began to pace again. "I can't believe I didn't see this sooner." He closed his eyes, jaw clenched. "I wasn't ready to propose. I wasn't even sure Maddison was the one." He looked at Jude, then stabbed a finger in the air toward Hollis. "Then *he* convinced me she'd be the perfect small-town bride. A permanent tie to Modest, a tribute to Grandmother."

Jude opened his mouth, unsure what to say or who to say it to. He wasn't really surprised — that was a move straight out of

503

the Hollis Worthington playbook. Manipulate, scheme, and connive at any cost. But the fact that this time it was directed toward Warner, and not Jude . . . now *that* was surprising.

Apparently, Warner thought so too. "It was always us, Dad." His voice quieted. "I can't believe you'd trick me like this — just to get your way."

"Enough with the guilt trip. I was doing it for you." Hollis waved his hand in the air. "You'll get swallowed up in Dallas full-time. No way would you last there alone."

"No, Dad." Warner made his way to the door. Jude could hear the emotion in Warner's voice, and his brother looked up at the ceiling, unshed tears brimming in his eyes. "I think you're afraid *you* wouldn't last without us, alone. But instead of saying so, you have to make everyone in your life a chess piece."

"Bull." Hollis scowled.

Sympathy for Warner made its way into Jude's heart, along with the subtle conviction Hannah had been tossing his way for weeks. *Love your enemies.*

Suddenly, Warner wasn't so arrogant, prideful, and bitter. He wasn't the face of an enemy. He was simply his brother — the same one who used to play sword fights with sticks and then cry when he got a splinter. The brother who once climbed one branch too high in Grandmother's old oak tree and refused to come down until Jude was there to catch him — just in case. The kid who would negotiate with Maria for an extra chocolate chip cookie, then share it with Jude.

When Warner spoke again, it was with resigned authority. "I'm canceling my nomination for mayor."

"Now, wait a minute. You can't do that." Anger clouded Hollis's voice as he tried to straighten the bed further. But it was at its max.

And apparently, so was Warner. His brother shook his head, pausing in the open doorway. "I can, and I will. I'm afraid that's the one thing you *can't* control." Then he gave the doorframe a final tap and walked out of the room.

Hollis looked at Jude with frustration. "What are you going to do about this?"

Love my enemies. Starting with his own family. Jude inhaled slowly. "I guess I'm going to go tell my brother I'm proud of him. Then I'll see if I can find you a Coke — diet, that is."

"Don't bother," Hollis huffed. "I've never been treated this way in my entire life."

505

"Which is exactly the problem." Jude walked over to the bedside and laid a gentle hand on his dad's arm, noting the purple veins and the IV taped to the top of his wrist. His dad wasn't an enemy to overcome either. He was only a man — a broken man, with fears and insecurities like everyone else.

A compassion he had never before felt for his father overcame him. Jude squeezed Hollis's hand. He didn't have to hold on to the resentment of his family name. He didn't have to internalize his mistreatment, get lost in old habits, and take them out on the people around him like his brother and father did. He could break the cycle — and hope and pray they eventually did the same.

He smiled at his father — the first time it'd felt genuine in a long, long time. "Feel better. Call if you need anything."

Hollis grunted.

"Love you, Dad."

Then Jude went to find Warner.

TWENTY-NINE

Jude hadn't responded to her DM. Not that she blamed him. What was there to say?

Rory tried to focus on the financial figures for Salsa Street occupying the laptop screen in front of her, but the lack of notifications on her display mocked her. The way she'd ended things with Jude hadn't exactly been conducive to further conversation. But she did want to talk to him. She hated the thought of him dealing with his father in a hospital alone — or worse than alone, with *Warner.*

But now, a week had gone by since that fateful party. That fateful kiss. That fateful goodbye in the hospital hallway. The local news reported that Hollis Worthington was fully recovered and that the rumors of Warner Worthington running for office were just that — rumors. That had been great news for Whit, who was now destined to win his much-deserved reelection. Everything was as back to normal as it could be, and she had no real reason to ever see or speak to Jude again.

Although she might need to talk to someone at the law firm soon — there was a particular legal document she needed to have drawn up.

"Order up!" Grady rang a bell — the new addition he'd brought with him on his first day back — and set a hot plate of tacos on the counter.

Nicole popped up from outside, resting her arms on the serving counter and glaring through the open window at them. "I can't believe you brought that thing." The late summer sun glinted off her blonde hair, turning it nearly white. She looked tan and rested and happy — and she'd been cooking all morning. Rory smiled at the irony. Who would have thought?

Grady faced off with his wife, spatula in hand. "What's unbelievable is that you never got me a bell the entire time I was sick."

"No, what's unbelievable is that you bought *yourself* one."

"Get off my truck, woman." His teasing smile removed any hint of seriousness from his words — not that Nicole would have obeyed anyway.

508

Rory squinted at the numbers in front of her, hiding her smile. *His* truck. Interesting turn of phrase. She and Nicole had worked the numbers over and over, and unless their calculator was wrong, this would be the perfect deal for everyone involved.

Nicole cast Rory a glance. "You mean, *our* truck."

"Ha." Grady snorted. "Look, you've been a relatively good sous-chef this past week, but don't go getting cocky. We all know this is still Rory's truck."

"Not anymore." Rory cleared her throat. "After next week's loan closing, Salsa Street is yours."

"Next week's *what*?" Grady's eyes widened as he looked back and forth from Rory, perched behind her laptop at the back counter, to Nicole, beaming from the window. Beans dripped off his spatula and plopped on the floor. "I think I might be getting sick again. I'm hallucinating."

"I applied for a loan." Nicole beamed. "Low interest — don't panic. And we were offered a very competitive price." She winked at Rory. "Turns out the owner was desperate to sell."

Grady's mouth opened, then shut. Then opened again. More beans dripped.

"You might want to clean that mess off

your floor."

"My floor?" Grady pointed at himself, bean juice splattering onto his white T-shirt.

"Looks like you're stuck with me as sous-chef." Nicole shrugged.

"Get in here and kiss me, woman." Grady waved the spatula. "And you!" He gestured to Rory. "Hug. And no mushy complaints." He caught Nicole in one arm as she rushed into the truck and pressed his lips against hers. "Are you sure? This is really happening?" His eyes lit with something that could only be defined as giddiness.

Rory took a deep breath. "Salsa Street has been yours for a long time, Grady. It's beyond time to make it official. We'll sign the papers next week, and then it's a done deal."

"I can't believe it." Grady squeezed her hard, the kind of hug that made Rory wonder why she'd avoided the mushy stuff for all those years. Affection was nice. Reassuring. It touched the ache deep down she hadn't fully realized she'd had all this time.

She was cared for. Maybe not by StrongerMan99 — Jude — anymore, but she had family. *True* family, thicker than blood. She could imagine Sophia's smile at Grady years ago, claiming him as her own. *Taco grease is thicker than water,* she'd joked. She was right.

Nicole linked her arm through Rory's. Instead of making an excuse to step aside, Rory moved in closer as her friend spoke. "Grady, you do realize that Rory won't be here every day to make you miserable."

"That's the downside." Grady frowned as he resumed cooking. "What are you going to do, hermana?"

This time, instead of grating on her, the nickname fit just right. "The paper gave me a great write-up for Warner and Maddison's party. Unfortunately, with the way the night turned out, it sort of got lost in the more interesting headlines." She shrugged. "But the attention motivated me. I know I did a good job, and I think I can make a go of an event-planning business with the right advertising."

Nicole squeezed her arm. "It'll work out. Look at everything that already has."

And everything that hadn't. Rory glanced at her laptop.

"You should ask Warner to promote you. Share your info with his hoity-toity friends and colleagues in Dallas." Grady set a tomato on the cutting board.

Rory grimaced. "I'd rather not talk to him again at all."

"He owes you that much. Think about it." He grinned and wiggled his head back and forth. "From one business owner to another."

"I'll think about it." Grady had a point. But the thought of approaching Warner and asking for any kind of favor made her skin crawl. She'd rather work twice as hard and do it on her own.

The next half hour was lost in the lunch rush, and Rory pitched in despite the crowded confines of the truck. She, Grady, and Nicole worked well as a team, and when the crowd dwindled, Rory went back to her laptop.

Until a familiar voice at the window ordered a beef taco — meat and cheese only.

She turned, heart in her throat, pulse pounding in her ears. *"Dad?"*

Jude checked the final desk drawer in Warner's office. Only a handful of paper clips and a rubber band remained. He shut the door and straightened. "You're sure about this?"

"Were you when you decided to change paths?" Warner asked, pulling a stretch of packing tape from the roller. Beams of afternoon sunlight shone through the window and into the empty office, highlighting all the spots the cleaning service had missed when last dusting.

Jude held the box closed. "Are you scared?"

Warner hesitated, then nodded as he secured the tape over the flaps.

"That's how you know."

His brother nodded again, a nervous twitch flexing his jaw as he stacked two more boxes on the dolly. Jude stepped back to give him room. Warner had come a long way in the last week. Standing up to Hollis — which was considerably harder to do when he wasn't lying in a hospital bed — and making the decision to move to Dallas despite their father's adamant protests. Apologizing to Maddison, getting the ring back — which she eagerly handed over — and putting his townhome up for rent. Not to mention shaking hands with Mayor Whit and easing the tension there.

His brother was finally growing up.

"I'm proud of you for doing this packing thing by yourself — well, almost by yourself." Jude grinned as he handed him the other tape roller. "I'm shocked you didn't hire it out."

"I tried, actually." Warner grinned sheepishly. "They were already booked on such short notice."

Jude smirked. "That makes more sense." Some things never changed. But noting their easy banter and seeing his brother's relaxed expression and carefree demeanor, well — it was evident some things did. He was doing the right thing.

"I think that's it." Warner taped the top of the box he'd loaded. "Man, I'm a pack rat."

"I threw out old magazines when you weren't looking."

"Thank goodness." Warner rested his elbow on the box, turning to give his office one last scan. "Sure you don't want this office?"

Jude scoffed. "This might literally be the last room in Modest I'd ever be interested in occupying."

"So you're going to keep the truck running. Storefront too?"

"Maybe one day." Jude shrugged. "Right now, I want to keep things small and manageable — at least until I can hire more help."

Plus, he hadn't told Warner, but he'd refused to keep his father's money from the contest winnings. Instead, he'd turned around and donated it to the town beautification fund. Jude had started out determined to make a go of this food truck business on his own, and knowing his father was the contest sponsor tainted that entire effort. The money — especially since his dad had stubbornly withheld his annual donation while pouting over the recent turn of events — would be much better suited for whatever town project Mayor Whit chose.

Warner shifted the top box so it sat more squarely on the one below it. "Are you going to let Alton work for you, after everything Dad tried to get him to do?"

"We talked. He confessed the entire thing — how Dad emphasized that if he really cared about Kimmy, he'd sabotage us so Cluck Truck would have a better chance of winning." Jude ran his hands over his jeans, brushing off the remaining packing dust. Too bad he couldn't brush off his father's words and toxic effect as easily. "I'm going to give him another chance. Plus, he couldn't actually bring himself to do it."

"Right — he got it in Rory's entry instead."

"When he was hanging out by the judging tables during setup, he panicked. Was trying to be subtle, which for Alton is sort of like putting clown shoes on a bull and marching it straight into a china shop." Jude shook his head. "Once he decided not to do it, he ended up accidentally spilling ghost pepper into Salsa Street's pozole instead. Then he couldn't bring himself to tell anyone what had happened because he couldn't do that without admitting his original goal. He's been guilt-ridden ever since."

Alton had promised he'd make it up to Rory — apologize, offer to help her for free in her food truck, whatever she wanted. Hopefully, she'd be more forgiving of the kid than she'd been of Jude and his family. Part of Jude wanted to clear the air with Rory, help Alton explain, and hope that in the meantime she'd realize Jude had had nothing to do with it all.

The other part of him realized that if Rory didn't know and believe that about him by now, she never would.

Warner sighed. "Poor kid. Dad really knows how to get in people's heads, doesn't he?"

No kidding. After several late-night talks with Warner — over coffee, *not* beer — they'd realized they'd both been victims of their dad's coercion and schemes over the years. Jude had determined to get out from under their dad and succeed on his own, away from the games, while Warner had been swayed to the other extreme to try to earn Hollis's favor. Those efforts had led to Hollis losing them both. So far, he remained unrepentant of those truths. But if the day ever came when he wanted to own up to it all, Jude was ready to forgive him.

Hopefully, anyway.

Warner kicked the dolly into a rolling position. "What about Rory?"

Jude tried to ignore the accompanying ache that Rory's name conjured. "She made it clear in her message last weekend she only wanted to be friends." If that. More like acquaintances.

"And you don't?"

A knot — the familiar one that always appeared when Rory was mentioned — formed in his throat. "I think it's more like I *can't.*"

"Understandable."

Warner nodded, but Jude had a feeling he didn't really relate. His brother hadn't loved Maddison. Jude had wanted to move forward with Rory until her last message. After everything they'd shared . . . all the vulnerable conversations, the inside jokes, the kisses . . . it would be unbearable to move backward into friendship.

As much as it hurt to lose her, a clean break was his only chance at healing.

Warner began to wheel the dolly toward the door. "Ready?"

Jude grabbed the one box that hadn't fit on the dolly, tucked a small faux fern under his arm, and gave Warner's office a final sweeping glance. The once-intimidating space of a brother he used to assume was an enemy was far less terrorizing now that it sat empty and dusty. Now it would become a fresh slate for someone else to fill — while he and Warner began to fill their own.

He turned off the light and nodded at his brother. "I think we both are."

If only his ache and knot would get the same memo.

"I can't believe you're here." Rory leaned against the interior truck counter, where her laptop still rested, and gripped the edges to keep the tension from her voice. It was good to see her dad.

Right?

After giving Rory's father his taco, Grady had shot Rory an understanding look, flipped the sign on the window to closed, and ushered Nicole to the picnic tables outside to give them space to talk in private. She wasn't sure if she wanted it or not.

Her dad wadded up a napkin with a few remaining shreds of cheese still clinging to it and tossed it into the wastebasket, looking out of place in the truck in his crisp dress shirt and navy slacks. How long had he been in town? Had he come straight here? So many questions, and she had no idea which to ask first.

"Are you happy?"

He beat her to it. She hesitated, rolling in her lower lip. "To see you? Or in general?"

Her dad studied her face, his expression soft and serious. "Both."

Her emotions began to spiral, along with the rush of memories that always showed up when she was in his presence. She didn't know how to respond. The truth would hurt him. But why did that fact make her paralyzed to speak it? Hadn't he hurt her by choosing to stay largely out of her life?

Then a calmness swept over her. He no longer had the right to jerk her emotions around. She wasn't an insecure little kid anymore, desperate to please her father and beg for his attention. She was a grown woman in the process of selling a business and starting a new career. She was a success, without him and his approval, and much more than just a pretty face. She'd proven it over and over. She no longer had to.

Despite the fluttering of anxiety in her chest, she lifted her chin and met her father's gaze. "I'm getting there."

He nodded. "To both?"

She remained silent.

He ran his hand over his thinning dark hair, now looking as uncomfortable as she felt. It was much like their awkward phone calls, but a dozen times worse in person. "I got in town a few days ago and wanted to surprise you."

He'd been there a few days and was only now coming by? "It worked."

"You seem mad."

"I'm not mad. I'm . . . cautious." She folded her arms over her T-shirt, studying him. He'd lost weight since she'd seen him last, but his eyes seemed more peaceful than she remembered. Something was different. "Are you staying long?"

"I might." He looked around, a gentle smile softening his drawn expression. "You've done a good job with this place. Sophia would be proud."

The compliment warmed her more than she wanted it to. But wasn't that what she'd always longed for from him? She tried to relax her guard. "It was mostly Grady. I'm actually in the process of selling it all to him."

Her dad didn't seem surprised as he brushed a few crumbs off the countertop. "That's a good idea. What will you do instead?"

"Dad, before we shoot the breeze . . ."

Rory tightened her grip on the counter and took a deep breath. "Why are you here?"

A mixed expression, full of both respect and regret, filled his face. "A coworker talked me into attending a weekend conference with him and some other men a few weeks back. I think he'd been seeing how down I'd become and was worried." He let out a sigh. "It's a long story, but the short version is, I had a big realization while I was there. One that has inspired me to do things differently."

A flicker of hope lit in her heart, which was almost immediately suffocate by fear. He'd made empty promises before, but never this specific. Could it be possible he meant it this time? "Yeah?"

"I've been running from grief for so long, hiding from the things that reminded me of it, that I was robbing myself of the good things I still had left — like you."

It sounded like he'd practiced that a few times. Which meant he cared enough to do so. Rory nodded, her throat thick.

"I want to be around more often. I missed so much time with my sister . . ." Her father's voice cracked, and he briefly closed his eyes. "I can't change that now, but I can with you." He hesitated. "That is, if you want me to."

She didn't owe him anything, but nothing could have stopped her from stepping into his arms, which he was holding open as an invitation. "I do." He smelled like peppermints and ironing starch, and in his embrace, a few good memories from the past tugged at her. The ones she'd never let herself remember before.

Maybe there was still time for new ones.

"I'm glad you're here." She meant it. And she meant it for his sake *and* her own, and not just because she'd finally proven what she needed to prove to herself about her value. After having done so, she could recognize that she hadn't needed to prove anything in the first place.

If only she could tell StrongerMan99 about her self-discovery. Her joy dipped at the remembrance of what she'd lost in his friendship. But this was a moment to celebrate, to be grateful for.

Her father pulled back slightly to see her. "I wanted you to know I really meant it, so I made a gesture. I —"

The truck door suddenly squeaked open, and Hannah strolled inside, computer bag tucked under her arm. She pushed past Rory's dad, giving him only a cursory glance as if she saw him frequently instead of every five to six years. "Hi, Uncle Perez."

Then she set her laptop in front of Rory and scooted hers out of the way. "Rory, I have something to show you."

Rory glanced at her father. "Hannah, this might not be the best —"

"No, no, go ahead." He patted Hannah's shoulder and smiled. "This seems important. I'm going to try to find Grady and swindle him into giving me a free dessert."

Rory struggled to focus on the computer Hannah was plugging in and opening in front of her, but her mind still raced with the turn of events. Her dad was back. And he was . . . happy.

Maybe she would be too.

"I mentioned this to you last weekend on the phone, but I don't think you were listening," Hannah pointed out in her charmingly blunt way.

Rory shook her head, trying to focus and not prove her cousin right a second time.

"Besides, I wanted to have a sale first before I showed you in person." She nudged Rory slightly out of the way and painstakingly typed out a web address in the browser bar. With a quick intake of breath, she hit the Enter key.

An adorable website filled the screen. Hues of yellow, peach, and pink, reminding Rory of sherbet, swirled together to create an inviting background to feature Hannah's painstakingly perfect origami creatures. Each animal was nestled inside its own bubble, complete with price listings. Hannah's short bio and beaming headshot, featuring her holding up an origami swan, sat in a text block toward the bottom of the screen, next to a "Contact to Purchase" form.

Her own business.

Awe and an overwhelming sense of pride filled Rory's heart, bringing happy tears in their wake. "Hannah . . . congratulations." She pulled her cousin into a hug. "I'm so proud of you. This is amazing."

Hannah's bright smile made her cheeks even rounder than usual. "It is."

"I always knew you were so talented."

She agreed again, nodding seriously. "I knew too."

Rory laughed and sniffed away the next round of tears. "Look at you — your first sale. You're going to do great." She couldn't stop staring at the sea of paper animals before her. What a great idea. Hannah could have more independence this way, could help pay for some of her own needs like she'd always wanted, and bring joy to others with her giftedness. It was perfect.

Hannah bounced on the balls of her feet

as if she couldn't contain the rest. "This is what Jude helped me with the other week. My own business."

"Wait. *Jude* helped you with this?" Rory cut a sharp glance at Hannah, her voice pitching in surprise. "So when he came to see you at Unity Angels, he was helping you make a website to sell your art?"

"Right." Hannah's matter-of-fact tone gave Rory no reason to doubt.

But it did leave her with a lot of thoughts. Jude had done this . . . and he hadn't told Rory. She swallowed hard, leaning back away from the computer. Which meant he hadn't wanted credit for it — and he hadn't wanted to use it to get to Rory.

He'd done it for Hannah.

She glanced up at Hannah's stoic expression as she scrolled her own website, mouth moving slightly as she read the descriptions beside each listed animal. It didn't add up that Jude would do something like that so secretly, then turn around and pay for Hannah's tuition with an obvious motivation like the one left by the donor.

But if Jude wasn't the anonymous donor, then who was?

A pretty girl . . .

Rory's stomach clenched. Her breath tightened at the memory of her father's recent words. *I made a gesture . . .*

Her heart splintered into a hundred shards of regret as reality ushered in the painful truth.

She'd been so, so wrong.

THIRTY

The Saturday afternoon sun had given way to a steady drizzle that evening, but Jude couldn't bring himself to stay in his house after work. He'd had a productive day at the food truck after helping Warner finish cleaning out his office. Alton had managed the late-afternoon crowd well, and Jude hoped to give him a raise soon if business stayed booming. In the meantime, he needed to move. To run.

Maybe the physical ache would ease the internal one.

His feet slapped the wet concrete, and he tugged the hood of his sweatshirt up over his head, lowering his chin against the gentle mist as he turned the corner of Maple Street and headed toward Main. The cooler air revived his lungs and cleared his head. But the clarity brought a painful awareness. Getting out of the house might have been good at first, but now it only reminded him that he had no one to go back home to.

His running shoes squeaked as he rounded the curve onto Clark Avenue. The gazebo at the end of the road loomed ahead. This was where he and Rory had ended their unofficial race that day. How many weeks ago had that been?

How many lifetimes ago?

Before he'd known who she was . . . before she'd known who *he* was . . . before the pride and the assumptions and the betrayals had chipped away at any chance of them getting together. Back when the only thing that had mattered was getting out of the family business and starting his own.

Funny how priorities shifted when the things you thought you needed the most turned out to be somewhat superfluous, after all.

He jogged past the hair salon where Maddison worked, wondering briefly how she was doing in his brother's wake — free from the burden of a ring she wasn't meant to wear. If Mayor Whit had anything to do about it, she wouldn't be lonely long.

Lonely. The word seared like a hot iron. But he shouldn't be lonely. He had a thriving new business, career goals. A renewed friendship with his brother, of all people. Brotherhood with Cody and Alton. He had a rich life, even if his bank account wasn't as well off as it had been or could have been if he'd catered to his father's whims. That was a no-brainer type of trade.

He neared the gazebo, then ran up the stairs and shook the rain off the sleeves of his waterproof hoodie. Panting for breath, he tilted his chin up and paced, hands on his hips, eyes closed as he fought for control. Fought to surrender.

Something brushed his elbow and he opened his eyes, whipping around.

Rory.

"You run fast." Her wet sweatshirt stuck to her slim shoulders, and her dark ponytail straggled down her back in wet knots.

He opened his mouth, but words failed him. Was she real? Had the emotional roller coaster of the last week finally tipped him over the edge?

She stepped toward him, caution and regret fighting for first dibs in her eyes. She extended a rain-soaked hand toward him, water dripping down her fingers. She was real. But what was she doing here?

"I've been chasing you since you left your house."

He finally found his voice. "That's several miles." The words strained in his throat.

"Tell me about it." She shivered as she

crossed her arms over her chest, her breathing heavy. "What are you running from?"

He studied her for a minute, a dozen emotions flooding faster than the rain. "You, apparently."

The man looked good wet.

Rory watched him watch her, wishing she could read the meaning behind his gaze. Heroic as he seemed and as handsome as he was in the rain, there was no way his patience should have lasted this long. How many times had she misjudged him? Assumed the worst? Misunderstood and stubbornly stuck to her misbeliefs out of fear of the truth?

This had been a fool's errand.

But regardless of her embarrassment, regardless of the pain that would surely accompany her all the way home, she had to do what was right. Jude deserved her sincerest apologies. This wasn't the movies. She didn't exactly foresee a happily ever after with a sudden blaring soundtrack as the credits rolled, but she had to at least give him the apology he deserved.

"Have you, by chance, not checked your messages in the last week?" She winced, knowing the question was ridiculous.

"I read it." His face, still stoic, revealed

nothing.

She opened her mouth, then closed it.

He shifted his weight, his arms a defensive barrier across his broad chest. "For the record . . . I wanted it to be you as well."

She closed her eyes. *Wanted* — past tense. The pain burrowed deep, and she nodded. "I understand." She deserved that. Now she had to move forward — which meant back home, to her lavender tea and new business plan and frozen meals for one. It would have to be enough. She'd blown it.

But she wasn't done with what she'd come to say. The message that had driven her from the food truck, away from her father's revelation. Away from Hannah's excitement about her new website and Grady's and Nicole's eagerness about the upcoming closing. This had to be done first or she'd be in limbo forever.

She summoned her courage and opened her eyes. His gaze had gentled, probably because of the death blow he'd just dealt, because Jude wasn't cruel. But he was honest, and that was all she needed. "I was wrong."

He quirked a brow.

"About you. About us. About . . . everything." She shuddered as the wind changed directions, blowing more rain into the gazebo. She would warm up at home, but this deep chill inside . . . that was going to last. "I feel like Elizabeth Bennet."

Jude frowned, still not speaking.

"You know. In *Pride and Prejudice,* where she realizes that she's been so wrong about Mr. Darcy. But she says it much more eloquently."

"I have courted prepossession and ignorance, and driven reason away."

He spoke Austen. Rory swallowed hard. "Yes. That." She nodded. *"Till this moment, I never knew myself."*

Now he looked agitated as he shoved his hands through his wet hair. "What are you *really* trying to say, Rory?"

"I was trying to protect myself." The words flew out faster than she'd ever meant to say them, like if they didn't escape all at once, they'd be trapped forever. "I thought I knew what men wanted with me. I thought I had you figured out from the start. Arrogant, wealthy, used to getting your way. Playing the games that I now see your *father* played." She shook her head. "I thought you were using the contest to get yet another silver spoon in your life. Then I thought you were using me, and then using Hannah to get to me — just like others have in the past. I thought you paid her tuition."

He looked confused. "Wouldn't that be a good thing?"

"It could have been, if the donor hadn't made sure to point out it was all for a pretty girl." Rory pressed her fingers against her temples. "I realize that sounds crazy. I knew you had gone to visit Hannah — she'd mentioned it to me — and I thought that was why. Now I know it was for the website. You helped her create her own business . . . and you didn't even tell me."

"Because it wasn't for you."

His quiet confirmation of what she'd hoped was true nearly burst her heart apart with happiness. "I know." Now. She knew *now*.

But it was too late. Which yanked her heart back into deep sadness.

Jude tugged at the string of his hoodie, his brow furrowed. "Earlier this week, after realizing my father had tried to rig the contest and hurt you instead, I tried to ask the judges for a recall. I begged Whit to make it happen."

Her breath hitched. "You did?"

He looked away, toward the water puddling on Clark Avenue. "Yeah. It was a no-go. Once they realized Hannah had helped you make the tamales for round two, they said you would have been disqualified anyway."

Disqualified? Her mind raced. "But why —" Then it hit her. The sous-chef rule. They were allowed only one. Hannah had helped Rory with Sophia's tamale recipe, but Nicole had prepped the rest of the food for their entry.

She closed her eyes as reality sank in. She'd have lost because of her own mistake — regardless of Jude. Regardless of any potential sabotage or family drama or presumptions. "I get it now. How did they know that part?"

"Hannah called the same day I did — only about an hour before. Apparently, she had the same idea to ask for a recall since she knew Alton had interfered."

"And the truth came out about her helping me that day." Because Hannah was the most truthful person Rory knew — and Rory wouldn't change a thing about her. But something still didn't make sense. "It wasn't your fault your father tried to sabotage everything, though, so why did you try to undo it? You won. You had everything you wanted."

"Almost everything." Jude took a tentative step closer to her.

Hope thudded her heart so hard against

her rib cage, she thought it might crack.

"You weren't the only one who made mistakes." He reached for her hand, his palm warm and calloused against hers. He threaded their fingers, and her heart plunged into her wet running shoes. "I was so preoccupied with getting out from under my dad's thumb, with getting what *I* wanted, that I ran right over your dreams."

"We couldn't both win."

"I feel like we both lost instead."

The words sank around them, cool and penetrating like the rain. Rory focused on the connection of their hands, grasping for grounding as everything she thought she knew — and thought she wanted — spun around her.

He continued. "I asked about the recall because I wanted to do something — to show you that you meant more to me than the contest or the truck or any career I could build. But it didn't work."

She tightened her grip on his fingers. "Jude, you didn't even know me a few months ago. You had no obligation toward me or my dreams."

"I'm pretty sure I did."

Her eyes cut to his, to the sincerity shining through.

"The moment I knocked on the window

of Salsa Street to ask you to teach me to cook, everything changed."

She let out a strangled half laugh, half cry. "I can't even cook, though." She remembered what Hannah had taught her and corrected herself. "I don't *like* to cook."

A teasing grin lifted the corners of his mouth, and he pulled her close. "But you're fun to cook with."

"More like humorous to cook with." His proximity made her heart race as her gaze swept over his stubbled jaw, raindrops attempting a rogue escape through the dark bristle. She smiled. "I think I've finally accepted that my lot in life doesn't involve a kitchen."

"Does it involve this?" Then his lips were on hers, tasting of rain and salt and happily ever after. She kissed him back, her fingers tangled in his damp hair, her heart soaring with the joy of forgiveness and second chances.

She eventually pulled back for a breath. "This isn't exactly ending like the movie did, you know."

Jude raised his eyebrows, only loosening his embrace enough for her to gesture.

"It's not sunny. And there are no flowers."

He looked around them at the rain running off the gazebo roof and providing a translucent curtain, then tugged her back against his chest. "No golden retriever either."

She pressed her lips together, holding back a smile. "I think I'm okay with that."

"Are you okay with the smell of cilantro?"

She tilted her head back, narrowing her eyes. "For how long?"

"We'll see." He shrugged, a twinkle in his eye. "Maybe for as long as we both shall live?"

Joy collided with hope and bubbled over. "Only if I can get that with a side of nachos."

"Deal."

His lingering kiss removed any further thoughts of Mexican food.

EPILOGUE

One Year Later

"That's way too much cilantro, babe." Rory tugged at Jude's arm in a futile effort to stop the inevitable.

"There's no such thing." Jude hastily swept a few more leaves into the sizzling taco meat on the food truck's stove.

"I disagree."

"That's what you do best, wife." Then he leaned down and kissed her, making her forget all about tacos and the fact that she hated cilantro. Mostly she just remembered that she loved him.

"Don't you two set the truck on fire now," Cody hollered from outside the open window.

Rory broke away with a laugh as Jude wiggled his eyebrows at her. Then he tossed in another handful of cilantro before she could protest further. But that was marriage. Give and take. Sort of like he'd given her a ring and she'd given him the motivation to open a storefront six months after the contest last year.

And about a month after *that,* Jude realized he didn't want to run a storefront, that he missed the food truck life. So he'd hung a sign on their leased space announcing a new business. Let's Give 'Em Something to Taco 'Bout — a joint venture featuring party and event planning with built-in Mexican catering. Rory had already been featured in multiple media outlets all over Texas and Louisiana and had a big New Orleans society wedding on the books in two weeks.

But that wasn't the biggest surprise.

Jude turned off the burners and transferred the meat expertly into a serving tray. She grabbed the bowls of diced tomatoes and freshly chopped onion, then followed him out of the truck and across the lawn to the picnic tables they'd set up for the party. Cody, Alton, and Hannah sat at one, admiring Hannah's latest advanced origami creation, while Grady and Nicole saved Jude and Rory seats at another. Maddison and Whit occupied a third table.

"Did you ever think you'd see this day?" She nodded to where both their fathers sat at another table a few yards away, shooting the business breeze. Her dad, having finally put on a little weight, munched fried appetizers while Hollis, now several pounds lighter, worked on a salad Jude had prepped for him.

"I really didn't. I had zero expectations of Dad coming around, but apparently he even sent Warner a 'how's it going' email the other day." Jude shrugged as he set the meat platter on the table beside the other taco toppings.

"Well, his wedding gift sure was generous." It'd been the only way they'd been able to afford the initial costs of getting their new business off the ground.

And maybe afford something else that was coming their way . . . Rory smiled as she joined their friends.

"Hey, you guys should have made barbeque, just to throw everyone off," Grady joked as he scooted over to make room on the bench seat.

Nicole adjusted the weight of the adorable dark-haired baby she wore in a front-wrap sling and smirked. "Don't quit your day job, honey."

Grady feigned offense. "To what? Be a comedian — or sell barbeque?"

"Either." She swatted at him, then paused and wrinkled her nose. "Oops. Your son needs you."

Grady let out an exaggerated sigh as he stood and reached across the picnic table. "I told you to tell him to stop doing that every day."

"That wasn't any funnier." She handed over the baby, then the blue plaid diaper bag.

"How many of those do you want?" Mayor Whit pointed as Grady hurried toward the public restrooms, baby in tow.

"How many food truck chefs?" Maddison swept her bangs off her forehead, her brand-new diamond ring glittering in the sunlight. Whit had proposed last week, and the entire town had sighed in relief. Finally.

"I hope zero. I can't cook very well." Whit's expression remained serious as he dragged a chip through a pile of salsa.

Maddison's white smile deepened. "I was joking."

"So was I." Whit straightened in his seat, brushing awkwardly at the back of his neck.

"No, you weren't, sweetie. But you butter toast really, really well." She rubbed his arm in consolation.

"You guys will need a bunch of babies." Rory reached over and stole a nacho from the appetizer tray in the middle of the table, the cheese stringing toward her paper plate.

541

She'd finally talked Jude into putting nachos on the menu permanently. Alton had been ecstatic.

Nicole agreed, folding her arms on the table as she leaned across to snag a chip. "Yes! Think about it — miniature politicians with fantastic hair."

Rory hid her smile behind a chip.

"Hey . . ." Alton suddenly stared at Rory from the next table over, his head tilted to the side. "You should, like, totally go as that Fiona Stone chick for Halloween. You're a dead ringer."

Nicole paused midchew to shoot a worried glance at Rory as Jude quickly shushed him. But the comment, for once, didn't make Rory want to run away. Instead, it made her look over at her father and feel . . . nothing. Except fondness and gratitude. She knew now he'd done the best he could over the years while navigating his own pain and loneliness, and he'd made a continued effort these past months to be more involved with not only her but also Hannah.

The wounds had healed. And while some days the scar tissue tugged tighter than others, overall, she was grounded in her worth. Jude did his best to remind her of it daily, but even outside of him, she finally knew who she was. And it turned out, she was a pretty good event planner . . . a fantastic wife . . . and in about six months, she'd hopefully be a really, really good mom.

She pressed her hands against her growing secret, then fumbled for her napkin as Jude glanced across the table at her with a loving grin. He didn't know yet. But he would in a minute.

"Why don't you go ahead and crack open the piñata?" She nudged the brightly colored llama closer to Jude. "I could go for some candy."

"Now?" Jude asked around a mouthful of taco. "Everyone hasn't even finished fixing their plates."

"Your wife wants candy, man. I'd listen to her." Grady walked back up, passing the baby to Nicole. She nestled their son in her arms and winked at Rory. Nicole was the only person who knew — mainly because she'd given Rory so many nausea-reducing tips over the past six weeks.

Rory handed Jude the baton that had come with the piñata. "Go for it."

"Wait. Alton really likes doing this." Jude hesitated, craning his neck to see Alton at the next table over.

"I think you should." Nicole used her newfound mom voice, and Jude shrugged.

"Candy it is, then." He slammed the baton

across the piñata, then a second time. Pink-and blue-wrapped candies spewed across the table, along with a handful of the tiny babies usually found in king cakes.

Alton, who had come closer to watch, shook his head in disappointment as he reached for a piece of bubblegum. "Dude, whoever filled that is an amateur. No Skittles? No Laffy Taffy?"

Jude stared at the colorful mess on the picnic table, then at Rory. His eyebrows rose, and a slow light of understanding began to shine. "Are you —"

She nodded eagerly before he could finish his sentence, and he was over on her side of the table in seconds, scooping her up with a whoop. "I'm going to be a dad!" He spun her in a quick circle that made her regret the nachos, then set her back down to stand on the grass. "And you're going to be a mom."

"That's how that works." She laughed as she clung to his arms for balance. The rest of their friends and family rushed their table, chattering over each other as they offered their congratulations.

After several handshakes, words of advice, and warnings, the group began debating the best way to do a gender reveal.

Ignoring the chattering chaos around

them, Jude pulled her close again and tucked a lock of hair behind Rory's ear, his eyes full of love as his gaze caressed her face. "I hope it's a girl."

She sucked in her breath. That'd be a little terrifying. "I hope it's a boy." She turned her cheek to rest against his palm.

"I hope it's twins," Nicole piped up, beaming as she fumbled in the diaper bag for a bottle.

Grady snickered. "I just hope they like cilantro."

"As long as he or she has your eyes," Jude countered.

Rory grinned. "And your cooking ability?"

"Absolutely." Jude paused, leaning down to brush a kiss against her lips. "Tacos for three."

ACKNOWLEDGMENTS

It's a blessing to have people in your corner — and my corner is incredibly crowded in the best possible way! I'm increasingly grateful with each new novel for my super-agent, Tamela Hancock Murray of the Steve Laube Agency, who is always only a phone call away from a prayer, a long-distance hug, or a wise word of encouragement.

The marketing and editorial teams at Revell are fantastic, and I'm blessed to work with them! Special thanks to Kelsey Bowen and Amy Ballor for their brilliant ideas, sharp eyes, and gentle nudging to make this story more than it was. You ladies are pure gold!

I don't think I could make it through a novel without Georgiana Daniels reading each chapter as I go and cheering me along. We've been crit buddies now for over a decade, and we're still going strong. You are the cilantro in my taco.

Amy Leigh Simpson — your faith inspires mine! Having you in my corner is a true gift.

Ashley Clark — your daily friendship is like sunshine. Without it, I'd shrivel up.

Mammaw Marie — you inspired in me a love of books at such a young age. Working with you in the church library are some of my favorite childhood memories. Thank you for always listening when I blabbed on about the latest Baby-Sitter's Club plotline.

Nicole Barnard — you fill my corner with coffee and Greek food. I'm so grateful the Lord crossed our paths as sisters-in-Christ.

My parents and my Sissy — you're always my biggest supporters and permanent corner-occupiers. Love you guys!

Topher, Audrey, and Addy — thank you for being patient with me when I'm on deadline, even when I say things like, "Don't interrupt me for the next two hours. If you're bleeding, find a Band-Aid. And if the house is on fire, just put it out." You guys are the best (even though you don't like cilantro).

Last but never least — a HUGE thank you to the readers in my corner! Without you guys, I wouldn't get to do what I do. I love interacting with you and am so thankful for your excitement and support with each new book (passes everyone a taco). Cheers!

ABOUT THE AUTHOR

Betsy St. Amant is the author of more than fifteen inspirational romances, including *The Key to Love,* and a frequent contributor to iBelieve.com. She lives in north Louisiana with her husband, two daughters, a collection of Austen novels, and an impressive stash of pickle-flavored Pringles. When she's not composing her next book or trying to prove unicorns are real, Betsy can usually be found somewhere in the vicinity of a white chocolate mocha — no whip. Learn more at www.betsystamant.com.